THE LEOPARDS OF NORMANDY:
DEVIL

David Churchill is the pseudonym of an award-winning journalist, who has conducted several hundred in-depth inter-views with senior politicians, billionaire entrepreneurs, Olympic athletes, movie stars, supermodels and rock legends. He has investigated financial scandals on Wall Street, studio intrigues in Hollywood and corrupt sports stars in Britain, and lived in Moscow, Washington D.C., and Havana. He has edited four magazines, published seventeen books and been translated into some twenty languages. *The Leopards of Normandy* reflects his lifelong passion for history and his fascination for the extra-ordinary men and women of the past who shaped the world we live in today.

THE LEOPARDS OF NORMANDY:
DEVIL

DAVID
CHURCHILL

headline

First published in Great Britain in 2015
by HEADLINE
An imprint of HEADLINE PUBLISHING GROUP

1

Cataloguing in Publication Data is available from the British Library

ISBN 978 1 4722 1917 6 (Hardback)
ISBN 978 1 4722 1918 3 (Trade paperback)

Typeset in Garamond MT by Avon DataSet Ltd, Bidford-on-Avon, Warwickshire

Printed and bound in Great Britain by Clays Ltd, St Ives plc

Headline's policy is to use papers that are natural, renewable and recyclable
products and made from wood grown in well-managed forests and other controlled
sources. The logging and manufacturing processes are expected to conform to the
environmental regulations of the country of origin.

HEADLINE PUBLISHING GROUP
An Hachette UK Company
338 Euston Road
London NW1 3BH

www.headline.co.uk
www.hachette.co.uk

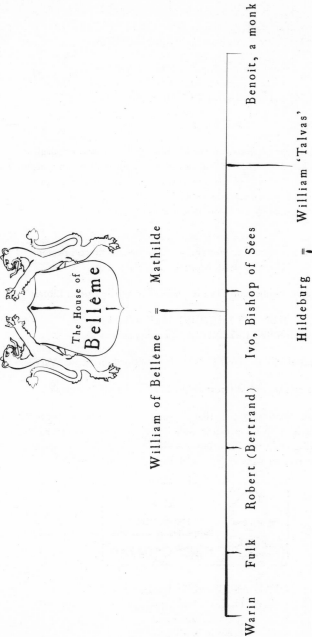

The House of
Bellême

William of Bellême = Mathilde

Warin   Fulk   Robert (Bertrand)   Ivo, Bishop of Sées   William 'Talvas'   Benoit, a monk

Hildeburg = William 'Talvas'

Mabel

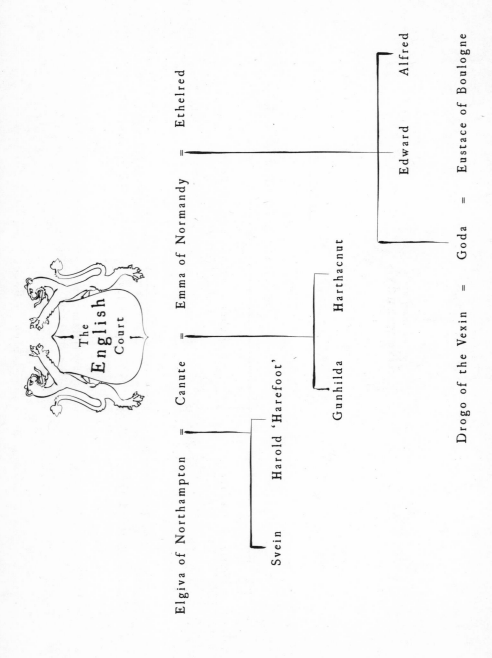

The **English** Court

Elgiva of Northampton = Canute = Emma of Normandy = Ethelred

Svein

Harold 'Harefoot'

Gunhilda   Harthacnut

Edward   Alfred

Drogo of the Vexin = Goda = Eustace of Boulogne

The House of Normandy

Rollo 'the Strider' = Poppa

William I 'Longsword' = Sprota

Richard 'the Fearless' = Gunnor

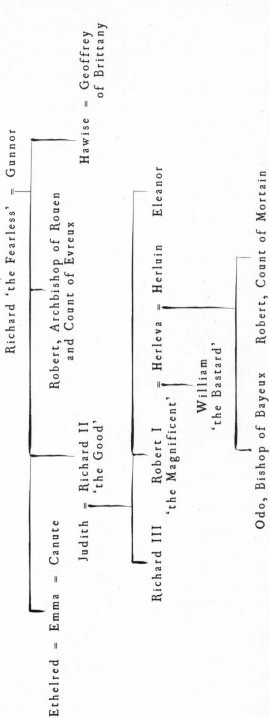

Ethelred = Emma = Canute

Judith = Richard II 'the Good'

Robert, Archbishop of Rouen and Count of Evreux

Hawise = Geoffrey of Brittany

Richard III

Robert I 'the Magnificent' = Herleva = Herluin

Eleanor

William 'the Bastard'

Odo, Bishop of Bayeux   Robert, Count of Mortain

List of Characters

Historical Characters

The First Dukes of Normandy

Rollo 'the Strider' (846–931)

William I 'Longsword' (900–942)

Duke Richard I 'the Fearless' (933–996)

Duke Richard II 'the Good' (978–1026)

The House of Normandy

Lady Gunnor:	widow of Duke Richard I
Duke Richard III:	son of Richard II and first husband of Princess Adela of France
Count Robert of the Hiémois, known as both 'the Devil' and 'the Magnificent':	Richard III's brother
Eleanor, sister of Richard and Robert:	married to Count Baldwin IV of Flanders
William 'the Bastard':	Robert's son by Herleva, the tanner's daughter
Emma of Normandy, Queen of England:	daughter of Duke Richard I and Gunnor

Robert, Count of Evreux and Archbishop of Rouen:	son of Duke Richard I and Gunnor
Ralph of Gacé:	Archbishop Robert's son and William's cousin
Mauger, later Archbishop of Rouen; and William, Count of Arques:	sons of Richard II by his second wife Papia, and William's uncles
Gilbert of Brionne:	William's cousin and guardian
Osbern Herfastsson:	steward to Duke Robert and William's guardian
William Fitzosbern ('Fitz'):	son of Osbern, later William's friend and steward
Thorold:	William's tutor

The Houses of Fulbert and Conteville

Fulbert the tanner:	William's grandfather
Doda:	his wife
Herleva:	his daughter, William's mother
Osbern and Walter:	Fulbert's sons, William's uncles and guardians
Herluin of Conteville:	close friend of Robert of Normandy
Odo, Bishop of Bayeux; and Robert, Count of Mortain:	sons of Herluin

The House of Flanders

Baldwin IV:	Count of Flanders
Baldwin V:	son of Baldwin and second husband of Adela of France
Matilda:	his daughter

The House of Brittany

Count Geoffrey:	married to Hawise, daughter of Richard I of Normandy
Judith:	Geoffrey's sister, married to Duke Richard II of Normandy and mother of his sons Richard and Robert
Count Alan III:	son of Geoffrey and Hawise, first cousin of Richard and Robert of Normandy and later guardian of William

The House of Bellême

Count William of Bellême:	ally of Duke Richard III, but rebel against Duke Robert
Mathilde:	his wife
Warin, Fulk, Robert ('Bertrand'), Ivo and Talvas:	Bellême's sons by Mathilde
Hildeburg:	Talvas' wife
Baron Arnulf:	Hildeburg's father
Gonthier:	a loyal retainer

The Kingdom of France

King Robert II, 'the Pious'

Queen Constance:	his wife
Henry (later King Henry I of France), Robert and Adela:	Robert and Constance's children

Bishop Fulbert of Chartres

The Kingdoms of England and Denmark

Ethelred, King of England:	Emma of Normandy's first husband
Edward and Alfred:	Ethelred and Emma's sons
Goda:	sister of Edward and Alfred
Canute, 'the Great', King of Denmark, Norway and England:	Emma of Normandy's second husband
Harthacnut and Gunhilda:	Canute and Emma's children
Elgiva of Northampton:	Canute's first wife/concubine
Svein and Harold 'Harefoot':	Canute and Elgiva's sons

The House of Wessex

Godwin, Earl of Wessex

Gytha:	his wife

Sweyn, Harold, Tostig Gyrth, Leofwin and Wulnoth	Godwin and Gytha's sons
Aethelnoth, Archbishop of Canterbury:	Godwin's uncle

Miscellaneous Characters

Guy of Burgundy:	boyhood friend of William, later his enemy
Warner of Rouen:	a poet
Drogo, Count of the Vexin:	friend of Duke Robert and first husband of Goda
Eustace of Boulogne:	second husband of Goda
Nigel, Count of the Cotentin:	loyal ally of the House of Normandy
Alfred 'the Giant' of Gavray:	mighty warrior
Rabel:	commander of Norman forces
Aelfwine, Bishop of Winchester:	friend to Queen Emma

Fictional Characters

Judith:	Herleva's best friend
Serlo:	Judith's father

Osmund:	a forester
Sybil:	his wife
Jarl the Viper:	a professional poisoner
Mahomet:	Jarl's Saracen companion
John:	a blacksmith's boy
Rolf:	an innkeeper
Johans of Perpignan:	a brothel keeper
Galiana:	a young prostitute
Brother Mark:	a monk, apparently
Moriella:	a woman of mystery
Tancred:	Duke Richard III's chamberlain
Rat:	a scullion at the ducal palace
Jean of Beauvais:	a blacksmith
Thurstan of Coutances:	a fishmonger
Guerech of Dol:	a Breton spy
Ranulf of Damville Orbec and Thierry of Breteuil:	Archbishop Robert's retainers
Otto of Cologne:	a wandering mason
Godfrey of Gacé and Lady Judith:	Ralph of Gacé's guardians

Prologue:
A Brace of Promises

1

Early morning mist rose from the river and drifted through the trees like cold grey smoke, blanketing the horsemen as they made their way along the bank and rendering them as shapeless and insubstantial as wraiths. The only sound was the gentle fall of hooves on the dewy earth, the puffing exhalations of the horses and the metallic chink of bridles and chain mail.

The men had been on campaign all summer, advancing from the mouth of the Seine to the gates of Paris itself. They had marched and fought together, a vagabond band of brothers, for more years than anyone could remember. Some of them were the sons and even grandsons of those who had gone before. Others were old and gnarled, with bald scalps scarred and pitted with the marks of a lifetime's battles. Yet although they were dusty, blood-spattered and caked with their own filth and sweat, and their matted beards stank of the smoke and rancid grease of countless campfire meals, still there was a wild extravagance to their appearance that only served to emphasise their outlaw status. Some had outlined their blue eyes in heavy black paint. Others had filed their teeth into points or tattooed swirling patterns and runic inscriptions on to their faces and shaven skulls. Others again wore their hair so long that it could be braided into intricate plaits that hung halfway down their backs. Their clothing was as exotic as their grooming. Many wore broad pantaloons, gathered below the knee, made from Chinese silk in gaudy colours and vivid patterns, acquired through the souks of Constantinople, Damascus and Arabia. Gold coins hung from chains around their necks. Their cloaks were clasped with silver pins, longer than a man's forearm, with jewelled heads and needle-sharp points. Even their axes and swords were chased with patterns in silver and gold.

Lesser men who dressed with such effeminate vanity and adornment would have risked derision. But no one dared mock or belittle this flamboyant display. For these were Vikings, or 'Northmen' as the people hereabouts called them: fearsome predators who had put all Christendom to the sword and the torch. They stood as tall and mighty as the pagan gods they worshipped. Yet the man who led them dwarfed them all.

His name was Rollo the Strider, so called because he always went on foot, there being no horse big or strong enough to carry his massive bulk. He was said to be in his sixty-fifth year, yet he carried himself like a man in his prime. In his time, Rollo had roved across the oceans as far as Iceland, leaving corpses without number in his wake and a wife and family on a cold, storm-racked Scottish isle. But for the past twenty years or more, he'd ceased his voyaging and concentrated his depredations on the lands of the Western Franks. Though the rich, fertile valley of the Seine had long been his favourite hunting ground, he and his men had slaughtered, raped and thieved their way across the lowlands of Flanders, the rocky seashores of Brittany and the fields and vineyards of Burgundy.

His raids had made him rich with plunder and furnished him with a concubine, too: Poppa, daughter of Berengar, Count of Bayeux. Rollo had stolen her, bedded her and seen no reason to return her. She pleased him well enough and had given him a fine young son, William, to be his heir. Poppa and the boy were waiting for him now, safe in the coastal lands between Rouen and the sea, where the Northmen had settled in their thousands.

This summer, however, Rollo had encountered an unprecedented reverse. An alliance of Frankish noblemen had managed to defeat him outside the town of Chartres. Now the king of the Franks himself, Charles the Simple, had summoned him to a parley. There was a deal to be done, and the fact that the Franks had been the ones to sue for peace suggested to Rollo that it might be to his personal advantage. After all, if the Franks had thought there was any chance of destroying the Viking threat once and for all, they would surely have attempted to do so. Instead, they seemed to regard their victory as something so rare and precious that it had to be exploited at once, before it could be overturned. By meeting him now, they were essentially surrendering, but on the best possible terms.

Rollo and his men had almost reached the appointed meeting place when the sun finally cut through the mist, the last wisps dissipated and the air cleared. Rollo strode out of the woods and found himself at a point where the river split in two, flowing on either side of a large island, perhaps two hundred paces long and fifty across, given over to grassland and the occasional small tree or bush. For this single day, both sides had agreed that it would be a place of truce, where lifelong enemies would talk, not fight. Whether either party would keep their word was another matter.

A line of stepping stones led across to the island. The Franks stood there now, waiting for the parley to begin. Nobles armoured in brightly polished mail bore shields whose heraldic emblems were echoed in the cloths that bedecked their horses and the pennants that fluttered above their heads. Around them massed a small army of foot soldiers, more than even Rollo and his men could cut down. And then, of course, there was the king.

Charles the Simple was a slender man, handsome in a thin, fine-boned way. He wore silken robes, dyed an imperial purple and trimmed at the cuffs and neck with snowy white ermine, and sat on a gilded wooden throne placed on a raised dais, below a richly embroidered canopy. But as Rollo strode up to the dais, he was not impressed by what he saw. This foppish young king had no natural power or authority beyond that conferred on him by his crown. There was no need to respect, still less fear him. Very well, then, let him make his best offer.

Rollo stood silent and massive, his head almost as high as the canopy under which the king was enthroned. An uneasy murmur rippled through the Frankish ranks. Evidently they were expecting Rollo to make the first move, and for it to be that of an inferior: a bowed head, a bended knee and a few murmured words of obeisance. Charles held up his right hand and wafted it limply, as if graciously giving Rollo permission to honour him.

Rollo straightened his back. He held his head high, looking down his nose as he caught the eye of the king. Still he said nothing. He was prepared to wait all day if he had to. He was completely indifferent to the glaring disapproval of the dukes and barons on either side of the dais. This was a simple trial of will, and as he had anticipated, it was the king who cracked first.

'You appear to forget that you come here in defeat,' Charles said in a tone that suggested he was more puzzled than offended by Rollo's attitude. 'We are the victors, and it is only because of our generosity and our sincere desire for peace that we are prepared to discuss any terms whatsoever, rather than wiping you and your men from the face of the earth.'

Rollo's silent stare remained impassive. 'Say your piece, King of the Franks.'

'Very well, then. I am prepared to make you an offer. In exchange for your sworn commitment to peace and certain other conditions, I will grant you lands in the county of

Flanders: all the coastline from the fishing village of Dunkirk to the island of Ostend and the line for five leagues behind it.'

There was a murmur of surprise among the Franks. They had not expected their king to be so generous to a defeated enemy.

Rollo replied with a blunt 'No. What do I want with mud-flats, marshes and sand? There's bugger-all else there. No people, no cattle, no sheep. So if we needed anything, we'd be back to plunder and pillage, and I don't reckon any of you would fancy that. If you want to live in peace, give us land that will provide us with everything we need without us having to steal it.'

'Do you have anywhere in mind?' the king asked, in a mocking tone that made his nobles laugh. For a moment they'd been worried he might give in to this barbarian.

'Yes, I do,' Rollo replied. 'Give me the land between the Epte and the sea' – he pointed to the river that ran around the island – 'and I'll give you a nice quiet life.'

King Charles could not believe what he had just heard. 'From here to the sea? That must be forty leagues at least.'

'At least,' Rollo agreed. 'And I've controlled it for years without your say-so. I just want what's already mine.'

'You've taken possession of that land as a thief. I'm the only one who can grant you ownership, and a noble title, and all the rights that come with it. And if I do that, I'll want something in return.'

Rollo said nothing. He had spent a lifetime on the move. His constitution had proved astonishingly resilient, but even he knew that he could not hold back time for ever. It would be good to find a place to rest.

'So what do you want?' he asked.

'I have a number of demands and all must be met if we are to have an agreement. The first is that you consent to defend the land I grant you and the territories around it from any more raids by your Northman cousins. You've been a burglar. Now

I'm appointing you my gatekeeper and I expect you to keep my kingdom untouched and my people safe.'

For the first time, Rollo allowed himself the indulgence of a smile. 'Don't worry. If I own this land, no one else is getting their hands on it. What's your second condition?'

'That you worship the Lord God Almighty and his son Jesus Christ. If you want to stay here, you'll do so without your pagan gods.'

'One god is very much like another. I accept.'

'Then you must display your acceptance by wearing the cross and taking a Christian name.'

Rollo shrugged. 'Doesn't matter what my name is, I'll still be the same man. Is that all?'

'No. My last demand is the most important of all. You must become my vassal and grant me your unswerving, unquestioning loyalty and obedience. I will be your king and you will kneel to me. So that is my command to you: kneel and accept me as your lord. Or reject my offer and know that a state of war will once again exist between us.' The king cast an eye over his nobles and troops and added, 'With immediate effect.'

Rollo grimaced. His heavy brow cast deep shadows over his sapphire eyes and his breath became heavy as if some great force were rising within him, making his massive shoulders heave with each expansion of his barrel chest. His men watched him nervously, knowing the signs of their leader's berserker rage and fearing its consequences.

'I kneel to no man,' Rollo said in a voice whose rumble, like the sound of distant thunder, sent a warning of a fearsome storm to come.

'Kneel, or we Franks will finish the job we started at Chartres.'

'I will not,' Rollo insisted.

'I beg you to consider the offer I have made you. I'm giving you land and a title. I'm offering you the chance of peace. Your men will be able to set their weapons aside, find wives and raise families. And all you have to do is kneel.'

Rollo shook his head. 'I will not kneel. But . . .' He let the word hang in the air. 'But I will accept your offer. I'll be your gatekeeper. I'll worship your God. When your kingdom is threatened, I'll bring my men to stand by you. I give you my word on all this and my word is all you need. So for the last time: I will . . . not . . . kneel.'

The Franks had listened with gathering enthusiasm to what Rollo had been saying. Few men, however bloodthirsty, did not welcome the coming of peace. Now they stiffened again, angered as much by the sense that they had been taken for fools as by the Strider's unrepentant insolence. Rollo observed the growing hubbub for a moment, then raised a hand to quiet it and spoke out more loudly than before, so that everyone could hear. 'But . . . since it's your custom for one man to crawl on his knees before another, I'll see if someone else is willing to do it.'

Rollo turned to his men and asked, 'Does anyone want to kneel before the King of the Franks? You all heard what the man said. If you want your share of that land, someone's got to get down and grovel for it.'

His words were met with sullen silence. Rollo's men were no more accustomed than him to bending the knee. Finally a single voice called out, 'How big a share exactly?'

The words came from one of the Vikings' most grizzled veterans, a scraggy beanpole figure whose ancient black cloak was ragged, shiny and green-tinged with wear.

'Ah, Olav the Raven . . . always wanting to know how full your beak will be,' Rollo replied. 'There'll be plenty of land for everyone. But if you do this service, old friend, then you'll be the first in line.'

'I'll need an ox to plough my fields.'

Rollo laughed. 'You can have two strong, fat oxen to pull your plough or fill your pot. How's that?'

Olav looked unimpressed. He grunted non-committally. Then he gave a world-weary shrug, clambered down from his horse and walked out on to the no-man's-land between the two forces, the feathery tatters of his cloak fluttering behind him as he went. He paused for a moment beside Rollo, who said nothing, simply extending an arm in the direction of the Franks. Olav looked at him with a grumpy twist to his mouth, uttered another wordless, disdainful grunt and ambled towards Charles the Simple, who rose from his throne to greet him.

The king lifted the hem of his purple gown and extended his right foot, the toe pointed as daintily as a dancing girl's. Olav stood before him and muttered, 'Now what?'

The king simply glanced down at his foot, raising an eyebrow as he did so. Olav harrumphed again and began with exaggerated care to lower himself, accompanied by catcalls from his fellow Vikings. With every movement, he grimaced and sighed at the toll being paid by his battered old joints and aching muscles. Finally he was down on his left knee, with his right foot flat on the ground in front of him.

'Why don't you ask him to marry you?' some wag shouted from the crowd.

Olav twisted his head over his shoulder and growled, 'Why don't you go fuck yourself?'

Then he turned back again, sighed, grabbed hold of the king's waiting foot and pressed it to his mouth. A great cheer broke out from both sides. The king beamed complacently, content that honour had been satisfied. Olav, meanwhile, was struggling to get up, his task not made any easier by the fact that he was still holding on to the king's foot. He made a massive effort to push himself semi-upright with his right leg. Then he tried to straighten the left one.

In the general excitement, no one seemed to hear the king's cry of alarm. For as Olav struggled to his feet, he lifted the king's foot higher and higher, forcing the royal knee up towards the chest.

Charles desperately waved his arms in a helpless bid to keep his balance. He was slowly toppling over, as surely as a tree whose trunk had been cut almost all the way through. As Olav finally straightened up, he let go of the king's foot, and that, like the last fatal blow of the woodcutter's axe, propelled Charles the Simple off his feet and sent him tumbling backwards into his throne. The gilded chair tilted back on to its rear legs . . . and kept on tilting until it looked as though it too must surely fall, throwing the king head first off the back of the dais.

For a moment the throne hung in the balance, and men reached for their swords, knowing that the instant it fell, the truce would be forgotten and the bloodshed would begin.

No one moved. The fate of men and nations hung on the tilt of that throne, and whatever gods they worshipped would decide it.

The throne trembled. It seemed on the very point of toppling over . . .

Then Charles gave a great convulsive swing of his arms, the balance shifted and his throne crashed forward again, back into place with the king still in it, humiliated but unhurt.

The clatter of the throne against the dais seemed to echo around the island. Every man was silent, waiting to see how the king would react. He was narrow-eyed and white-lipped with rage. If he leapt to his feet screaming insults at the Vikings, his subjects would rush to defend his honour. An insult to their king was an insult to the Franks as well.

The king rose slowly and glared at the Raven, who looked right back at him, saying nothing.

'Get back to your horse, Olav,' said Rollo, breaking the

silence. He waited for his man to withdraw, then took a step towards the king. A thousand Frankish hands reached for their swords. Rollo lifted his palms away from the hilt of his own blade and held them up beside his body to signal that he had no hostile intent. He kept walking until he was right in front of King Charles, and though the king was standing on his dais, Rollo still towered above him like a father over his infant son.

Rollo placed his hands on the king's shoulders, causing the Franks to gasp at his blatant contempt for the body royal, then leaned down and spoke in a low rumble too soft for anyone else to hear. 'I am going to offer you my hand. Take it and I will leave in peace, accepting our agreement in full. Reject it and . . .' He pressed his fingers a little more strongly against the king's bony shoulders, feeling them shudder under his grasp. 'My men are not afraid to die. Yours are.'

Rollo let go of the king, took a step back and held out his hand. 'Well?'

Charles the Simple, King of the Franks, looked at him. A spasm of distaste flickered across his refined features and then, reluctantly, he clasped the Viking's hand in his own.

And so Rollo the Strider became the first Duke of Normandy. He took as his crest two golden leopards on a red field, and created a dynasty bred and reared – like leopards – to hunger, to conquer and to kill.

2

Rouen, Normandy, August 1026

Rollo the Strider was followed as Duke of Normandy by his son
William Longsword. Then came two Duke Richards; the first,
Richard the Fearless, who ruled Normandy for half a century,
brought strength, peace and prosperity to his duchy and was
followed by his son Richard II, 'the Good'. Early in his thirty-
year reign, Richard the Good's forces fought off an attack on
Normandy by the English. Having tasted victory on the battlefield, he secured peace by marrying his sister Emma to the
English king, Ethelred. Thus a daughter of the House of
Normandy became the crowned Queen of England, and not
just once, but twice, for when Ethelred died, Emma married the
man who then seized the throne, Canute the Great, King of
England and Denmark.

Now Richard the Good was forty-eight years old. He was
the undisputed master of a rich and powerful land. He could
stand alongside the kings of England and France, if not as an
equal, then as a man who had earned their respect. But none of
this counted for anything any more. For Richard the Good was
dying.

His final days were passed in his chamber at the ducal
palace in Rouen, the capital city of Normandy. Though it was
a hot August day, a great fire blazed in the room and the
duke lay beneath a pile of fur and woollen rugs. Yet still he
shivered with the bone-deep chill brought on by the shadow
of death.

Richard's family were gathered around the bed. His fifteen-year-old daughter Eleanor rearranged the covers in a futile bid to make him warmer, then withdrew into the shadows. His mother, the Dowager Duchess Gunnor, perched on the bed beside him and gently stroked his forehead. His younger brother Robert, Archbishop of Rouen, stood nearby. He was known as Robert the Dane, for his strapping, tow-headed looks and Viking blood alike. But there was now as much silver as gold in the archbishop's blond hair, and his once square shoulders were starting to hunch, for he was barely a year younger than the dying duke.

Richard looked at his mother through cloudy, semi-blind eyes. 'Is Emma coming to see me?' he croaked.

Gunnor took her son's hand. His flesh was even more shrivelled than her own, and his veins and bones more clearly visible beneath his virtually transparent skin. She shook her head sadly. 'No, my darling. I wish she were here too, but His Majesty forbade it.'

Richard's only response was a soft grunt as he closed his eyes and gave a fractional nod of the head. He knew full well why Canute would never allow his wife to return to her native land; even so, he had hoped that somehow God might have led the king to a more compassionate frame of mind. But compassion was not an indulgence a king could always afford. Not if he wanted to stay on his throne.

With a grimace of effort, Richard raised a hand and gave a feeble wave in his brother Robert's direction. 'Sit by me,' he said.

The archbishop swapped places with his mother.

'Do you think Our Lord will allow me to enter heaven?' Richard asked.

'Of course,' replied the archbishop. 'You have served Him well, Richard. You ruled the duchy justly. You were devout in your worship, and you gave generously to your abbeys and churches. Your soul will take its place in the kingdom of the Lord.'

The hint of a contented smile played at the corners of Richard's mouth. 'That's good,' he sighed. 'Judith is there, I know she is, and I long so much to see her again.'

The mention of his dead wife seemed to light a spark in the duke's mind. He gripped his brother's hand and said, 'Promise me you'll look after my boys. Richard will need your help. He's a good lad, strong and brave. But he's got no experience, no understanding of how to win people over. All he knows is fighting. He needs you to guide him. And Robert, too . . .' The duke paused and smiled again. 'He's got a winning way, that one. But he's impatient. He wants everything, all at once. He's got to be taught to bide his time.'

'Don't worry, brother, I'll keep my eye on both of them. Have no fear, if they step out of line, I'll shove them back on to the right path.'

'And find a good husband for Eleanor, someone who'll be useful to Normandy.'

'I'll find as good a match for her as you did for Emma.'

Richard forced an exhausted smile. 'Thank you. It makes it easier to go, knowing that you're still here to watch over the family.'

'Always.'

'Now I need to talk to my boys . . .'

And so the two brothers on whose young shoulders the future of the House of Normandy depended stepped towards their father's bedside. Richard was clearly a scion of Rollo's blood, a tall young man in his early twenties, heavily built, with a clenched, pugnacious expression more likely to intimidate men than seduce women. Robert, meanwhile, was as long-limbed as his brother, but at the age of just eighteen there was still a boyish air about him, and his face was far more likely to be wreathed in a charming, self-confident grin than twisted into a snarl.

For the first years of Robert's life, his brother Richard had liked him well enough, if only because he hardly noticed his presence. But as Robert grew older and, instead of showing Richard the respect that was his right, seemed, on the contrary to take pleasure in finding new ways to tease and irritate him, so the friction between the two had grown. Richard might still be the stronger, but Robert was quicker and more nimble in both body and wit. Since the one quality they had in common was their family's absolute refusal to concede defeat, no matter what the circumstances, a peaceful resolution to their sibling rivalry was never likely to be found. Duke Richard knew that as well as anyone. But even so, as his final act upon this earth, he was going to try.

'My two fine sons,' he said, with a voice infused with his love of them both and the pain he felt at their mutual hostility. 'Richard, you will be my successor as duke. I bequeath you all the revenues from taxes and fiefdoms; all the proceeds of customs and toll booths; all the ducal palaces, castles and estates. The Norman Militia will be under your command, and every knight and baron in the duchy must swear you his fealty – and that includes you, Robert.'

He turned his attention to his younger son. 'I will make you Count of the Hiémois, with all that county's lands, villages, towns and castles. In return, you will be your brother's loyal vassal. You will show him the respect and obedience that is due to a duke. You will obey his commands and answer his call to serve the cause of Normandy in battle. In return, Richard, you will protect your brother, as a liege lord should protect all his subjects.'

Richard darted a sharp, acidic look at Robert and then

turned his eyes back to his father. He did not so much say as grunt the single word, 'Yes.'

Now the duke addressed them both. 'I know what it's like to be at daggers drawn with one's own brother. Do you think your uncle Robert and I were always close friends?'

'Bitter enemies, more like,' the archbishop laughed.

'Very bitter,' the duke agreed. 'But when we became men – true, serious, grown men – we set our differences aside. And you know why? Because we learned that our petty disputes counted for nothing.'

Duke Richard grimaced with effort as he forced himself to sit up in bed and pour the last of his energy into his words. 'All that matters is our family, our dynasty and our legacy. This is our land, our duchy, and no one is going to take it from us. We are the House of Normandy and we must stand together against our foes, or they will pick us off one by one. Promise me that you understand?'

'Yes, Father,' the two sons replied, in unison for once.

The duke slumped back, exhausted, on to his pillows. He looked towards his brother, the archbishop. 'Now read me my last rites,' he said. 'I have nothing more to say.'

The duke was buried at the Abbey of Fécamp. He was succeeded by his namesake son, who became Duke Richard III.

Robert, meanwhile, headed south-west from Rouen to his newly bequeathed territory in the Hiémois. The county seat was Exmes, where a modest wooden castle stood, but Robert ignored it and made his way instead to the county's other large town, Falaise. Beside him rode his oldest and closest friend, Herluin the Orphan. Herluin was as short and stocky as a bulldog, but his face was open, honest and good-natured. His mother had died giving birth to him, and his father, a knight who had devoted his entire adult life to the service of the House of

Normandy, was killed in battle when Herluin was still a very small boy. Duke Richard took the newly orphaned lad into his household as a companion for Robert and the pair had been inseparable ever since. Herluin had inherited his father's loyalty, to which had been added his gratitude for the kindness and generosity the duke and his family had shown him, and his devotion to Robert was as deep as his friendship.

The two young men reined in their horses atop a hillside overlooking the town. Below them a cluster of houses and churches stood at the foot of a high, rocky spur, topped by a large castle whose keep, gatehouse and inner walls were all fashioned from stone.

'So there's Falaise,' said Robert. 'What do you think, Herluin, is it part of the Hiémois?'

'I think so,' Herluin replied.

'I think so too. And my father said that all the land, and the towns and castles of the Hiémois belonged to me. So that would make Falaise mine, wouldn't it?'

'I suppose so, yes.'

'So the castle must be mine, too.'

Herluin grimaced nervously. 'Well I'm not sure. I mean, I thought your father bequeathed all the ducal castles to Richard.'

'He did, along with the ducal estates. But he made a specific exception for the Hiémois. And we agree that Falaise is part of the Hiémois and the castle is part of Falaise. So the castle belongs to me.'

'If you say so.'

'I do. And now we're going to ride into that castle, and I'm going to claim it and it's going to be mine.'

And with those words, Robert spurred his horse and rode along the hilltop towards Falaise, blithely unaware of what the consequences of that ride would be.

Book One:

The Making of the Man

Autumn 1026–Early Spring 1027

1

Falaise, Normandy

Right at the heart of the ancient forest lay a glade where the interlaced canopy of oak and ash trees, elms and chestnuts thinned and the land dropped away into a deep circular depression. Its sides were steep and virtually bare of vegetation, with just the occasional stunted sapling managing to cling to the rock face, while the bottom was scattered with bracken, brambles, bushes and small trees. The local people called it the Mouth of Hell, for it was an easy matter to lose one's bearings when travelling through the forest by night or in a thick fog, then fall over the lip and tumble to one's death. There had even been cases of bolting horses, spooked by a smell or sound in the forest, plunging headlong into the abyss, carrying themselves and their riders to their doom.

A small group of horsemen, most of them high-born sons of noble families, were standing at the edge of the drop doing their best to calm their nervous mounts while they peered down into the depths. They were flanked to one side by a pack of snow-white Alaunts, short-coated hunting dogs bred for their muscular build, flat skulls and mantrap jaws. The dogs were barking with an excitement bordering on frenzy, milling around, barging and snapping at one another while their handlers shouted commands and lashed out with whips and sticks to keep control of the pack.

There had been a frost overnight and it had yet to melt away, so the fallen leaves were still white-dusted and crisp beneath boots, horseshoes and paws, while the air was filled with the steamy breath of the hunters and their animals alike.

'There he is!' called out Herluin the Orphan. He pointed down into the Mouth, towards a briar rose on which the hips stood out in scatterings of bright scarlet against the thorny green-black stems. 'Just to the right of that . . .'

Robert of Normandy narrowed his eyes as he followed his companion's directions. Within the shadow cast by the plant there was a movement, one blackness inside another, yet visible to a sharp, well-trained eye.

'Yes, got him! Well spotted, Herluin!' The words were delivered with boyish excitement and energy, yet Robert sat tall and proud in his high double-girthed saddle. There was an easy confidence to the way he held his courser's reins in one hand and his hunting spear in the other, letting it rest against his right shoulder. And the body beneath his wolf-skin cloak and the padded leather surcoat covering him from shoulder to mid calf was lean and strong.

'By heaven,' Robert went on, 'he's a mighty beast, isn't he? A good six feet nose to tail, I'd say. Tough old fighter, too, to survive a fall like that.' Now it was his turn to point. 'Look over there, at that stump growing out of the cliff face. That's freshly broken. He must have come racing out of the woods, gone over the edge and hit the tree on the way down. That's what saved him. What incredible luck. It would have been a sorry end to the hunt if our quarry had died from a damned fall.'

'Kind of him to provide us with a moving target for archery practice, though.'

'Archery? Come on, Herluin, you can't be firing off arrows like a common bowman. The only way for a knight to kill a magnificent old monster like that is by hand, with his spear and his sword. And since you'd never get a horse down there, it'll have to be done the true warrior's way: on foot.'

22

Robert dismounted, leaving his horse for his squire to tend. Not wanting to be encumbered, he took off his cloak and gave that to the young lad too. A little way off, a narrow path, barely wide enough for a man to walk down, wended and twisted its way down the side of the cliff. He had taken a couple of steps towards it when he was stopped in his tracks by Herluin's voice. 'Good luck, my lord . . . God be with you.'

Robert grinned back with a young man's easy certainty of his own immortality. 'Don't worry. I may be descending into hell, but I've got no intention of staying there.'

He made his way to the dogs, whose barks had now given way to sullen, menacing growls, and gestured at one of the men standing guard over them. 'Give me Bloodfang and Snow.'

'Yes, m'lord,' the kennel hand replied, stepping into the pack of dogs and cutting out two of the biggest and most menacing.

Robert gave a piercing whistle and faced the dogs, slapping his thighs. They bounded towards him and he gave them each a rough, affectionate scrub of his gloved fingers around their ears before walking towards the point on the cliff's edge where the path began. As he looked over the side, Robert wondered for a moment whether it had really been such a good idea to be so brazenly bold, for the bare stone was slippery with half-melted frost and the drop was higher than any castle battlement on which he had ever stood. But it would not do to show the slightest sign of fear in front of the others, so he called to the dogs and urged them down the path ahead of him, laughing aloud as the two animals stood at the top of the uninviting track, sniffing the ground suspiciously and showing little sign of wanting to set foot on it.

'I'm sorry, m'lord,' the kennel man called out, 'but they're hunting dogs, not mountain goats!'

'We'll see about that,' Robert replied.

He grabbed Bloodfang by the scruff of his neck and almost threw him down the path. The Alaunt gave a yelp of fear as his paws scrabbled for purchase, then he got his footing and set off downhill, tentatively at first but then with gathering excitement as he caught the wild boar's scent. Snow followed in his wake, and as their barking echoed around the walls of the Mouth of Hell, Robert went after them, doing his best to affect an air of devil-may-care jauntiness. He discovered to his surprise that the more he acted like a man who felt no fear, the more his worries seemed to disappear, so that he was taken in by his own deception. By the time he reached the bottom of the path and stepped out into the middle of the Mouth of Hell, Robert of Normandy's confidence in his ability to kill his quarry had been fully restored.

The boar must have caught the deadly scents of dogs and men, for he raced away on short, spindly legs that looked oddly insubstantial beneath his massive shoulders and barrel chest. He was powering through the bracken, moving so fast that he only just managed to skitter to a halt before he smashed into the face of the cliff. He turned and trotted along it in a futile search for a means of escape, so engrossed in his task that he barely noticed the dogs' approach until they were almost upon him. Then, unable to run away, he turned to face his pursuers.

The Alaunts were fast, powerful dogs, well able to run down and savage a man if trained and commanded to do so, but even they were no match for a boar this size. Robert watched as they darted up to their quarry, barking, snarling and snapping at its legs. The boar gave an outraged squeal – a high, feeble sound from such a massive beast – and swung its huge head from side to side, sending the dogs fleeing from the rapier tips of its tusks as they scythed through the air.

All the time, Robert crept closer. He came forward in a low, crouching gait with his spear held in front of him, angled upwards, his eyes fixed on the boar, which was now directly in front of him, less than ten paces away.

The dogs made another attack, and this time Bloodfang got close enough to snap his jaws at the powerful muscles bunched around the boar's left shoulder, tearing through the tough hide and leaving a splash of crimson against the black-brown coat. The boar howled again, and made a desperate, stabbing lunge of its head towards Bloodfang, meeting nothing but fresh air as the dog leapt backwards. The boar stood with the weight of its body leaning backwards, poised for further retreat; Bloodfang's head was still stretched forward, snarling defiance through foaming lips and gore-spattered teeth.

The boar was hurt, enraged and distracted. It had forgotten about the second dog, Snow, which had crept round behind it and now attacked, snapping at one of the boar's hind legs, drawing another carmine streak of fresh, warm blood. The boar howled in pain and leapt away from its tormentor, and as it did so, it caught sight of the man standing right in front of it, barely moving, presenting an unmissable target. The animal charged, its skinny little legs shifting its huge bulk with astonishing acceleration as it raced straight for Robert.

The earth seemed to tremble beneath the pounding charge, but the young lord did not flinch. He stood his ground, his eyes fixed on the tiny patch of the boar's chest visible beneath its long snout as it came ever closer. The beast would be on him in an instant, yet time had suddenly slowed to a crawl and Robert's senses were so sharp that he could distinguish every bristle on the boar's coat and feel its steaming breath on his skin. Somewhere in the back of his mind he heard the voices of the men up above shouting warning and encouragement, but they seemed so faint and distant that their words were indistinct. All his concentration was focused on the danger close at hand.

He aimed the finely honed and polished blade of his lance at a point below the boar's throat, right in the middle of its chest, and watched as the animal ran directly on to the steel. The blade pushed against the thick hide for an instant and then it was through, cutting into the body of the beast just as the dogs' teeth had done. But the spear went much further, deflecting off the breastbone, finding a path between two ribs and passing deep into the great barrel torso.

The momentum of the boar's charge was so great that the spear might have been buried to its full length, like a roasting spit, bringing those deadly tusks right up into Robert's face, were it not for a cross-guard at the bottom of the blade that was specifically designed to prevent such an occurrence. It slammed against the boar's ribs, cracking two of them, but stopping the spear in an instant.

The whole process had taken just a fraction of a second, but now the spear was moving as fast as the boar, right back towards Robert. The shock of the impact drove the weapon from his hands, and had he not had a young man's reactions, as yet unburdened by time, wine and physical decay, he could never have flung himself to one side of the onrushing animal as it thundered past, slashing its tusks just a hair's-breadth away from his body. He hit the frost-hardened ground with an impact that jarred his bones and drove the air from his lungs.

The wounded, maddened boar kept racing forward, the part-buried lance pointing ahead of it and bouncing along the ground in a grotesque porcine parody of a charging knight in armour. But then the handle of the spear hit a rock that protruded from the ground. It jammed hard against the unyielding stone and for a moment the boar seemed to be flying through the air as the spear briefly acted like a lever, lifting it off its feet. But the weight of the animal proved too much for the wooden shaft, which snapped in two. The boar thudded back down to earth and stood there for a second, its chest heaving, every exhalation sending a fine spume of blood into the air. The spear had pierced its lungs and it was mortally wounded. But a dying animal could still take an unwary hunter with it to the grave.

Robert did not have the slightest concern for his own safety. The proximity of death and the thrill of his survival had left him drunk with the joy of being alive. He was laughing as he sprang to his feet, punched the air and gave a wild, exultant, triumphant yell. By now the two dogs had caught up with the boar. The metallic scent of its blood was filling their nostrils. They could tell the end would not be long and were skulking around the stricken animal, waiting for the moment to make their final attack. The boar was waiting too, slowly drowning in its own blood, its chest heaving with the effort of dragging air into flooded lungs, the spray from its breath turning a darker, richer red with every exhalation.

But Robert did not wait. He drew his hunting knife and ran straight at the boar, dashing between the dogs. The boar turned and tried to run away, but its strength was fading and it had managed only a few stumbling strides before Robert caught up with it. He leapt full length on to its back, slamming his face into the crest that ran like an abrasive scrubbing brush along its spine.

He winced as the bristles scoured his skin. As the boar bucked, trying to throw him off, he wrapped his left arm around one side of its thick neck, grabbed a handful of rough hide and clung on. His knife was in his right hand and he reached down and slashed it back towards him, hacking at the boar's exposed throat once, twice, and then a third time before he finally cut through the windpipe.

The animal collapsed with Robert still on its back, his head lying flat against the boar's in a strangely intimate embrace. In its last few seconds Robert saw the terror, the agony and the bafflement in its eyes. The excitement he had felt just a few seconds earlier drained from his body and he was left with a deep sorrow and even shame at being the cause of such suffering. But then he was getting to his feet, patting and praising the two excited Alaunts and answering the cries of his hunting companions and servants as they made their way down the narrow path towards him. The boar would make a fine feast for his household. There would be toasts to his courage and skill as a huntsman. He would tell the tale of how he had slain the giant beast in the Mouth of Hell, and the story of it would spread across his corner of Normandy and grow with every telling.

When he thought of it like that, Robert felt certain that the boar had died a fine and noble death. His spirits began to rise again. By the time Herluin reached him a minute or two later and gave him the first of many congratulatory slaps on the back, the grin across his face was just as gleeful as ever.

'So what are you going to tell Father?' Talvas, the youngest son of the Count of Bellême, asked his older brother Warin as they watched the triumphant hunter make his way back up the path.

'Hard to say, really . . . Robert likes hunting, I suppose, but who doesn't? He's pretty pleased with himself, living in Falaise Castle, but so would I be. What else is there?'

Now Talvas knew for certain why his father had told him to accompany his brother on their spying mission. Talvas might only be sixteen and Warin six years his senior, but there was no doubting which of them had the sharper mind. From the moment they had arrived at Robert's gatehouse, explaining that they were travelling from Bayeux back to their family's castle at Alençon and requesting shelter for the night, Talvas had kept his eyes and ears open.

'The way he went after that boar shows that Robert's brave

but impetuous, and arrogant too,' he said. 'He always thinks he'll win, no matter what. That's why he's in Falaise. He wanted it, he took it. But can he hold it? He doesn't have very many men – far fewer than we do. Wait . . . here he comes.'

Robert was still smiling as he strode towards the Bellêmes. 'Did you see the kill? That boar put up a hell of a good fight.'

'It was really exciting!' exclaimed Talvas, feigning an air of boyish enthusiasm far removed from his true nature.

Robert laughed. 'It was a bit too exciting from where I was standing! So are you staying another night? We'll be eating the boar at dinner. It'd be a pity to miss it.'

'I'm sorry, my lord,' said Warin. 'We're expected back in Alençon tomorrow. So we'll be on our way very soon and aim to reach Sées by nightfall.'

'Have a safe trip, then. If you'll excuse me, I've got to find a way to get that boar from down there to up here.'

Warin and Talvas rode away through the forest. 'I wonder why Father wanted us to visit Falaise,' Talvas mused. 'He must have something in mind, but what?'

'I haven't a clue,' said Warin. 'But you know the old man. Whatever plans he has, they'll be nothing but bad news for Robert of Normandy.'

2

The dead boar was far too heavy to manhandle along the narrow path that ran up the side of the Mouth of Hell, so the carcass had to be gutted and crudely butchered where it lay, then brought back up in pieces that were piled on a woodman's cart for carrying back to Falaise Castle. Robert and Herluin rode a little ahead of their men, locked in conversation as they tried to recapture every instant of the hunt. As they reached the edge of the forest, almost at the outskirts of Falaise itself, Robert suddenly pulled on the reins and brought his horse to a halt. He held up his hand to indicate that Herluin should stop too. Then he cocked his head, as perfectly still as one of his hunting dogs catching a scent, twisted his face into a quizzical grimace and said, 'Wait! Did you hear that?'

'What?' asked Herluin.

Robert paused a second, trying to catch the sound again over the sigh of the breeze in the trees, then nodded and said, 'That!'

Sure enough, there were girlish voices singing and peals of high-pitched laughter, somewhere up ahead of them. Now Robert's eyes lit up. He put his finger to his lips and walked his horse down the path as slowly and quietly as possible. A few seconds later, he and Herluin emerged from the trees on to a stretch of open ground, beyond which stood the stockyards where cattle brought to market were held, the slaughterhouses where they died, the skinners' and fleshmongers' premises, and the wooden sheds of the tanneries for which Falaise was famous across Normandy. The wind shifted for a second and drove the vile, excremental stench of the leather vats towards them, making both men cover their mouths and noses with their hands until, to their relief, the wind changed direction again and the air was fresh once more.

Now they could concentrate on the girls. There were three of them and, evidently long accustomed to the reeking tanneries, they had not paused for an instant as they sang their song, and spun across the frosted ground in a whirl of twirling skirts and flying hair.

One of the girls started a new verse:

> Pretty lady fair of face
> How I love you so-oh.

A second girl joined in, repeating the opening lines while the first continued:

> Sweet and gentle, pure and chaste,
> Pretty lady fair of face.

Robert had often heard his mother and sister sing these very words. He smiled at the memory and joined in under his breath as a third voice took up the first line of the roundelay while the first sang:

> I'd give my life for your embrace,
> Please don't let me go.

But then something caught his eye, and all his nostalgic memories vanished in an instant as the three singers united for the final refrain:

> Pretty lady fair of face,
> How I love you so-oh.

They finished their song with more shrieks of laughter, still so rapt that they had not noticed the two horsemen. Then one of the horses whinnied and the spell was broken. The girls realised that they had been observed by men, and noble ones at that, and became uncertain, shy and embarrassed.

'Mother of God, she's beautiful,' Herluin gasped.

'She's mine,' said Robert, not for an instant doubting which of the three Herluin was talking about, nor his own right to try her first.

He kicked his mount into a walk and approached the girls with Herluin in his wake. His expression was so serious, so intense that it unnerved one of the trio, a plain, dreary creature, as tall and thin and featureless as a broomstick. 'We're very, very sorry, my lords,' she pleaded. 'We didn't mean no harm.'

'No need to apologise,' said Herluin kindly. 'We greatly enjoyed your singing.'

Robert said nothing. The second girl was little more than a tavern wench in the making, with a buxom figure, a mass of unkempt curly black hair and a lascivious smile cloaked in an unsubtle attempt at coyness. He did not pay her a second glance. All his attention was focused on the girl beside her. She was wearing a deep blue hooded cloak. It was held at her neck by a silver clasp, and for a moment Robert thought she might be of noble blood. But no, if that were the case he would surely have heard about her long before: a fine-born maiden this beautiful could not have been kept a secret.

Her hood had fallen down as she danced to reveal a tumbling mass of hair that seemed to match the burnished copper and blazing orange of the autumn leaves all around them. Her eyes were as clear and blue as the sky above and they looked directly into his own with a gaze that seemed to cut right through to his heart, even to his immortal soul.

Robert tried to think of something to say. He prided himself on being ready with a quick response to any situation, but for once his wits had deserted him. He sat mutely astride his horse, inwardly cursing his own stupidity while the girl looked back at him. And was it just his imagination, or was there the faintest hint of a smile at the corner of her mouth? In all of heaven there could not be an angel more beautiful, nor in hell a devil more tempting, and Robert could only pray that something, anything would break the spell she had cast over him.

He heard a cough beside him and then Herluin's voice saying, 'My lord . . .'

Robert did not reply. The girl was a sorceress. She had robbed him of the power of speech.

'We really should be going back to the castle . . .'

Finally Robert spoke. 'Yes. What?' He was grunting like a simpleton. 'The castle . . . yes . . . of course . . .'

He pursed his mouth, trying to summon the strength to leave, offered a curt, wordless nod in the direction of the three girls, then gave a desperate tug on his rein and pulled his horse away from them as if it had been enchanted as completely as he had. Robert had the distinct feeling that Herluin, too, was trying to suppress a smile. He had made a fool of himself in front of the most wondrous girl in all creation. At the moment when he should have been at his absolute best, he had failed utterly. He rode on for fifty paces or more, slumped in the saddle as elegantly as a sack of turnips, sinking ever deeper into self-pitying despondency. Then he heard the sound of whistles and catcalls from behind him, accompanied by increasingly excited barks and yelps.

He turned round and saw the rest of the hunting party coming down the path. The column was just passing the spot where the girls had been dancing. It had slowed to a crawl and the men, their spirits buoyed by the morning's triumph, were expressing their appreciation for the young women in the most blatant fashion while the hounds, picking up on the humans' arousal, strained excitably at the leash. Two of the women had stopped to face the men, and Robert heard harsh, high-pitched peasant accents, answering with words as crude as they'd been given. The third, though, was hurrying down the path, her cloak pulled tight around her, trying to escape the scene.

Robert could not see her face at this distance, nor even a flash of her hair, but he did not need to.

He wheeled his horse round. 'Don't wait for me,' he said to Herluin, then dug his heels into his mount's flank and urged it forward, moving from a walk to a canter to a full gallop in barely a dozen strides.

He was already riding flat out by the time Herluin called out to him, 'Where are you going?'

Robert did not slow his pace for an instant as he shouted back over his shoulder, 'Hunting!'

The men were becoming more hostile as Herleva the tanner's daughter refused to acknowledge them. They'd stopped professing their love and lust for her. They'd even given up asking her to smile and cheer up. Now they were merely venting their frustration with insults, saying she was a stuck-up, frigid little bitch and telling her she should be more like her friends.

She didn't care. She was used to the things men said and the feel of their hands as they made a grab for her when she went to fetch her father from the tavern, or shopped at the market stalls; even as she took her pew in church on Sunday mornings. She'd grown used to being the object of other people's desire. Every lad in the village had tried to win her heart and take her to bed, and most of their fathers too. But now the tables had been turned. She'd recognised Count Robert at once, of course. He'd taken up residence at the castle at the beginning of September, just days after the death of his father, the late duke, whose property it had been. Since then he'd become a hero to every young female in Falaise and the topic of countless breathless conversations.

Nothing, though, had prepared Herleva for the effect of his actual flesh-and-blood presence. He'd looked so fine astride his courser, like a living sculpture or a young god, that all she could do was stare at him, the way boys usually stared at her. She'd lost herself in his eyes, trying to decide if they were grey or blue or green, for the colours seemed to shift and change like the gleam of a pebble in a sparkling sunlit stream. She must have lost her wits too, for she'd managed not a single word of greeting. No wonder Robert hadn't bothered even to say goodbye. Why would he care about a stupid village girl who couldn't pay him the slightest respect?

And then she heard the sound of a galloping horse. She looked up and there he was, charging down the forest path towards her, taking her breath away as he pulled up in front of the other men, scarcely five paces away from her, and shouted, 'That's enough! Leave these maidens alone. Say a word, any of you, and by God I'll make you regret it.'

He aimed a furious glare at the hunting party. 'Move on!' he commanded them, pointing away down the path. 'Now! Come on . . . move!'

The column got back under way. When the last straggler had gone by, Robert jumped down from his horse and, ignoring the other girls completely, walked straight across to Herleva.

'I apologise on my men's behalf,' he said. 'Their behaviour was disgraceful.'

Herleva just about managed to stammer, 'Th-thank you, my lord.'

He was so close to her she could have reached out and touched him; close enough to see the splashes of dried blood on his leather gloves and the sleeves of his tunic; close enough to feel the size and physical presence of him. Robert was tall and broad-shouldered. From the way his brow glowered, the muscles in his jaw clenched and his eyes blazed, it was easy to understand why men feared his anger. Yet there was something almost feminine in the sensuous curve of his mouth and the fullness of his lips. And there was a shyness, too, about the way his brow was now tilted a little to one side and those same eyes seemed more vulnerable and uncertain.

There were little scratches, she could now see, across one side of his face. It was all Herleva could do not to take that one last step between them and kiss the marks away.

The young lord took a long, deep breath, almost as if he were summoning his courage before battle, and then quietly but with heartfelt intensity said, 'I want to see you. I have to . . . this evening. I . . . I command it. There's a postern gate, round the back of the castle. It's very private. Go there an hour after sunset, once it's properly dark. I'll make sure that you're let in.'

'No, my lord, I will not do that.' The words came to Herleva without thinking. If she had given herself even a second's reflection, she would surely have bitten her tongue.

Robert looked as though she had slapped him. She could see the temper rising in his eyes and quickly said, 'I . . . I . . . have to ask my father's permission.'

'Then tell him from me he'd better grant it.'

'And . . . and there's something else . . .'

Robert frowned suspiciously. 'What?'

'If he says that I may come, I don't want to use the postern. I want to come in by the main gate.'

'But everyone will see you.'

Herleva nodded, but was too afraid to speak. She cursed her rashness and stupidity. She had made the Count of the Hiémois angry. It was not only a matter of what he could do to her; he had the power to banish her whole family from the town. They

36

would lose their home. Her father's business would be stripped from him. Oh Mary, mother of God, she prayed silently, please don't let my family suffer because of what I've done.

But then Robert took her completely by surprise. He smiled, not just any smile, but a grin that lit up his face and made her feel that she and he were conspirators in a wonderful, wicked little plot. The way he directed his complete attention towards her, the full force of his personality, was intoxicating. She felt a little breathless. Her heart was racing, her lips were burning hot and she seemed to be melting inside. No man had ever had that effect on her before. What had he done to her?

'Very well,' said Robert. 'You shall come in by the front gate. And I will be waiting at the top of the steps, by the door to the keep, especially to meet you.'

He turned without another word, mounted his horse and rode away.

Her friends had been hanging back, not daring to intrude, but now they ran up to her, squealing with excitement. Herleva felt as though her heart was doing somersaults of joy, flipping over and over inside her chest. They showered her with questions: 'What did he say?' 'Does he want to see you?' 'Why was he smiling like that?' 'What did you do?'

Finally, when they'd all calmed down enough for Herleva to make herself heard, a triumphant smile crossed her face as though she were the cat that had got the cream, and the fish and a nice fat mouse to boot, and she said, 'He likes me . . . Almost as much as I like him.'

One of the girls hurried off home, desperate to be the first to start spreading this spectacular bit of gossip, and Herleva was left alone with Judith, her best friend. Judith was by no means as beautiful as Herleva, but her abundant curves and come-hither manner ensured that she received just as much male attention: more of it, in fact, once boys discovered that she was only too happy to trade flirtatious banter and even the occasional cuddle or kiss.

'Come on,' she said. 'Tell me all and leave nothing out. I want every word, every dreamy look he gave you!'

At first, Judith responded to what Herleva had to say with giggles and little cries of 'No!' 'My God!' or 'I don't believe you!' But when she came to her promise to go to the castle that night, Judith stared at her, gawping in disbelief. Finally she gasped, 'And I thought I was the biggest slut in Falaise!'

3

'You said WHAT?!' Fulbert the tanner exclaimed, when his daughter described her chance encounter with Robert of Normandy, told him she'd agreed to meet the count that night and announced her plan to walk through the main gate of Falaise Castle for all the world to see.

Fulbert was a man bent on self-improvement. Over the years he had worked his way up from apprentice to tradesman and was now the master of his own tannery, curing cow and pig skins into the leathers without which horses could not be ridden, nor fighting men clad. He was blessed with a wife, Doda, whose shrewd, calculating nature was the perfect foil to his more straightforward abilities, and the couple had two strong sons, Osbern and Walter.

They were decent, honest lads, but there was nothing particularly special about them; nothing that would lift Fulbert's family on to a higher social plane. Herleva, though, was another matter. All fathers thought their daughters beautiful, but Fulbert knew his was, and he was well aware what her beauty was worth. He was determined to preserve Herleva's virtue intact and unsullied until the day she married a man with enough money, status and power to carry her away to a better life. Under their marital bed he and Doda kept a stout chest containing their most precious possessions, including a bag of silver coins they had saved for Herleva's dowry. All his hopes rested on her. Which explained the stomach-churning, jaw-dropping horror that seized him now.

Herleva, however, seemed blissfully indifferent to his suffering. 'Well it just didn't seem right, going in secretly, round the side, as if I was doing something shabby . . . something dishonourable.'

'And what do you call marching in like a brazen strumpet?' Fulbert retorted. 'Just how honourable is that? You're not a little girl any more. You must know there's only one reason a man like that calls for a girl like you . . .'

'What do you mean, "a girl like you"?' she replied indignantly. 'You're always saying I should be proud of who I am. Why do you want me to be ashamed now?'

'Because . . . because . . .' Fulbert adored his daughter. He'd been wrapped around her little finger from the first moment he'd looked into those lovely blue eyes, and nothing had changed in the sixteen years since. And she knew it. She always found a way to win him round, no matter how angry he was to begin with. He gazed helplessly at his wife. 'You tell her, love . . . tell her what I mean.'

Doda patted the wooden bench next to her. 'Come here, sweetheart.'

Herleva did not move for a second, to show that she could not easily be ordered around, then sat herself down beside her thin, dark, beady-eyed mother.

Doda reached out, took one of Herleva's hands and stroked it gently. 'What your father is trying to say,' she began, looking Herleva in the eye, 'is that you're a very beautiful girl and anyone can see it. His lordship certainly can and he . . . well, he wants to take advantage of you.'

'That's not what he said! He said he wanted to see me,' Herleva protested, not even convincing herself.

'Well, what a young man says and what he thinks are two very different things, 'specially when he's a mighty lord looking at a humble maiden like you.'

'But I know he cares about me,' she said, meaning it this time. 'I could tell. He . . . he didn't know what to say. The very first time he saw me. We just looked at each other and neither of us could speak. Not a word.'

Now Herleva grabbed Doda's hands and squeezed tight as she said, 'It was wonderful, Mama. And he felt it too. I know he did!'

She gazed at her mother imploringly. The older woman looked back, her lips pursed shrewdly, assessing what Herleva had said. Then she looked up at her husband and said, 'I wonder . . . Maybe we're wrong to object. This might be the moment we've been praying for. Our little girl may just have landed the biggest prize in all of Normandy.'

Her husband gave a dismissive snort. 'Heavens above, woman! When did you go soft-headed? That Robert is the duke's brother. His wife'll be some fancy princess, not a common lass he spotted on a hunting expedition.'

He looked at Herleva with a plaintive expression on his face: 'Sorry, love, but that's the truth of it.'

'Who said anything about marriage?' asked Doda. 'And why shouldn't a lord fall for a common lass he met out hunting? The count's grandfather, the first Duke Richard, did. I remember my mother telling me all about it when I was a little girl . . .'

'We don't have time for your mum's gossip now,' Fulbert protested.

'Oh yes we do . . . just you wait and see.'

'Please, Mama, tell me what happened to old Duke Richard,' Herleva begged, sensing that the story might work in her favour.

'Well, Duke Richard the Fearless, as people called him, had a wife, but she died so then he was alone again. There was a forester who watched over some of the duke's hunting grounds and he was married to a woman named Sainsfrida, who was famed for her beauty. So the duke went hunting in that particular part of the forest and made sure that he stayed overnight in the forester's house. Sure enough, this Sainsfrida was just as lovely as everyone had said, and the duke told the forester that he wanted her brought to his bedchamber.'

'But that's awful!' Herleva exclaimed. 'She was the forester's wife!'

'Yes, and Richard was the duke, and if he wanted her, he was going to have her. So the forester had to go to his wife and tell her what the duke had commanded.'

'I'd have knocked his head off, duke or no duke,' muttered Fulbert.

'And then he'd have had you imprisoned and most likely killed and where would that have got your family? Anyway, it didn't matter because Sainsfrida had a plan. She sent her sister Gunnor, who was a virgin and even more beautiful than her, to the duke instead. And Duke Richard was captivated by Gunnor's beauty, just like you say young Robert has been captivated by you.'

'What happened next?' Herleva asked, thrilled by the idea that a common girl could win a duke's heart.

'Ah well, that's just it,' said her mother. 'Duke Richard fell in love with Gunnor and made her his concubine and she gave him four fine sons and a few daughters too. And one of them was Emma, who's the Queen of England!'

Doda paused for breath before continuing in a much more calculating voice. 'I ask you, Fulbert, if Gunnor could do all that, why shouldn't Herleva win Count Robert's heart? And if she did, just think what that would do for our family. This town is full of people looking down their noses at us, going on about what a smelly, disgusting business it is being a tanner. They'd change their tune fast enough if we had the ear of Count Robert. And it would be good for business, too. I'm sure Herleva could make sure that any leather the castle bought came from your tannery.'

'Well, that would certainly be worth a bit,' said Fulbert, who was no slower than his wife to spot a business opportunity.

'And why should you be a tanner all your life, eh? Play your cards right and it won't be long before we have a little estate of our own, even a title for you or one of the boys if we're lucky . . .'

She stopped mid flow and looked about her, frowning. 'Where's that blasted girl gone? Hey, Fulbert! Did you see where she went?'

Doda got up and stood with her legs apart, hands on hips, glaring at her surroundings as if she could will her daughter to reappear. 'By God, I swear if that little madam has gone off to see Count Robert without so much as a by-your-leave, I don't care if she marries him this very evening. I'll smack her pretty little backside so hard she won't sit down for a week!'

'There's no need for that,' came a voice from right behind her.

Doda spun round to see Herleva standing by the door to her parents' bedchamber. She was wearing a plain white linen chemise and over it a dress made of the finest Flanders cloth. It was a dazzling scarlet, belted at the waist by a girdle of woven leather and embroidered with a delicate pattern of white and yellow flowers at the neckline and the hems of the sleeves. She gave a little twist of her hips that set the skirt swirling around her legs. Then she looked at her mother and asked, 'Will he think I look pretty if he sees me wearing this?'

'But that was going to be your wedding-day dress. I've been keeping it specially . . .'

'I know, Mama, but I just want to look nice for Robert. I can't bear him to think he's made a terrible mistake and—'

Herleva broke down in sobs and Doda took her in her arms.

'There, there,' she said. 'I'm sure Count Robert will think you're the loveliest girl he's ever seen.'

Doda only spoke the words to comfort her daughter and stop her crying. But it struck her now that they were no more than the simple truth. Any red-blooded man with eyes in his head and a cock between his legs would take one look at Herleva and want her in his bed. Once she was there, it was simply a matter of exploiting the relationship to make sure she and Fulbert derived the full benefit from it. True, their girl would no longer be a virgin. But any future husband would be likely to forgive that if the man who'd had his bride first was the brother of the duke. In fact it might even make Herleva more desirable as a prospective wife, not less.

That red dress had been bought as an investment. And tonight, Doda gratefully concluded, it would deliver a most handsome profit.

4

The vaulted storerooms beneath the keep of Falaise Castle were crammed to bursting point with food. Bulging sacks of flour, oats, barley, wheat, nuts, dried beans and turnips were piled from floor to ceiling. Woven baskets were filled with autumn crops of leeks, mushrooms, apples and pears. Huge sides of beef, pork, mutton and horse hung from iron hooks, alongside cured joints of ham and bacon and all manner of sausages. There were shelves piled with massive round cheeses; earthenware jars filled with honey; great quantities of dried, smoked and salted fish; a stone tank in which live eels and lampreys writhed and seethed; huge wooden tuns of wine and beer that stood as tall as a man.

Robert of Normandy examined the entire magnificent display. 'It's not enough,' he said.

The castle cellarer frowned, as if unsure what his response should be. Might the count be attempting some kind of a joke? He could surely not have meant what he said. The man gave a little laugh, playing along with the young master's conceit, and replied, 'I do assure you, my lord, that we are very well provided for.'

'Nevertheless, you will need more,' Robert insisted.

So he was being serious. The cellarer did not like that at all. He was a proud man with decades of experience of looking after the castle and its inhabitants. Robert, on the other hand, was nothing but an inexperienced youth, who'd only been in the castle for a few short weeks. Thus far he'd not shown the slightest interest in its provisioning. Yet here he was now, for no good reason that the cellarer could see, telling him how to run his own storeroom. That would not do.

'The supplies that you see here, my lord, are considerably greater than we would normally have at this time of year,' the cellarer explained carefully, trying to maintain at least a facade of politeness. 'I have, additionally, taken account of the requirements imposed upon us by your arrival here. I am allowing, of course, for the normal purchases of dairy products and fish that will continue through the winter. Add to that meat provided by hunting – like the fine boar you so bravely slew today – and there will be more than enough here to see us through to the springtime.'

Robert did not want an argument and the cellarer's irritation was evident, so he adopted a more conciliatory approach.

'Master cellarer, I should explain myself. My father's tragic death will be taken by some as an excuse to make mischief. They will see my brother on the ducal throne and, perhaps unaware of his prowess as a leader of men, they will scent weakness.'

He put his arm around the cellarer's well-padded shoulder and spoke in a low, conspiratorial tone, as if letting him in on secrets to which only the mightiest were privy. 'You may have heard that a messenger arrived from my brother a few days ago. He had ridden hard from Rouen, a day and a night without rest, bringing me urgent news. There are signs that Brittany, Maine and Anjou are planning to move against us in the New Year. These invaders will have to come by Falaise and take this castle if they wish to go any further. But we won't let them, will we?'

'Er, no, I suppose not . . .'

'Good man. What I'm counting on you to do – and I'll give you the silver you need to achieve it – is very quietly and gradually to start buying more than usual, so that little by little our stores will increase.'

'Just little by little . . .'

'Exactly! I knew a man of your experience and wisdom would understand it at once.'

Oh yes, I understand all right, the cellarer thought as Robert bade him good day. You're spoiling for a fight, young master count. Well you shall have it, and your soldiers will be well fed. But I won't be here to see it.

Herluin had been waiting for Robert by the storeroom door. 'Good thing you didn't reveal the real reason for those supplies,' he said quietly as they walked away.

Robert gave a sigh of frustration. 'I still hope it won't come to a fight.'

'You could just leave this place. Then there'd be nothing to fight about.'

'You know I could never do that,' cried Robert, outraged. 'How can you call yourself my friend and even think such a thing? I'm a count, for heaven's sake. I've got to have a proper castle. Come on, let's inspect the fortifications. If they're not in decent condition, there's no point storing up supplies. We'll be kicked out long before we get to eat them.'

The next two hours were spent walking around the castle. It stood on an outcrop of solid rock that rose over the town of Falaise. The outline of the castle walls was roughly the shape of a boot. An inner fortress occupied the foot, with the gatehouse standing at the heel and the keep at the toe, which was the highest point of the outcrop. Both buildings were constructed of stone, as were the walls of the inner fortress, and the two young men checked them all for cracks and loose mortar. To Robert's alarm, they weren't hard to find.

The leg of the boot was taken up by the outer bailey, a large expanse of open ground dotted with housing for castle workers and men-at-arms, as well as stables, the blacksmith's forge, pens for pigs and sheep and a large vegetable garden. A high wooden palisade enclosed this area. Half a dozen watchtowers, linked by a walkway around the top of the palisade, formed defensive strongpoints, and a second, smaller gatehouse – the only stone building in this part of the castle – allowed direct access from the bailey to the town of Falaise. Robert and Herluin examined every timber in the palisade, searching for the earliest signs of rot. Once again, the evidence that the castle had not been properly maintained was all too plain to see.

When the survey was complete, they returned to the keep. 'We're going back up to the top ramparts,' Robert said. 'I want to look down over the whole castle to see if there's anything we've missed.'

As they climbed the narrow, claustrophobic staircase that wound up through the heart of the keep's outer wall, Robert called back over his shoulder. 'We need every mason or carpenter for leagues around. I don't care what they're doing or who they're working for. We need them all here as soon as possible. Every repair to the castle has to be made by the beginning of April, at the very latest.'

'That could be difficult,' Herluin warned him. 'They can't dress stone and work wood outside in the dead of winter any more than an army can fight.'

'I don't care. Get the men we need and tell them that they work through wind, rain, snow, through the crack of doom itself if they have to. The job must be done. And meanwhile, we have to think about soldiers. How many armed men do we have at the moment?'

'Thirty-three, when they're all fit and well, which they never are all at once.'

'We won't hold the castle for ten minutes with that number. We need more – a lot more.'

Herluin paused, partly to give himself time to think, but also to gather his breath before he replied. 'I can probably get a dozen men down from Comteville, maybe twenty if we're lucky.'

'That's a start, and I can summon men from my own estates, but there won't be many of them, and they'll all want to go straight back to their farms when it's time to start sowing their fields.'

They emerged on to the battlements atop the keep. Barely three hours had passed since their midday meal, but already the sun was low in the sky and a biting wind was blowing in from the north. Robert paused and looked off into the distance, as if he might see an army of men coming to his aid. 'I'll have to pay for mercenaries, that's all there is to it. A couple of companies of Breton archers will make this place a great deal easier to defend. I only wish we had time to put up proper stone walls round the bailey as well.'

'Come here,' Herluin said, leaning between the stone battlements and looking straight down past the walls to the precipitous rock face below them. 'Imagine trying to climb that cliff while those Bretons fire their arrows at you from all along the walls. It'd be a massacre, and if anyone does manage to get to the top, there's not enough room to charge a battering ram. Even putting up a ladder could be a tricky job. So we don't need anything new. God has given us stone walls higher than any man could ever build.'

'Thanks, Herluin,' said Robert, giving his friend a slap on the back. 'That was just what I needed to hear. If we do a halfway decent job of defending it, this end of the castle is virtually impregnable. But that's not what I'm worried about.'

He pointed towards the bailey and crossed the keep to the opposite wall so that he could overlook it. 'There's our problem. Look how the land slopes much more gently down towards the town. By the time you get to the furthest wall, by the gatehouse, it's practically flat and there's only a wooden wall to defend it. If I were Richard, that's where I'd attack.'

'So what are you going to do about it?'

'Make him regret it,' Robert replied, with the same sort of blithe, grinning confidence he'd displayed when setting off to kill the boar single-handed. 'Come on, let's get back downstairs and find out if that girl's accepted my invitation to dinner.'

'Ah . . . I have some news about that,' said Herluin, following him.

He sounded a little shamefaced, as though there was something he didn't want to admit. Robert stopped dead in his tracks, so abruptly that Herluin almost bumped into him, and spun round with a frown on his face. 'What kind of news?'

'Well I've discovered her name, for a start. It's Herleva. Her father's called Fulbert. He's one of the local tanners.'

'Who told you that?'

'Her brother – a big strapping lad called Walter. He came up to the castle just after you'd gone off to talk to the cellarer.'

'And . . . ?'

'And whatever it was you asked the girl to do, the answer is yes.'

'You bastard!' Robert said, punching Herluin in the shoulder and laughing as he did it. 'Why didn't you tell me that hours ago?'

Herluin did his best to look serious. 'Because, my lord, you had important work to do inspecting the castle's defences and I didn't think it wise to distract you.'

'Oh didn't you now?' Robert said and then laughed again. 'Fair enough. I'd never have been able to concentrate on cracked stones and rotten planks if I'd been thinking about . . . what did you say her name was?'

'Herleva.'

Robert gave a long, thoughtful sigh, rolling the name around in his mind. Then he clapped his hands and rubbed them together in eager anticipation. 'Well, Herleva, you're about to get a night to remember.'

5

It was already dark when Herleva reached the foot of the bluff beneath the castle keep. Thanking heaven for the clear skies overhead, she picked her way up the path that twisted up to the gatehouse and was let in without delay. A messenger was sent to the keep to alert Count Robert to her arrival, and as he sprinted away, another of Robert's men, bearing a flaming torch, approached her. 'Let me escort you, miss. The path gets very slippery in this cold weather and we wouldn't want you to fall.'

By the time she arrived at the steps that led to the entrance of the great stone keep, Robert was waiting for her just as he had promised. He had changed out of his hunting clothes and was wearing a deep green cloak swung casually across his shoulder. He gave a brief nod of dismissal to the soldier and Herleva curtseyed before him, eyes modestly lowered, wanting to behave properly this time. As she rose again she said, 'Good evening, my lord.'

Her heart was pounding and she felt almost sick with nerves. She offered up a silent prayer: Please God, let him like me.

With exquisite formality, Robert gave a little nod. 'Good evening, my lady,' he said. 'You've arrived at the perfect time. We're just about to have dinner.' Then he offered her his arm and she took it, thrilled by the intimacy of the gesture.

As she walked through the door into the keep's great hall, Herleva was met by ranks of huge trestle tables flanked by benches packed with Robert's retainers. At once, every man and woman in the room leapt to their feet and stood in respectful silence as their master and his maiden walked past. Herleva could sense them all looking at her and it made her feel naked and exposed, so that she lowered her head and cast her eyes down towards the floor.

'Hold your head up,' Robert murmured. 'Walk proudly . . . like a noblewoman.'

Herleva took a deep breath, lifted her chin and straightened her spine until her head was high and she was looking down her nose at the world around her as haughtily as if she were the Duchess of Normandy herself.

Robert gave her arm an encouraging squeeze. 'Well done,' he said, his mouth so close to her ear that Herleva could feel his breath with every word that he spoke. She clung to him even more tightly, and as he led her to the high table and placed her at his right hand, her senses were overwhelmed by the strength of the muscle beneath his sleeve and the musky, male smell of his body.

'I must apologise,' Robert said. 'The cooks didn't have time to prepare a proper feast in your honour. You'll have to make do with whatever meagre fare they've chosen to serve us, I'm afraid.'

There followed a dizzying succession of fish, fowl and red meats, accompanied by all manner of pies, vegetables and cheeses and washed down by sweeter, richer, more intoxicating wine than had ever before passed Herleva's lips. The highlight of the meal was the head of the boar that Robert had killed that morning, surrounded by great piles of its roasted meat. Herleva applauded with everyone else when the trophy was borne into the room on a huge silver platter, with an apple in its mouth. Yet she barely ate a bite when a slice of boar, swimming in rich gravy, was placed before her. She had been so busy trying to say the right thing and behave like a woman who deserved to be sitting next to a great man, and so consumed by excitement, anxiety and the sheer delight of being in Robert's presence that her appetite had deserted her.

Finally the servants ran out of dishes to put before them. Robert stood, offered her his hand once again and led her back past the silent standing crowd. This time, however, they did not walk in the direction of the door, but towards a huge wooden partition that stretched across the width of the keep.

Ahead of them a heavy woollen curtain, richly embroidered with hunting scenes and fantastic mythical animals, hung from a wooden rail. Robert drew it aside to reveal a door studded with black iron nails. He opened it and led Herleva into a chamber illuminated by a host of beeswax candles whose sweet honey scent filled the air. The walls were covered with magnificent tapestries whose vivid colours glowed in the soft, flickering candlelight. A massive bed, far larger and more ornately carved than the one on which her parents slept, dominated the room. Soft, thick, rippling furs were strewn across its surface.

Robert shut the door, led Herleva a little deeper into the room and then his arms were around her. As she tilted her head up towards him, she caught a glimpse of the fierce, predatory hunger in his eyes, and then he pressed his mouth to hers and there was nothing else in the world but their kiss.

So many times Herleva had wondered what this moment would be like. But there had never been any boy she could even imagine wanting to love, so her fantasy partner had been a faceless, bloodless shadow. She had practised kissing once or twice with her closest girlfriends, though their attempts to imitate the passion of a man and woman had ended in hysterical shrieks and giggles. Nothing had prepared her for the breathless ecstasy of being held in the arms of a man she adored, feeling so tiny and insubstantial in the face of his size and power. His right hand cupped her buttocks and pulled her against him, pressing his hardness against her stomach, and she moaned with an instinctive, animal lust. She was shocked by the intensity of her desire. This hunger for him was sinful. She would be damned for it. And yet she didn't care. At this moment, in this bedchamber, with this man, she'd happily exchange an eternity in the flames of hell just to feel the passion he ignited in her.

Their lips and tongues explored and devoured one another, drawing them together so closely that the boundaries between their bodies and souls seemed to dissolve and they became one being.

He was thrusting his pelvis against her, rubbing up and down her belly, faster and faster, and then he pulled his head away from hers, his breath ragged, panting with exertion before uttering a final ecstatic groan.

He took a step back, out of her arms, and stood bent over, his hands on his knees, his chest heaving like an athlete at the end of a gruelling race.

Herleva was left feeling pent up and frustrated. It had all been wonderful, but now it was horribly unresolved: a story that had not been given a final chapter. She wondered if she had done something wrong. There was no passion or desire in the way Robert was looking at her now. He seemed furtive and even embarrassed. What was the matter? Did he want her to go? Was he angry with her?

She was, she realised, very angry with him. How could he take his own pleasure and leave her like this?

They stood in silence, neither one of them having any idea how to break the tension that had sprung up between them. Finally Robert stuttered, 'I . . . I . . . er . . . I don't know what happened. It's just . . . I mean, you're so gorgeous, and it felt amazing . . . I just couldn't stop myself.'

And then Herleva understood that this was a kind of victory. Here she was, a humble tanner's girl who'd grown up amidst the stench of leather and shit, and yet she had driven the brother of the Duke of Normandy himself so wild with desire that he had lost all self-control. All her life her looks had been nothing but a nuisance. But now she realised that they could be a source of power. It delighted her, too, that she had been able to give such pleasure to this beautiful young god, and her happiness was so great that she burst out laughing.

That was a mistake.

He thought she was mocking him. She could see the anger in his eyes and she ran to him, taking his face in her hands and fixing his eyes with hers, planting kisses on his lips and murmuring, 'I'm sorry . . . I'm sorry,' until she saw the rage receding. And then he kissed her back, and wrapped his arms around her, and she giggled with delight as she felt him rise and harden, and then his mouth met hers and it started all over again.

6

As the feeble morning sun cast a cold, dull light across the chamber, Robert propped his head on his elbow and gazed at the treasure that lay before him. He could hardly believe that she had let him kiss those honey lips, and kissed him back with a desire that burned like his own. She had not protested as he ran his greedy hands over the soft skin of her perfect breasts, but had gasped and shivered with pleasure as he played with her nipples and then moaned as his hands ventured lower, over her smooth flat stomach and that gentle mound covered in soft curls and into the sweet, warm, liquid flesh beyond. She had given a little cry of pain when they first made love, but then clung to him so tightly, drawing him deeper and deeper into her until they seemed to become a single being. They'd spent the entire night exploring one another's bodies and the delights they offered, exulting in the limitless energy and appetites of youth. And when they weren't sharing their physical passion they lay in one another's arms, talking, laughing until they finally fell asleep.

Now Herleva's face crumpled in a frown and she made a soft little sound and then another, almost as though she were distressed. Robert was alarmed. He couldn't bear to see her unhappy and he feared that some kind of sleep demon might be plaguing her. Should he wake her up? What if she was still plagued by the demon when she woke? He didn't know what to do. Damn this girl! She was turning him into a dithering ninny. Well, they said it was best not to wake a sleeping dog. Perhaps the same applied to sleeping girls. Robert rolled on to his back, gazed up at the ceiling and tried, without much luck, to think about something other than Herleva.

She could feel something stirring, deep inside her belly. It moved and it itched and no matter how hard she scratched, the feeling wouldn't go away. And then she knew that it was a seed growing within her, the seed of a great tree like one of the massive old oaks that stood in the depths of the forest. And suddenly the tree had emerged from her body and she could see it rising up and up into the air. As it grew, its branches spread until they seemed to cover the whole sky above her. Now she was looking down on the tree from up in the sky, like a bird flying high above the ground. She could see the branches, still growing, reaching out wider and wider until they covered all of Normandy and then out across the sea to an island. And though she had never seen England, nor had much of an idea where it really was, she knew somehow that the tree had grown so far that the whole of England was in its shadow. Something told her, with absolute clarity, that this was a message, and she wanted to tell Robert and ask him what the message was, but she couldn't move. And suddenly the weight of the tree was overpowering. She was lying beneath it and it was bearing down on her and crushing her. She was trapped. She couldn't breathe. She writhed and struggled desperately to get free . . .

And then, quite suddenly Herleva was awake and her distress disappeared and was replaced by a happy, sleepy smile as she saw Robert's worried eyes looking into hers. They kissed and she stroked his face, feeling the scrape of his stubble beneath her fingertips.

'I had such a strange dream,' she said.

'Tell me all about it, my lady.'

'Am I your lady?' she asked, excited, but a little apprehensive, hardly daring to believe it could be true.

'Yes, you are . . . Now tell me about your dream,' Robert said, limitless in his curiosity about her.

Herleva snuggled even closer, laid her head on his chest and said, 'There was a seed deep inside me and it grew and grew into a tree—'

But before she could say any more, the privacy of the bedchamber was invaded by a knocking on the door, followed a moment later by the sight of Herluin striding into the room. He was clearly in a state of some agitation that only increased when he saw Herleva lying in bed next to Robert.

'Oh, I'm sorry, I didn't mean to disturb you,' he said.

'It doesn't matter. We were awake anyway,' Robert replied. 'What is it?'

'A messenger has come from your brother. He's ridden through the night. He says he has to speak to you, in private, as soon as possible.'

'Dammit!' Robert angrily threw his bedcovers aside and got up. 'I suppose I'd better hear what he has to say.' He started pulling on his hose and looking around for the boots he'd kicked off in a lustful frenzy the previous evening.

'Has something happened to Duke Richard?' Herleva asked anxiously.

Robert laughed. 'I'm sure my dear brother's in perfect health.' He wrapped his cloak around his shoulders, leaned over the bed and kissed her on the forehead. 'He just wants his castle back, that's all.'

7

Rouen, Normandy

'I trust you're well, Mother,' Robert, Archbishop of Rouen, said as a servant poured hot mulled wine from a silver jug into crystal goblets. The intoxicating winter scent of cinnamon, ginger, honey and cloves filled his small private study, mingling with the smoke from a blazing fire.

'Very well, thank you, my dear,' replied the dowager Duchess Gunnor. For the best part of half a century she had participated in the highest councils in the land as the concubine and then wife of the first Duke Richard, and the mother and grandmother of his successors. Now, in her twilight, she liked from time to time to be carried in her covered litter from her dower house to the archbishop's palace for a reviving drink and a chat. For his part the archbishop found it a great relief that there was someone even wiser and more experienced than him on whom he could rely for good conversation and sound advice.

Gunnor was very old and somewhat frail, but there were still traces in her fine high cheekbones and the elegant lines of her brow, nose and jaw of the beauty that had captivated Duke Richard all those years ago. Soft cushions had been placed on her chair and a warm blanket draped across her lap. She patted it contentedly as she enquired politely, 'And how about you, my dear, and those fine boys of yours?'

'All very well, thank you, Mother.'

As a clergyman the archbishop had an obligation to be celibate, so when he was in residence at the archbishop's palace in Rouen, as he was at the moment, he lived alone. But he was also the Count of Evreux and as such bound by an equally solemn requirement to produce at least one heir to his title. It was therefore necessary and very agreeable when at the castle of Evreux to perform the duties of a married man. There was, he well knew, a growing movement of reform calling for all priests and monks, no matter how high their rank, to spend their lifetimes in unwed celibacy, but he felt no need to bow to it. He had better things to worry about.

The archbishop saw himself as the power behind the ducal throne. He had, after all, given his late brother his sworn promise to keep an eye on the young Duke Richard III and the seething crowd of nobles, scattered across Normandy and beyond, who were constantly seeking to grab more power, more land or more castles from his hands. The archbishop took that promise all the more seriously now that the seething nobles included his other nephew, his namesake Robert. And he could think of no one better equipped than his mother to offer him advice on how to handle an increasingly unstable situation.

'I wanted to have a word with you about this whole Falaise business,' he began. 'In my view, Richard is perfectly entitled to insist on Robert vacating the castle. It's a ducal property and my brother's words, which we both heard, clearly implied that Robert should content himself with the castle at Exmes.'

'Well it's not quite that simple,' said Gunnor. 'I heard what your brother said too, remember, and unfortunately his words could be taken two ways. He said Robert could have all the castles in the Hiémois—'

'But that obviously excluded Falaise, since it is a ducal castle and therefore belongs to Richard.'

'Well in that case he made Robert Count of the Hiémois and then denied him use of the finest castle in the area, where the count should obviously live. And that's hardly sensible, is it?'

The archbishop took a deep, calming breath. 'Perhaps not, Mother,' he said. 'But you know as well as I that if Robert were given that castle along with his title, he would possess too great a power base and would therefore threaten Richard's position.'

The old lady was undaunted. 'You're wrong,' she declared, waving a bony finger at her son. 'There are two things that threaten Richard. The first, which no one can do anything about, is that Robert is clearly the finer of the two boys. Anyone can see that. He's much better-looking, has a quicker, brighter mind and the people adore him.'

'The women adore him, you mean.'

'Women are people too, even if men don't like to think so. But that is not the immediate problem. What you seem to be ignoring is that the surest way of setting Robert against Richard and making him a threat to the duke's position is to deny him Falaise Castle. If Richard leaves his brother alone, he'll be perfectly happy playing the lord of the manor, hunting with his friends and bedding every girl for leagues around. But if Richard tries to evict him, or makes threats, then the consequences don't bear thinking about.

'Robert won't leave. Richard won't back down. We'll have a civil war on our hands. The family divided. The duchy split in two. And all our enemies licking their lips knowing how easy it will be to let our boys destroy one another and then step in and pluck Normandy like a ripe apple from a tree. I know I'm a fussy old lady who'll soon be joining her husband in the grave, but as long as there's breath in my body, I will not stand by and let such a tragedy happen to this family.'

The archbishop said nothing. He could see the sense in what his mother had said and he knew his own flesh and blood well enough to be certain that she was right: if the brothers ever fought, they would not stop until both of them were destroyed and the duchy of Normandy with them. Even so, one had to consider the fundamental rights and wrongs of the issue.

'I take your point,' he conceded, 'but I don't think you're being entirely fair to Richard. He has his qualities too. He's strong, reliable and a fine soldier, all of which are excellent attributes in a duke.'

'That may be so, but he's also boring. And like a lot of boring people, once he gets an idea into his head, he can't get it out again.'

'Perhaps we should put another idea in there to replace the one you don't like,' the archbishop suggested. 'It's not long till Richard's wedding. I have no reason to doubt that he's a perfectly normal, red-blooded young man. Once he's got that little French girl in his bed, I'm sure she'll take his mind off Falaise.'

'Let's hope so,' said Gunnor, holding up her goblet to be refilled. 'But I'm not sure that Princess Adela will be particularly enthusiastic about satisfying Richard's needs in the bedroom, even supposing that she has the faintest idea how to do such a thing, which I very much doubt.'

'She's going to be Richard's wife. It's her duty to please him.'

'For pity's sake, Robert, a woman doesn't find a man desirable simply because she's made a vow. Adela's spent her whole life expecting to marry young Baldwin of Flanders, most of it living in Bruges with his family. Suddenly she's being dragged away to marry a Norman she's never set eyes on . . . Of course a girl of her kind understands that her husband will always be chosen for political reasons – your sister Emma never had any illusions on that score, though I believe she's actually quite happy with Canute. But I shouldn't expect Adela to be brimming with joy as she walks up the aisle to meet her new husband.'

'Then it's a good thing I've found someone who'll cheer the two of them up,' said the archbishop. 'Do you remember the poet I sent you, Warner of Rouen? He wrote that shocking poem about a fellow called Moriuht and then had the nerve to dedicate it to you and me?'

'Of course . . .'

'I hope you didn't find it too vulgar.'

'My dear boy,' Gunnor protested, 'a little vulgarity never hurt me. People forget that old ladies have been young women in their time. And besides, Warner was clever enough to include lots of nice things about me in his poem.'

'I'm glad you approve, because I thought we might ask him to perform *Moriuht* as part of the entertainment at Richard's wedding.'

'I wonder what my dear grandson Edward will make of that. I never met a young man who disapproved of carnal pleasures the way he does. Quite unlike the rest of the family.'

Edward and his brother Alfred were the sons of Emma of Normandy and her first, now deceased husband, King Ethelred of England. Their banishment to Normandy had been a condition of Emma's marriage to Ethelred's successor Canute. Now their presence in the ducal household was a constant reminder that Canute was only king by conquest, not birthright.

'King Edward, if you please, Mother,' said the archbishop, underlining the point. 'He insists that he, not Canute, is the rightful king of England, and we are supposed to be on his side after all.'

'Ha!' Gunnor gave her son a look to let him know that she was far too old and worldly-wise to go along with such foolishness. Then she smiled as a thought struck her. 'Mind you, Edward's not the only one. The King of France will have a fit! There's a reason they call him "the Pious", you know. I hear his palace is more like a monastery than a royal residence these days. He spends his time writing music for his choir and conducting endless services while they sing his compositions, and the entire court has to sit and listen to it all.'

'All the more reason to tease him, then.'

'You should welcome piety. You're supposed to be a man of the cloth, you know.'

'Exactly, Mother. I am a consecrated archbishop. I serve God, as do the bishops and priests under me. And we can't have laypeople, even royal ones, acting as though they rather than we have the keys to the kingdom of God. It's not right.'

'Well I must admit, I do look forward to seeing the king's face as Warner's poem becomes more and more disgusting. Of course, Queen Constance will simply lap it up. It's just the sort of thing she'd enjoy – both the poem and the effect it has. Nothing gives her more pleasure than causing chaos wherever she goes.'

'She's a wicked woman!' said the archbishop with feeling, causing Gunnor to raise an eyebrow; it was rare that anything penetrated her son's carefully cultivated air of imperturbable sangfroid. 'You do know she had Bertha of Burgundy murdered because she couldn't keep her hands off the king.'

'It was he who couldn't keep his hands off Bertha,' Gunnor replied tartly. 'He wasn't so pious when she was around, that's for sure.'

'I swear Queen Constance is possessed by devils,' the archbishop went on. 'She attacked her own confessor, Father Stephen, with a stick and poked his eye right out. The Bishop of Chartres wrote to me recently to confess that he's been frightened away from royal occasions by Constance's savagery – that was the actual word he used. He said the only time she can be trusted is when she's threatening harm.'

'One can only hope Adela doesn't take after her.'

'Fret not, Mother, I made sure to ask about that and was

assured that Adela is very much her father's daughter. And as you say, she's spent more than half her life in Flanders. That's enough to dull even the most fiery spirit.'

'In that case,' said Gunnor, 'if she can't bewitch Richard with her lovemaking, perhaps she can dull his spirits too – send him into a deep, thoughtless stupor. Anything to take his mind off war with his brother!'

8

Winchester, England

Godwin, Earl of Wessex, rose with the rest of the congregation of humble townsfolk, prosperous merchants, minor landowners and mighty nobles crowded into Winchester Cathedral for Mass on Christmas Day. From the west door of the cathedral came the voices of Benedictine monks, whose richly sonorous plainsong chants rose high into the soaring stone vaults and thence to heaven itself. The finely carved pew that was reserved for Godwin and his family stood in a place of honour, closest to the choir and altar, so he had to peer right back down the nave to see the incense bearers, the singers and behind them the Bishop of Winchester, the abbots of the city's monastic houses and a great horde of priests. Every wall and column in the cathedral was decorated with ornate patterns; portraits of Christ, the saints and the prophets; and scenes from Bible tales painted in every colour of the rainbow. But many of these images were hidden, for the walls on either side of the nave were hung with a forest of wooden stools and crutches: thousands upon thousands of them, discarded by cripples who had come here to be cured by the relics of St Swithun. The only heat in the building came from the bodies of the people within it, and their breath hung in the chilly air, so that as Godwin looked at the procession, it seemed to move towards him like a company of pilgrims in the mist.

Finally, after all the men there came a woman: a tall, haughty, magnificent beauty. She wore a purple cloak trimmed with ermine, and the long white veil that covered her hair was held in place with a golden coronet studded with rubies, emeralds and garnets. Time had robbed her complexion of the soft, clear radiance of youth, but the lines of experience faintly etched between her brows and beside her lips only added to her dignity, and the fractional thinning of her flesh brought out the regal elegance of the bones beneath her skin.

This was Emma of Normandy, twice-crowned Queen of England and Queen Consort of Denmark besides. As she proceeded past the congregation jammed into the cathedral's pews – all standing, some bowing as she passed, others staring in open-mouthed awe – she seemed more like a living deity than a mortal woman. Even the bishop, bearing his shepherd's staff before him, with a tall mitre on his head and a cope embroidered with dazzling gold thread around his shoulders, seemed overshadowed. And though her ladies-in-waiting, bringing up the rear of the procession, were drawn from the grandest families in the land, they were like mere house cats beside a lioness.

As the procession moved closer, Godwin heard a sound he knew well: the wordless little noise his wife Gytha made when she wanted him to pay attention to her, without actually having to ask him to do so. He turned his head and saw that Gytha was staring down the nave, directly at the queen. But her face held none of the awed admiration that shone from so many other eyes around them. In fact, he thought he saw disapproval in her expression. Was this just a matter of straightforward female jealousy?

Gytha had many virtues in Godwin's eyes, but great beauty was not one of them. She was a sturdy lass, more handsome than pretty, and could certainly be forgiven for resenting Emma's dazzling charms. But the more Godwin considered it, the less that seemed a plausible explanation. Gytha had been his wife for six years now, and he knew her forthright, practical character well enough to be sure that she would not waste her time worrying about that sort of thing. Nor had she any reason to feel hard done by. Her brother Ulf had married Estrith, sister of King Canute, thereby making Gytha part of the royal household. Canute's offer of her hand to his loyal subject Godwin, who had fought alongside him on campaign in Denmark, had thus been a sign of great favour to bride and groom alike.

Godwin had only been nineteen at the time. The son of a noble Saxon line that had fallen out with King Ethelred, he was determined to restore the family fortunes under Canute. Gytha was younger still, but it soon became apparent that her nature was as fiercely ambitious as his. The two newly-weds wanted to create a dynasty, not just of earls, but of kings. Gytha understood from the start that her primary role in this enterprise was to be Godwin's brood mare, and she took to that task with a will. Her broad hips and robust constitution had already produced three sons, Sweyn, Harold and Tostig, and a daughter, Edith, and the making of the children had pleased her and Godwin just as much as their arrival.

Other men complained that their womenfolk were cold and unwilling, and when Godwin had first taken Gytha to bed he had feared that she might be the same, for she fought against him as he tried to take what was his by husbandly right. But soon he learned that she was simply setting him a challenge, demanding proof that he was fit to master her, and the harder the fight, the sweeter the pleasure for both of them when she at last surrendered. In Godwin's experience, nothing made a woman more content than being well satisfied in bed, and that being the case, what reason would Gytha have to care about another woman's appearance?

Perhaps it had something to do with money. Another of Gytha's qualities was her talent as a businesswoman. She operated a flourishing business selling pretty young English slaves to traders from all across the Viking world, and made more than enough from her activities to buy herself clothes and jewellery – not that Gytha was over-concerned with either of those fripperies – without Godwin having to dip into his own income to fund her.

For all her commercial acumen, however, Gytha's profits from trading were only a fraction of those Emma had amassed from men. The Queen had been a girl of fifteen when her brother, Duke Richard, had given her to King Ethelred, providing her with a dowry large enough to display his own wealth and importance. Not wanting to be outdone, Ethelred had then showered her with gold and land, all of which she'd kept when he died. When she'd married Ethelred's conqueror, Canute, Emma had negotiated her own price and added still further to her fortune.

As a result, she was the richest woman in England, perhaps in the whole of Christendom. Only a short walk from the cathedral, in the chapel of the New Minster abbey, there stood a cross she had donated made from three hundred pounds of silver, fifteen pounds of gold and an extraordinary profusion of jewels. Godwin could imagine Gytha envying that kind of wealth, despising the means by which Emma had come by it and disapproving of her giving it away with such flagrant profligacy. But if so, why had she never mentioned it before?

Godwin gave up. He leaned close to Gytha and murmured, 'You look perturbed, dearest. What troubles you?'

'Nothing, my lord,' she muttered.

That was plainly not true. 'Tell me.'

'You'll only say I'm a foolish woman, spreading gossip and tittle-tattle.'

Why, Godwin asked himself, were women so impossible to deal with? 'Just tell me,' he repeated.

70

The choir were very close to them now and it was hard to make themselves heard. Gytha motioned to her husband to bend his head to her level, cupped her hand and spoke into his ear. 'It's the queen. I fear that all is far from well with her.'

'What on earth makes you say that? She seems magnificent to me. Look at the way everyone stares at her. If ever there was a woman born to be queen—'

'She is majestic, my lord, I will not deny it, and far more beautiful than I could ever dream of being. But I do not envy her position. She's locked away her heart and buried it in ice. Forgive me, my lord, but when I look at Queen Emma, I see a lonely, loveless woman weighed down by a grief so deep I fear it might destroy her.'

At that very moment, Emma turned her head and looked right at Godwin. He had the terrible feeling that she had heard him and Gytha talking, and as he bowed his head in her honour, he was only too grateful for the chance to hide the shocked expression on his face. It had never occurred to him that Gytha might look on the queen with pity as well as contempt.

All through Mass he paid little attention to the service and barely tasted the wine at Communion. He was consumed with what Gytha had said. By the time they left the cathedral, he had worked out why his wife had voiced such an apparently unfounded opinion and, to his surprise, decided that he agreed with her.

'Thank you,' he said to Gytha as they walked to the royal palace of Winchester, where the queen was hosting a splendid Christmas feast.

'Why, my lord?'

'Because you have told me where the queen is vulnerable.'

'Have I?' she said innocently, as though that had not been her purpose all along.

'So what should I do about it? You're a woman. Tell me how to take advantage of another woman's weakness.'

'Well don't do what most men would do. Don't try to get her on her back while her husband isn't looking.'

Godwin laughed. 'I wouldn't dare! If Canute ever found out, he'd kill me. And if you ever found out—'

'I'd kill you before he did,' Gytha interrupted, enjoying the feeling of being her husband's co-conspirator. 'In any case, Emma is far too shrewd to fall for such an obvious approach, and what's more, she loves her husband. You're still a boy in her eyes and that's what you should play on. Now, Emma has three sons: Edward and Alfred from Ethelred, and Harthacnut with Canute.'

'Thank you, my dear, I already knew that.'

'But think! She hasn't seen any of them in years. Ethelred's boys were exiled to Normandy. Harthacnut's been packed off to Denmark. She must miss them desperately. So be her son. Befriend her. Support her. Show her sympathy. She will be far more vulnerable to that than she would ever be to a more obvious approach.'

'So what you're saying is I should sneak up on her from the flanks, instead of charging head on at her defences.'

Gytha laughed. 'If you say so, my love. You're the soldier, not me.'

'I am, and if my next campaign is victorious, I will owe it all, dear Gytha, to you. Now, let's go and have our dinner. I don't know about you, but I'm ravenous.'

Canute had, as so often, left England's relative peace and quiet for other, more troublesome corners of his far-flung empire. In his absence, Godwin was seated in the place of honour next to Queen Emma. When a number of dishes had been served and the queen had drunk a goodly amount of sweet strong mead to wash them down, he put on his most thoughtful, concerned expression and said, 'Your Majesty, at this time of year, when we are all celebrating Christ's coming with our families around us, I know how hard it must be for one such as you who has sacrificed so much in the service of her people.'

He hesitated for a moment, to make sure he had not offended her, but she did not upbraid him or look in any way insulted, and so, emboldened, he continued: 'You have always put your duties as a queen and a wife ahead of your needs as a woman and a mother. To maintain peace and unity in the kingdom you bade your own children farewell. To ensure that there is a steady royal hand guiding the affairs of England you remain here alone while your beloved husband is away. So I hope you know how much we all appreciate your service. And how I, as your loyal Earl of Wessex, appreciate you above all.'

Queen Emma was not given to displays of emotion or frailty; she regarded them as essentially one and the same. But as he watched her face, Godwin was almost certain that he saw a flicker of something that might be called distress. Gytha was right. This was a lonely, unhappy woman, and thus a woman in need of a man.

'Thank you, Godwin,' she said, as coolly as ever. 'Your words are as welcome as they are comforting.'

Then she changed the subject to the latest developments in the Holy Roman Empire, and the upcoming coronation of the new emperor, Conrad of Germany. 'I have received a letter from His Majesty the king. He tells me that he will be travelling to Rome to attend the ceremony. Perhaps Prince Henry will also be there to see his father become emperor, and maybe even Gunhilda, too.'

Gunhilda was Canute and Emma's daughter. She was just six. A year earlier, the king had betrothed her to Conrad's son Henry, Duke of Bavaria, and sent her to be raised at the German royal court. Given the distance between them, it was extremely unlikely that Emma and her daughter would ever set eyes on one another again. For a second even Godwin felt sorry for the queen, and there was genuine sympathy in his voice as he said, 'I'm sure that both the king and Princess Gunhilda would enjoy that very much.'

But his own moment of weakness soon passed, and as Emma gave him a sad, perfunctory smile, Godwin was thinking: Gytha was right. This woman's there for the taking. And once I control her, I'm halfway to controlling the kingdom.

9

Falaise, Normandy

The New Year's Eve feast had lasted late into the night, yet Judith awoke before dawn. She shared a garret room beneath the great keep's roof with four other girls, all of whom were getting up and preparing for another day's work, with only a quick drink of small ale and whatever stale crusts of leftover bread they could scavenge from the castle kitchen to sustain them through their first few hours of work. The great hall would need cleaning and all the tables had to be put out before Count Robert's household assembled for their breakfast: porridge bread and gruel for the lower orders, with a selection of meats, fish, eggs and pastries for the count and the other gentlefolk.

Life as a castle servant was hard, but then again, all life was hard. Judith's father was a skinner, with little talent for his trade and a terrible habit of drinking away his meagre earnings in any tavern he could find. So she had long been used to days or even weeks when there was barely any food in the pot, and accustomed to the black moods that descended upon their hovel, when no one was safe from the rough edge of Father's tongue or the hard blows of his fist. Even the meanest scullion at Falaise Castle lived better than her family had done, so she was only too grateful for the offer of employment, particularly since she was rather more than a scullion.

The hall floor had been swept, new rushes laid and almost all the tabletops carried from the side of the room and placed upon their trestles when Count Robert strode by, on the way to the stables for his regular morning ride. New Year or not, his routine remained the same. A few moments later, Herluin dashed by, running to catch up with his friend, swiftly followed by two more young nobles who were staying at the castle.

They would not be gone for long, for Count Robert liked to ride hard and fast, returning in no time at all, bursting with energy, with his steed half spent and lathered in sweat beneath him. He expected his guests and the senior members of the household to be ready then to accompany him to a brief morning Mass in the castle chapel before they broke their fast.

Judith did a little more work in the hall. Then she let the other servant girls know that she had to leave them and made her way to the curtain that covered the door into Count Robert's chamber. She slipped behind it and, taking great care to make no noise, opened the door and went inside.

Count Robert had discarded a wine-stained tunic on the floor beside the bed, but that was none of Judith's business. Instead she picked up the long chemise of fine white linen lying nearby. There were dirty marks at the end of the sleeves, which were cut tight to the arm and buttoned at the wrist, and along the hem of the skirt. Nearby were fine woollen hose. At home such garments would be worn for weeks or even months, but standards were different at the castle. That can all go to the laundry, Judith thought, picking the clothes up and then dropping them by the door to take with her when she left the room.

A beautiful silk gown, its flared sleeves decorated with embroidered bands of gold and silver thread dotted with seed pearls, had been thrown across a carved oaken chair beside the bed. Judith picked it up, marvelling at the beauty of the Anglo-Saxon embroidery and wondering what it must be like to wear something so beautiful, bought for a sum that would have kept her family fed, clothed and housed for years. She took it across to a chest filled with half a dozen equally splendid dresses, folded it and put it away. From another chest she extracted a woollen day dress and from a third fresh underclothes. She brought them with her as she walked back towards the bed and placed them neatly over the back of the chair.

Stepping right up to the bedside, she stopped to look at the sleeping face she knew so well, and that glorious blaze of hair on the pillow. Then she pulled back the fur rug a fraction and very gently shook the naked freckle-dusted shoulder until the body beneath it began to stir.

'It's time to wake up, my lady,' she said, pitching her voice just loud enough to be heard without being aggravating.

There was a wordless little grunt of acknowledgement.

Judith waited a moment until her mistress had opened her eyes, got her bearings and propped herself up on her elbows before she gave a little bob and said, 'Good morning, my lady. I hope you slept well.'

Herleva gave a sleepy smile. 'Mmm . . . very well, thank you, Judith.'

'His lordship left for his ride a little while ago. I've laid out your clothes. Would you like me to help you dress?'

'Yes please.'

Judith set to work again, kneeling at Herleva's feet and holding out the hose for her to step into; doing up the laces and fastenings on her dress; brushing her hair and then arranging her veil and the headband that held it in place. The two young women made inconsequential conversation, with Judith taking great care never to contradict anything Herleva said, nor make a remark that could possibly be taken as disrespectful to any of her betters. For that was how it was now between them, and Judith couldn't help wondering whether a time might come when they simply couldn't remember things being any other way.

She had been summoned to the castle within a week of Herleva's arrival there. Count Robert lacked a housekeeper, wife or even a mother, and so it had fallen to him to deal personally with something that would normally have been an issue for the lady of the house. When Judith arrived, he was in the great hall, warming himself by the fire, with Herleva beside him. The two girls exchanged nervous, uncertain smiles. Judith bowed her head and curtseyed, then waited to discover why a senior member of the ducal family had requested her presence.

Robert cleared his throat. He looked more like a nervous boy than a mighty lord, and she had the distinct impression that he would rather be hunting, fighting a battle or doing almost anything rather than talking to her. 'As you know, ah . . .'

'Judith, my lord.'

'Yes, of course . . . Judith . . . Well, as you know, the Lord God in his infinite wisdom has a plan for us all. Isn't that so?'

'Yes, my lord.'

'Good . . . very good.' Robert nodded and then began speaking again, not talking normally to Judith so much as reciting a carefully prepared little speech.

'We each have our purpose in God's creation and it's not for us to question His will. If one man is a king and another a lowly shepherd, that's because God wills it so, and we must all obey those who have been set over us, even if we love them. I mean, I loved my father, for example, but he was my duke as much as he was yours and I had to bend my knee and obey him, just as you would have done. And my father, in turn, had to bow down before the King of France. And even the king has to bow down before God, when he stands before him to be judged, just as every single one of us will do. Do you follow me?'

'I think so, my lord.'

'Good, because my point is . . . well, I've asked Herleva to stay here with me, as part of my household, and she's honoured me by accepting my, ah, invitation. She also suggested that she'd like to have someone with her who she knows from, you know, her previous life. A companion, you might say. She suggested you and I could see the sense of that, but as I pointed out to her, a person has to have a purpose. Even the noblewomen who attend a queen have to serve as her ladies-in-waiting. So if you are to stay in the castle, eat my food and drink my ale, you'll have to earn your keep as Herleva's handmaiden.'

'Oh,' said Judith, who for once in her life was lost for words. Whatever she had been expecting, it hadn't been that.

'I want you both to understand what that means,' Robert went on, glancing at Herleva while Judith tried to calm her scrambled mind enough to pay attention.

'You can't be friends like you used to be. Herleva will be your mistress. And if you are to stay here, Judith, you must do so as her loyal and obedient servant. You will love her, as any good servant should love her mistress, but the way you show that love will be in the devotion of your service to her. You must call her "my lady" and do her bidding, no matter what she demands of you, no matter when. If she asks for your opinion, perhaps on some trivial matter of clothing or appearance, you may give it. But always do so modestly, respectfully and without the slightest hint of criticism.'

He looked at Judith, who said, 'Yes, my lord,' though she could not imagine how she could ever think of Herleva as her mistress. This was a tanner's daughter who'd grown up surrounded by the piles of dung and vats of animal piss her father used to cure the skins; who'd lived in a cottage where the door faced south-west in a desperate attempt to capture the prevailing breeze and blow away the stomach-churning stench. Suddenly here she was in a castle, dressed like a noblewoman, and Judith was being told to call her 'my lady'. It didn't make sense.

Robert seemed entirely unaware of the turmoil his words were causing. 'Now, Herleva,' he continued, growing in confidence, 'you have to learn about the treatment of servants. You are, of course, free to do whatever you want. Your servants are your chattels and you may be as cruel or capricious with them as you like. But I was always taught that one should care for one's servants as a parent cares for their children. A parent provides a child with food, clothing and a roof over their heads. A parent praises a child when they are good. But a parent also punishes a child who has done wrong, so you must never be afraid to punish a servant who's lazy, careless or disobedient. After all, if you don't punish them, how will they ever learn to do better?'

Herleva put her hand to her mouth and stared at Judith wide-eyed, both of them equally shocked by the thought that one of them was being told to obey and the other to punish. Robert had been surrounded by servants from the moment he was born. He gave orders as easily as he breathed and took it for granted that they would be followed without question. Now he was asking them to enter his world, but at very different levels.

Robert finally noticed Herleva's anguish and walked across to her. He placed his hands on her shoulders and, when she turned her eyes away from his, tilted his head to follow her, so that she could not escape his gaze.

'I know this is hard, my darling, but you can't be Judith's friend now, any more than she can be yours. She needs to know where she stands and there can be no confusion about her position. It would be cruel, actually, to pretend that she's your equal when she isn't, do you see?'

Herleva nodded mutely and Robert stepped away from her.

'And since you now have power,' he said, 'you must exercise it by deciding Judith's fate. Do you want her to stay here as your servant? Or would you prefer her to be sent away, back to her family?'

'I . . . I don't know,' Herleva stammered. 'I mean, I can't . . . it's not . . . I just can't.'

'You must,' Robert said, softly, but with unbending firmness. 'Tell us now: does she stay, or does she go?'

Herleva made a visible effort to pull herself together. Eventually she said, 'Please, Judith, will you stay?'

'Don't answer her!' Robert snapped. All trace of the boy who had greeted Judith had disappeared. He was a tall, strong, dominant young noble, taking absolute command of the situation. 'This is not a decision for Judith to make. It has to be your command. You must tell her: stay, or go?'

Herleva swallowed hard and in a barely audible voice whispered, 'Stay.'

'Good,' said Robert. 'We have a decision. And you, Judith, have a new mistress. She has bestowed her favour on you. So what do you say?'

'I . . . I don't know, my lord.'

'You say thank you, of course. You approach your mistress respectfully. You bend your knee to her and you say, "Thank you, my lady." And if you do not, you will regret it.'

'Yes, my lord.'

'Then do it.'

'Yes, my lord.' Judith walked past Count Robert and stood in front of Herleva, who looked utterly distraught, barely able to restrain her tears. She gave a jerky little bend of the knee and muttered, 'Thank you, my lady.'

'You will have to improve your manners, Judith, if you are to remain in my household,' Robert said. 'Now, the steward will explain your duties and find you space to sleep in. You can

81

ask for him in the kitchens, through that door over there. Someone will know where he is.'

Judith turned to go, but Robert stopped her. 'Wait. Your mistress hasn't dismissed you.' He glanced at Herleva. 'Do you require her any longer?'

Herleva shook her head.

'Then tell her she may go.'

It struck Judith that Herleva was, at this minute, as much under Robert's command as she was, and when she heard the softly murmured 'You may go,' she made a point of saying, 'Yes, my lady,' in a clear, respectful voice, just for Herleva's sake.

'Much better,' said Robert, and Judith walked away to the kitchen, her life entirely altered.

So now she was a handmaiden, and it was becoming so automatic to call Herleva 'my lady' that she hardly knew whether she would be able to address her by her name even if that were allowed. She found herself becoming strangely protective of her new mistress, as if she were the parent and not, as Robert had suggested, the child. On the rare days when she was allowed out of the castle and down to the town, the girls there rushed up to her and bombarded her with questions about Herleva and Count Robert. Already stories were spreading, becoming more elaborate with every retelling, about their meeting at the forest's edge and Herleva's first journey to the castle. Judith, whose status among her other friends had actually gone up as a result of her new position, dismissed every rumour as nonsense and resolutely refused to give away a single secret about what went on between the count and his new love. And God forbid that anyone should show insufficient respect to Herleva, or slander her reputation, for if they did, Judith rounded on them with furious indignation.

But as she walked down the castle passage carrying her

mistress's underclothes, it struck Judith that she possessed one piece of information that would cause a sensation, not just in the taverns and market stalls of Falaise, but across the entire duchy. For in all the weeks that Judith had been making Herleva's bed and looking after her clothes, she had never once seen a single spot of blood. The moon had waxed, and waned, and waxed again, and yet Herleva had shown no sign of it. And that could only mean one thing.

Herleva the tanner's daughter was carrying Robert of Normandy's baby.

10

Jarl the Viper was a nightwalker, a hider in the shadows, a silent and unseen harbinger of death. His appearance was a mystery, for none had ever seen him, and Jarl took very good care to preserve that invisibility.

It was said that there was a tavern in Vaudreuil, down by the dockside where the rivers Seine and Eure met, to which anyone seeking Jarl's services might go. First, of course, one needed courage enough to brave the wharf and warehouse workers, the seamen, smugglers and slave traders, the ferrymen and chandlers who frequented the place and had little time and less sympathy for any stranger who crossed the threshold. Then one had to approach the tavern-keeper, whose diminutive size was more than made up for by the ferocity of his temper and the savagery of his fists and feet. It would not do at all to be specific about the nature of one's requirements, nor even the name of Jarl himself. Either would result in a swift and painful exit. Instead one had to speak in riddles: 'I seek a man without a face,' perhaps, or 'I'm looking for one who cannot be found.' If the tavern-keeper was convinced of one's seriousness and his palm was crossed with sufficient silver, then he might just grunt his assent and mutter, 'Come back in seven days' time. Maybe I'll have news for yer, maybe I won't. I can't promise nothing.'

In the days that followed, a sign would be left for Jarl at the tavern. What it was, only the tavern-keeper knew, and he wasn't talking. Various rumours pointed to a light in a window, an old wine barrel left upside down, or a mark on a whitewashed wall. Whatever the signal, if Jarl responded, his would-be client would be directed to make their way alone to a meeting place a league or two out of town. They were all warned that they would be watched along the way. This not only guaranteed their safety, but ensured that if they were accompanied by anyone, their meeting with Jarl would be immediately and irrevocably cancelled. At the rendezvous they found a donkey and cart waiting for them. The client was helped up into the cart and blindfolded before being led away. At the end of their journey, they were helped back down to the ground, still blindfolded, and led into a building. There, sight was restored to them and they found themselves in any one of a dozen small, unattended, somewhat decrepit rural churches. Jarl's manservant and bodyguard Mahomet would always be standing there, a huge Moor with skin of ebony and a scimitar of gleaming Toledo steel.

Mahomet was a deaf-mute and thus unable either to hear or repeat anything that was said by either party in the conversation that followed. For the client was now led to the confessional box. He, or sometimes she – for women were just as likely as men to wish a person killed, and were less able to carry out the act themselves – would explain what they required. The Viper, whose voice was surprisingly light and pleasant to the ear for one with so venomous a calling, would ask for information about the putative target's routines, surroundings and defences. A price would then be quoted, a portion to be paid immediately and the rest upon the successful conclusion of the killing. Thus far, all the Viper's missions had ended in success, and all his fees had been met in full. His clients knew that if they failed to pay, they would be sent straight to Hades and could pay the Devil instead.

As the death-seekers left the church, the vast, menacing

85

presence of Mahomet deterred them from any temptation to look inside the priest's half of the confessional box. Only when the coast was quite clear would Jarl emerge, his body as slender and boyish as Mahomet's was massive and his skin as pale as the Moor's was black. Together they would journey back to the manor house built amidst the ruins of an old Roman villa where Jarl made his home, along with a small band of devoted disciples who worked his gardens and assisted with both the preparation and the execution of his work.

For Jarl was a poisoner. He carried a light, razor-sharp dagger and it had tasted blood often enough, but only in the cause of his self-defence. When he set out deliberately to kill, he did it with powders, pastes and tinctures derived from the deadly substances with which he surrounded himself. To the innocent eye, for example, the flowers in his garden might seem to have been chosen for their beauty. But Jarl had not planted beds of foxgloves for their spires of pretty pink, white and pale blue flowers, but for the vomiting, madness and paroxysms of the heart induced by the digitalis he extracted from the plants. Likewise the dazzling scarlet and mauve blooms of the poppies were only of interest for the milky sap contained in their seed pods, a miraculous substance that when dried could ease pain, bring sleep, induce a blissful delirium or, if taken in sufficient quantities, ease a man into the deep, dreamless sleep that had no end. The leaves of deadly nightshade provided Jarl with belladonna, while the fine, lacy leaves and tiny white flowers of the conium shrub produced the hemlock that had killed Socrates fourteen hundred years before. Nodding white and yellow daffodils, the autumn crocus with its purple flowers and bright yellow stamens, the glowing golden buttercup, even the lily of the valley could be harvested for crops intended to end life rather than sustain it. And when autumn came, the mushrooms and toadstools in Jarl's meadows and woodlands were as deadly an arsenal as any vault packed to the rafters with lances and bows.

Jarl was not reliant on his garden alone for his toxins. He and Mahomet made regular journeys across the lands of the Franks, over the Alps and down into Lombardy to the city of Pavia. There traders from Arabia and the Orient brought spices, fabrics and minerals that had travelled the full length of the Silk Road from China, crossed the deserts of Arabia and sailed the oceans from lands where no Christian had ever ventured. Jarl purchased rocks of cinnabar and antimony and, late at night, when both he and the Syrian who sold them wore fabric wrapped around their heads and faces in the style of desert Arabs, small bronze vessels filled with arsenic.

He could conduct these transactions in the Arab tongue, for though he had been born on a Varangian longboat, sailing down the Dnieper river, he and his mother had been captured by Khazar bandits and sold into slavery. His mother had died before his fifth birthday and he was passed from one owner to another until, by the age of thirteen, he found himself in Baghdad, the most populous city in the world. He became the indentured servant and bedmate of Zaid al-Zuhairi, a Syrian apothecary who also considered himself a surgeon and alchemical researcher. The scientific learning of the Byzantine and Islamic kingdoms was far beyond anything known in the cold, wet lands of the north, and Jarl, who was gifted with sharp eyes, a bright mind and a retentive memory, absorbed it all. So much so, in fact, that at the age of eighteen he was able to kill his master with a slow, steady and ultimately fatal programme of arsenic poisoning.

The apothecary finally passed away as the muezzin was calling the faithful to Isha, the night-time prayers. Jarl filled a purse with gold and a sack with the rarest and most precious elements in al-Zuhairi's inner sanctum. He hung the purse from a belt around his waist, covered it with a loose djellaba and slung the sack over his shoulder. By the time the pre-dawn Fajr prayers had been spoken, he was just one among a crowd of travellers waiting by the great iron doors of the Damascus Gate. The city's inner walls were more than forty paces thick, and higher than fifteen men standing one upon another. Beyond them stood another set of even mightier fortifications and a moat as wide and deep as a river. Jarl walked through the entrance tunnels cut into the walls and crossed the bridge over that great expanse of water. Then he set off on the long road west to Damascus and, beyond that, the sea.

On the second night he met Mahomet and performed some simple magic tricks that made the Moor's eyes bulge wide in wonder and delight. By the time they reached the port of Acre, they had developed a friendship of opposites, secured by a wordless form of communication, a system of signals, gestures and expressions that became so fast and so subtle as to be a sort of mind-reading.

A dozen years had passed since then, though they had left no trace on Jarl's smooth, unlined features. Now he was no one's slave, nor would he have anyone in his service who was not present of their own free will. And because his face was unknown to the world at large, he could travel wherever he willed. His eyes and ears were still as acute as ever, his mind and memory as powerful. So now he studied the politics and power struggles of his new adopted land, learning so much that he often knew who would call upon his services before they did themselves.

Jarl's current interest was the evident rivalry between the two sons of the late Duke Richard. The young one had occupied a castle to which he was not entitled. Clearly this was an act of provocation. Equally clearly, it would be taken as an act of rebellion, too. The second son resented the fact that his older brother was the duke, as any second son would. For his part, the new duke was furious that his brother had dared to defy their father's will and, in so doing, defy him too. It was obvious to Jarl that the ducal family were expecting trouble. Carpenters and masons were being paid ridiculous wages to work through the winter, fortifying the castle. Servants in the archbishop's palace had heard their master and his mother discussing what to do about the row.

Nothing much was going to happen now, not in January, with the duke's wedding just a few days away. But come the spring, hostilities would surely commence. The duke would have more men, but his brother would have the best defensive position in Normandy. A stalemate was therefore more than likely.

At that point the warring sides would surely look to something, anything that might break the deadlock. Jarl confidently expected that his services would be quietly mentioned to those who needed to hear of them, and an emissary would be sent bearing a commission and the gold with which to fund it.

The only question that remained was: which brother would it be?

11

Rouen, Normandy

Richard of Normandy's wedding feast had not yet begun and already he was blind drunk. He'd got through his first flagon of wine before the service, just to give him the strength to bind himself in marriage to the bride his uncle had procured for him. It was bad enough that he had been given strict instructions to stop his wenching until he had produced a legitimate heir. Why the hell should a duke have to take orders from anyone, let alone his damn uncle? But to be forced to restrict himself to this sour, sexless child made him wonder what he'd done to deserve such a miserable fate.

As he'd strode into Rouen Cathedral – his walk perfectly steady, for Richard was as strong as a strapping young ox and held his drink as well as any man in the duchy – he'd caught sight of his brother Robert. The devious little shit had had the brass nerve to bring his common whore to this royal occasion. And what made it far worse – and accounted no doubt for the smirk that was smeared across Robert's face – was that the little trollop was as beddable a female as Richard had ever seen in his life. He'd even caught the archbishop eyeing her up during one of the psalms. That's right, Uncle, thought Richard, take a good look at those fine plump tits and her soft pink lips . . . By God, he'd give his duchy to have that sweet, warm mouth around his cock! . . . and then tell me why you thought a flat-chested stick of a child like Adela of France would do for me.

'A drop more wine, Your Grace, just to celebrate this great occasion?'

The Count of Bellême, father of Warin and Talvas, and master of a great swathe of land in the south-west corner of the duchy, was standing with Richard in the ducal palace, by the door to the great hall. All the guests, bar the King and Queen of France and their closest retainers, were gathered inside, awaiting the arrival of the bride and groom and the royal party. Bellême was a balding, paunchy, unappealing man who was old enough to be Richard's father. He and his family had done very well out of their loyalty to the previous duke, and from the way Bellême was sucking up to Richard, it was clear that he planned to be just as close to the new one, too. Richard did not particularly care for Bellême's style – there was something unpleasant lurking beneath his sycophancy, like a wasp inside a rotten strawberry – but right now he had brought Richard the one thing in the world that he most wanted: a servant armed with a fresh pitcher of Burgundy. Bellême flicked his fingers and the servant poured half its contents into the capacious pewter tankard – a vessel intended for ale or mead rather than wine – from which Richard was drinking.

'Oh yes,' sneered Richard, 'let's all celebrate . . . And let's start by sticking my little brother on a sword like a pig on a skewer. Then while he's trying to put his guts back into his belly, we'll take that ginger-haired harlot of his off somewhere nice and quiet, see if the hair on her cunt is as red as it is on her head, and show her what it feels like to be fucked by a real man . . . or two . . . or three . . . or every damned man in Normandy, because you know they'd all like to do it.'

'An excellent plan, Your Grace!' said Bellême. 'But I fear Duchess Adela might not approve.'

'Duchess Adela . . .' said Richard with slow deliberation, scarcely believing the words. 'Where is my young wife anyway?

It's time we went in. No one can start eating until we arrive, and they won't thank me for keeping them waiting.'

'As you recall, Your Grace, she is with her handmaidens, adjusting her costume and preparing herself for the feast . . . and the night that will follow it. I'm sure she wants to look her very best for her husband, as any good wife would.'

'I wish her luck with that,' said Richard. He saw a flurry of movement at the other end of the corridor and Adela appeared with her mother, Constance of Arles, the Queen of France, beside her. Adela was a nervous, mousy slip of a girl and hopelessly outshone by Constance, who was as predatory a creature as ever walked the earth, with black eyes and raven hair and a mouth as cruel as it was enticing.

I wonder what it's like being married to that witch, Richard thought. By Christ, she terrifies me, but I'd take her over her daughter any day.

Behind the two women came the King of France and his two surviving sons. The king's face had worn the same look of sour disapproval all day, as though nothing in Normandy came up to his exacting standards of holiness and decorum. Or perhaps he was simply miserable at losing the only one of his children who had not yet risen up against him. All three of his sons had rebelled a year earlier, egged on by Constance, and though the eldest, Hugh, had died, the other two had yet to put down their arms. Why would they? Richard thought. They're winning.

A more puzzling question was why the king still tolerated the presence of a wife who so publicly conspired against him. Either he's too scared to get rid of her, for fear of what she'd do in revenge, or he's still got enough red blood in him that he can't stand the thought of not having her around to fuck. Maybe both, Richard concluded. But he wasn't impressed by either explanation. A man who couldn't win his battles, control his sons or master his woman was not one a Norman duke was ever likely to respect. Still, Richard bowed deeply when the king approached and nodded his head to the queen. Adela, in her turn, gave a little curtsey to her new husband. 'I do apologise, my lord,' she said. 'I hope I haven't kept you waiting.'

Richard gritted his teeth and did his best to maintain the pretence, at least, of graciousness. 'Of course not, my dear, I was just passing the time with my good friend the Count of Bellême – man's talk, I'm sure you would have found it very dull.'

Bellême, in his turn, paid due homage to the royal family.

'I do hope that you will soon become my good friend too, my lord,' said Adela.

A sickly smile appeared on Bellême's face. 'That would be my very great pleasure, Your Grace. I'm only sorry that my dear wife could not have been here today. I know she would have been enchanted to meet you. Sadly, her health did not allow it.'

'I'm so sorry to hear that. Please send her my best wishes for a speedy recovery.'

'I will, Your Grace. I know she will be deeply touched by your concern.'

Had Richard been sober, or even slightly disposed to see good in Adela, he would have noticed how graciously she had spoken to Bellême and perhaps even given her a quiet word of congratulation. But his meagre stock of charm had run dry and the best he could do was to stick out his arm for Adela to take, not even glancing at her as she did so. Oblivious to the disappointment in his young bride's face or the dagger glare in her mother's eyes, he brusquely tugged her closer and, with a muttered 'Might as well get this over and done with', led the way into the great hall.

12

Herleva had told Robert that she might be with child as they were leaving Rouen Cathedral after the wedding service. Three weeks had passed since Judith had tentatively raised the subject: 'I don't wish to say anything I shouldn't, my lady, but I've noticed that there's not been any blood on your sheets, and . . .'

She hadn't needed to finish the sentence. Herleva knew exactly what she was talking about. Another two weeks went by, and still no bleeding. That had never happened before. But then she'd never spent every night in bed with a man before, either. It took a few more days to raise the courage to tell Robert and try to find the right moment to give him the news. It was only as they were walking down the aisle towards the great west door that she suddenly, without any real warning to herself, let alone him, said, 'I think I'm going to have a baby.'

There was a terrifying moment of what seemed like absolute silence, though the church was filled with the hubbub of a large congregation chatting and laughing as they made their way from the service. But then, without any sign of panic, or even surprise, Robert wrapped his arms around her and held her tight. 'This is wonderful news, a gift to us from God and the Blessed Virgin.'

Herleva felt tears of joy and relief welling in her eyes. 'I'm so glad you're happy. I was worried that you'd be cross.'

'Don't be worried . . . don't cry . . . I love you and will never, ever forsake you, or our baby.' Robert paused and waited for Herleva to wipe the tears from her face. Then he looked her in the eye. 'Now listen to me,' he said. 'You mustn't say anything about this to anyone today. Not a word. There'll be enough talk about us as it is without them all having that to gossip about as well.'

A little later, when Herleva took her seat next to Robert at the high table – placed, as he laughingly pointed out, as far away from the bride and groom as was possible without falling off the end – there was a finely crafted silver strainer with a spoon-like handle hanging from a chain around her neck. It was a badge of acceptance into Robert's life and his world, for it was the duty and privilege of high-born ladies to serve their menfolk's wine at feasts and celebrations, using the strainer to sieve out the sediment as they did so. She was pouring Robert his second large cupful, taking great care to make sure that the wine never spilled over the side of the strainer, when there was a sudden commotion from the side of the room, the huge doors opened and Duke Richard led his new bride across the hall towards them.

Herleva had been sharing Robert's bed and his castle for almost two months now, yet she still found it impossible to believe that she was in the same room as the King of France, his family and the mightiest nobility of France and Normandy alike. That they would soon be sitting at the same table as her was even more extraordinary. And yet these people, so great that they were almost like gods to a girl of her lowly birth, were now revealed to be very human. There was Queen Constance, reaching out to fiddle with her daughter's dress, with an irritated little purse of her lips, and Adela closing her eyes as she felt her mother's hand, as if she could wish it away.

This was how it must always have been, Herleva thought: the daughter never quite managing to live up to her mother's standards and expectations. How Adela must have longed to escape! Marriage must have seemed like the perfect opportunity. But when the unhappy bride opened her eyes again, her face looked numb and lifeless and the obvious effort she put into the smiles she directed towards people calling out good wishes only betrayed how bitterly her hopes had been dashed.

Richard, meanwhile, seemed completely indifferent to his wife's feelings; her entire existence, in fact. Herleva remembered the sheer joy she had felt when she first walked arm in arm with Robert, and felt a deep pity for Adela. What was the point of being a princess, of growing up in a palace surrounded by servants, of marrying in a great cathedral if you had no love in your life?

Herleva had just turned her attention to Richard when he happened to look in her direction. He caught her eye for a second, then turned his gaze on Robert, who was showing no interest whatever in his brother's entrance. The hatred in Richard's eyes hit Herleva like a fist in the belly and a hand round the throat. She was stunned, unable to think or move until she finally found the strength to shake Robert by the shoulder to attract his attention.

He smiled at her, still glowing with the thought of his impending fatherhood. 'Mmm . . . ?'

'Your brother,' she said.

'What about him?'

'He hates you.'

Robert's grin grew even wider. 'Well I don't need you to tell me that, my sweet.'

'No, you don't understand. He really hates you . . . and me too.'

'Oh come now . . .' Robert reached out, grabbed Herleva's arm and pulled her down on to his lap. 'You're imagining things. Richard and I have always fought, but it's nothing too

96

serious. Really . . .' He stroked her cheek very softly. 'Don't trouble yourself with these silly thoughts.'

Herleva said nothing. The last thing she wanted was an argument. But she knew what she had seen. Richard's face had borne the look of a man who didn't just want his enemy beaten. He wanted him dead.

13

The archbishop could not remember when he had attended, let alone conducted, a less encouraging wedding. He had to admit that Adela was not at first glance the most desirable bride for a young man like Richard. But if his nephew had taken even the slightest interest in her, or applied a mere fragment of imagination, he might have seen what was clear to the archbishop: there was more to this girl than first met the eye. She had withered and faded in the deep shade cast by her mother, but if a man were to give her some light and love, then she would repay it tenfold, if for no other reason than gratitude. And she was still very young and undeveloped. When she bloomed into full womanhood, she might very well possess many of the qualities that were so sadly lacking now. She just required a husband prepared to be kind and patient and wait for her to come into her own.

Richard was clearly not that man. He had taken one look at her and made no secret of his angry disappointment. It hadn't helped that Robert had brought his concubine to the wedding. The boy had only done it to provoke. He couldn't resist an opportunity to tease and taunt his elder brother. But he was just as stupid in his own way, just as blind to his long-term interests. The archbishop would have to deal with them both today, and the thought of the effort that would take and the slim likelihood that it would end well filled him with a deep weariness. Why did he put himself through all this? Why not resign the archbishopric and retire to a monastery to spend his last years in gentle contemplation?

But there was still so much to do, so many threats to counter. Until and unless Richard and Adela managed to produce an heir, the dukedom's line of succession would not be secure. The longer it took for a son to arrive, the greater the temptation for someone else to try to depose Richard and seize the duchy for themselves. And if Richard was idiotic enough to go to war with his own brother, that would give any potential rebels an ideal opportunity to strike.

So there really was nothing for it, the archbishop concluded: he would have to settle the argument over Falaise Castle this very day. First, though, he needed someone to use as a go-between, a man both brothers would trust. Looking around, he caught sight of the perfect candidate for the job, his first cousin Osbern Herfastsson. Now there was a man to rely on. The archbishop waved him over as if summoning a servant. 'Osbern, how very good to see you. I wonder if you could give me a moment or two of your time. There's something I need you to do . . .'

As one lavish dish followed another, Robert passed the time by telling Herleva about the other guests, all of whom seemed tied to one another by blood, marriage or both. When she pointed this out to him, he immediately agreed. 'Absolutely. In fact the only thing I'm not sure about is whether all the people here belong to lots of different families that happen to be connected, or one giant family that's gone off in different directions. Just look around . . . within a few paces of us there are half a dozen fellows our age, two of them my half-brothers and the rest cousins, and they all probably think they've got a right to be the duke themselves one day. And if the title ever falls vacant or looks vulnerable enough to be there for the taking, believe me, they won't hesitate to make a move. In fact here's one of them now, coming to say hello . . .'

Robert stood up to greet a compact, swarthy young man with thick, wavy black hair. 'Alan!' he said, giving him a back-slapping hug. The new arrival was shorter than Robert, but as Herleva got to her feet too, she couldn't help noticing that his physical presence was just as powerful, and when he smiled, his teeth gleamed white against his olive skin.

'Come now, Robert, where are your manners?' Alan said. 'Aren't you going to introduce me to your ravishing companion?' He fixed Herleva with eyes so dark a brown they were almost black. 'I must tell you, my lady, that you're the one I've come to see, not my cousin here. The whole wedding is talking about you. They say Duke Richard is infuriated that you are so much more lovely than his bride. And I can see exactly why he thinks he's been hard done by.'

'Count Alan of Brittany, may I present Herleva of Falaise,' said Robert, very pointedly putting himself between the two of them. 'You know, Alan, we were just talking about you.'

'Oh really, and what were you saying?'

'Well, I was trying to decide whether the guests here belonged to a host of different families, or just one great big one. Take you and me, for example: are we family, or not?'

Alan nodded thoughtfully. 'Interesting . . .' Herleva felt his attention turn to her again with unnerving but not entirely unpleasant intensity, 'You see, my lady, though Robert and I belong to different houses, we are actually cousins twice over. Our fathers each married the other one's sister. Our grandfathers thought it would bring peace between Normandy and Brittany, because how could two men who were practically brothers possibly go to war?'

'Now there's a question,' said Robert wryly.

100

'And did your grandfathers' plan work, my lord?' Herleva asked.

Alan's eyes crinkled in knowing amusement. 'So far, my lady . . . so far.'

'I think it's frightening,' said Herleva, after Count Alan had gone back to his table. 'Here we all are at a feast. Everyone should be enjoying themselves, feeling happy to be together, but underneath they're all busy plotting against each other.'

'Well they're not all plotting now, but they might do one day,' Robert replied. 'And is it different to any other big family? I'm sure you could go to a wedding in Falaise full of tanners and skinners and who knows what else, and there'd be just as much rivalry and jealousy there, people conspiring with one another to get at someone else.'

Herleva looked at him and sighed. 'But you're talking about people fighting over the whole of Normandy.'

'Not just Normandy, my darling. There's a pair of brothers down the table who want the crown of England.'

Robert was about to say more, but his attention was caught by the arrival of a new guest at the feast, walking up the middle of the hall, making straight for the high table. He was a thin, nervy man, with feverish, staring eyes and a mess of unkempt tangled hair. He was dressed in a bright red tunic and sky-blue leggings and he held a small drum or tambour in his hand. As he passed between the other tables a steady murmur of recognition and amusement started building, and Robert too now let out a loud whoop and gave half a dozen hard, steady claps of his hands. Then he turned to Herleva and said, 'This is Warner. He's a poet. The dirtiest poet you'll ever hear.'

Warner of Rouen reached his destination, directly opposite the centre of the high table. He bowed deeply and paid his respects to the assembled royalty and nobles, ending with a few flowery

101

phrases in honour of 'the beautiful princess who has so graciously honoured us all by taking the hand of Normandy'.

As the guests clapped and cheered, Adela gave a shy, sweet smile that brought new life to her face. She could actually be quite pretty, thought Herleva. If only Richard would kiss her. Go on, you fool! Let everyone see that you love her, or are proud of her, or like her even a little bit. It would make her so happy and everyone will cheer. Go on . . . !

She could see from the desperate little glance Adela darted at her new husband that she was longing for the same thing. But Richard sat impassively, staring straight ahead of him, and the moment was lost.

'With Your Majesties' and Graces' permission,' Warner went on, 'I should like to tell the tale of a certain . . . Moriuht.'

There was another burst of applause from the mass of guests at the lower tables. Tankards were thumped against the wood and drunken voices bellowed, 'Mori-uht-uht-uht.' Herleva looked around her and noticed that even on the high table there were broad smiles on the Norman faces. She saw Gunnor and Archbishop Robert glance at one another, and for a moment the stately dowager duchess and scheming churchman were two more happy revellers, looking forward to the evening's entertainment.

'The story I am about to recount,' Warner began, 'concerns a certain Moriuht, a poet like myself, who came from the distant shores of Ireland. Travelling here to Normandy with his wife and daughter, he somehow lost his family, his possessions, everything that was dear to him. And so, as my tale begins, he is wandering the roads, going from village to village and town to town, trying to find the woman he loves, while still enjoying the pleasures of sweet young maidens, pretty boys or, if he has no other choice, any sheep or goat he can catch . . .'

Robert leaned over and whispered in Herleva's ear, 'Have you ever heard the story of Moriuht?'

She shook her head and then, for no other reason than the fact that she loved him so much, leaned across and kissed him. Robert gave her a sly, wicked smile and she felt his hand beneath the table slide across her thigh. She opened her legs a fraction, cursing the folds of silk and linen that lay between his skin and hers, then trembled as his hand burrowed between her legs.

'Well you'll love it,' he murmured.

Herleva's whole world was contained within the space she and her man occupied. Somewhere far away in the distance Warner started declaiming his verses, beating out the rhythm on his little drum.

He had an old goatskin in front of his prick and another
one over his arse.
His balls were quite bare
And his black pubic hair
Made the ladies all scream as he passed.

His butt was as big as a barrel and it had a great gaping hole.
There was enough room up there
For a cat, dog and bear,
His crack could have swallowed them whole.

14

Warner's epic ballad was a torrent of sex-obsessed smut from beginning to end and Alfred the Atheling, one-time prince of England, responded to it like any normal fifteen-year-old boy: with helpless, hysterical laughter. His elder brother Edward, however, was not amused. 'For heaven's sake control yourself!' he snapped. 'This vile insult to poetry is nothing but ungodly filth. This feast is supposed to be a celebration of the holy sacrament of marriage. It makes me sick to see it sullied by such gross carnality.'

'Don't be stupid,' Alfred replied. 'How can you have a marriage without carnality? Cousin Richard has just promised Princess Adela that he will worship her with his body. She's promised to be gentle and obedient to him in bed. I know what that really means. They're going to fuck each other and make babies. So don't lecture me about ungodly filth. We wouldn't be here without it.'

'And don't lecture me about theology,' Edward replied, his voice bitter with years of accumulated resentment and self-pity. 'I know a lot more about that subject than you do. And I wonder whether you can tell me where, in any of those vows you seem to care so much about, it tells a wife to throw the children of one marriage away the moment she finds another bull to tup her?'

'Not that again . . .' Alfred moaned. 'I just want to enjoy the poem and have a good time, like everyone else. Do I really have to hear you whining on about Mother again? Today of all days . . .'

'On the contrary, today of all days I can't help but think about the way our mother betrayed our father's memory and abandoned you and me, her two sons, her own flesh and blood, so that she could go chasing after that Danish usurper.'

'For Christ's sake, she didn't abandon us. She saved us. It's obvious! She had to get us out of the country or Canute would have killed us.'

'If she cared about us more than she cared about staying on the throne, she'd have come with us. But instead she cares about power, and men's cocks and that is all.'

Alfred muttered, 'Shut up!' through tightly clenched teeth.

Edward ignored him. 'They say that when she and the usurper rut, the sound of her screaming echoes through all the rooms of Winchester Palace. That woman may style herself Queen of England, but I know she's nothing but the Queen of Harlots.'

'So what does that make you? You call yourself King of England. King of Fools, more like. For the thousandth time, Edward, the only way our mother could save us was by making a deal with Canute. And the only thing she had to offer him was herself. If I can see that, at my age, why can't you understand it when you're supposed to be an adult?'

Now a woman's voice cut in on the conversation from the opposite side of the table. 'He's quite right, you know, Edward. Mother was acting in our best interests.'

'Thank you, Goda,' said Alfred to his sister, the oldest of Emma's three children. She had left England with her brothers and was now married to Drogo, Count of the Vexin. His lands lay between the border with Normandy to the west and Paris to the east, spreading Emma's dynastic influence into France as well as England, Denmark and Germany.

Edward looked at Goda with something close to disgust. 'Keep your empty-headed opinions to yourself, sister, they are of no value to me. I hope our mother roasts in the fires of hell for what she did.'

'Don't say that!' Alfred shouted. 'Don't talk about our mother like that!'

'Or what? What exactly can you threaten me with? Still, if it makes you any happier, I will tell you that the Jezebel you so foolishly insist on defending has done me one great service at least. She's cured me of any carnal desire for women. I know Eve for a friend of the serpent and deceiver of men. I know her cunt to be an acid well filled with demons, and I shall never venture there.'

'That's disgusting! I'd rather listen to Warner than you. At least his filth is funny.'

Not far from the two young Englishmen, the archbishop rose from his seat, made polite apologies to Duke Richard, his bride, the king and queen and discreetly slipped away from the table and out of the hall, leaving by a side exit.

Warner, meanwhile, had arrived at the verses that the guests who knew the story of Moriuht had been looking forward to most of all. For never before had the great lady they described been present when they were spoken. And so the cheers redoubled as he declared:

To blest Lady Gunnor now Moriuht came, to our
lady most noble and wise.
He begged her, 'My queen,
Have you perhaps seen
That wife of mine that I prize?'

'I know where to find her,' said Gunnor.

'She's just been sold as a slave.
In Vaudreuil you can see her
Just say that I'll free her
And your broken heart you may save.'

Robert was thoroughly enjoying the feast. His belly was full of food. There was excellent wine in his goblet. His mouth was on his woman's lips and his hand was up her skirt. But then the day took a turn for the worse as Osbern Herfastsson appeared, coughed politely and said, 'Excuse me, my lord, but His Grace the archbishop would be very grateful if you could spare a few moments to speak with him.'

'Can't it wait?' Robert asked, disengaging his mouth from Herleva's. 'I'm having a very nice time right here . . .'

'So I see, but His Grace was very keen to see you as soon as possible at his palace. He apologises for making you take a short walk, but feels it would be more private there. He's asked me to fetch Duke Richard as well.'

'Richard? Really? Does my uncle propose to meet us both together?'

'That was his intention, my lord, yes.'

'Well, that should be interesting . . .' Robert took Herleva's hand. 'I'm so sorry, darling, I'll try not to be too long. Don't do anything wicked while I'm gone. And watch out for those French courtiers. They're not much good at fighting, but they're absolutely ruthless when they see a beautiful woman . . .'

He gave her a peck on the forehead and followed Osbern away across the hall. Herleva sat for a minute or two absorbing the scene and wondering what to do next. The only other person she knew here was Herluin and she wasn't at all sure that he liked her: he was always perfectly polite, of course, but he'd never been particularly friendly. She was beginning to feel unnervingly conscious of men's eyes looking at her and fearing that they would soon be followed by the men themselves, making drunken advances, when a woman's voice spoke over her shoulder. 'May I join you, my dear? You look as though you could do with a little company.'

She glanced up to see the tall, slender figure of Lady Gunnor beside her, looking very old and delicate yet at the same time imposing and even a little frightening. Herleva sprang to her feet feeling hopelessly flustered and dipped into a very clumsy, unbalanced curtsey. 'I'm so sorry, Your Grace, I'm afraid I didn't see you.'

Gunnor smiled. 'It's quite all right, there's no need to apologise. I just thought it might be enjoyable for you and me to talk. You see, of all the people in this great gathering, I am the only one who understands exactly how you feel. I know just what it's like to meet a great nobleman, fall hopelessly in love and suddenly find oneself in a world quite unlike anything one has ever experienced or imagined before.' She paused for a moment and fixed Herleva with a kind but shrewd look. 'You do love my grandson, don't you?'

'With all my heart, Your Grace.'

Gunnor took Herleva's hand and patted it gently. 'Good, I'm very glad to hear it. And I'm not in the slightest bit surprised. The men in that family are all the same: impossible, but irresistible. Well, most of them, at any rate – a few are just impossible. And of course they all take it for granted that they must have their way over everything, all the time, and are as sulky as spoilt children when they can't.'

Herleva laughed. Gunnor had just summed up Robert in a nutshell.

'So now you must tell me everything about this wonderful story of yours. Is it true, as people say, that Robert spotted you from the castle walls, dancing with your friends, and summoned you that very instant?'

'It is almost true, Your Grace. I was dancing, but Robert was on his horse and had just been out hunting. And he did summon me that very instant, but I didn't go to the castle until later that night and . . . oh!' She suddenly realised that she'd given too much away. 'I'm so sorry, Your Grace . . . You must think I'm wicked and—'

'Nonsense! I was no different. I know it must seem impossible for you to believe, but I was once just like you – a pretty little thing from a very humble home. My father was a merchant. He'd made a bit of money, and made a lot more in later life, but he came from a modest background back in Denmark. And then I met Duke Richard and . . .' She smiled wistfully at the memory.

'Did he make you happy?' Herleva asked.

'Yes, my dear, most of the time he did. We spent almost thirty years together and had eight children. Of course, he had another four or five with other women . . . Don't look shocked. I'm afraid that sort of thing is only to be expected. These Normans are real men. They're strong and brave. They'll keep you and your babies safe. They'll love you, provide for you and make every other man you meet seem feeble and insipid by comparison. But if you fall in love with a stallion, you shouldn't expect to be his only mare.'

Herleva didn't know quite how to reply to that, but was saved from the need to do so as Lady Gunnor said, 'Ah, I think our poet is coming towards the end of his great work. Shall we listen to his final verses?'

Warner was sweating like an overworked mule. His voice was hoarse and he barely had the strength left to keep beating his little drum. He took three deep breaths, drew himself up straight and made a final burst for the literary finishing line:

To Vaudreuil poor Moriuht hurried, to find his wife
in that city.
Her master, so rude
Gave her no clothes or food
And nothing to cover her titties.

15

There was a knock on the door of the archbishop's study. It opened just enough for Osbern Herfastsson to poke his head into the room. 'I have His Grace the duke and Count Robert here as you requested, Your Grace,' he said.

'Bring them in,' replied the archbishop with a little wave of his hand.

Osbern opened the door wider to let Richard and Robert through, and then closed it behind them so that they were alone with their uncle.

It was immediately plain to the archbishop that both brothers had consumed a great deal of drink. That did not in itself alarm him. It was only to be expected at a wedding feast, after all. What was more concerning, however, was the different effect that intoxication had had upon the two of them. Robert greeted him with a cheerful 'Hello, Uncle!', looking for all the world as though he, rather than his brother, was the happy bridegroom. Richard, on the other hand, was silent, brooding and clearly simmering with the sort of pent-up drunken rage that might at any moment erupt into outright violence. And the way he was glaring at Robert left no doubt who would be on the receiving end.

The archbishop knew that he had to take immediate control of the situation before any small hope of a reasoned negotiation was lost. He rose from his chair, approached the two men, held out his right hand, palm down, fingers slightly bent, and gave a single word of command: 'Kneel!'

The ducal family of Normandy made a point of their Christian devotion, not least because their Viking ancestors had all been pagan. Richard and Robert dropped to their knees without a moment's hesitation and each in turn kissed the massive gold episcopal ring on the archbishop's fourth finger. While he stood over them, the archbishop gave a solemn warning: 'Remember that you speak now in the presence of Almighty God, and any vow you make will be witnessed by Him. He will hear you and judge you, and any insults, or threats, or sinful words uttered here, within His palace, will be held against you when you stand before him on the final Day of Judgement.' He paused for a moment to let the words sink in, then, in a much milder tone, said, 'You may rise.'

Two wooden chairs had been placed a couple of paces apart in front of the archbishop's. 'Please take a seat,' he said. He waited for a few moments while the young men made themselves comfortable and then went on, 'I apologise for taking you away from the wedding feast. Rest assured I won't keep you long. But I didn't know when there would be another opportunity to talk to you both face to face, in the same room, and it would have been remiss of me to let this one go.'

'Yes, yes,' said Richard with surly impatience. 'Just tell me what's so damned important and let's deal with it. I don't want to spend any more time than I have to in the same room as him.' He gave a jerk of his head towards Robert and added, 'Or his damned whore.'

Robert smiled amiably. 'I do apologise for my brother's rudeness, Uncle. I think he's upset by the comparison between the divine beauty of my lovely Herleva and the more, ah, modest attractions of his new wife. Though I think she looks perfectly charming . . . in a homely sort of way.'

'I don't have to sit here and listen to this,' said Richard, rising unsteadily to his feet.

'Enough!' the archbishop roared. 'You!' He pointed at Richard. 'Sit back down at once. And you,' he turned his eyes on Robert, 'will address me at all times as "Your Grace", for I am your archbishop and you will not forget it.'

Richard slumped back down into his seat more like a recalcitrant schoolboy than a reigning duke. The archbishop waited a few seconds for his words to sink in and then continued more calmly, but with an intensity that not even the most befuddled ear could miss. 'The two of you are a disgrace to our family. Your father, my brother, spent thirty years fighting to make the duchy of Normandy greater and stronger, and our family with it. His father before him was dedicated to the same task for more than fifty years, building on the legacy first created by your great-great-grandfather Rollo when he was given these lands. And now you two, you spoiled, self-indulgent brats, are going to throw it all away.'

Richard leaned forward in his chair and was about to protest, but the archbishop jabbed a finger at him and said, 'No! Not a word. I will say my piece and only then will you talk . . . I want to deal, here and now, with this whole ridiculous business of Falaise Castle . . .'

This time it was Robert who opened his mouth to speak, though a single furious glance from the archbishop was enough to shut it again.

'Can't you see how it harms Normandy to have the duke and his brother at odds? Do you really want our enemies watching in glee while the two of you fight to the death? This matter has to be settled. So let us agree on the central point first: Falaise Castle forms part of the ducal estate and it belongs to the reigning duke unless he, or one of his predecessors, has specifically entitled someone else to live in it. Second point: His Grace Duke Richard II did not grant anyone else the right to live in the castle and thus it belongs to the reigning duke.'

'Precisely,' said Richard, suddenly feeling much happier. 'Tell him to get out of there and let that be an end of it.'

'Not so fast,' the archbishop warned him. 'I have not finished outlining the truth of the case as I see it. For it's also clear that the castle stands in the lands known as the Hiémois and is, indeed, the principal building in the region. So it follows that the Count of the Hiémois should reasonably expect to hold the castle as his seat.'

'Thank you,' said Robert. 'That's what I've said all along.'

'Now the question arises, what are the motives of someone who occupies the castle in defiance of the duke? Some people might see it as an act of rebellion. Falaise would make a fine base from which to mount an attack on the duchy itself. So I shall ask you directly, Robert, bearing in mind that you speak in the sight and hearing of God, do you have any intention to overthrow your brother?'

'Of course not!' Robert replied indignantly. 'All I want is somewhere better to live than that pathetic shack of a place at Exmes.'

'And will you swear a solemn oath of fealty, made on the Holy Bible, promising to be your brother's true and loyal subject?'

Robert crossed his arms, pushed his lips into a sullen pout and muttered a reluctant 'Yes . . . I suppose so. If I have to.'

'Very good,' said the archbishop. 'So, Richard, can I ask you this: if Robert swore allegiance and promised to serve you faithfully, would you consent to let him stay at Falaise Castle?'

Silence fell upon the room. The archbishop looked at Richard. He in turn leaned back in his chair and appeared to find something fascinating on the study ceiling. Robert said nothing. The castle was almost in his grasp. He had no intention of doing anything to let it slip.

Richard lost interest in the ceiling. He lowered his eyes and looked at Robert with raw loathing. Then he glanced back at the archbishop and said, 'No. As long as I am Duke of Normandy, he will never, ever be allowed to occupy Falaise.'

The archbishop cupped his face in his hands, rubbed his eyes, looked up and made one last attempt at diplomacy. 'Richard, think again, I implore you. What harm does it do you to show generosity to your own kin? If you reject Robert's offer of fealty, you make him your enemy. And I say again that if you two go to war, no good will come of it. Not for either of you, nor for any of us.'

'I don't care,' Richard replied. 'Father left the castle to me. If he'd wanted to leave it to Robert, he could have done, but he didn't. So it's mine. And you know what, brother dearest? I might have considered giving it to you, just to please our uncle archbishop. But then you had to bring that woman here . . . As if I wouldn't know what you were doing, showing off to the world that you think you're so much better than me – the pretty boy who gets all the girls and learns all the fancy Latin words—'

'I'm also a much finer horseman and far, far better with a sword. Don't forget that,' Robert pointed out, with a casual arrogance calculated to make his brother even more furious.

Richard got to his feet and for a moment it looked as if he might launch himself at Robert and settle the question there and then, for whatever his shortcomings, he was certainly the bigger and stronger of the two. But the archbishop sprang to his feet with surprising agility for a man of his age and stood between the brothers, barring Richard's way. He was tall enough to look the duke in the eye as he said, 'Go back to your wedding. Make sure your guests are entertained. And try to show some small shred of kindness to your wife, if you're man enough to do it . . . Go!'

He waited until Richard had left the room and then turned to face Robert. 'I'll get Osbern to fetch that woman of yours and any retainers you may have at the feast. I'll send my stable boys to find your horses and get them prepared. And then you will leave Rouen immediately, and if you have any sense at all, you will vacate Falaise too.'

'Never,' said Robert. 'I'll be on my way now, don't you worry about that. I don't want to spend another second in my brother's presence. But if he wants that castle, he's going to have to come and get it.'

The archbishop's face fell. 'In that case, there will be war. And may God have mercy on all our souls.'

Adela, Duchess of Normandy, cried herself to sleep that night. Her new husband had drunk so much that he could barely manage to walk up to their chamber for the formal blessing of the marital bed. The archbishop was too senior to conduct this part of the ceremony, so the job was left to a mere priest.

He made the sign of the cross over the bed and intoned, 'Bless O Lord this chamber and all who dwell therein, that they may be established in thy peace and abide in thy will, and live and grow in thy love, and that the length of their days may be multiplied.'

Richard put a hand to his mouth and tried to suppress a belch as the priest continued, 'Watch over these thy servants who rest in this bed, guarding them from all fantasies and illusions of devils, guard them waking that they may meditate on thy commandments; guard them sleeping that in their slumbers they may think of thee; and that here and everywhere they may ever be defended by the help of thy protection.'

When he had finished, the priest sprinkled both the bed and the newly married couple with holy water, and then they and the considerable crowd of guests who had crammed into the chamber to witness this conclusion of the sacrament and celebration of marriage all intoned a final 'Amen'.

At this point in most weddings it was customary for men and women alike to offer encouragement, advice and even a dash of mockery, the cruder the better, to the happy couple. But this couple were so obviously *un*happy and the spark of desire was so clearly absent that no one had the heart to make merry. Instead they all filed out, leaving Richard and Adela alone.

Like any girl, Adela had wondered what this moment would be like. Never had she imagined it would be like this. In the end, when Richard proved too sodden with drink to make even an attempt at consummating their marriage, she felt a sense of relief. That torment at least she had been spared. But the thought of an entire lifetime spent in this Norman purgatory was more than she could bear.

16

Alençon Castle, the County of Bellême

'You know, it's not often I feel sorry for a man who's about to get a free fuck, but I've never in all my days seen a man who looked more miserable than Duke Richard on his wedding night.'

The Count of Bellême burst out laughing at his own fine wit. Of his six sons, four were with him that day and they all dutifully joined in. He was about to say more when he was distracted by the smell of hot roast meat wafting across the private chamber in the keep of his castle at Alençon. A haggard old menial was standing just inside the door on the far side of the chamber. Her dress looked like a hand-me-down from a much grander lady, for though it was frayed and coming apart at the seams, the stuff of which it was made was fancy enough. She had untidy grey hair and a drawn, anxious face, and she was so nervous in the presence of the count and his sons that the platter she was holding, laden with a freshly cooked joint of pork, was shaking in her hands.

The terrified drudge made a visible effort to summon up the courage to speak. 'Er . . . er . . . excuse me, my lord, but Cook thought you might like something to eat.'

'Well then for God's sake bring it here, woman, before you drop it on the floor and we all die of hunger.'

She managed to deliver the food to the table around which the men were standing, and then stood there looking down at

118

the floor in case his lordship should have any further commands. Bellême unsheathed the dagger that hung from his belt and cut off a rough slice of pork. He took a couple of lusty bites, then, with his mouth still full of half-chewed meat, said, 'I want wine . . . now!'

'Yes, my lord, right away.' The woman bobbed respectfully and scuttled out of the room.

'Right,' said Bellême, 'let's get down to business. I spent a good long time talking to Duke Richard, and he told me, in strictest confidence, that he's going to go to war against his upstart young brother. He's marching on Falaise in the spring with the firm intention of kicking that little shit out of the castle. Obviously I told him he could count on the full support of the House of Bellême. When I said we could put almost three hundred men in the field, the duke was impressed and, I might add, very grateful. I also pointed out that this would entail a significant expense on our part for which we would need to be suitably compensated. And then I suggested, very casually, that Falaise Castle would need a new tenant once the boy Robert had been kicked out, someone the duke could depend on absolutely. Well, he's not exactly a genius, Richard, but he's not so thick he couldn't see what I was getting at. So he told me that if we come on the campaign with him and help him take the castle, he'll give very serious consideration – and then he said it again, "very serious" – to letting us have the tenancy of Falaise.'

'So what are the chances of Duke Richard taking the castle?' asked Talvas. He had been christened William, but he preferred to be known by the nickname he'd acquired as a small boy, which meant 'shield'. A group of children had found a bird hopping and flapping about on the floor of one of the storerooms in the basement of Alençon Castle. It had got in somehow, injured its wing while trying to escape and was now incapable of

119

flight. The children were arguing, trying to decide whether to carry the bird up into the open air and set it free, or put it out of its misery.

William had walked in on them by chance. Without saying a word or displaying the slightest sign of emotion, he'd walked over to the bird, picked it up and dashed out its brains against the storeroom's bare stone wall. Then he'd handed the corpse to one of the other children and said, 'Give it to the dogs. They'll eat it.'

Later that day, Bellême heard what had happened. He had looked at his youngest son and said, in a tone that mixed pride with an odd thread of apprehension, 'By God, boy, you're a hard one. As hard as a warrior's shield.'

From that day on, William had been Talvas, and he'd more than lived up to his name. He had a cold, ruthless mind, untroubled by scruple or sentimentality, so his question now was no innocent enquiry. He wanted to know the odds of success, the better to judge the deal his father had made.

'Of course Richard'll take Falaise,' Bellême replied, slicing off another hunk of meat. 'I was with him when his old man sent him off to Burgundy to teach Hugh of Chalon a lesson. Hugh shut himself up in Mimande Castle – which, let me tell you, makes Falaise look like a peasant's shack. He reckoned there was no chance anyone was ever going to prise him out, especially not some wet-behind-the-ears pup of nineteen. But Richard marched through Burgundy, stealing or raping everything that moved and burning anything that didn't. When he got to Mimande, he didn't bother with a siege. He attacked straight away, took Hugh totally by surprise and had him on his knees by sunset, with a saddle strapped across his back, grovelling in the dirt and begging for mercy. He'll do the same thing to his own brother, you mark my words.'

'Hmm . . .' Talvas did not look as impressed as Bellême had

hoped. 'Does Count Robert know the story of Richard's attack on Mimande?'

'I should think so. What of it?'

'If he does, he's not going to fall for the same trick. Not unless he's even thicker than his brother, and I know for a fact that he isn't.'

'You watch your tongue,' Bellême snapped, stabbing his dagger in Talvas' direction. 'Richard'll take Falaise. You'll all be there to see him do it. And that's only going to be the start for us . . . Look at this.'

A scroll of parchment was lying on the table. Bellême moved the food out of the way and unrolled it, stabbing the far end with his knife to hold it in place. 'Right,' he said, 'time I gave you whelps a lesson. This is a map. I had one of the monks draw it up for me. No point paying for a whole damned monastery if you can't make those idle bastards take their hands off their pricks and grab their pens instead, eh?'

'What's it a map of?' asked Warin, while Talvas wondered idly whether if he cracked open his brother's skull he'd find anything at all inside.

'It's the land around us,' Bellême replied. 'Look, here's Alençon and our castle, where we are right now. And here's Bellême itself, just to the right of Alençon.'

'How do you read all those names?' asked Fulk, another of the brothers.

'I don't. The monk told me and I remembered. But it's simple once you understand that you're looking at the world from up in the sky, the way a bird or an angel does. So up here, at the top of the map, that's the rest of Normandy. Look, here's Sées. Can you see, the monk even drew the bishop's palace with your brother inside.'

Another of Bellême's sons, Ivo, had been given the bishopric of Sées when he reached the age of eighteen, round about the time the family had received permission to build their castle. It had all been part of a deal old Duke Richard II had made to buy their loyalty.

'Down below where we are, that's the county of Maine, and underneath that, Anjou. So we're right in the middle, where Maine meets Normandy. And look at these lines, lads. What d'you reckon they are?'

There was a long, heavy silence. Eventually Talvas could bear it no longer. He gave a long sigh of exasperation at the dimness around him and said, 'Roads. Isn't it obvious?'

'Don't you take that tone with me, young man!'

'I wasn't,' Talvas protested. 'I was taking it with my idiot brothers.' He looked at them insolently, daring them to take him on. None of them moved.

Bellême grunted non-committally. 'Well you're right, anyway. Those are roads. Some of them go back to Roman times. That's why they're so straight. Six of them meet at Bellême – see? They stretch out right across Normandy. Then there are more here at Alençon. This one's the old Roman road from Le Mans to Falaise. And there's the one that goes up towards Vieux, through the gap in the hills between here and Domfront. The reason I wanted to show you boys this map was so you'd understand why the land around us is so important.

'Duke Richard needs us because we guard his southern border with Maine. And the lords of Maine and Anjou need us because if they want to get into Normandy, they've got to come through here. So if we control even more land hereabouts, and all these roads, we can put ourselves in a very strong position. And if Duke Richard is kind enough to let us have his fine castle at Falaise, we'll be even stronger. Strong enough perhaps to create a little duchy of our own, where no one can look down on us and even the King of France himself has to show us respect.'

The Count of Bellême looked at his sons. 'And that is what I intend to do. With your help, boys, I'm going to create the duchy of Bellême.'

Talvas was thinking, no, you're not going to create that duchy . . . but I will, when the door opened and the old drudge came back in, hanging on for dear life to a tray on which stood five goblets and a large earthenware pitcher full to the brim with rich red wine. The men watched her with smirks on their faces.

'What'll you lads wager me the whole lot goes flying before the dried-up old slapper gets to the table?' Bellême called out, and the woman blushed at the mocking laughter that followed. Somehow she managed to reach the table and place the tray upon it. She passed out the five goblets and then started serving her master the count. Her hands were shaking again, so much so that the lip of the pitcher bumped against Bellême's goblet and knocked it over. The cup was not even a third full, yet there was enough wine already inside it to splash on to the table. Some ran off the side and dropped to the floor. But two or three thin red snakes writhed across the tabletop and on to the map.

The woman looked on in helpless horror as she saw what she had done. She looked around, desperately trying to find somewhere she could put the wine jug down so that her hands were free to clear up the mess. But in her panic she could see no suitable resting place, and so she stood there shaking, making wordless little squeaks and sighs of anxiety with each of her rapid, shallow breaths.

Bellême regarded her with bottomless contempt. 'You stupid . . . pathetic . . . incompetent old slut,' he said, not even bothering to raise his voice. He gave a sharp flick of his right arm and slapped the helpless drudge hard, backhanded, across the side of her face. The force of the blow knocked her back a step, but Bellême moved with her and swung his hand back the other way, hitting her just as brutally with his palm. The woman did not raise her hands to defend herself. They were both wrapped tight around the wine jug, which she was clutching to her body, knowing that if she dropped it and it smashed on the floor, the punishment she had received thus far would be nothing compared to what would follow.

Nor did she cry out. She took her beating silently, as she had learned to do over the years. There was no point in weeping, still less protesting. It only made him angrier.

Still holding the pitcher, she fell to her knees at his feet. 'I'm very sorry, my lord. Please forgive me. I was clumsy and foolish, I know. You were right to punish me. I'll try to do better in future, my lord, I swear I will.'

The man leaned down and grabbed the beaten, humiliated woman by her hair. He pulled it until her head was bent back, her eyes looking straight up into his as he towered over her.

'See that you do, or next time I will be less merciful.' He looked her up and down, his face wrinkling in disgust at what he saw. 'By Christ, you're an ugly bitch. Get out of my sight!'

'Yes, my lord, thank you, my lord.'

The Count of Bellême watched the woman get slowly to her feet and shuffle away from him, hunched and defeated. He waited until she was halfway to the door before calling out, 'Wait!'

She stopped and looked back at him, on the edge of breaking into the sobs of despair she could finally release once she was out of the room. She sniffed, gulped and then quavered, 'Yes, my lord?'

'Stop snivelling, woman!' the count said. 'You've forgotten something. Guess what it is.'

Her eyes widened. Again she looked around her in something close to terror. Had she left something behind? And then she realised: the mess on the table. 'I'll clean it up right away, my lord. I'm sorry. I'm so very sorry . . .' She scuttled back towards them.

'Stop!' Bellême shouted, even louder this time, and the others burst out laughing as the woman tried to bring herself to a halt, skidding on the floor rushes and almost losing her balance in the process.

'No, you pig-ignorant whore. I don't want you to clear it up. You'd only make even more of a mess. I want you . . .' he waited for a moment, grinning at the smirking faces of the other men, 'to give me the godforsaken wine jug.'

All five men burst into helpless laughter, so that Bellême almost dropped the pitcher himself when the woman handed it to him. He couldn't hit her again because his hands were full, so he lashed out with his feet and kicked her towards the door.

As the Countess of Bellême left the room, her husband turned to her sons, shook his head and said, 'God only knows why I married that cunt.'

Book Two:

Battle in the Blood

Spring–Autumn 1027

1

Falaise, Normandy

In the grey half-light before dawn, two servant girls clad in patched and faded dresses, with rough woollen shawls draped over their heads and shoulders to ward off the chill of an early morning in April, slipped out of the postern gate of Falaise Castle. A man followed, unshaven and equally shabbily dressed, leading a donkey bearing their meagre possessions and two large canvas sacks. They were almost the last of the staff to leave, the others having departed two days earlier as news came that Duke Richard's forces had left Rouen and were bearing down upon them.

The track ran around the edge of the bluff on which the castle stood, with the walls rising to one side and the drop – steep in some places, virtually sheer in others – falling away to the other. It was, by design, very narrow, and being seldom used was not worn down, making it hard to follow, especially in such meagre visibility. They were forced to proceed in single file, and only the donkey was sure-footed enough to amble along without the slightest sign of nerves. Finally they hit the path that led from the castle gate down to the town below and were able to make their way more quickly. There was no one else to be seen as they hurried through the streets of Falaise. It was still very early, and besides, many of the population had fled as word spread that a battle or, even worse, a siege was in the offing. They were completely undetected as they passed by the stock-yards and crossed the fields that lay between them and the forest.

Some while later, Count Robert left the castle for his usual morning ride. Most of the stable staff had departed along with everyone else, and those that remained, the grown men with military experience, were now quartered with the other troops. The morning rations were being doled out. Soon they would be conducting exercises in the castle yard, sharpening up rusty sword-fighting skills and sparring with long wooden staffs. So Robert watered, fed and saddled his stallion himself and took a second courser with him, held on a leading rein.

He caught up with the three travellers not far from the Mouth of Hell. As he rode towards them, the familiar surroundings took him back to the day he had fought the boar and then, riding this same horse, first set eyes upon Herleva. And there she was now, the woman who was carrying his baby, with Judith and Herluin beside her. He leapt down from the saddle, and as Herleva ran towards him, he caught her in a fierce embrace and they kissed with the desperate hunger of lovers who knew that they must soon be parted and might never see one another again.

Herluin tethered the horses to some trees that were far enough away from the trail to be safe from passing travellers' eyes, but kept hold of the donkey as Robert led the four of them into the trees, following a stream as it wound through a narrow gully. They walked in silence, subdued and apprehensive, until they came to a point where a long-dead tree, blown down in a storm, had fallen across the gully, blocking their path. There they climbed back up on to the forest floor and turned away from the stream. No path was visible to the naked eye, yet Robert strode ahead, turning occasionally to the right or the left as they passed through the undergrowth, around thickets of bracken, bramble and hawthorn and between the sturdy trunks of chestnut trees.

They had been walking for some while when Herluin asked,

'Are you sure you know where you're going?'

'Of course I do,' replied Robert, but even his certainty was beginning to fade when at last there came the sound of dogs barking somewhere in the distance. He grinned. 'What did I tell you? We're almost there.'

They followed the sound of the dogs until they reached a clearing in which stood a stout cottage made of sturdy wooden logs, the walls and roof alike, with vegetable beds, a pigpen and a chicken run outside. Three large mastiffs chained to a post were straining at their leashes and baring their teeth as the sight of the strangers they had previously only smelled drove them into an even louder frenzy. The cottage door opened and a man with silver hair and weather-beaten skin as brown and leathered as one of the hides in Fulbert's tannery strode out, stood before the dogs and snapped, 'Quiet!' The barking subsided into a low, angry snarl. The man pointed towards the post and issued another command: 'Sit!' and the dogs skulked resentfully away.

'Good morning, Osmund Forester,' said Robert, and then, seeing the figure of a woman appear at the door, added, 'And to you, Mistress Forester.'

Osmund stepped forward, gave a respectful nod of the head and held out his hand. His grip when Robert took it was firm, and the muscles of his forearm strong, honed by a lifetime of hunting and woodcutting. 'We are ready to do your bidding, as we promised, my lord,' he said.

Two weeks earlier, when he knew that the long-awaited conflict with Richard would soon be upon him, Robert had taken the forester aside and asked for his help. 'I'm requesting a favour, not giving an order,' he had said. 'I know your home is far away in the woods and none but you and your family know where to find it, and I need somewhere safe, where something very precious to me can be hidden. I may be putting you in danger, so if you refuse me, I won't hold it against you. But if you consent, I'll forever be in your debt.'

The forester had formed a good opinion of Robert from the fearless way he faced even the wildest animal himself, rather than asking others to do it. So he agreed, without asking what it was that his lordship wanted to hide. A few days later, when Robert was out riding, they had met on the forest trail and Osmund showed him how to get to the cottage, pointing out the signs scratched on tree trunks, invisible to anyone who did not know what to look for, that marked the way.

'So, this treasure of yours,' Osmund said, walking over to the donkey. 'Is it in these sacks?'

'No,' said Robert, 'she's standing by my side. This is Herleva, the daughter of Fulbert the tanner. She is my woman, and in her belly she carries my child. And this is her maidservant, Judith.'

The woodman looked thoughtful. 'Hmm . . . I know Fulbert Tanner. I've bought his leather. It was good and his price was fair. You are welcome here, Miss Herleva. But why are you and your baby safer here than in my lord's fine castle?'

'Because my brother, Duke Richard, means to attack that castle and take it from me,' Robert said. 'He's marched from Rouen and will be here sometime today. I'm certain he'll try to take the castle at once, but I intend to stop him. So then he'll put us under siege, possibly for months. In time his men will grow hungry. They'll take the crops from every field for leagues around, kill all the farm animals and then come into the forests and take every deer, boar and even rabbit they can find.'

'They'll not come poaching in my woods,' Osmund said, angrily.

'They won't be poaching. They'll be acting on the orders of the duke. These are his forests, not yours, and they're his animals, too. He can do with them as he pleases. So don't try to stop the soldiers taking whatever they want. Lie low and keep these women well hidden. And don't on any account, for any reason, speak to anyone until this whole business is over. Not unless you absolutely can't avoid it. And even then, not a word about Herleva.'

'Don't you worry, my lord,' Osmund's wife Sybil piped up. 'I'll keep my husband's mouth well shut, and I'll take good care of your young lady. And if her baby arrives, I'll see to that and all. God's not blessed us with any children of our own, but I have three sisters and I've seen them all through more birthings than I can count.'

Robert gave Osmund a small leather purse. 'There'll be twice as much again if Herleva is safe and well at the end of all this, and three times as much if our baby is with her. There's food for you all in the sack: oats, beans, dried ham and so on. Now I must go, or Richard will get to the castle before me and all will be lost. Goodbye, my darling.'

He gave Herleva one last quick hug, kissed her lightly on the lips, then remounted his horse. Herluin took the spare. 'Let's go,' Robert said. He had protected Herleva as best he could. That aim was accomplished. His mind was now concentrated on the far more dangerous tasks that lay ahead. In a few moments he and Herluin had disappeared into the woods, vanishing as completely as if they had never been in the clearing at all.

2

Duke Richard had sent an advance guard ahead of the main body of his troops. He very much doubted whether Robert would have set any ambushes for him – he couldn't possibly have enough men to spare for that – but only a fool would run the risk of a surprise attack, however slight it was. The Count of Bellême had established himself as Richard's closest ally and observer, and so he sent a dozen of his men, under the command of his son Warin, up the road to reconnoitre. They encountered no opposition and reached a copse on the outskirts of Falaise, within sight of the castle itself. Warin led his men into the shelter of the trees, where they could not be observed by anyone on the battlements, then sent a rider back to let the duke know that the way ahead of him was safe. He was about to give the order to dismount, so that his men and horses could rest until everyone else had caught up with them, when he saw movement about two hundred paces away. A pair of men were emerging from the forest on horseback, going at a steady canter, with a donkey trailing on a lead behind them.

Warin thought he recognised the man on the leading horse. He screwed up his eyes to sharpen his vision, hardly believing what he was seeing. 'By God, it's Robert,' he muttered, 'the treacherous son of a whore.' If he could kill or capture Robert now, the castle's defenders would give up at once. The castle would be his before Richard had even arrived and he would be the hero, wallowing in the glory and all the rewards that went with it.

He charged out of the copse with his men behind him, aiming to cut across Robert's path and block his way to the safety of the castle. Twelve men were chasing two, and their quarry had not yet seen them coming.

Robert had ridden from the forest to the castle so many times that he could practically do the journey with his eyes shut. In truth, he was hardly watching where he was going now. All his concentration was devoted to planning the first, decisive action that he knew would take place today. He was trusting to his horse to get him home safely. And then his reverie was broken by a shout from Herluin. 'Robert! Horsemen! Up ahead to the left!'

There were a dozen of them at least, riding right across his path. Robert saw the three red crescents of Bellême on the leading rider's shield and recognised Warin. He was fully armoured, as were his men. Robert and Herluin had swords with them, but were otherwise completely unprotected. On the other hand, that made them lighter, so their horses would be faster and more agile. If they could use their speed to evade Warin and his men, they would live. But if they were caught and surrounded, they would most certainly die, or at best be taken prisoner and thrown upon their knees before Richard. Even death would be preferable to that, Robert thought. But escape would be better yet.

Up ahead were the stockyards, a maze of wooden fences, as high as a man's chest, with narrow paths between them. They were all completely empty, any cattle having long since been slaughtered or taken as far away as possible to escape the oncoming army of hungry soldiers.

The road into Falaise swung away to the right, looping around the stockyards before it entered the town itself. Warin was aiming to cut him off at the point where the road curved, but Robert had no intention of falling into that trap. He spurred his stallion into a flat-out gallop, heading straight for the stockyard fence. Warin immediately responded. The two groups of horsemen were closing on each other at right angles, the gap between them narrowing with every stride. Robert still had the donkey's lead tied to the rear pommel of his high wooden saddle. The poor beast, free of any weight on its back, was just about managing to keep up, but it was already starting to slow him and it would only be a matter of seconds before its strength failed entirely. Worse than that, if it fell, or was hit by a spear or sword, it would become a dead weight and Robert would be helpless.

He switched his reins into his right hand and with the left reached back to untie the donkey, his fingers fumbling with the knotted leather.

They were now within twenty strides of the fence.

The knot still wouldn't come loose.

Warin had reached the stockyard boundary and was riding alongside it, so close that if Robert turned his head to one side he could look into his pursuer's eyes. Behind Warin, one of his men raised his arm and flung his spear. It flashed straight towards Robert. He ducked and felt it whistle over his head.

The fence was almost upon them.

Another spear flashed past, somehow missing Robert, the donkey and Herluin alike.

'Surrender, you traitor!' Warin shouted.

Robert felt the knot give beneath his fingers. It came undone, but he kept hold of the rein. Just a few seconds more.

A third spear passed just in front of him and slammed into the fence.

There was no time to steady his horse, or correct its stride pattern. He would just have to trust the animal's skill and his own dumb luck.

He heaved on the donkey's rein with his left arm fully extended, bringing it round in a circle and swinging the poor exhausted creature into the space between him and the on-rushing Warin. Then he dropped his hands down to his horse's neck, leaned forward in the saddle and flung himself and his mount at the fence, clearing it by a whisker. Herluin followed.

Behind them the panicking donkey dashed to and fro, braying in terror and forcing Warin and his men to slow right down as they manoeuvred their way around it. They reached the point where Robert and Herluin had jumped the fence and milled around for a few seconds. A man on horseback in heavy chain mail could barely jump a narrow ditch, let alone a fence. There was nothing else for it. They would have to go round the long way.

Robert whooped with triumphant glee and flashed a huge exhilarated grin at Herluin. 'We did it!' he shouted.

They jumped out of the far side of the stock pen, rode along one of the paths and leapt into the final pen. One more jump and they would be back on the road and into the town, with enough of a gap between them and their pursuers to be sure of reaching the castle ahead of them.

They were so close to escaping unscathed: just this last fence. The two men approached it side by side. Herluin flew over, but Robert misjudged the distance; only by a fraction, but it was enough. His horse was too close to the fence when it took off. Its forelegs caught the top rail and it toppled forward, flinging Robert from his saddle, and suddenly he was flying through the air, totally out of control, with no helmet or armour to protect him from his fall.

It was the fleeing citizens of Falaise who saved him. The spring rains had softened the ground and the mass of carts and pack animals heading away from danger had churned some parts of the road into a thick, clinging stew of mud. Robert landed in the deepest morass. He was winded. He was filthy. But he was still in one piece.

Herluin wheeled his own horse around. 'Quick!' he shouted. Robert got to his feet, grabbed hold of Herluin's outstretched hand and hauled himself up on to the horse's back. He was still scrabbling for purchase as Herluin kicked on. Robert clung on to his friend for dear life until his legs were finally set and his seat was secure. He turned his head. Warin and his men had caught up much of the ground they'd lost and were shouting and cheering, knowing that the odds had suddenly shifted in their favour. An armoured man on horseback could never hope to catch a rider who was lightly dressed. But two men on the same horse were far, far easier prey.

The road wound through Falaise, across the market square and then up the low, gentle slope of the hill towards the castle. There were no obstructions along the way, no more opportunities to play tricks, no stray animals or fences to come to Robert's aid.

It was a race, pure and simple.

3

Robert had ordered lookouts to be set at every tower on the castle walls: young lads whose sharp eyes would spot an enemy approaching at the furthest possible distance. John the blacksmith's boy was on duty atop the keep that morning, and even when they were mere specks in the distance he recognised Robert and Herluin's horses emerging from the forest – he'd shod them often enough. He also saw the horsemen springing from the copse and bearing down on the count. 'Watch out! Look to your left!' he shouted at the top of his voice, though he knew the riders were so far away they could not possibly hear him.

But one of the other lookouts, down below on the castle walls, could. He looked up at John and called back: 'What's happening?'

'It's Count Robert, and Master Herluin. They're in trouble!'

In an instant, the word spread around the castle. A runner was sent down to the bailey gate to make sure the men there were ready to open it and let the count in.

Soon John had been joined on the castle roof by a group of Robert's knights. One of them looked at him. 'You know where those Breton archers live?'

'Yes, sir, their barracks are right by the forge.'

'Then get down there, fast as you can, and tell that Conan fellow that if he and his lads want to get paid, they'd better make sure Count Robert makes it back to the castle in one piece. Got that?'

'Yes, sir!'

'Then what are you doing standing here? Move, boy, move!'

John raced off, praying that he could find Conan. He was one of the few Bretons who spoke Frankish. Most only had that gobbledegook of their own that no one else could make head nor tail of. He'd never be able to tell them what was going on.

The men on the keep's top battlements forgot about John the moment he vanished from their sight. All their concentration was on the chase unfolding before their eyes.

'Is that the Bellême crest on their shields?' one of the men asked.

'Reckon so.'

'Bastards, the lot of 'em.'

They watched Robert as he sent the donkey into the path of the oncoming riders then followed Herluin through the animal pens. They groaned in horror as he lost his horse and then shouted encouragement as the two men dashed through the town on Herluin's mount, racing desperately for the bailey gate. The road they were on looped round to within a stone's throw of the castle walls. All they had to do was turn right for one final dash to the safety of the gate that was even now swinging open to meet them.

'By Christ, they might just make it!' someone called out.

And then another, quieter voice said in a tone of near despair, 'I don't think so. Look.'

The men of Bellême had divided their forces. Most were still in hot pursuit of Robert and Herluin, but three riders had broken away from the main group and were riding through the town, racing between the houses, taking a more direct route towards the castle. They were going to cut their quarry off. And the terrible thing was that only the spectators high up on the keep could see what was happening. The town's buildings were

140

acting as perfect cover for the riders on their way to ambush Count Robert. Neither he nor Herluin could see them, nor could the men by the bailey gate.

The siege of Falaise Castle was about to be over before it had even begun.

Herluin could see the castle now. Behind him, Robert waved his right arm frantically above his head, trying to attract the defenders' attention.

'Help!' he shouted. 'For God's sake, someone help!'

They both saw movement on the castle walls and people waving back from the top of the small stone gatehouse that broke the bailey's wooden walls. The gates opened a fraction, inviting them in.

Robert glanced back over his shoulder. Warin and his men were gaining, but not fast enough. He and Herluin were going to beat them to the castle. And then something caught his eye, a flash of light from behind a building up to the right. He looked again and saw something else: a large black shadow passing across the gap between two houses, barely more than a flicker, gone as fast as the blinking of an eye. But it was all he needed.

'Men! To the right! We're cut off!'

Herluin said nothing, but he reacted instantly. He pulled his horse to the left. Instead of aiming for the bailey gate, they would now have to go halfway round the castle and try to make it to the steep, winding path that led up to the main gatehouse in the shadow of the keep.

But that was a lot further away. And the further they rode, the greater the advantage to Warin and his men.

Robert heard shouts behind him, immediately answered by more to his right. The men who'd ridden round to ambush him weren't making any secret of their presence now. They came out from behind the shelter of the buildings, bearing down upon the two men clinging to a single horse.

And the horse was tiring. Its chest was heaving, its flanks lathered with sweat, and its pace was slowing. Robert drew his sword and smacked it down flat against the exhausted beast's haunches, startling it into a brief spurt of speed. They were alongside the castle now, almost at the start of the path. But he could detect no signs of life on the walls. Had everyone been down at the bailey gate? Surely not. He hardly had a huge army, but there were almost two hundred men and boys inside that castle. Some of them must have noticed what was happening. So where were they all?

He looked back again. Warin's men were no more than ten horse's lengths behind them now and gaining with every stride. Robert saw the nearest rider draw back his arm and fling a spear, which fell only just short.

They were at the path. It went up a few strides and then immediately made a switchback. Herluin pulled at the reins and the horse somehow managed to negotiate the sharp uphill turn without stumbling. But now they were riding back towards Warin and his men, albeit at a slightly higher level. Another one of the Bellême soldiers pulled on his mount's reins. Letting his comrades ride on ahead of him, he stopped, took careful aim and threw his spear.

It missed Robert and Herluin but hit their horse at the point of its hip, just a couple of handspans behind Robert. The horse whinnied in pain as its rear leg gave way and it crashed to the ground. Robert, unhindered by a saddle or stirrups, jumped free, landed on his feet and stumbled a couple of paces before regaining his balance.

Herluin was not so lucky. He was trapped beneath the thrashing beast.

'Run!' he shouted. 'Run for the gate!'

'No!' Robert knew there was no point even trying to flee. He would be cut down within seconds. Better to stand and fight. The path was narrow. They could only come at him one at a time, and Herluin's horse, now desperately struggling to get back on its feet, would act as a living barrier for the few seconds that it took the men of Bellême to dispatch it. 'Get behind me!' he shouted as Herluin crawled out from under the horse.

Robert stood, legs apart, sword held in both hands in front of him, and prepared to fight to the death.

Warin of Bellême had reached the turn in the path and was coming up towards him, his reins in one hand, sword in the other.

Forget the man, get the horse, Robert told himself.

Two more spears hit Herluin's horse, killing it.

Warin jumped the dead animal. He and his mount filled Robert's entire field of vision. Two more strides and they'd be right on top of him. Suddenly a great calm descended upon him, just as it had at the boar hunt: that same feeling of time stretching out and every sense being sharpened to an extraordinary degree. He looked Warin straight in the eye and saw a flicker of uncertainty there. Robert began to smile. He'd take their leader with him before they cut him down.

And then, from high above him, he heard a man's voice utter a single word in a language he did not understand. Suddenly the air was filled with arrows, turning Warin of Bellême's horse into a huge living pincushion and throwing him to the ground. Robert took a pace forward to engage his enemy, but then he felt a sharp pull on his shoulder and heard Herluin say, 'No, my lord! Let the bowmen do it. You must get back to the castle.'

As Robert ran up the path, he saw Warin throwing himself down the slope to join the rest of his men as they turned tail and fled. One had already been killed and his corpse was hanging from a single stirrup as his horse dragged it along the ground. Warin cut the body free, pulled himself up on to the horse and raced away, somehow evading all the arrows that were fired in his direction.

Moments later, Robert and Herluin were surrounded by their own men, who formed a ring around them for the last dash through the castle gate.

They ran along the passage between the two internal walls before emerging into the yard beneath the keep. As people clustered round, Robert answered their shouted questions with a simple 'I'm alive and unhurt.' Then he raised his hand for silence. Virtually every one of his men was now gathered around him.

'Listen,' he said. 'We don't have much time. My brother the duke will be here with his full army before the next church bell tolls. So pay attention. We've made our preparations for the duke's arrival. You all know what you have to do. Just follow your orders and all will be well. Chaplain!' Robert waited while a priest emerged from the crowd. He gestured towards him: 'Come here, Father. Say a blessing for us, if you will. We shall kneel in prayer . . . and may God grant us victory.'

4

The first red banners, emblazoned with the two gold leopards of Normandy, were spotted soon after midday. Robert stood on the battlements watching them approach and tried to work out how many men his brother had mustered. There were certainly several hundred of them, maybe even a thousand. At any rate, the odds were not good. But he had the castle, and that in itself was enough to give him hope.

He had already dressed for battle in a coat of chain mail that hung down to his knees, with mail leggings over his shins and the tops of his feet. The coat was hooded, with a square flap, currently hanging loose on his chest, that could be pulled up and tied to the hood to cover the lower half of his face. The back of his head and neck had been shaved to make the steel helmet he was currently holding under his arm sit more comfortably. It was not a particularly warm day, but the armour was heavy and retained all the sun's heat, so that before he had unsheathed his sword he was already hot and sweaty.

'Do you think he'll go straight on the attack?' asked Herluin beside him.

'I'm certain of it,' Robert replied. 'Richard knows there are only two good times to take a castle. One is right at the end of a siege, when the defenders are hungry, exhausted and down to their last few men. The other's right at the start: catch them by surprise, when they're still unprepared. If it works, that's the best way, and it'll be Richard's way too. He's angry and he wants to teach me a lesson, so he won't hang around.'

'He's done it before.'

'Exactly. And it worked, so he'll do it again.'

'We'd better hope he attacks the way you think he will.'

Robert turned his eyes away from the approaching column and looked at Herluin. 'What other way is there? The keys to this castle are the two gates. We learned that lesson this morning. And if you have any idea about where the castle stands and how it's laid out, which Richard does, then there's only one sensible way to attack. The thing that keeps bothering me, though, is whether my brother's capable of being sensible. If he is, we've got a chance. But if he's either so stupid, so angry or, God forbid, so brilliant that he does something else, and catches us by surprise, then we might be in serious trouble.'

Richard attacked. His men arrived in full armour, ready for battle. He did not waste time making a camp. He did not even wait for the trebuchets to be set up, the great siege engines that could catapult huge boulders against a castle's walls. He sent two hundred men towards the main gatehouse. Some of the foot soldiers scrambled straight up the steep rocky hillside. But the ones carrying ladders came along the winding path. So too did the crew of a battering ram, hidden beneath a frame of light saplings lashed together and covered in a thick leather skin that had been soaked in water to prevent it catching fire if hit by burning arrows.

There were forty bowmen and fifteen men-at-arms under Herluin's command waiting to meet them. A great cauldron had been set up behind the battlements, directly above the main gate. It was suspended over a fire of burning coals that were glowing red as John the blacksmith's boy and his master worked the bellows that fed the flames with air. More youngsters were posted by bundles of arrows, tied with twine, ready to carry them to the archers when their quivers were empty.

One of the Bretons loosed an arrow. It landed harmlessly on the hillside, missing the duke's men as they climbed in an open skirmishing formation.

'Wait!' shouted Herluin. He strode across to one of the very few archers who spoke Frankish. 'Tell the men that they're not to shoot a single arrow until I give the word. Watch for my hand. And aim for the ones with the ladders first.'

He went back to his position and raised his arm. As long as it stayed in the air, the bowmen and the men-at-arms waited, feeling their guts twist and tighten with every second that passed until the duke's men were almost within touching distance of the wall. Only then did Herluin finally call out, 'Now!' as he swung his arm down. Suddenly the air was thick with arrows and the men on the hill below were holding up their shields to defend themselves, while those carrying the long bulky ladders broke into a clumsy run in their desperation to escape the death flying at them from the castle walls.

Within seconds the ground was littered with the corpses of dead men and the writhing, screaming bodies of those who had been injured. Two of the ladders were lying on the ground, abandoned by troops who had either been hit or run away. But most of Richard's soldiers were still moving forward towards the gatehouse and the castle walls, and though the protective screen above the battering ram was so spiked with arrows that it looked like a giant porcupine advancing up the path, both it and the men beneath were intact and unharmed.

The first ladder had reached the top of the path. Half a dozen men formed a protective shield ring around its base. Two more manoeuvred it into position against the castle wall while Herluin's men pushed it away from the battlements, trying to make it topple backwards. But now there were men racing up the ladder and their weight was pressing it hard against the stone, making it impossible to shift.

'Time to go to work, blacksmith!' Herluin called, and the giant smith grabbed an iron bucket with hands covered in thick leather gauntlets and dipped it into his cauldron. A thick, stinking concoction of tallow, pitch and sulphur was bubbling and belching inside, and even the smith grimaced at the heat and the smell as he scooped it into his bucket. Then he reached down to the floor, picked up a short-handled shovel and plunged it into the fire, filling it with burning hot coals.

'Quick, mate, over here!' someone yelled as the first attacker's head and shoulders poked up over the battlements. The man was skewered with a lance and fell backwards, screaming, but there was another attacker to replace him, and he had a sword in his hand and was sweeping it from side to side before him, keeping the defenders at bay.

The blacksmith walked with a steady, purposeful gait towards the ladder. He was wearing no armour, nor carrying a sword or shield. He simply had the bucket in one hand and the shovel in the other. When he reached the ladder, he stood a couple of paces away from the attacker, who was now climbing between the two battlements and about to set foot on the walkway behind them. The smith put down his bucket, grasped the shovel with both hands and flung the coals straight at the soldier's face. He howled in agony and raised his hands to his face as his cheeks, nose and eyelids were instantly burned to a blistered crisp, then doubled up as he took a spear to the guts. The blacksmith reached out and pushed his victim off the battlements to the mercy of an instant death on the rocks below. Then he picked up his bucket and emptied the scalding, sticky mess over the ladder and the men climbing up it.

But there were more ladders and more men, an overwhelming surge of them, and now the battering ram was almost at the gate. Herluin did not bother to give another command. He was already in position by a rope anchored to the stone walkway by a steel ring. It was stretched almost to breaking point as it disappeared between two battlements. He swung his sword against the rope, and then swung again and again until the last tattered threads gave way and the rope disappeared like a fleeing snake. A second later there was a thunderous crash as the boulders that had been suspended in a great net to which the rope was attached fell to earth and smashed into the frame around the battering ram, pulverising it and the men beneath it.

Herluin had no time to enjoy his success, for suddenly there was a cry of 'Behind you!' and he spun round to see a knight just a footstep away from him, raising his sword for a killer blow. Herluin swung his own blade up to meet it and felt the jarring impact of steel upon steel vibrate through his body. The two swords jammed against each other. Herluin was conscious of the snarling face opposite his, and felt the strength of his opponent pushing him back. He planted one foot to give him leverage and shoved back. Both men put all their weight into the struggle, knowing that whoever cracked first would die. The knight was taller, with a longer reach, but Herluin was more compact. He pushed up and out, every muscle straining, until finally the other man was forced to take a backward step that turned into a stumble. Suddenly the pressure on Herluin's sword was released and he was the one moving forward and scything his sword into the knight's flank, opening him up above the hip and then striking again with a two-handed stab into his belly.

All across the gatehouse and along the wall to either side, similar battles were taking place, one man against another in brutal hand-to-hand combat. And all the while the archers maintained their relentless rhythm of loading, bowing, aiming and shooting.

The battering ram was picked up again, by a new team of attackers, and slammed against the castle gates. But then the great cauldron was tipped over and its remaining contents ran out into a gully that led to a spout poking out above the gate. A stream of scorching, scalding liquid poured down on to the ram and the men carrying it. Some died instantly. Others were set on fire and ran blindly down the hill, their heads ablaze like demons from the bowels of hell, their terrible screams echoing across the battlefield.

It was then that the assault finally broke. The men at the feet of the ladders, shocked to the depths of their souls by the horrifying sight of the burning men, turned and fled after them. The ones up on the castle walls, seeing their comrades running, tried to get back on to the ladders and make good their escape, but they were cut down where they stood, or forced over the walls until they fell to their doom.

Suddenly it was over. A ragged, exhausted cheer broke out among the defenders. A handful of Robert's men were dead and others were nursing wounds, but most were still alive and in fighting condition. And that was just as well, thought Herluin. For this had only ever been a skirmish, a feint. The real attack would be made against the other gatehouse. That was where Robert was fighting and where the battle would be decided.

Herluin left half his men to guard the gatehouse, just in case the enemy should mount another attack. The other half he took with him as he went to the aid of his friend.

5

Richard of Normandy had many faults, but he was neither a fool nor a coward. He did not need to be told that the bailey gate was the weak point in the defences of Falaise: anyone who had ever set eyes on the castle could see that. The gate stood on relatively flat land, and was flanked by a wooden palisade, making it far easier to assault. Once into the bailey there was still another wall, stone this time, to get over. But even if one could not manage that, the very fact of holding the bailey deprived the castle's occupants of all their fresh food and provided a perfect site for siege engines of all kinds, making the inner castle and keep incomparably more vulnerable.

So that was where Richard launched his main attack, leading it if not from the very front, then from the head of the cavalry charge with which he intended to follow his initial assault. And it all went incredibly well. While his diversionary force were tying down the defenders at the main gatehouse, his men got to the bailey gate with only minimal casualties from the scattering of archers positioned there. They advanced in overwhelming force and found that the gate had already been abandoned and was hanging loose on its hinges. The second it began to swing open, Richard spurred his mount and led a column of horsemen, galloping towards the gatehouse like a great iron fist.

Up ahead he could see the castle's defenders desperately running away, racing from the top of the gatehouse and along the walkway behind the spiked logs that formed the palisade. A triumphant grin spread across his features as he thought of the killing and the victory to come. His sword was hungry for blood and he intended to sate its appetite.

Richard aimed for the slowly widening gap between the two doors of the gate. He plunged into the shadow cast by the palisade. He hurtled through the gate and under the arch of the gatehouse, emerging into the open ground of the bailey, his men behind him driving him on. The enemy were nowhere. His triumph was complete.

And that was when he realised that he had ridden straight into a trap.

Everything that Robert had done was based on the certainty that he would be greatly outnumbered. He therefore had to create ways of evening the odds. And that meant a war of subterfuge and deceit, of ambushes rather than direct confrontation. So when he had assembled his team of masons and carpenters, they had not merely done everything possible to shore up the existing defences at Falaise, they had added something new: a second palisade, slightly lower than the external one, and therefore invisible from the outside. It ran from one side of the bailey to the other, cutting it in two and creating an enclosure like a gladiatorial arena, roughly fifty paces in diameter, ringed by sharp stakes.

More than eighty archers were arrayed around the perimeter, mounted on walkways from which they could shoot their arrows down on to the trapped horsemen. Their apparently pell-mell retreat had been nothing but a ruse. Now they stood, calm and purposeful, loosing five hundred arrows a minute at point-blank range into the ever-growing mass of the duke's finest mounted troops as more and more poured in through the gate, making it impossible for those already inside to get out.

Robert was waiting behind the second palisade with all the mounted knights he had at his disposal. Sooner or later, Richard's men would stop piling into the enclosure. At that point, anyone already inside who had not been finished off by the archers would finally be able to find a way out. And that was when he planned to strike, finishing them before they could escape. He was waiting for a sign from Conan, the Breton captain, up on the palisade.

And here it was. Conan jabbed his hand towards the enclosure, telling Robert to get in there. Now the final element to the trap was sprung.

One section of the inner palisade consisted of five vertical logs, bound together by ropes and hinged on one side so as to create a crude gate, held in place by a horizontal plank. Two of Robert's foot soldiers lifted the plank out of the cradle in which it sat. Two more heaved on ropes attached to the hinged logs. The gate swung open and now it was Robert's turn to lead a charge, straight into the melee.

He rode with his lance in the couch position, held under his armpit so that it pointed ahead and down, all the better to skewer an enemy soldier. The scene that greeted him was one of carnage. There were dead and wounded everywhere: animal and human alike. The air was filled with the frenzied neighing of injured horses and the screams of agony and pleas for help of men crippled, blinded and gutted by arrows. In the middle of the enclosure, a small band of men were trying to make their way back on foot to the gate, holding up their shields to protect themselves from the hail of arrows.

The bowmen stopped shooting as Robert and his knights entered the fray. Robert saw a shield being lowered as one of the retreating men tried to see what had happened. He caught the look of wide-eyed panic on the man's face as he realised that one form of torture had ended only so that another could begin, and then Robert stuck him like a pig on the end of his spear.

What had been a tightly disciplined knot of men unravelled

into a mob as each tried to save his own skin. And that was when Robert saw his brother. He had somehow lost both his helmet and his shield. Blood was seeping between the links of his mail, close to his left shoulder, and the arm below it was hanging uselessly by his side. Robert let go of his spear and jumped down from his horse. If he was going to settle matters, he would do it face to face. He still had all his armour and was physically unharmed: that was more than enough of an advantage without being mounted as well. He hacked his way through the fighting, barely noticing the men he struck until he reached his brother.

Neither man said a thing. They simply circled one another, swords at the ready. Richard was breathing more heavily and he winced once or twice as the motion jarred his wounded shoulder. Robert saw that the sword in his other hand wavered whenever this happened, only for an instant, but that was enough. The next time it happened, he sprang forward on the attack, smashing his sword down on Richard's and striking it so hard that the blade broke, leaving Richard holding nothing but the hilt.

He threw it away and stood helpless in front of Robert. 'Come on then,' he snarled. 'You want to be Duke of Normandy. So do it. Kill me. You'll never get a better chance.'

Robert knew he was right. It was no sin to kill a man in battle, especially if that man had started the fight. All he had to do was stick his sword into his brother's body and he would have everything he wanted: not just Falaise Castle, but Normandy itself. He would be duke and Herleva his duchess. Their boy-child would be his heir.

But first he had to kill his brother.

And he couldn't do it.

Something stayed his arm. Some deep sense of family loyalty, or perhaps a long-lost crumb of love, prevented him from taking the life of his own flesh and blood. It took only a second's hesitation, maybe less, but that was enough. Three of the duke's men barged their way between the two brothers and grabbed Richard. Two of them draped his arms around their shoulders and took him away, suspended between them.

As he was carried from the enclosure, Richard turned his head, looked Robert in the eye and spoke a single word: 'Weakling.'

Some of Robert's knights tried to prevent the duke getting away, but he had a dozen men around him now, and more coming in from outside, forming a ring around him. The archers started shooting again and took out three more attackers, but it was too late. Richard, Duke of Normandy, had escaped.

The defenders of Falaise Castle had won a remarkable victory, yet it seemed more like a defeat. Their leader, Count Robert, had devised a brilliantly successful strategy, the castle was intact and the enemy had lost almost a hundred men, killed and wounded, yet already the duke's forces were putting up tents and lighting fires in a ring around the castle. They might have been given a bloody nose, but the siege was still going ahead anyway.

Robert and Herluin stood on the battlements as they had done a few hours earlier, looking down at the lights of the campfires. Neither Herluin's loyalty to Robert nor their friendship had been broken. But he was unhappy, and for once he could not hide it. 'My father has a saying he's drilled into us since we were knee-high to him: "There's only one thing that's never permitted in war, and that's kindness." You were kind to your brother, my lord, even though he's your enemy. We can only pray that he doesn't give you cause to regret it.'

6

London and Winchester, England

Emma groaned as her husband entered her. She wrapped her legs around him and tilted her hips to let him go deeper. It had been so long since he'd been inside her. She wanted all of him; to feel that wonderful sensation of both taking and being taken; to be joined with him again.

When she had seen Canute at the dockside, finally back in England after almost a year of travelling, she had been as excited as a girl of eighteen, rather than a mature woman in her forty-third year. He was so tall, with his mane of thick blond hair, and the absolute confidence that seemed to surround him as impenetrably as the strongest armour. She longed to rush up to him, throw her arms around his neck and let him pull her close against his body. But this was a public event and he was both her husband and her monarch, so she had to curtsey before him and maintain a fitting air of modesty and obedience.

Their conversation was polite. 'Did you have word of our dear daughter Gunhilda, Your Majesty?' Emma had asked, showing no sign of the pain it had caused her when Canute had given their daughter to be raised far from her home and family as a German princess.

'His Imperial Majesty was pleased to tell me that she is in very good health and plays very happily with the other children at the court. She and Prince Henry appear to be perfectly content in one another's company. There is every reason to suppose that they will make a very satisfactory marriage.'

156

'That is very good news, Your Majesty. And was Harthacnut well, when you saw him in Denmark?'

'Very well, and grown so much that I hardly recognised him.'

These agonising pleasantries completed, Emma remained silent while Canute conducted his business with the great nobles who had also come to welcome him back to the kingdom. At dinner she had served his wine and then departed to eat with the other ladies of the court, leaving the men to get on with their feasting and drinking in peace. Only when the king retired to bed could his wife finally have him to herself.

Emma had not expected to love Canute. Having spent almost fifteen years in a cold, oppressive marriage to Ethelred, a man she'd loathed, and who frequently treated her with contempt and even violence, she could barely conceive of what a happy union might be like. She therefore entered into negotiations with Canute with the sole intention of saving her sons' lives and securing her own position. The king's first wife, an Englishwoman called Elgiva of Northampton, had given him two sons – or at least had produced two boys, Svein and Harold, whom she claimed were Canute's. Malicious palace gossips suggested that Elgiva was infertile and had in fact bought her 'sons' as babies from a lowly peasant woman who could not afford to keep them. Emma, who had no reason to doubt her own fertility, presumed that she and Canute would have children, and wanted to ensure that they had precedence in the order of succession. She insisted on keeping all the money and land she had accumulated as the result of her first marriage, and she expected Canute to add to it. Beyond that she saw marriage, and all that went with it, as an unavoidable duty. A woman's job was to serve her husband and bear his children. If she was lucky, her husband would be kind and childbirth would not kill her. But she might not be lucky. It was just the way things were.

157

To their mutual surprise, she and Canute had discovered that theirs was more than a marriage of convenience. Emma found herself entranced by the strength of her new husband's personality. He was immensely clever, and his intellect was matched by an instinctive shrewdness, an understanding of people and how to get them to do what he wanted. He could be thoughtful, considerate, surprisingly amusing when it suited him to be so, and yet iron-willed, ruthless and merciless in the pursuit of his objectives. She admired him greatly and also feared him a little: not because he had ever harmed her in any way, but because he could do so, and would without a second thought if he ever felt it necessary.

Above all, she craved him with a physical desire that both aroused and infuriated her. She was helpless with longing for him. In the long months when they were apart, she missed the feel and smell and taste of him so badly that her body ached. Her entire life had been a struggle to free herself from the command of men and give herself such wealth and power that no man could hurt her. But with Canute, none of that made any difference. She was his woman. He could do with her as he pleased.

Or so it had always been. But tonight there was no passion in his lovemaking, simply a wordless, perfunctory thrusting that culminated in a climax that felt like no more than a crude physical excretion. He might as well have been having a shit. Emma felt cheated, frustrated and also, very suddenly, so sad that she found her eyes filling with tears. After all the months apart, all the nights she'd dreamed of having him back, was there to be no more than this meagre show of physical affection?

She felt him about to withdraw and held him to her again. 'Stay, Your Majesty,' she whispered. 'Please stay.'

Canute was usually as perceptive about Emma as he was about everything else. But now he either misunderstood what

158

she was saying and feeling, or simply chose to ignore it. He rolled away and lay beside her, making no attempt to hold or console her, even as she sniffed and reached for a kerchief, making it perfectly obvious that she was upset.

'I can't,' he said. 'I'll be here in London for a week, but all my time will be taken up inspecting the ships I've commissioned from the yards at Rotherhithe. After that, I'll be campaigning in Scotland for most of the summer, then I need to attend to Norway. The people there are calling on me to be their ruler. I intend to establish a new kingdom there. I was thinking that Elgiva could be my regent. She can take her boy Svein with her. It'll do him good.'

Up to now, it had been the wife in Emma that had been hurt, the woman whose love and body had both been taken for granted. But now she was outraged as a politician, for whom the maintenance of her status, and that of her own son Harthacnut, was of paramount importance. She stopped crying and gathered her thoughts. This was no time for emotion. She needed her wits about her.

'You show Elgiva great favour, Your Majesty,' she said, gently stroking his chest. 'May I ask what led you to this decision?'

'I need to keep her happy,' said Canute, lying on his back as motionless and unresponsive to her touch as a marble statue on a tomb. 'She can cause great trouble among the English if she chooses. She's one of them, after all, which neither you nor I are.'

'The people think of me as English. I have been their queen for a very long time.'

'Precisely. You are the Queen of England. Elgiva will merely be regent of Norway. She will be a very long way from here, and her power to influence events will be greatly reduced as a result. It is not for you to question my decisions . . .'

'Of course not, Your Majesty.'

'But in this case, I should have thought you would be pleased. Now, if you will excuse me, I have had a long day and the journey from Denmark was very tiring. I would like to go to sleep.'

Canute rolled over, turning his back on Emma, who was left wondering what on earth was going on. She could not deny that if Canute made Elgiva his regent in Norway, it would exclude her from affairs here in England, but on the other hand, it would give her the chance to turn Norway into her own private fief, a base from which she could plan her return to England. So why was Canute favouring her in this way? They surely could not be having a love affair, could they? Elgiva had been no closer to him than Emma over the past nine months, and he would hardly be sending her off to Norway if he wanted her for his mistress.

Actually, Canute had been right: Emma would normally have been pleased to see her rival effectively banished. But not tonight, not when she felt as though she'd been exiled in her own bed. She had sacrificed so much and lost so much. Not one of her five children lived in the same country as her, and there was no reason to suppose that she would ever see any of them again. The one sure joy in her life had been her love for Canute and his for her. If that too were lost to her, what point would there be in living at all?

7

Emma's unhappiness was as obvious to Godwin as it was to the entire court. She sat at the high table as glum as a criminal awaiting execution, though she naturally denied the faintest hint of dissatisfaction when he gently enquired whether anything about the meal was displeasing her. Then one evening at Rotherhithe, after a long day spent inspecting keels and discussing hull sizes for the new warships that were being built there, Canute let slip the reason for his queen's bad mood.

'You know, Godwin,' he confided, 'just because a woman's got a crown on her head and noble blood in her veins it doesn't make her any less unreasonable than a common fishwife.'

'They're both women, Your Majesty, whatever their rank,' Godwin agreed.

'Exactly, and just as likely to drive a man mad. I thought the queen would be pleased because I'd decided to pack Elgiva off to Norway. The two of them can't stand each other, so it seemed like the perfect way to solve two problems at once. Elgiva would be pleased because I'd given her and Svein the status of regents, and Her Majesty would be thrilled to see Elgiva sent away to my most distant kingdom, where she can't wield any influence on events here in England. But no, all that Her Majesty can see is that Elgiva's a regent and she isn't.'

'Her Majesty's as good as a regent while you're away from England, sire. She attends every meeting of the royal council, hears cases and signs charters. She hardly lacks for influence.'

'Thank you, Godwin. I'm glad someone can see this from a logical point of view.'

'A woman's idea of logic is very different from yours or mine, sire.'

'Yes, well, perhaps that's why I feel so much more at ease on campaign with my army than at home with my wife.'

Yes, thought Godwin, don't you just? It struck him then that Canute was the type of man for whom lust for power was much more interesting and absorbing than lust for women. Godwin, on the other hand, regarded the two things as two sides of the same coin: he sought power in part because it made so many more women available to him. But he also knew that women, and his ability to use them, could bring him more power. They made up half the world, after all. A man was a fool if he didn't give them at least some of his attention.

'Look at that shameless, vulgar tart,' said Emma bitterly. 'She doesn't think for a single moment that she's losing anything by leaving here. She thinks she's getting a chance to prove she can rule a country. And the infuriating thing is, she's right.'

The ships had been built. Canute had sailed them up to Scotland and was now submitting yet more territory to his will. Elgiva, meanwhile, was about to leave with Svein to take up her post as regent of Norway. First, though, she had organised a great feast at Canute's palace in Winchester, to see her on her way. Emma attended, if only to deny Elgiva the satisfaction of being the most important woman there: both had married the king, but the crowned queen took precedence.

Now, though, as the assembled guests and their hostess gathered in an antechamber before the feasting began, Emma was furious, and it was Godwin's task to calm her down. He idly considered telling her how unflattering her frowning brow and downturned mouth were to her appearance. With his own wife, Gytha, he might have risked it, but with Emma a more diplomatic approach was required.

'Not necessarily, Your Majesty,' Godwin said respectfully. 'She's being packed off to a cold, barren outpost of the king's empire, a very long way from here. The English are only interested in what happens in their own country, or even their own village. Most of them have no idea where Norway even is, assuming they've heard of it at all. What Lady Elgiva does or doesn't do there is no concern to anyone.'

Emma showed no sign of having heard a word he'd said. 'And look at those two boys. I can't see any resemblance whatsoever between either of them and the king. Svein looks marginally less like a peasant farmer's boy, but I don't believe Harold has a single drop of royal blood in him. Look at him standing there with his mouth hanging open like a village idiot. The boy's supposed to be twelve, but he's got spots all over his face and thick black hairs as coarse as hog's bristles sticking out of his chin. The other palace lads call him "Harefoot", you know. I gather he spends so much time running away from them that he's developed quite a turn of speed.

'I'm sorry, Godwin,' she went on, finally acknowledging his presence. 'It's beneath my dignity to go on like this, I know, but it's just too much having to look at that woman, and her two pretenders, knowing that I may never again see my own sons, who are truly royal, and truly fit to sit on the throne of England. It's not right.'

'But it must be God's will, Your Majesty,' Godwin assured her. 'Who knows what His purpose is, or who he'll anoint to be the next king. He has His plans and we cannot judge them. But if the Lord wishes to work through us to ensure that the king's true son inherits the crown that is his birthright, then all we plan or do will surely be blessed with good fortune.'

'Thank you, Godwin,' said Emma. 'Those are very wise

words, and very reassuring ones, too.'

'I'm glad to have been of service, Your Majesty. And now, if you will excuse me, I must find my wife so that we can pay our respects to Lady Elgiva. Please rest assured that it is purely a matter of proper behaviour. I shall not breathe a word to her of our conversation.'

My, you're looking old and bitter tonight, Elgiva thought, meeting Queen Emma's eyes and flashing a cold, tight smile in her direction. I can see just why Canute's been bedding me so often these days. He wants to feel a real woman beneath him, not a raddled old crone.

Her thoughts were interrupted by the arrival of two guests. 'Why, Earl Godwin, Lady Gytha,' she said. 'How very kind of you to come.'

8

'Do you think he's all right?' asked Herleva for the umpteenth time that summer. She was sitting on the grass outside the forester's cottage while Sybil and Judith worked away weeding the vegetable beds. The sun was blazing, there wasn't a breath of wind, and with less than a month before her baby was due, she felt huge, baking hot and thoroughly miserable. 'I can't bear it, not knowing whether Robert's alive or dead, or what's happening at the castle. What if he never sees his baby and the poor little thing's born without a father?'

Sybil sighed, stood up straight and wiped a bead of sweat from her forehead. 'Don't you worry your pretty head, my lady,' she reassured her, as she had so many times before. Slightly out of breath from her exertions, she leaned on her long-handled hoe. 'My Osmund was telling me only yesterday that he'd followed a dozen of Duke Richard's soldiers blundering around the forest looking for game. They were making that much noise and commotion, there wasn't so much as a field mouse for leagues around. They didn't have a clue Osmund was there, the silly sods, and he heard them moaning about what a miserable time they were having, how their rations were rubbish and their tents let in water when it rains, all that sort of thing. So the siege is still going on and that means Count Robert must be alive, or the castle would have fallen by now.'

'But how much longer can it hold out?' Herleva asked, her voice rising with anxiety. 'I know Robert was worried about whether he had enough supplies. And he must be running out of money, too. How is he going to pay all his soldiers?'

'Well they won't be walking out on him if they're stuck in that castle, will they?' Sybil pointed out. 'Not like the duke's men. Lots have deserted him, apparently, gone back home to their farms to get ready for the harvest. And half the ones that are left are going down with siege sickness in their guts. It sounds disgusting, from what Osmund told me. They can't keep food or water down at all. It just comes right out at both ends, if you get my meaning.'

That was a mistake. It only put new fears into Herleva's mind. 'So Robert could be sick too, couldn't he? Maybe he's lying there wasting away, with no one to look after him . . .'

Sybil had had enough of this wailing, even if Herleva was a nobleman's fancy. 'You just calm down, my girl,' she said, sharply. 'Fretting like this won't do any good for you or the baby.'

Judith had been on her knees, pulling out weeds with her hands from around the raspberry canes. Now she sat back on her heels and spoke for the first time, acting the peacemaker. 'I'm sure she's right, my lady. My mother always says that there's no sense worrying about something if you can't do anything about it. You just have to accept it and get on with your life.'

Sybil nodded approvingly. 'Your mother's a very sensible woman, Judith. Now, Herleva . . . my lady . . . we were all told not to speak to anyone while the siege was going on, so's not to attract attention. But I don't think anyone expected things to drag on this long, and all this not knowing is wearing you down. So I wonder if maybe Osmund should go into town – apart from anything else, people will start to wonder what he's getting up to if he doesn't ever show his face. And while he's there, he can ask around and see what he can find out. I mean, if

166

someone saw Count Robert walking along the battlements yesterday, as healthy as can be, well, then at least you'll know he's not poorly.'

'But won't people ask Osmund what he's been doing?'

Sybil shrugged. 'Probably, but if they do, he'll say he's been just like all those forest animals, keeping out of danger and minding his own business.'

'So why's he coming into town now?' Herleva asked.

'I don't know, my lady . . . Maybe he's bored of being stuck with me for months – that's probably true enough! – and he fancies a drink with some mates. Or he's got furs to sell and seed to buy. And of course he's curious about what's going on up at the castle, because who wouldn't be?'

'Will there be anyone left in Falaise that Osmund knows?' Judith asked. 'Most people had already got out if they could, even before we left the castle.'

'Oh, there'll be people in Falaise, don't you worry about that,' Sybil assured her. 'There's always some that can make money from having an army camped nearby: tavern-keepers, blacksmiths, loose women, all sorts of ne'er-do-wells. Then others come back after a while, just to see what's happened to their property. I've seen a few sieges in my time – I didn't always live stuck away in a big dark forest, you know! I could tell you a story or two.'

'Ooh, please do!' exclaimed Herleva, who was cheering up at the thought of getting news about Robert.

'Oh no,' said Sybil. 'The things I've seen – and done, too, come to that – they're not for the ears of a young lady like yourself. Specially not in your condition.'

Something caught her eye and she looked out towards the forest. A figure had appeared at the edge of the clearing. 'Ah! Here's my Osmund now, coming home for his lunch.' Sybil waved her hand above her head and received a wave back in reply, then turned towards Herleva again. 'Let's have a word with him in a moment and see what he thinks about a little trip to Falaise . . .'

9

No one could pretend that Count Robert's orders had not been clear: no talking to anyone unless it was absolutely unavoidable. But Osmund had been cooped up in his house with nothing but women for company for more than three months now, and it was driving him slowly mad. So when they all started going on about how he ought to go down to Falaise, and it wouldn't do any harm, and Robert wouldn't mind if he knew, Osmund didn't need much encouragement to put a few coins in his purse and start walking.

A couple of hours later, he emerged from the forest on to the open land that lay between the trees and the town. The first thing that struck him was the smell. There wasn't any – not at first, anyway. The tanneries and slaughterhouses had all been abandoned for the duration of the siege so that the stink that usually welcomed him to Falaise had disappeared. Within a few more minutes of walking, however, it had been replaced by an equally disgusting odour: the foul-smelling midden of an army encampment in the middle of a long siege.

Osmund didn't have to be told what that would be like. He'd been on enough campaigns as a young man, watching the shit pile up outside each tent before it turned liquid in the rain, sending foul brown streams through the camp until the ground underfoot was sodden with filth. He thought of the flies at this time of year and gave an involuntary shudder. There weren't many advantages to getting old, but leaving that side of military life behind for good was one of them.

By the time he reached the first tavern, he was starting to blot out the smell from his mind and thinking more about the thirst he'd worked up on his walk. He got himself a large wooden cup of ale and started up a conversation with Rolf the innkeeper, whom he'd known for years.

'Does that camp look as bad as it smells?'

'Ha!' Rolf gave a wry laugh. 'You're well out of it, Osmund Forester, hidden away there in the woods. So what brings you here anyway?'

'Well, I need a few things. You know, seed for my winter vegetables, some salt – nothing fancy. I was hoping some of the shopkeepers were still trading.'

'No chance! They ran off months ago, taking their stock with them. We don't even have a market here any more. The nearest place you'll find one of them is L'Oudon.'

Osmund grimaced. 'I can't get there and back in a day . . . The hell with it, we'll just have to make do with what we've got. So . . .' he leaned forward on the counter, 'what's going on up at the castle, then, eh? I mean, who'm I going to be doffing my cap to and calling sir when the hunting season starts again?'

'Your guess is as good as mine, mate,' Rolf replied. 'They say that if Duke Richard wins, he's promised the place to the Count of Bellême, in exchange for all the troops Bellême's brought with him.'

'And will he win?'

'Dunno . . . He's made six attempts to get over those walls and been knocked back every time. That young Robert's fighting like a man possessed. He's working miracles holding on to the place, 'cause he's not got half as many men as his brother. But each time a big attack comes, he loses a few more and he's that much weaker the next time. They're getting hungry in there, too. They've started slaughtering horses. You can hear the poor beasts from here when they're killed.'

'And every horse that's dead is another that can't be ridden into battle.'

'Exactly.'

'Sounds like it's only a matter of time before the castle falls, then.'

'Not necessarily. The duke's got his troubles too.'

'Is that so?' said Osmund thoughtfully, sipping on his ale. He thought about telling Rolf what he'd heard in the woods the other day, but decided against it. The fewer people who knew he was spying on the duke's soldiers the better. 'What troubles are they, then?'

'Oh, the usual. You've been to war, you know how it is – more people dying of gut ache and fever than ever get killed by the enemy. Lads quietly slipping out in the middle of the night and never coming back.'

'Fucking sieges . . . it's never about who wins. It's about who doesn't lose.'

Rolf chuckled. 'That sounds about right. Another ale?'

Osmund nodded and handed over his cup to be refilled.

'Oi, Osmund Forester! Aren't you going to buy me one too?'

Osmund swung round to see who had spoken to him. There were four soldiers playing dice at the only table that appeared to be occupied, and none of them looked remotely familiar.

'Over here!' the voice called again. And then Osmund saw a man sitting alone at a table in the furthest, darkest corner of the tavern. 'It's me, Serlo . . . Serlo the skinner. Jesus Christ, Osmund, I've bought you enough drinks in the past. Don't go pretending you don't know me now.'

Osmund grimaced into his ale cup. He knew Serlo Skinner all right, and a nasty piece of work he was too, especially when he was drunk. But if he snubbed him, that would only provoke him, so he bought another ale and took it over to Serlo's dismal corner.

'You're a good mate,' Serlo said, grabbing the cup like a desert wanderer dying of thirst. 'Always thought you were one of the best.'

'So what keeps you here, then, in the middle of all this?' Osmund asked, for want of anything better to say.

'Nowhere else to go, have I? And then there's my daughter . . . my lovely, beautiful, innocent little girl.'

'What, is she here too?'

'Well that's the question, isn't it?' Serlo answered. He grabbed Osmund's arm. 'That's the whole fucking question. Where is she? That's what I want to know. Where's my little girl?'

'Is she lost, is that it?'

Serlo held up his hands in bafflement, a stupid expression on his face. 'Search me. She could be lost. She could be captured, forced to do terrible things for some bastard of a soldier. She could be dead, the poor little darling. I just don't know, see? No one knows . . . No one has a fucking clue where my little girl has gone.'

'What's her name?' Osmund asked.

'Judith,' said Serlo. 'Lovely girl, sweet nature, kind . . . Amazing tits, too. Big ones. Gets them from her mother.'

Osmund made his face a mask. Judith hadn't talked much about her home life. He'd got the impression it hadn't been particularly happy, and now he had the terrible feeling that he knew why. 'So when was the last time you saw her?' he asked.

'About a week before all this madness started. She was working up at the castle for that stuck-up little slut Herleva, the tanner's girl. One minute the two of them are best friends, giggling and gossiping – you know what girls are like. The next Herleva's got herself tucked up in Count Robert's bed, legs wide open, and she's telling Judith she has to be her servant and call her milady. My girl, bowing and scraping to the town tart . . . It made my blood boil, mate, I can tell you. Christ, I could use another drink. Be a pal . . .'

Osmund got them both ales. It was either that or punch Serlo's teeth out.

'So anyway,' Serlo said, wiping his mouth with the back of his hand, having knocked back half his cup in one go, 'the last time I saw my Judith . . . Well, she was in the market, wasn't she? Talking to a couple of other lasses. I thought about going to have a word with her, like, but I didn't want to interrupt her conversation.'

Didn't want to get a flea in your ear, more like, Osmund thought.

'See, the thing is . . .' Serlo said, reaching out for Osmund's arm again, 'I thought I'd see her again in a week or two and I could talk to her then. But I never did. All the other girls from the castle got out before the trouble started. But Judith wasn't with them. She just disappeared. And now . . .' Serlo's voice cracked and Osmund began to worry that he would start to cry. He could already sense that the soldiers were looking in their direction, and he didn't want to get anything started with them. 'And now,' Serlo repeated, almost wailing now, 'I don't know what's happened to my baby. So I'm just waiting here for her to come home and asking everyone I meet if they've seen her.' He stared with manic intensity right into Osmund's eyes. 'Have you seen her, Osmund Forester? Have you seen my Judith?'

'Of course not,' Osmund replied. 'I've been stuck in the forest, just me and the wife. Haven't seen a soul apart from her.'

Serlo said nothing. He kept staring at Osmund. And then, in a low, rasping, poisonous growl, he said, 'You're lying. You're telling bloody lies.' He got to his feet, glaring down at Osmund, his voice rising in volume and pitch. 'You've seen her, haven't you? You've seen my little girl!' He grabbed

Osmund by the shoulders. 'What have you done with her, you bastard?'

Osmund ripped Serlo's hands off his body and stood up, throwing the table aside as he did so. The two men were standing face to face, glaring at each other.

'I've not done anything to her,' he answered, his voice deliberately calm. 'I told you. I've been in the forest, keeping my head down. Just me and the wife.'

Rolf the innkeeper rushed up, holding a large cudgel, and forced his way between the two men. 'I've just about had enough of you,' he said, poking Serlo in the chest with the end of the club. 'Get out of my tavern. Now. And don't come back, or I'll crack this over your thick skull . . . Go on – out!'

Serlo spat on the ground between him and Osmund. Then he looked at Rolf. 'Fine,' he said. 'Your ale tastes like piss anyway.' He walked towards the door, muttering, 'What are you fucking looking at?' to the soldiers as he passed their table. Just as he was about to leave, he turned, looked back at Osmund and jabbed a finger at him. 'You know what happened to my Judith. I can tell. And I'll get you for it. I'll get you good and proper. Just you bloody wait . . .'

'Ignore him,' said Rolf. 'The man's a gutless coward, always has been. Never had the balls to follow through on any of his threats. Just took it all out on his wife and kids. You ask me, the girl's putting as much distance between herself and that bastard as she can, and I don't blame her. Here, why don't I get you another drink? On the house.'

Osmund shook his head. 'No thanks, I'll be on my way. It's a long walk back home and I want to be there before sunset.'

The next morning, Judith announced that she was going to do the laundry. 'What on earth for?' Sybil asked. 'I only did it all a couple of months ago.'

Judith laughed. 'There's laundry done almost every day at the castle. I feel like doing it. We can take it down to the stream. It'll be fun.'

The three women went down to a brook that ran through the forest less than a hundred paces from the cottage. They chatted and laughed as they kneaded the dirty clothes and linens in the fresh, cool water, with Herleva insisting on joining in with the other two.

And all the time, Serlo the skinner watched them from the undergrowth nearby, just as he'd watched Osmund arrive at the cottage the previous night, and then leave in the morning with his dogs; just as he'd watched Sybil, Judith and Herleva make their way down to the stream. It wasn't difficult. He'd spent his entire childhood playing in the woods, and then, when he was older, poached rabbits, birds and once even a young deer. He could move so silently and invisibly through the trees that even Osmund didn't know he was there. And now it was all he could do not to jump out from behind the bush where he was hiding and have a bit of sport with the women: give his daughter a proper beating, just to remind her he was still in charge; pay back that lying bastard Osmund by giving his fat old cow of a wife a good fuck; and as for Herleva, he'd . . . he'd . . .

Serlo jammed his own hand against his mouth to stop himself from cheering. Because he'd just realised what he was going to do to Herleva. Oh yes, he'd fuck her all right. He'd fuck her and her fancy boyfriend. Fuck them good and proper.

He took one last look at the three women doing their laundry, then he turned and disappeared into the forest once again.

Two hours later, Serlo reached Duke Richard's camp. He was stopped by two guards and asked his business. 'I need to see the duke,' he replied.

'I'd like to fuck the duchess,' one of the guards replied. 'But that's not going to happen either.'

'I know something,' Serlo insisted. 'Something that could put the duke in the castle by nightfall.'

'Oh yes? What is it – a secret gate at the back of the castle? Because we know about that already.'

'No, better than that. It's something that'll make Count Robert open the main gate – the only thing that'll make him do it.'

'So tell us what it is?'

'No. I tell the duke, no one else.'

The guards were Bellême men. They conferred for a moment and then said, 'We'll take you to see our lord. He's the duke's right-hand man. If you're telling the truth, maybe he'll persuade the duke to see you.'

'And if I'm not telling the truth?'

'Do you really need to ask?'

10

It was mid afternoon, and Herleva was fast asleep. She'd come inside to get out of the heat, lain down on her bed and drifted off the moment her head had hit the canvas sack filled with chaff that served as a pillow. It was the frenzied barking of the dogs that woke her, but she was still not fully conscious as Osmund burst into the cottage and shouted, 'Run! Run! The duke's men are here!'

The next thing Herleva knew, Judith was almost pulling her out of the bed. She was dimly aware of Sybil screaming at her husband, 'How did they find us? How did they know?' and Osmund, much more quietly, saying something that sounded like 'It's my fault . . . It's all my fault.' And then she was out of the bedchamber and in the main room of the cottage, where Osmund was reaching for his old sword, left over from his time as a soldier, and saying, much more calmly now, 'Go, all of you. I'll try to hold them for as long as I can. For God's sake, go!'

Sybil paused just long enough to look her man in the eye and say, 'I love you,' and then they were racing out of the door, round the back of the cottage and into the woods. Now Herleva could hear other sounds: the pounding of hooves, the harsh shouts of unknown men and the clash of steel upon steel.

'Split up!' gasped Sybil, who was already struggling for breath, pointing in different directions as she ran. 'Harder for them to catch us.'

The three women peeled off. Herleva heard Sybil calling out, 'Follow me, girls!' and knew she was trying to draw the pursuit towards her, and then she was alone in the forest and the loudest noise was the rasping of her own breath and the pounding of her blood in her ears. Like Serlo, she had known the forest all her life and over the past few months had become familiar with every detail of the land around the cottage. She was naturally fleet-footed and nimble and under normal circumstances would have had the speed to evade an armoured soldier on foot and the agility to go where no horseman could follow.

But now she was within a month of giving birth. Fear, and the burning desire to protect her baby no matter what, seemed to fill her with a surge of energy, so at first she moved with a speed she would never have imagined possible. Even so, her distended belly weighed her down and unbalanced her. It made her feel clumsy and bulky, as if she was in someone else's body. She couldn't see the ground beneath her feet and it only took one tree root snaking across in front of her to bring her crashing to the ground, sliding uncontrollably down a short slope into the gully of a dried-up stream.

She came to a halt in a haze of dust and fragments of dried leaves. She coughed a couple of times and then her hands went to her belly. Somehow it didn't seem to have been hurt in the fall, and the hefty kick her baby gave her suggested that it was still in one piece too. She gave a little half-laugh. 'Sorry,' she whispered. 'I didn't mean to shock you like that.'

She put a hand down to the ground, pushed herself up on to her knees and then tried to get to her feet. At once a searing pain shot through her right ankle. She must have twisted it, perhaps even broken a bone. Too bad. She couldn't stay where she was. She could already hear the men's voices, getting closer. 'We're coming for you, tanner's daughter,' someone shouted. 'We know you're here. Come out. There's no point running.'

Herleva had lost her sense of direction. From where she was, below the forest floor, it was impossible to see any of the familiar trees or bushes she used as landmarks to guide her. She didn't know which way to run. She looked up and down the stream, then began making her way, part limping, part hopping, along the gully. Every step hurt, and when she looked around after what seemed like an age, she realised to her despair that she had barely made any progress. She gritted her teeth and fixed her stare ahead of her, then started moving again, almost crying with pain. And then she heard a voice from above her: 'Stop!'

She ignored it and kept going.

'Stop . . . now . . . or you'll never take another step.'

Herleva knew she stood no chance. But she kept on, forcing herself to ignore the pain.

And then there was the twanging of a bowstring, a feathery whirr in the air, and an arrow landed just in front of her and stood quivering in the dry, dusty soil of the stream bed.

This time she stopped. She looked up and saw a horseman with three crescents on his shield looking down at her. Two bowmen stood one on either side of the horse, aiming their arrows straight at her.

There was nothing fine or handsome about the rider's face, but from the charger he was riding and the armour in which he was clad, Herleva could tell he must be of noble birth. He was young, still not yet fully a man, and that made her think of the first time she had seen Robert. She wondered if she would ever see her love again.

More men had come rushing to join the group on the bank. 'Go and get her,' the horseman said, and then four of them were scrabbling down the crumbling slope towards her, grabbing her and dragging her away.

Herleva's hands were tied, the rope attached to the pommel of the horseman's saddle, and she was led back through the woods, chewing her lip to stop herself crying out at the agony that stabbed through her ankle with every step. Before she got to the clearing where the cottage stood, she smelled the smoke coming through the trees and then felt the heat of the flames.

The cottage was ablaze. Osmund's torn and bloodied body was lying face down on the grass. Sybil was reaching out towards it, desperately trying to escape the grasp of a soldier, who laughed at the futility of her struggle. Judith was screaming insults at a shabbily dressed man who was making a big show of indifference. Herleva heard the words 'What kind of a father does a thing like this?' and then realised that the man was Judith's father, Serlo. He must have led the soldiers to their hideout. But how had he known where to look?

Then Herleva remembered that Serlo was a drunk who spent most of his time in taverns. And Osmund had been to a tavern yesterday. She could not believe that the forester would knowingly have betrayed them, but he must have let something slip. That was why he'd said it was all his fault.

It wasn't, she said to herself, looking at Osmund's body, knowing that he had sacrificed himself for her sake.

Herleva, Judith and Sybil were lined up together. 'Put the count's whore in that,' the horseman said, pointing towards Osmund's cart. 'She won't manage the walk. And bring the other women, too. They'll provide good sport, if nothing else.'

Several of the men cheered. 'I'm having the young one,' someone shouted. 'What do you reckon, lads? Do I stick my cock in her pussy first, or between those big fat tits?'

There were more shouts, more raucous laughter that only ended when the horseman snapped, 'That's enough!'

'What do you want us to do with him?' a soldier asked, pointing towards Serlo.

'Kill him.'

'But your father promised me money!' Serlo cried.

'More fool you for believing him. Let's go.'

The sun was low in the sky and the air had lost a little of its heat when the lookouts on the battlements above the main gate of Falaise Castle saw a man leave the duke's encampment and walk up the path towards them, accompanied by a young lad carrying a white flag.

'Hold your fire!' the watch commander said in Breton, as his men started raising their bows.

'I come under the protection of parley,' the duke's man said when he was within earshot of the castle. 'Fetch your master, the Count of the Hiémois. My lord the Duke of Normandy wishes to speak to him. He has an offer. He believes his brother will wish to hear it.'

Robert took his time getting to the battlements. He did not want to appear desperate, though in truth he was very close to it. For more than a week now the castle's few remaining defenders had been living on little more than a weak gruel of barley and vegetable scraps. The last of the horses had been butchered and consumed. Even water was running perilously low. Unless it rained soon, they'd be defeated by thirst.

But he held his head up as he came into view of the forces besieging him and there was no sign of his hunger, fatigue or despondency as he called out, 'I am Robert, Count of the Hiémois. What is this offer you wish to make me?'

The messenger did not reply directly. Instead he turned and called back down the path. 'Bring them up!'

Another man walked up from the camp. He was holding a rope that extended behind him. It was tied around the necks of three women, who were being led like a line of donkeys up the path. One of them was limping heavily. As the women came closer, and Robert saw who they were, his blood ran cold, and then the horror was replaced by rage and it was all he could do to stop himself jumping down from the castle walls and charging in a berserker rage at the men who were mistreating his woman so cruelly.

He looked down at the messenger. 'Let those women go. Let them go now, or by God I'll make you pay for it.'

The Bretons around him might not have understood every word Robert had said, but they caught the gist of it clearly enough. They raised their bows.

'You don't want to hurt me,' the messenger said. 'Not if you want to see your child born.'

Robert was breathing heavily, the fury building inside him. Herluin had reached the battlements now. He placed a calming hand on Robert's shoulder and said, 'Listen to him . . . for Herleva's sake.'

Robert glared at him and then nodded. 'Very well,' he called down to the messenger. 'Tell me what my brother has to say.'

'It's very simple. You will vacate the castle by sunset, crawling out through the main gate with a saddle upon your back. And then you will go into exile until such time as Duke Richard sees fit to let you return.'

'And if I do not?'

The messenger smiled. 'Then your concubine, her servant and the forester's wife will be taken back to the duke's camp. They will be used by his men until they are on the point of dying. Then they will be slaughtered like pigs. You surrender, Count Robert, or they die. It's a very simple choice.'

11

The parley took place on the plain before the castle. Robert went down to meet his enemy accompanied by a dozen of his men, all covered by the bowmen lined up along the gate-house battlements and the ramparts on either side. Before the sally port was opened to let them out, he turned to his companions and said, 'We've fought together for all these months. I trust you with my life and I hope you trust me too. Now you may hear me say things you don't like. But have faith. I'll never give up. I'll never surrender. And when this parley ends, this castle will still be ours.' They prayed briefly, asking for the Lord's guidance in the negotiations, then stepped out from the shadow of the gatehouse into the clear late-afternoon sunshine beyond.

The three women had been led back from the foot of the path, just far enough away from Robert that he could still see them, but with so many guards around them there was no chance of attempting a rescue. Herleva would be killed long before Robert could get to her. But all the way down the path he kept his eyes upon her, and she looked right back at him with her head held high. He remembered the first time he had led her into the great hall, how frightened she had been, but how bravely she had raised her head and walked as proudly as if she'd been born to be a great lady. So now, though he had intended to give her hope that he would find a way to save her, he found that the exact opposite was happening. Just seeing her made him feel stronger and gave him the faith he needed to make his case and win his brother over.

Robert's concentration on Herleva was so total that it was only when he reached the foot of the hill that he realised that Richard had not come out to negotiate with him. Instead it was Bellême who stood there, exuding malice; and the soldiers watching over the women, and all those who now stood opposite him, their hands hovering over the hilts of their swords, wore the crescents of Bellême, not the leopards of Normandy.

'Where is my brother?' Robert asked.

'Taking his leisure in his tent,' Bellême replied. 'He trusts me to speak on his behalf.'

'Does he now? Well tell His Grace the duke that if he wants to make demands of me, then he must make them in person. And tell him this too . . . To kill three innocent, helpless women and a child in its mother's womb would be a mortal sin no priest could ever absolve. God will damn him to an eternity of suffering for such a crime – and damn you all for conspiring in it.'

Some of the soldiers flinched at that, for the threat of damnation was enough to fill any man's heart with fear, but Bellême was unmoved. 'If these women die, it will be your treachery and your arrogance that kills them,' he said. 'Surrender. Crawl on your knees before the rightful Duke of Normandy, and your whore and her child will both live. Defy him, and their blood will be on your hands.'

Robert wanted to strike Bellême dead for the insult to Herleva, but he knew that the count was trying to provoke him. He had to keep a cool head if he was to win this verbal contest. So he took a deep breath and paused before raising his head and speaking like a true scion of the House of Normandy.

'You forget yourself, Bellême, and you evidently forget who you're talking to. If I am to parley, I have the right to do it with

184

my brother, not with some rabid, flea-bitten dog who lies at his feet hoping for scraps from his table. But if it helps, you can tell him that I want peace between us. I want an end to the killing . . . but only once we have talked.'

Richard, Duke of Normandy, had been squatting miserably over a large beaten-copper commode when Bellême first came to his tent to inform him that Herleva and the other two women had been captured. The duke's page looked on with disgust on his face as Bellême told Richard how he planned to use the women to force Robert to surrender, though whether the boy's expression was due to moral outrage at Bellême's lack of scruple or distaste for the vile task of emptying the commode was impossible to say. Duke Richard had spent much of the past three days either voiding his bowels or lying curled up on his bed groaning piteously, his skin grey and lathered in sweat as he wrapped his arms around his tortured guts.

Two prostitutes had arrived from Rouen several days earlier. The most prized employees of the city's finest brothel, they were both southern girls, born and raised on the Mediterranean coast, with olive skin, dark brown eyes and coils of raven hair tumbling about their shoulders. Richard had been in no condition to enjoy them, but no one dared send them back in case he should recover and demand to be entertained. So they had been left in the sweltering, reeking tent to pass the time gossiping, playing games of dice and languidly grooming and petting one another like a pair of pretty black cats.

Their native tongue was Catalan, a language quite foreign to a northern duchy like Normandy, and they could be as disparaging as they liked about their sickly, self-pitying, shit-encrusted client.

'At least he's not at home making his wife's life a misery,' one said.

'Poor Adela,' the other agreed. 'Can you imagine what it must be like for a girl with Provençal blood to have to bed down with a filthy Viking like him?'

'I don't think she does bed him,' the other one giggled. 'I had the palace steward a few weeks ago. He swore blind the marriage hasn't ever been consummated.'

'Well that's a relief to her, I'm sure!'

The two of them were still chattering away, and Richard, after a brief interlude on the bed, had returned to his vigil over the commode when Bellême returned.

'Your brother wants to negotiate. But he'll only talk to you. Also, he wants you to know that God will damn you to hell if the women are killed.'

'Tell my brother to go fuck himself. He knows the deal. He admits defeat or the women die. There's nothing more to talk about.'

'He also says he will kneel, and that he wants peace,' Bellême said grudgingly, not wanting to be deprived of the chance to abuse the women then take the castle from Robert regardless.

'He wants to save his skin, more like.'

'Unfortunately the men liked the sound of peace.' Bellême grimaced. 'They won't be happy if you don't deal with your brother face to face. You're their leader. You started this campaign. They need to see you finish it.'

'Well they can't. I'm sick. I've barely got the strength to shit, let alone do anything else.'

Bellême took two strides across the room, grabbed Richard by his soiled, damp nightshirt and pulled him upright. He looked his duke in the eye and snarled, 'Then find some new strength, fast! You promised these men victory. You promised me Falaise Castle. If you want to keep the throne of Normandy, you'd better deliver on those promises. Now.'

Richard pulled off his nightshirt, wiped his arse with it and

186

threw it to the floor. His body looked shrunken and shrivelled; the muscles had all wasted away and every bone in his ribcage was clearly visible beneath the skin.

'Get me some clothes,' he muttered to his page, who began helping him into his leggings, boots, undershirt and surcoat.

'Will you wear your mail, Your Grace?' the boy enquired.

Richard shook his head. 'Too heavy. But bring a chair. A duke does not stand when he hears a traitor's plea.'

Richard of Normandy did his best to maintain a lordly warrior's stride on the walk from his tent to the place where his brother stood waiting for him. But when he got there, he collapsed into the high-backed wooden chair and sat there breathing too heavily to speak.

'You look unwell, brother,' Robert said. The old teasing tone had vanished from his voice. He was too tired, too hungry to summon it up. 'I can smell the sickness in your camp. I hope you've not been too badly afflicted.'

Richard looked at him through bitter, feverish eyes. 'Huh!' he grunted. 'Your concern for my health doesn't fool me. You want me dead, and you know it.'

Robert shook his head. 'If I'd wanted you dead, I'd have killed you when I had the chance. Or I'd challenge you to combat now. But I wouldn't want to be seen killing a man too feeble to wear armour, or even lift his sword to defend himself. I'd rather we both lived. And so I will swear my fealty to you . . .'

There were gloating cheers from the duke's supporters, convinced that their enemy was about to give in, but though Robert could sense his own men bristling with frustration, their discipline held. There were no complaints or suggestions of dissent.

'Then put a saddle on your back and crawl,' Richard said.

But Robert had not finished his sentence. 'I will swear fealty . . . on the terms our uncle Robert, Archbishop of Rouen, suggested.'

Richard gave a puzzled frown. 'What terms? I don't see him here.'

'You know perfectly well what I mean,' Robert said. 'But others here will not, so I will explain myself . . .' He looked around the assembly and, summoning the last dregs of his energy, raised his voice so that everyone could hear him.

'On the day of Duke Richard's wedding, he and I were summoned by Osbern Herfastsson to attend our uncle archbishop – Robert the Dane, as he is also known – in his private chambers. The archbishop is a wise, far-sighted man and he could see the conflict brewing between my brother and myself. Is that not so, Your Grace?' He looked back down at Richard, slumped in his chair. The duke grunted again and feebly waved a dismissive hand as if to say, yes, but so what?

'He begged us . . . no, he ordered us not to fight,' Robert went on, still looking at his brother, though his voice was clearly audible to everyone around them, 'for he could see the harm that such a quarrel would do to us, our family and the whole duchy.' He paused for a moment, letting silence fall before he said, 'Look at us now – me half starved, you half dead. Think of all those of our comrades who have died, and who may still die if we fight on, and tell me he was not right.'

Still Richard said nothing. Now Robert straightened up and looked around him, focusing on one small group of men and then another as he continued his story.

'The archbishop asked me to swear in the sight and hearing of God Almighty that I meant neither harm nor disloyalty to my brother Duke Richard. And I swore that to be so. Then he proposed a simple agreement: that I should go down on one knee and pledge my fealty to His Grace the duke, and that the duke in his turn should of his own good will grant me occupation of this castle.'

He looked back down at Richard. 'Is that not so?'

Now his brother found his voice again. 'It is, but what of it?'

'And did I not agree to those terms and offer to pledge my fealty?'

'Yes . . . grudgingly. But you insulted my bride first.'

'If I offended her, or you, I apologise. But tell me this: when the archbishop asked you whether you would allow me to live here at Falaise, knowing that I had sworn my allegiance to you, how did you reply?'

Richard gripped the arms of his chair and the beads of sweat stood out on his forehead as he pulled himself to his feet and finally looked Robert in the eye. 'I said that as long as I was Duke of Normandy you would never be allowed to occupy Falaise Castle. And by God that is still what I say!'

His voice was too weak to carry far, but a ragged cheer sprang up from those of his men who were close enough to have heard him.

'And, by God, I still say that I will abide by the terms put to us by the archbishop,' Robert replied. 'It's funny, Richard, but I don't see our uncle's standard anywhere in your army. He's not sent you men from Evreux. He's not come here to conduct a single Mass, nor even to pray for the welfare of your men as they sicken and die. He thinks your cause is wrong.'

'Why should I care what an old man thinks?'

'Because that old man is a representative of God. You are fighting here without the Lord's blessing. That's why your camp is ravaged by disease, while I and my men are still healthy, however hungry we may be.'

The mood among the besiegers shifted like a sail in a changing breeze. Robert's words made a terrible sense. They had been cursed by disease brought to them by demons and evil vapours while God had stood by doing nothing to protect them. There had to be a reason for that.

Richard knew he was in danger of losing his men's faith. 'And you think God favours a Judas?' he snapped back, doing his best to shout. 'You can't dictate terms to me, you treacherous little turd. Crawl and grovel and beg me for forgiveness, or I'll give your women to my men to be used until they long for the mercy of death.'

Now the verbal battle had been joined. The spectators fell silent, watching and listening intently as tension tightened its grip on them all.

'Then what?' Robert asked. 'The world will know you for a coward who rapes and slaughters the innocent to seize by blackmail what he cannot capture in battle. And when I kill you, which by God I will, people will thank me for ridding the world of your infamy.'

Robert's men whooped, with relief as much as approval. It was good to hear his fighting spirit again.

But when he next spoke, his tone was almost plaintive. 'In the name of Jesus and all the saints, Richard, is that what you want? No man in our family has ever bent his knee, except before God. Rollo would not kneel before the king himself. But I am offering to kneel before you, here, in plain sight. And when I do, you can leave with your honour and your good name intact. Your men can go back to their homes and their families without another drop of blood being spilt. And all I ask in return is all I have ever asked: to be allowed to live here in peace with my woman and my child.'

He stretched out an arm towards the captives as he addressed the men, his own and Richard's alike: 'Look at these women. See my love, Herleva, and her companion Judith. They are simple Falaise girls. They could be your sisters, or your daughters. And see good Mistress Sybil, the wife, though I fear she is now the widow, of Osmund Forester. She is a decent, respectable woman.'

Now he stepped towards Richard's men, and the nearest ones recoiled at his approach. 'What harm have any of them ever done you?' he asked. 'What quarrel do you have with them? I say they should live. What do you say: should these innocent women live?'

'Yes,' a few voices responded, half-heartedly.

Robert raised his voice. 'I said: should the women live?'

This time the reply was a little louder: 'Yes!'

'And do you want to go home to your womenfolk, too?'

'Yes!' came the shouted response, and there was real enthusiasm now, and laughter too, as a few men shouted out ribald suggestions about what they'd do once they got there.

Robert let the hubbub die down before he asked, 'So should I kneel before the duke and accept him as my liege lord?'

'Yes!' the men shouted, enjoying the call and response so much that when Robert immediately asked, 'And should he leave me here, to live in peace?' they automatically yelled back, 'Yes!'

'You heard them, Your Grace. Will you consent to their plea?' Robert walked up to his brother and almost whispered in his ear, 'For pity's sake, Richard, do it. They will love you for it.' Then he dropped to one knee, his head bowed.

'Ha!' muttered Richard, with a bitter, derisory laugh. 'These bastards won't love me for anything.' Nevertheless, he laid a hand on Robert's shoulder and called out, 'Very well, I agree. Count Robert of the Hiémois, I accept your fealty as my loyal vassal.'

A great cheer rang out, from both sets of fighting men, and redoubled as Richard added, 'Bellême, free the women!'

'But Your Grace . . .' Bellême protested.

'I said let those women go.'

Herleva was released, and Robert ran to her side and took

her in his arms. The fear, the pain and the grief that had built up inside her over the day were finally released, and she broke down in tears, her chest heaving as she nestled her head against his shoulder and sobbed. Robert stroked her hair and tried to comfort her, telling her again and again that he loved her, that she was safe and that no one could hurt her now. When she had calmed a little, he lifted her off her feet and carried her through the throng of soldiers, back towards the castle gate.

Duke Richard was also being carried away from the scene. The sight of Robert on his knees before their leader had been enough to convince Richard's troops that, even if they had not stormed the castle, they had certainly not been beaten. So a small group of them picked the duke up and bore him away on their shoulders in the direction of his tent.

The cheers of Robert's men, applauding him and Herleva as they made their way uphill, merged with those of Richard's army until it was impossible to distinguish one sound from another. Of the men who had first confronted one another on the day the siege began, barely half were still alive and relatively unscathed by injury or disease. Now they too became caught up in relief that the war was over and that they had survived. The two forces began to mingle. The first flagons of wine, cider and beer were produced. Someone started picking out a tune on a crude wooden flute, the beat was picked up by a drummer and soon raucous voices were joining in with the song. A few of the older, wiser campaigners sighed to themselves, knowing that the drinking would carry on late into the night and would end, as such things always did, with arguments, fights and even a death or two. Better that, though, than the slaughter of further attacks on the castle, or yet more lives lost to siege sickness.

As the festivities got under way, however, there were some who did not feel inclined to join in the celebrations.

Talvas of Bellême cast a sardonic eye over proceedings, watching as his father followed the knot of men bearing the duke away in triumph, then turned to his brother Warin. 'The old man looks even more disgusted with the world than usual.'

'Are we really not getting the castle?' Warin replied, as slow as ever on the uptake.

'Not unless Count Robert feels like giving it to us. Maybe if you ask him very nicely . . .'

'But the duke promised it to us.'

'Yes, he did.'

'So he broke his word.'

'That's certainly how Father sees it. He thinks he's been cheated. He's very unhappy. And someone's going to suffer for it.' Talvas paused for a moment and then added, 'I think I'd like to see that, wouldn't you?' Then he walked away towards the ducal tent.

The Count of Bellême, meanwhile, had supervised proceedings as Richard was laid, exhausted, on his bed. It was all Bellême could do to stop himself taking out his sword and slaughtering the duplicitous bastard right there and then. He had to remind himself that there were too many witnesses. Even if he ordered everyone else out, so that he was left alone with Richard, who was now writhing around, moaning feebly as his body was racked yet again by the aching in his guts, that would do him no good. If Richard was put out of his and everyone else's misery by a steel blade plunged into his feverish belly, there could be no other suspect but Bellême. And in any case, all that would achieve would be to give the dukedom to Robert.

No, he had to be patient and wait. He would make Richard pay for letting him down, but not yet. Time was required to plan the job properly, so that no guilt could be laid at his door. And perhaps it would not be necessary. Richard and Robert were reconciled for now, but whatever Robert might say, his eyes were still fixed on the dukedom, and it would not be long before he tried to seize it.

These calculations were enough to stay Bellême's hand. He made no assault on Richard. On the contrary, he took care to let everyone see his concern for the duke's health, ordering fresh bedclothes to be brought for him, and a bowl of clear beef broth to give him strength.

It was then that Bellême caught sight of the two brothel girls sitting silently in the shadows. It was obvious that they were trying not to be noticed. There were plenty of other women around the camp, but most of them were cooks, washerwomen or cheap, rough sluts as filthy and disease-ridden as the men themselves. If anyone should ever discover that two such fine young specimens were present in the camp, they would be in for a very torrid time indeed.

Bellême got a little hard just thinking about the abuse they might suffer. But why leave them to the common soldiery? Talvas and Warin had just made their way into the tent. Bellême had no doubt which of the two would be best suited to the task he had in mind.

'Talvas, come here!' Bellême watched his son as he walked towards him. A few months of fighting had done him the world of good. The boy had become a young man. 'The duke has no need of his playthings. You may have them. Do with them as you will.'

'Yes, Father.'

'And when they've been dealt with, I want a full account.'

Talvas smiled and wondered what to do to the girls. It had to be something so imaginative in its depravity that even this disgusting old bully would be shocked, or better yet, impressed by his account. But for now he just nodded politely and said, 'Of course, Father, that would be my pleasure.'

12

Falaise and Rouen, Normandy

The dog days of August had brought a heavy, sultry heat. Out in the fields beyond the town, the crops of rye and barley, sown before the siege began but then left unattended for months, were now being harvested, and though the peasant labourers cursed the sun as it beat down upon their backs, they knew that the warm, dry weather was perfect for the crop and so they thanked God for providing it.

Herleva, however, did not feel quite so thankful. She was fast approaching the time of her confinement and every part of her was swelling. It was bad enough that her belly and breasts now felt ready to burst, but her back ached from all the extra weight it had to bear; her ankles, hands and face were puffy; and her baby seemed to give off heat like a living furnace, so that she was baked from inside and out. There were times when she could do no more than lie on her bed, red-faced, with her hair sticking damply to her forehead, while Judith did her best to soothe her with cool compresses.

Her physical discomfort and the sudden surges of emotion that pregnancy seemed to have brought in its wake combined to make her unreasonable and short-tempered. She found herself snapping at Judith over trifling complaints, and somehow the fact that her servant could not argue back only seemed to enrage her even more. Her criticisms became ever crueller and more wounding, only to be followed by tears of guilt-ridden apology as she realised what a bully she had become.

Even Robert occasionally caught the rough end of her tongue, for as much as she loved the fact that he still desired her, his fascination with her overripe breasts made her wonder whether he was remotely interested in any other part of her. But then he would lay his hand very gently against her skin and call out in delight as he felt the baby kick against it, and she'd be caught up in the excitement brought by the prospect of new life. He'd tell her how proud he was of her, how brave she'd been on that awful final day of the siege, and what a wonderful mother she was going to be to their child. And he'd tell stories of all the great deeds that their son – for Robert was absolutely certain that the baby was a boy – would accomplish, the adventures he would have, the kingdoms he would rule and the maidens who would swoon at his feet. 'Although, poor lad, he'll never find another woman as beautiful as his own mother.'

It gave Herleva a profound sense of security to know that her baby would have a father, after all the months when she'd feared it might not, and it seemed to her that she and Robert had entered a new phase of their lives as well as their love. He was now officially the master of Falaise Castle and she was acknowledged as his lady, and thus the castle's mistress.

The staff came to her wanting to know what dishes should be prepared for dinner, or what vegetables and fruits should be grown when the gardens in the bailey, wrecked during the siege, were replanted. Though the fighting had not reached the inside of the castle keep itself, the presence of so many armed men, paying no heed whatever to their surroundings, and the absence of any servants to clean or maintain the place had left the furniture, tapestries, carpets and wall paintings filthy at best, and in many cases completely destroyed. And it was Herleva who was expected to have ideas about how they might be replaced. Even the management of a great estate and the gathering of the harvest was the lady's responsibility rather than the master's. He, after all, was bound to spend much of his time away, either politicking at court or fighting campaigns on his own or his liege lord's behalf.

Of course, no one expected Herleva to be inspecting the harvest and checking the granaries while she was in her present condition, but next year she might have to. The prospect of such responsibility was daunting in the extreme, and she still found it extraordinary that someone born so humbly could have found herself in such an exalted position, but it was undeniably exciting too. She soon discovered that the more she threw herself into all these activities, the easier it was to ignore the discomforts of her pregnancy, until the point came when the combination of heat and fatigue finally forced her back to her chambers to rest.

Robert increasingly treated her as a true confidante, privy to his deepest emotions and most carefully guarded secrets. 'There's something you need to know,' he said late one night, as they lay naked on the great bed, praying for a waft of breeze to cool them. 'My treasury is empty. I spent so much fighting for this castle that now I can't afford to keep it. Those Bretons bled me dry, and I'd already used up most of my fortune preparing our defences and buying provisions.'

'It doesn't matter,' Herleva said. 'I love you whether you're rich or poor. And I can live without all those beautiful jewels and dresses you've given me. Sell them if it would help.'

Robert kissed her and stroked the hair away from her forehead. 'I could sell every scrap of clothing you possess and it wouldn't even scratch the surface of my debt.'

'So what are you going to do?'

'I don't know. I can ask my uncle for help, or even my grandmother, Gunnor. They're both rich. But they'd just say it was my fault for fighting my own brother. Or I could go to the

Jews of Evreux or Antwerp and beg them for a loan, but they'd want security, and I don't have any.'

'What about the castle?'

'I don't own it, my darling. Richard has let us live here, but it still belongs to the Duke of Normandy, whoever he may be.'

'Then why don't you go to Richard? There wouldn't have been a war if he hadn't attacked you. Surely he should pay for that.'

Robert laughed. 'I'd be better off with the Jews!'

'If only *you* were Duke of Normandy. Then you'd own the castle and you could get the money.'

'If I were Duke of Normandy, my love, I wouldn't need to borrow anything. I'd be richer than the King of France himself.'

'Well maybe you *will* be duke. Richard's been very ill. Who knows when God will claim his soul?'

'Don't say such a thing! It's practically treason. Anyway, Richard's as strong as an ox. He'll get better, you wait and see.'

'Did you know that tanners also embalm corpses? My father does that and he says that he's lost count of the number of times he's gone to get a body and the people there have said, "Oh, we thought he was getting better." That's often the most dangerous time of all.'

'Well I don't want Richard to die.'

'He wouldn't say the same thing about you. I know he wouldn't. I knew it the moment I saw the way he looked at you at the wedding.'

'All my problems would be solved if I became duke, that's true,' Robert mused.

'Well if God wills it, you will be.'

Herleva rolled over on to her side, as though the matter had been settled. A few moments later, she was asleep. But Robert lay awake late into the night, with the same thought going round and round in his mind: if Richard were dead, all his problems would be solved.

The archbishop and his mother were taking a stroll around the cathedral cloisters. 'Well at least it's over, we must be thankful for that,' Lady Gunnor said, with a sigh that suggested her own gratitude was in short supply.

'Over for now, maybe,' the archbishop replied, 'but the essential problem isn't solved, merely in abeyance. If anything it's become worse.'

'You mean the conflict between Richard and Robert?' Gunnor asked, then went on, not expecting a reply, 'I take the point, of course. But as I suggested months ago, Robert is happily ensconced with his concubine and will soon be doting over a child. He has no reason to pursue the quarrel.'

'He needs money,' the archbishop pointed out. 'He spent more than three months stuck inside that castle and every day was costing him more. That makes him weak, but also desperate.'

'Well we can help him if we have to,' said Gunnor. 'We can't have one of the family begging on the streets.'

'I hardly think it will come to that, Mother.'

'You know what I mean. Perhaps we can prevail upon Richard to be generous. He can't want to start fighting his brother all over again. What would he have to gain?'

'It's more what he stands to lose. That fool of a boy promised Falaise Castle to the Count of Bellême, in exchange for Bellême's support in the campaign. Bellême provided that support. I gather that towards the end, when Richard was shut away in his tent feeling sorry for himself, Bellême was practically running the siege. It was certainly he who came up with the idea of threatening to kill the girl, whatever she's called . . .'

'Herleva, and a sweet child she is too, and much stronger, I suspect, than she yet knows.'

'Well, Bellême was the one who threatened to kill her, and knowing him he'd have done it, and what's more enjoyed it. But Richard lost his nerve and accepted Robert's offer of peace – which he could have had seven months ago for nothing, without a single life lost – and now Bellême is feeling cheated. I can't say I blame him, and if I were in his shoes I'd be expecting a very substantial recompense.'

'Do you think he might try to take Falaise for himself? Robert must have sent his men home by now. And from what you say, he can't afford to hire more. So the castle would be relatively easy to take, and Bellême must know it.'

The archbishop paused by a wall painting that showed Christ making his way to Calvary bowed down by the weight of the cross, the crown of thorns around his head and his face running with blood. There were days, the old man thought, when the burden of retaining his family's grip upon the duchy felt as heavy as that cross, and as prickly as those thorns.

'Robert?' Gunnor said, interrupting his reverie.

'I'm sorry, my mind was distracted by the sufferings of Our Lord. So . . . the castle . . . Yes, I'm sure Bellême has considered the possibility of simply going and claiming his reward by force. But he's surely perceptive enough to see that that's the one thing that might unite our two brothers. If Robert went to Richard as his vassal, requesting help, Richard would be bound to provide it. And since he's also the castle's owner, he'd want to come to its defence. Bellême's powerful and can put hundreds of men in the field, but if both halves of the House of Normandy were united, he'd have little chance of beating them.'

'If he's thought that through, he'll only feel even more frustrated, and thus more angry,' Gunnor said.

'And more resentful towards Richard,' concluded the archbishop. 'So unless Richard finds a way to placate Bellême very soon indeed, he's going to have a powerful and very bitter enemy on his hands.'

'Is Richard in any condition to fight another campaign? I saw him a couple of days after he came back from Falaise and he looked ghastly. His skin was grey. His eyes were feverish. I put my hand to his forehead and it was burning. And can you believe it, he had some painted half-naked trollop in the room with him – with his own wife left completely ignored just a few paces away in her own chamber. I'm hardly unfamiliar with the ways of men, Robert, but even I was disgusted by that. It's just so stupid. Whatever Richard thinks of Adela, she's the daughter of the King of France . . .'

'And of Queen Constance, who frightens me a great deal more than her husband.'

'I can't bear it!' Gunnor exclaimed, casting aside her usual self-possession and giving vent to her feelings. 'Everything I most feared is coming to pass. This is what happens when a family fights against itself. It ends up weakened, divided and easy prey for its enemies. And the worst of it is, I simply can't see things getting better as long as Richard is duke.'

'Which rather raises the question: how long will that be?'

13

Somewhere near Vaudreuil, Normandy

Jarl the Viper slipped into the confession booth just as the cart containing his latest customer trundled into the churchyard. In some ways this was the most satisfying part of the whole process. No one was more fascinated by the nature of life than someone whose profession was taking it, and Jarl was an endlessly curious student of human nature and all the various ways that mortal men and women found to distract themselves from the inevitability of oblivion.

Every prospective customer came in search of the same end, yet no two supplicants were ever quite the same. Some were arrogant and demanding; others desperate and pleading; others again quite calm and matter-of-fact. Their intended targets were family members, business partners, or rivals for advancement at ducal or royal courts. Some wished death upon their cheating spouses; others were adulterers who wanted husbands or wives removed so that they could be free to marry their lovers. And as they laid out their requirements, explained the reasons for their request and gave Jarl the information necessary to determine the time, place and means of the murder, so they revealed every detail of themselves.

In Baghdad, Jarl had watched doctors dissect human corpses, flaying the skin to reveal the extraordinary complexity of organs, tissues and bones that normally lay hidden to the naked eye. These confessional conversations, far more honest and more detailed surely than any priest would hear, fulfilled a similar revelatory function and were just as gratifying. One learned so much from them. Almost as much as one did from the process that led up to that final, ecstatic moment when a victim swallowed the poison that would kill them, and their eyes played out that extraordinary journey from realisation, shock and terror through desperation and futile resistance to the ultimate moment of death itself. How ironic that in all God's creation there was no moment quite so perfect as that final instant when the divine spark of life was extinguished for all eternity.

Jarl heard footsteps on the flagstone floor of the church: from their pace and weight they were obviously male, with a confidence about them that suggested a man sure of his place in the world. There was a shuffling sound as the visitor passed through the curtain into the booth, and Jarl saw the indistinct outline of a tall, bulky body through the wooden lattice that divided the two compartments of the booth, then heard a grunt as the man lowered himself on to the cold, bare stone bench.

The priest was supplied with a cushion: an apt commentary, Jarl thought, on what the Church really thought about its flock. He said nothing. It was always best to let the new arrival start the conversation.

The man gave a brisk cough, as if to wake Jarl up. He waited to be asked about his business and then, when no question came, said, 'So, do I tell you what I've come about, then?'

It was a soldier's voice: abrupt, even harsh, but by no means stupid. There was an undercurrent of discomfort. This was a man who liked to fight his battles face to face. He was not at ease with underhand tactics. He has come at someone else's command, Jarl thought, which meant that the man or woman giving the orders was both powerful enough to have a man like this at their beck and call, and well known enough to fear being identified if they made the request themselves.

'Right, well, it's like this . . .'

Jarl smiled. A speech had been prepared and, no doubt, practised. A man whose every instinct was to say what he meant and then act upon his words as directly as possible would be forced to speak as evasively as a conniving courtier. Entertainment was assured.

The soldier cleared his throat and then began. 'The person who sent me here feels that certain matters have not transpired as well as they might have done. And he, this person, feels that for his own good, and the good of the whole duchy, action has to be taken to . . . to rectify matters. But this action has to be taken, er, discreetly, in private, so that no one really knows what happened, because if they did know, then the consequences could be very harmful, both to the person and also to the duchy as a whole. There could be conflict between the great families of Normandy. The King of France himself might get involved. It would end in war, which no one wants. So that's why it's best if everything is done . . . privately.'

'I see,' said Jarl the Viper, who understood precisely what the soldier was trying so hard not to say, and knew what the answer to his next question would be. He asked it anyway. 'So who exactly is the person against whom this action is to be taken?'

Jarl sensed the soldier stiffen. 'You swear to me no one else can hear us?' he heard him say.

'No one.'

'And I can trust you to keep your mouth shut?'

'Of course.'

'Because if you blab, I'll slice you open like gutting a fish.'

Jarl gave a soft, light laugh. 'No you wouldn't. Still, I understand your concern. You say you require discretion. Be assured, you will get it from me. But if I am to undertake work on your master or mistress's behalf, I have to know the identity of the target.'

'The duke,' the soldier said abruptly. 'God forgive me, it's Duke Richard of Normandy.'

'I see. You understand, of course, that I will require a very large fee for such a risky enterprise against a man who is so powerful and well guarded.'

'Don't worry, poisoner, you will get your gold.'

Jarl was amused by the bitterness in the soldier's voice. No man wanted more desperately to feel morally superior to another than when he knew he was doing wrong.

'Indeed I will, for only a fool would try to bilk me. Now, when do you want the duke to die?'

'Soon. He's been very ill, but he seems to be getting better. Now, if he dies before he's got his full health back, people will understand. That's normal. But if he's completely better one day and dead the next, no one's going to think it's anything but murder.'

'Very well then, this is a matter of urgency. So I need to know where the duke is now and what his plans are for the next ten days or so.'

'He's at the palace in Rouen and that's where he's staying, as far as I know, at least till he's well enough to go hunting again.'

'I've heard tell that the duke and his duchess do not share a bed. Is that true?'

'Not once,' the soldier said. 'Not in all the months they've been married.'

'But he is a normal man, I take it. He enjoys the company of women.'

'I don't know who enjoys it – not the women, that's for sure! But yes, they were there, even when he was as sick as a dog, spewing out his guts at both ends.'

'Who are they, these women? Does the duke have one favourite in particular?'

'I don't know for sure. People say there's one of the duchess's handmaidens that he's got his eye on. And he has his pick of the servant girls, of course. But most of the time he pays for them. Has them brought in from a place in the city.'

'Good, that makes it easier. Tell the person who commands you that I will take the commission. It will be an interesting challenge. But I have certain requirements that must be met, and at your cost, not mine. I need to know the identity of the pimp or madam who provides the duke with company. I need precise details of the location of the duke's bedchamber, the stairs and hallways that lead to it and the rosters of the guards and sentries within the palace and stationed at its walls and gates. My fee will be fifty pounds, weight, in gold.'

'What?' the soldier exclaimed. 'You could outfit an entire army for less than that!'

'Nevertheless, that is the fee,' Jarl said, in an imperturbably calm, almost gentle tone of voice whose pitch and lightness was such a stark contrast to the soldier. 'We will meet twice more. On the first occasion, which should be as soon as possible, you will provide the information I require and leave half the gold behind as you depart. On the second occasion, after the work has been completed, you will leave the other half of the gold. Be sure that it is weighed, and carefully, too. I will not be happy if I am short-changed. Can I take it that we have an agreement?'

'Yes,' the soldier replied.

'Very good. Then you can tell your superior not to worry. As far as I am concerned, the duke is already dead.'

14

Falaise and Rouen, Normandy

Herleva screamed – a long, keening howl of agony as desperate as an animal caught in a snare. The terrible sound echoed around the bedchamber at Falaise Castle and cut through the wooden screen that separated the chamber from the great hall, where Robert was pacing back and forth along a path of bare flagstones, the rushes that normally covered them having long since been worn away.

'For God's sake, what are they doing to her?' he cried out. 'I can't stand it any more. I'm going right in there and I'm telling that witch they call a midwife to stop her tortures now!'

'Calm yourself, my lord, I beg you,' said Fulbert the tanner, reaching out to restrain him.

'Take your hands off me, man. Let me go!' Robert shouted.

Fulbert stood his ground. As calmly as he could, he said, 'My lord, this is woman's work, and it's long, hard, bloody work too. There's nothing a man can do but wait for it to be over.'

Robert's chest was heaving as though he'd just raced a league or done an hour's hard practice with sword and staff. 'I don't believe it. There must be something. If I was in there with her, maybe I could calm her, or distract her, or do something to stop her screaming like that.'

'No, my lord,' said Fulbert, more like a father to his son than a tradesman to his noble master. 'I've been through this five times – three that lived and two that didn't, God bless their souls – and I know how it is. Herleva's got her mother and Judith as well as the midwife to help her through this. She doesn't want you to see her the way she is now. Leave her be.'

'But it's been hours! We'd barely eaten our midday meal when she was taken into the chamber, and now it's the middle of the night. That baby should have been out hours ago!'

'That baby'll come when it's good and ready. Some slip out nice and easy, like an otter into a stream. Others take their time. My Doda was up all night producing Herleva.'

Robert's expression, already anxious, now took on a look of even greater alarm. 'You mean we could be here for hours yet?'

Herluin stepped up and put an arm around his friend's shoulder. 'He's right, Robert, there's nothing we can do. Come on, let's get some more wine. See if that helps soothe your troubled soul, eh?'

'Some wine, yes,' said Robert, who was already the worse for wear. 'That might do the trick.'

Johans of Perpignan was a scrawny man with long, skinny limbs and ill-proportioned features. His nose seemed too big for his face, his chin too pronounced and his smile, which seldom possessed any trace of genuine mirth, too wide. His scalp was balding and such hair as remained hung in limp strands to his shoulders. He had grown up beneath Mediterranean skies, but more than twenty years spent in this cold, damp duchy had left him with a sallow, yellowish complexion. But then he rarely saw the sun any more, even when it was shining. Most men had been up and working for hours before Johans' day even began, and he seldom ventured outside the splendid premises, carpeted with soft Moorish rugs and hung with tapestries fit for a prince, where his stable of women plied their trade.

Johans pampered his customers with pastries sweet with honey and dates, olives from his southern homeland and heady

wines from the vineyards of Burgundy. It pleased him that his
house should be an oasis of civilisation in a land whose
inhabitants seemed to him to be little better than barbarians.
But there were times when he was obliged to conduct his
business beyond his own four walls. Tonight, for example, he
was accompanying his latest, potentially most precious
acquisition to her very first night's work.

His new girl, Galiana, was just thirteen years old and barely
past the time of her first bleeding. There were plenty of whores
who pretended to be virgins, but the delicious combination of
naivety, apprehension and just a little excitement in Galiana's
huge dark eyes was enough to confirm that she was the real
thing, even had she not been demonstrably intact. And she was
such a tasty little morsel, too: as slightly built as a child, and yet
as ravishing as the most seductive courtesan.

This was a girl worthy of a connoisseur. Instead she was
being wasted on a crude, boorish Norman ape. But this particular ape happened to be Duke Richard, and even if his
henchman Bellême and his poisonous viper of a son Talvas had
left two of Johans' best girls so ruined in mind and body that
they were no longer fit to be anything more than brothel maids,
still it would be unwise to deny the duke the pleasure of taking
Galiana's innocence.

There was a side gate to the ducal palace where late-night
visitors for whom discretion was an important consideration
could enter without being seen. From time to time one of the
household staff would be waiting there to guide anyone new to
the building to the duke's chamber. But on this occasion, Johans
and his human merchandise were greeted not by a servant, but
by the hooded figure of a monk, or rather a novice, for this was
a smooth-chinned adolescent who could only have been a year
or two older than Galiana herself.

'Are . . . are you, er, Johans of Perpignan?' the boy asked, evidently tongue-tied by embarrassment at the sight of the beautiful girl. The lad might have taken his monastic vows, but his cock wasn't paying them any attention.

'I might be. Who are you?'

'I . . . I'm Mark of Avranches. Prior Hugo asked me to meet you to tell you that Duke Richard has been taken sick. He is unable to, ah, fulfil his obligations this evening . . .'

Johans laughed aloud. 'Obligations! That's the first time I've heard it called that!'

'Yes, well, the duke is too ill to . . . to meet anyone. I've been asked to give you this, in recompense for any trouble you may have gone to.'

The boy held out a purse. Johans took it and was gratified by its weight. He opened it and peered inside. Even in the moonlight, the glint of gold was unmistakable. Little Galiana had earned him more by being turned away than she would have done by sleeping with Duke Richard. And her maidenhood was still available for sale to another customer. All in all this would be a very profitable evening. But why . . . ? Before his mind could finish formulating the question, Brother Mark was answering it.

'The prior asked me to point out that the duke's health is a very private matter. His present infirmity, which with God's grace will soon pass, must remain entirely confidential. He said that your discretion would be very much appreciated.'

So he was being paid for his silence. Well, Johans regarded himself as a man of honour. The fee was a generous one, and he would earn it. 'Tell your prior that I understand. I'll not breathe a word, and nor will this young lady, or she'll have me to answer to.'

Brother Mark looked at Galiana, who returned his gaze with coy upturned eyes. Ah, how charming, thought Johans, not entirely cynically. The whore and the monk: two novices falling

210

in love. Some minstrel should write a song about it.

'Very well, then,' he said, 'we'll be on our way. Pass my best wishes to the duke. I wish him a speedy recovery and look forward to being of service to him when he is back to his full strength and vigour. Good night to you, Brother Mark.'

'Good night, sir . . . and, er, miss,' the boy replied. 'And may the Lord's blessing be upon you this night and for ever more.'

As Johans and Galiana turned and walked away towards the brothel, Mark of Avranches went back into the palace, his errand done.

Not long afterwards, a lowly palace scullion, known by no other name than Rat, saw a woman slipping through the shadows towards the duke's private chamber and shook his head ruefully. There's just no sense to it, he thought. There's a duchess what's all alone in her chamber, waiting for a husband that never comes. There's a duchy what needs an heir. And there's that damn duke what's wasting his time with whores.

Duke Richard felt cheated. Johans had promised him an innocent young virgin, just ripe and ready for him to deflower. The brothel-keeper had gone into great poetic detail about the girl's plump little lips, how they were as soft and pink as rose petals, and how their colour exactly matched that of the nipples on her budding little tits, and of those other lips, all wet and glistening, down below. It had made Richard hard just thinking about it.

And now this.

Johans had described this virgin of his as small and dark, but the tart standing in front of Richard now was tall and willowy, with bright flaxen hair. True, her skin was as unlined as an innocent maiden's, but she was very evidently a grown woman. You could see it in the serene self-assurance of her dark blue

211

eyes and the calm, beautifully mannered way she had conducted herself since being admitted to his chamber.

Richard had seldom seen a woman who looked less like a slut than this one. But when she looked him in the eye and said, 'Good evening, Your Grace, my name is Moriella,' there was something in her soft, sweet voice that was so seductive, so intoxicating that it was all he could do to stop himself grabbing her, throwing her to the floor and taking her there and then.

And yet Richard did stop himself. For he understood somehow that brute force was not the way to get the best from this woman. He could take her if he wanted to. Even now, when he was still far from fully healthy, he was strong enough to overcome any resistance she might put up. And why would she resist? She was a prostitute, after all. She was being paid to give herself to him. But Richard had fucked enough women to have learned a little about them, and he could see that this Moriella was setting him a sort of challenge. Yes, he could have her whenever he wanted. But if he wanted to get the best from her – and something about the merest hint of a smile flickering around the corners of her mouth told him that her best might be very good indeed – then he would have to employ a more subtle approach.

'Very well, Moriella,' he said, 'perhaps you would care to serve us both with wine. The servants have left some over there, I believe.'

He waved in the direction of a side table, on which stood a carafe and two jewelled goblets.

'Certainly, Your Grace, that would be my pleasure,' Moriella replied, as if she were a high-born noblewoman rather than a common tart.

Somehow she turned the simple act of walking across the room into a performance as graceful as a dance, and when she turned her back to him for a moment and busied herself with the drinks, Richard felt bereft that he could no longer see her face, nor the gentle swell of her breasts beneath her dress. She seemed to read his mind, for she turned her head and, looking back over her shoulder, smiled at him with a look of such warmth that it gave him a sudden feeling of real pride that he had passed her first test.

As Moriella turned and walked back towards him, holding the two goblets, Richard felt better than he had done in months. This beautiful woman would be his before too long. That much was certain, and the anticipation of it had his blood pounding and the breath rasping in his chest. But that wasn't enough. What mattered most to him now was not just to have the lovely Moriella, but to have her begging for more.

15

How could anything hurt this much? Herleva had thought she'd experienced pain when she'd been forced by Talvas of Bellême to walk on a wounded ankle. The shooting, sick-making agony of it had been enough to make her cry. But that was nothing compared to childbirth. She could not imagine that even the vilest torture was as cruel as this, or could last as long. She felt as though her whole body was being ripped to pieces. She was going to die trying to get this baby out. She knew she was. She was actually going to be torn in two. And the only way she'd avoid that miserable fate would be if she died of exhaustion first. So she screamed and moaned and wept and shouted out in a rage born of suffering and terror. Somewhere far in the distance she could hear the voices of the midwife and her mother telling her to be calm, to keep taking deep, steady breaths and above all to push. And Judith screeching, 'I can see its head! Oh, Herleva – I mean, my lady – I can see its little head!'

For a few more minutes the pain and the voices and the breathing and pushing all continued, the pain if anything reaching new heights of torment. Then, quite suddenly, the pressure seemed to be lifted and there was an extraordinary slithering sensation inside her and cries and squeals of excitement all around her and high-pitched shrieks of 'It's a boy! It's a boy!' Then came the sound of a newborn infant crying. Except that this was no feeble mewling. This was the deafening, full-throated bellow of a young male announcing his presence to the world.

Herleva propped herself up on her elbows and saw him in Judith's arms, still slick with blood and afterbirth. He was looking at her with an indignant expression that made her smile, and she sat up and held out her arms so that Judith could give her the child. And the moment she held him, all the pain and fatigue simply melted away, to be replaced by a sensation of love so pure and so profound that she knew it would never leave her until the day she died. Somehow she had created this miracle, with his bright blue eyes and his little cap of burning red hair. As the midwife looked on with the satisfaction of a job well done, and her mother Doda cried, with Judith weeping beside her too, Herleva felt awestruck by her own achievement. She placed the baby to her breast and he suckled greedily.

The midwife sat down on the edge of the bed and began rubbing the base of Herleva's belly. 'He's a fine big greedy lad, that one,' she said, watching approvingly as the baby tucked in. There was one last, bloody stage of proceedings as the umbilical cord was cut and the afterbirth expelled. Then the three women busied themselves with cleaning Herleva and the baby and tidying up all the gory evidence of the act of childbirth.

'It doesn't do to let the fathers see all this,' the midwife said as she gave her orders to Doda and Judith. 'They're only men. They can't stand the sight of it.'

Herleva managed a weary laugh. 'Robert's a soldier. He's been to war. A little bit of mess from my tummy won't shock him.'

'You'd be surprised, my lady. I've seen tough old soldiers, all covered in scars, faint clean away when they came into the birthing chamber.'

The midwife kept a beady eye on the other women's efforts until she was satisfied that mother, baby and the room itself were all ready for inspection. 'Very well, Judith,' she said. 'You

215

may fetch Count Robert. I imagine he'll want to meet his new son.'

Richard was shattered. His body was slick with sweat. His tongue was exhausted from the sweet labour of licking and eating and straining ever deeper into Moriella. The muscles in his stomach, thighs and lower back ached from the strain of riding her for longer and harder than any woman he had fucked in his entire life. Somehow she had found ways of taking him to the very brink of ecstasy and then easing him back down before beginning the whole process again, until finally, when his heart was pounding so fiercely he feared it might burst through his ribs and every fibre in his being was crying out for release, she took him over the brink and for a second he wondered whether he might have died, for surely pleasure such as this could only exist in heaven.

Moriella shuddered and gave a final soft, sweet moan. 'Oh, my lord, my master, my king . . . you have conquered me . . . I am your slave.' She looked at him, and even though the room was almost dark, Richard could swear he saw a devotion in her eyes so deep that it might be love. She stroked his burning forehead and whispered, 'Are you thirsty, my lord?'

Richard nodded, too exhausted to talk.

'Then let me fetch you some more wine.'

She rose naked from the bed and he watched the sway of her buttocks as she made her way to the carafe and refilled his goblet. As she walked back, his eyes feasted on her face, her breasts and the dark triangle between her legs before she clambered up on to the bed beside him.

She placed one hand under his head and lifted it up to take the goblet that she held in the other hand. 'Here, drink, my lord,' she said, and as he gulped down the sweet red wine, she purred, 'Drink deeply. Restore your strength. Oh, you are such a man, so powerful, so virile, and you leave me so helpless before you . . .'

Richard smiled drowsily. He felt a blissful, sleepy warmth spread through his body, taking all his aches away.

'Tired,' he mumbled, 'so tired.'

'I know you are, my lord,' Moriella whispered, laying Richard's head back on the pillow. She stroked his hair, like a mother soothing a child. 'There, there, go to sleep . . . a deep, deep sleep.'

She waited a while as Richard's breathing slowed and all the tension left his body. Then she rose from the bed, gathered up her clothes and shoes and got dressed before tiptoeing to the door and letting herself out of the chamber.

As she stepped out into the corridor, Moriella heard a cough. She looked in the direction of the sound and saw the outline of a man standing no more than ten paces away. He hooked his index finger and beckoned her towards him.

'What is your name, woman?' he said as she reached him.

'Moriella, sir,' she said, in a much more humble, lowly tone than she had ever used towards Richard.

'Well, Moriella, I am Tancred, the duke's personal chamberlain. I take it you have spent the evening with His Grace?'

There was a skin-crawling relish in the chamberlain's voice as he spoke. He had a fat, jowly face with soft, plump lips made glossy by the moistness of his tongue. He looked at Moriella with unabashed greed as she replied, 'Yes, sir.'

'And how was he?' Tancred asked. He let the question's double meaning hang in the air for a while, then licked his lips again and added: 'His health, I mean. Did His Grace seem well to you?'

'Oh yes, sir, very well, sir. His Grace was very . . .' she frowned, searching for the right word, 'vigorous, sir.'

'And he dismissed you, did he?'

'Well, sir, he fell asleep, and he looked so peaceful I thought it was best to just slip out, to let him rest. I didn't want to disturb him, sir.'

'Very sensible. Now run along.'

'Yes, sir,' said Moriella, and she hurried away down the stairs towards the servants' door at the rear of the palace.

Tancred watched her go, thinking to himself that this Moriella was a much comelier girl than the rough southern strumpets that Johans of Perpignan normally supplied. Then he walked to the door of the chamber, opened it and peered towards the duke's bed. He could see nothing more than the outline of his body beneath a linen sheet, but he did not need the evidence of his eyes to be sure that all was well. Duke Richard of Normandy was snoring in slow, steady ripples of sound, like a contented old boar who'd just taken full advantage of his sows.

Little by little the snores became softer and further apart until, with a last little cough, they ceased altogether. The duke was asleep, and he was content; that was all his loyal chamberlain needed to know.

Early the following morning, Duke Richard's squire went to the bedchamber expecting to help him dress. The lad was not surprised to find his master still abed. On the contrary, it was far more of a surprise these days to find the duke up and clearheaded. The squire murmured a gentle 'Your Grace . . .' and then a little more loudly, 'It's time to rise, my lord.'

Only when that failed to provoke any response at all – not even the angry grunt of protest with which he was sometimes greeted – did the squire begin to feel the first hint of panic gnawing at his guts. 'My lord . . .' he was almost shouting now, 'wake up! Please! I beg you! Wake up!'

Finally, in desperation, he reached out and grabbed the

duke's shoulder, intending to shake it until he awoke. But the moment he touched the cold, waxen skin and felt the stiff, lifeless flesh beneath, he knew that the only thing that would ever wake Richard of Normandy would be the trump of doom on the final Day of Judgement. The boy's hand recoiled and he fled the chamber, shouting for help as he went and crying out, 'He's dead! Duke Richard is dead!'

In this moment of crisis, it fell to the archbishop to take charge of the situation. He soon established that the last man to have seen Richard on the night of his death was Tancred the chamberlain, who assured him that the duke had been alone in his chamber, sleeping peacefully. Tancred also told the archbishop about the whore Moriella, adding that she couldn't have done the duke any harm, unless the sheer strain of lovemaking had later proved to have overtaxed a constitution already weakened by siege sickness.

'At least he died happy; we should be grateful, perhaps, for that small mercy,' the archbishop remarked, before telling Tancred that there was no need to mention the whore to anyone else, or to make any further enquiries with Johans of Perpignan. 'The duchy is facing a grave enough crisis without adding to it with rumour and gossip,' he said. Though even as the words passed his lips, the archbishop knew that the speculation would already have begun into the cause of the duke's untimely passing.

All the more reason, then, to get another duke on the throne, and fast.

It was hungry work, becoming a father, and an achievement worth celebrating, too. Robert told the kitchens to provide the castle community and their guests with a particularly hearty lunch, with plenty of ale, cider and wine to wash it all down with. He would treat his friends, relations and all the many people who served him to an impromptu feast, and all they had to do in return was listen to him go on and on at inordinate length about the astonishing beauty and brilliance of Herleva; the impressive size, not to mention evident courage, strength and naturally masterful bearing, of the fine son that she had given him; and his own, not inconsiderable role in fathering the boy in the first place. Toasts were proposed, tankards raised and many a drink was downed. A couple of braver souls got to their feet and attempted to give short speeches, while the castle chaplain managed a somewhat slurred blessing.

'I ought to send a messenger to Rouen,' Robert said to Herluin, as the meal came to an end.

'Is there any need to inform Duke Richard right away?' Herluin replied. 'He might not be overjoyed to hear that you have produced a son and heir when he and the duchess have not.'

'Perhaps someone should tell my dear brother that if you want to make a baby, it helps to be in the same chamber as the woman you're making it with. But forget Richard; at least my uncle will be pleased by the news, and my grandmother. She's very fond of Herleva. So find a good rider, stick him on a fast horse, and get the news to the archbishop. I'll let him decide when to tell Richard.'

That matter settled, Robert got to his feet. He was about to leave the table when the door to the great hall suddenly burst open and a man stumbled in. He was at the end of his tether, barely able to stand. Every inch of him was covered in dust, except for the rivulets down his face where sweat had washed the dirt away. 'My lord,' the man said, looking at Robert. He stretched out his arm, in which a sealed scroll was clasped, but the effort proved too much, his arm fell limply to his side and he slumped exhausted to his knees.

'In God's name, won't someone help that man!' Robert

cried, and at once, three or four of the castle guard got up from the benches on which they were sitting and ran to his aid. Together two of them held the man up between them, with his arms around their shoulders, and practically dragged him up the hall to the foot of the dais on which the high table stood.

When they got there, the man rose unsteadily to his feet, shooed the two guards away and made a monumental effort to hold himself up straight as he addressed Count Robert.

'My lord,' he said, with a voice as shaky as the rest of him, 'I have ridden this day from Rouen . . .' The diners in the hall started at that: Rouen was usually two, even three days of travel away. 'I bring you news of Duke Richard.'

'Mother of God,' groaned Robert, 'what now?'

'My lord, your brother is dead.'

'What?' gasped Robert. The atmosphere in the room changed in an instant, all thought of celebration forgotten as the news of the duke's death hit home. 'That can't be right. The last I heard, he was getting better. He'd been very ill, I know. I saw it with my own eyes. But he was getting better. I know he was.'

'That is true, my lord,' the messenger said. 'But His Grace seems to have had some kind of relapse. His death was painless, at least; we can give thanks for that. He was asleep when God took him to join the angels in heaven.'

'The demons in hell, more like,' some wag yelled out.

'Silence!' Robert shouted. He looked at the commander of the guard. 'Have that man taken outside and whip some manners into him.'

Now Robert looked at the messenger. 'You're sure he's dead?'

'Yes, sir. I'm afraid there can be no doubt at all. And my lord, there is something else. His Grace the archbishop has commanded me to tell you that you must come to Rouen at once. The duchy requires someone to rule it. Unrest will spread if there is not a duke on the throne. And my lord . . . Your Grace . . . you are the new Duke of Normandy.'

16

Falaise, Vaudreuil and Rouen, Normandy

Baby William was much talked about in Normandy. It was said that when he was placed on the floor, he would grasp the rushes in his hands, and that his grip was already so strong, his nurse had a hard time prising open his little fists. His father Robert had apparently horrified his womenfolk by placing his sword, unsheathed, beside his son. But William had not cut himself. Instead, he had stretched out a pudgy arm and grabbed hold of the hilt like a born warrior.

It was just a pity that the duke's son was illegitimate. It only took days for him to acquire the nickname that would haunt him all his life: William the Bastard.

Jarl the Viper received his gold, but it was handed over grudgingly. The same shadowy soldier who had commissioned the killing of Duke Richard delivered it, though the confessional booth in which he and Jarl spoke was in a different church. 'I don't believe you killed him,' the soldier said. 'And what's more important, my master doubts you too.'

'What possible reason can there be for that?' Jarl asked, more amused than annoyed, having had many similar conversations with other clients. That was the inevitable disadvantage of committing murders that had no obvious cause of death. 'You asked that Duke Richard should die by a certain date,' he continued. 'I assured you that he would. Now the duke is indisputably dead. It could, in theory, be coincidence, but I assure you it is not.'

'But you can't have had anything to do with it,' the soldier protested. 'The only person who got anywhere near the duke that night was a woman, one of his tarts. No one saw you, that's for certain.'

'I should hope not. Mine is a trade that depends upon invisibility, and on uncertainty, too. If I had left a dagger sticking out of Duke Richard's back, or had his head smashed open with an axe, then it would be perfectly obvious that he had been murdered. Sometimes it's necessary to make one's point that way. But in this case you . . . your master can explain that the poor man passed away in the night, having taxed his body too greatly too soon after a serious illness. And who's to say otherwise?'

'The people,' the man grumped. 'They all say he was murdered.'

Jarl laughed aloud. 'So I did kill him after all! Come, come, sir. You cannot with one breath maintain that I did not carry out the killing, and with the next complain that the people think their duke was murdered.'

'So if you did kill him, how did you do it?'

'Perhaps I didn't do it. But I certainly caused it to happen, since it was I who concocted the potion that did for Duke Richard and I who devised the means of getting him to ingest it.'

'I need to know more than that.'

'No you don't' said Jarl, more firmly now. 'You just need to pay me what I am owed, or risk the consequences of crossing me.'

'All right, all right!' the soldier protested. 'You'll get your money. I just wish I knew what you were actually getting it for.'

'For putting a new duke on the throne in Rouen, and a much better duke, too.'

* * *

The new duke had no need of prostitutes. Johans of Perpignan knew that for certain the moment that he, along with a huge crowd of Norman folk, from mighty barons to the humblest peasants, saw Robert, Herleva and their baby son William arrive at the ducal palace. It was plain from the way the duke and his woman looked at one another that the fires of lust as well as love were still burning very brightly between them.

We might get a visit from him when the second baby comes along, Johans thought, then changed his mind. No, not from that lad, he'll never have to pay for it. Wouldn't want to, either. Not his style. Mind you, that tanner's daughter would fetch a pretty penny if she ever came to work for me.

But neither she nor anyone else would be working for Johans in Rouen. For more than a week he had spent half his time assuring everyone he met that the mysterious woman seen leaving Duke Richard's room on the night of his death had not been one of his stable. Luckily there were plenty of witnesses ready to say that he and Galiana had returned early, having been turned away at the gate of the palace and never entered the building. So no direct suspicion could fall on him.

But that had not eased his nerves. He had made discreet enquiries among some of his ecclesiastical customers and discovered that not a single soul from the priory of Saint-Gervais, let alone Prior Hugo himself, had attended Duke Richard on the night of his death. Nor had anyone ever heard of a novice monk called Mark of Avranches. The conclusion was obvious. There had been a conspiracy to murder Duke Richard, and the fake monk and prostitute were both part of it.

Anyone willing to go to such lengths to achieve their ends would have no qualms about silencing a potentially embarrassing brothel-keeper. So Johans of Perpignan sold his premises in Rouen, loaded all his possessions, including his women, on to a

225

line of ox-drawn carts and left the city. Within a matter of weeks he had reopened his business in Bruges, the capital of Flanders. The weather there was, if such a thing were possible, even more miserable than in Normandy, but the merchants were many and rich and the traders who came to the city's great markets and wool fairs had bulging purses. It was not long before Johans was prospering more mightily than ever. And little Galiana had lost her virginity on more than twenty occasions.

Johans was not the only one heading north. 'What do you plan to do with Adela?' Gunnor asked the archbishop a couple of weeks after Richard's funeral. 'She's too young to be a widow. She has no children to occupy her. And she's no use to herself or anyone else wasting her life away in Rouen.'

'Well, we could just pass her on to Robert,' the archbishop said. 'But I'm not sure the French want her having anything more to do with our family. So I thought I'd send her back to Flanders. She was always intended for young Baldwin, after all.'

'Will they have her back?'

'I don't see why not. She's still a virgin, after all.'

'Well, one good thing came of Richard refusing to go anywhere near her, then.'

'Quite so. And she's still the daughter of the King of France, too. She's a splendid match, and it's not as if Baldwin's married anyone else in the meantime.'

'Nor has his father the count,' Gunnor observed. 'He's been alone ever since poor Ogive died. Such a charming woman . . .' She stopped and looked at her son. 'Why have you got that great smirk on your face?'

'Because, Mother dearest, you seem to have read my mind. The Count of Flanders is, as you say, in need of a new wife. And we have a daughter of our house, Eleanor, for whom I was

226

ordered to find a husband. So our two spare females can be given to Flanders' two single men, and everyone's problems are solved.'

'Well that's all worked out very nicely, then.'

'I thought so too. Now all I have to do is find a suitable bride for Robert.'

'Don't!' said Gunnor, gripping her son's arm with a strength that conveyed the intensity of her feelings. 'He's got a woman he loves. She's given him a son. For God's sake don't start meddling in something that's actually working. There are plenty more urgent problems to be dealt with.'

'I'll have to find him a proper bride eventually,' the archbishop insisted. 'He's the Duke of Normandy. He can't spend his life with a commoner.'

'Your father did.' Gunnor glared at her son. 'When I look at Robert and Herleva, I see Richard and me. I think of all we achieved together. Leave them be and they will achieve just as much.'

'I disagree. That tanner's girl is no match for you, and Robert is half the man my father was. He will need a noble bride to complete him.'

'Over my dead body.'

The archbishop sighed. 'Come now, Mother,' he said, in the way adult sons condescended to their aged parents, 'let's not even think about that.'

It was left to Robert to say a formal farewell to Adela before she and his sister Eleanor departed for Flanders. 'I wish you and Lord Baldwin great happiness, Your Highness,' he said. 'I can only apologise for the mistreatment you suffered at my late brother's hands. I don't know what demons led him astray, but God has been merciful and found you another husband – the one, perhaps, you were always meant to marry. I am sure that in

227

years to come, your family and mine will have reason to meet. We will be neighbours, after all. And in the meantime, I hope that you will not think ill of the rest of us Normans.'

'I don't think ill of the Norman whose poison freed me from the marriage,' Adela replied, looking directly at Robert.

'It was not poison that killed my poor brother, Your Highness. He died from the illness he acquired while besieging me. To that extent, I was responsible for his death. And believe me, I take no pleasure in it.'

Yet for all Robert's denials, Adela was not the only one to presume that he was instrumental in Robert's murder. Rat the palace scullion had been telling anyone who would listen about the mysterious woman he had seen making her way to the duke's bedchamber. 'What if she was a witch, or a demon in human form?' he asked the other servants who had gathered to hear his tale. 'What if she killed Richard with an evil spell, or maybe poisoned him?' he speculated.

A heated debate soon began, to be echoed in every tavern, workplace and home in Normandy. 'Why did the witch kill the duke?' someone asked. 'What was in it for her?'

'Maybe she was sent by the King of France,' another voice suggested. 'He can't have been happy about the way Duke Richard was treating his precious daughter.'

'Nah,' another replied. 'The girl's not his business no more – not once she's married. Anyway, the king's too busy fighting his sons to worry about his girl.'

There followed a catechism of murderous reasoning.

'So who *did* want Richard dead?'

'Someone who stood to gain from it.'

'Yeah, but who could afford to get a witch to do it?'

'Someone rich and powerful, obviously.'

'Well then, who's rich and powerful and stood to gain from Richard being dead?'

It did not take long for an answer to be found: the man who would have the dukedom once Richard was gone – his brother Robert.

And of course that stood to reason. Everyone knew that Richard and Robert hated one another, and always had done. Richard had gone to war against Robert. He'd taken Robert's woman hostage and threatened to kill her, even though she was pregnant.

Plenty of people, men and women, thought that Robert was perfectly entitled to take his revenge for that. 'I'd want my man to do that for me,' one of the cooks said, to nods and murmurs of approval. Others, though, took a different line. They insisted that it was wrong to kill, even worse to kill a duke, and more evil still to kill one's own flesh and blood. To them their new duke was nothing more than a murderer.

And they called him Robert the Devil.

Book Three:

God and the Concubine

1028–1030

1

Rouen, Normandy

There were in those days two types of bishop in Normandy. The first were lifelong clergymen who had, after many years of particular devotion, holiness or political chicanery, ascended to episcopal rank. The second were the junior sons of great aristocratic clans whose fathers installed them in bishoprics they controlled. The archbishop was a perfect case of the latter group: he owed his position entirely to the fact that he was Duke Richard the Fearless's second son. Ivo of Bellême, Bishop of Sées, however, was a combination of both categories. He was the fourth son of the Count of Bellême and his father had given him his bishopric when he was little more than twenty. It was a sign of his disapproval. 'The boy takes after his damn mother,' the count would say, meaning that he was feeble, lily-livered and insufficiently violent. A more charitable view might have been that Ivo of Bellême was a genuinely devout, modest and well-meaning man who was, as it turned out, perfectly suited to his job.

He was also possessed of a conscience, which was what brought him to Rouen some eighteen months or so after the start of Robert's reign as Duke of Normandy, ostensibly to seek advice from his superior, the archbishop.

'It is very good of you to see me, Holy Father,' Ivo said as he settled himself into a chair in the archbishop's study.

'Not at all, my son,' the archbishop replied. 'I know how hard it can be in the early years of one's ministry, having to

233

shoulder so much responsibility when one has so little experience. What can I do for you?'

'Well, I have come by certain information, intelligence of someone's plans. On the one hand, I feel that it would be wrong for me to do nothing, since the plans in question involve actions that might harm His Grace the duke. On the other hand, I do not wish to betray the source of my information.'

'I see . . .' murmured the archbishop, who had been expecting to hear a self-pitying tale of insubordinate priests and resentful abbots making life difficult for a young, aristocratic bishop. This, he suspected, was going to be altogether more interesting. 'Tell me,' he asked, 'did you come by this information in confession?'

'No, it is not covered by any confessional privilege.'

'And you did not seek to unburden yourself in a confession of your own?'

Ivo looked directly at the archbishop. 'No, I felt it better to discuss it with you face to face. It seemed to me that we could both have – how can I put it? – a less restricted dialogue that way.'

'Quite so,' the archbishop replied, increasingly impressed by the young man's subtlety. Whatever information he possessed, he wanted it to be known. But he didn't want to be the one who was seen to be spreading it. Now it was time to get to the heart of the matter. 'So what is the matter that troubles you so?'

'My father wants to depose Duke Robert. Whenever I am in Alençon, I hear him ranting and raging, cursing His Grace for depriving him of the castle of Falaise, claiming that . . .' The young bishop paused for a moment. 'I apologise, Holy Father, for I understand how painful this must be for you, but my father claims that His Grace murdered his own brother, or at any rate had him killed.'

'There are some – and now *I* must apologise, for this may

234

offend you – who believe that Duke Richard's death was arranged by your father, as an act of revenge for the late duke reneging, as he saw it, on the promise of giving him Falaise. From what you say, however, the blame for that, at least, does not lie in Bellême.'

'I do not believe so. My father is a furious, intemperate, even vicious man, but his rages are never fabricated, or insincere. His anger towards Duke Robert is entirely genuine.'

'But is it only anger? Of course, it is a very serious matter for one of the duke's vassals to stir up insurrection. But even so, a man may say things in his own home that he would not repeat anywhere else, or act upon in any way.'

'No, Holy Father, these are not idle words. My father spends a great deal of time huddled away with my brothers and other fighting men who are loyal to the House of Bellême. I am not privy to their deliberations, but I'm quite certain that they are plotting a rebellion.'

'And you come to me out of loyalty to the duke.'

'Yes, Holy Father.'

'But you worry that you are being disloyal to your family, which is why you do not know what to do . . .'

'That's one of my worries, yes. But it's not the only one. For all his faults, I love my father. I owe everything to him. And I love my brothers too. I worry what might happen should they attempt to take on Duke Robert. He was able to defend Falaise with a handful of men against a much larger force. Now that he is duke, he has all the might of Normandy at his command. If my family defy him, I fear for their survival.'

'Your concern does you great credit, Bishop Ivo,' the arch-bishop said, 'as does your reading of the military aspects of the problem. But I sense that they do not provide a full explanation. Perhaps I am wrong. Perhaps I am being unfair, but for all your undoubted good motives in coming to see me, I sense that there may be a darker force at work as well. To commit what some might see as an act of betrayal suggests a degree of hostility, perhaps of revenge. Tell me, my son, is there anything you wish to confess?'

Bishop Ivo's head slumped, but the archbishop could see his brow furrowing and his mouth pursing and twisting as if he were wrestling with something deep within him. Finally the young cleric fell forward from his chair on to his knees and clasped his hands together. 'Bless me, Holy Father, for I have sinned. I wished harm upon my own father, the Count of Bellême, in vengeance for the harm he has done my dear mother. He beats her. Her abuses her and casts her down. He treats her worse than the lowliest kitchen maid. I confess, I was so moved to anger when I heard what he had done that I vowed to hunt him down and hurt him as he hurts the wife he has sworn to love and honour. She herself begged me not to, knowing that my other brothers would side with him and that I was bound to be defeated. I have prayed again and again to the Lord to smite down my father for the wrong he has done. But still he lives, and sins without the slightest remorse. And I must have some way to make him pay.'

'It is not for us to determine what punishment a man should suffer for his crimes. That is for the lawmakers here on earth, and Almighty God in the world to come. You are guilty of anger against your father, and of pride in assuming the right to stand in judgement against him. As an act of penance you will spend a day and a night, during which time you will neither eat nor drink, kneeling in prayer before the altar of your cathedral in Sées, meditating on your failings and begging God for his forgiveness. Your sins, however, are as nothing to your father's. And while your anguish and penitence are plain to see, his lack of them only adds to his transgressions.

'For now, however, we must concentrate on the matter at

hand and find some way of nipping this rebellion in the bud, before it has a chance to wreak havoc on both sides. As men of the Church, we must strive always for peace and reconciliation. I will give some thought as to how this may be accomplished. But for the moment, let us ask our Father in heaven to guide us towards the path of righteousness.'

The archbishop now knelt as well and led them both in prayer. When they rose again and the archbishop was bidding Ivo farewell, he made a point of telling the younger man, 'You did well to come to me, my son, and I will not forget it.' And though Ivo did his best to hide it, the glint in his eye told the archbishop that for all his conscience and good intentions, he was no more deaf than any other man to the siren's call of ambition.

Robert was not surprised to hear the archbishop's news. Bellême had always made it plain that he regarded the struggle for Falaise Castle as unfinished business. And he was by no means the first man in Normandy to test Robert's strength and resolve, or to take advantage of his youth and inexperience. Barons waged small wars against their neighbours, fighting for territory and erecting castles from which they could dominate the surrounding countryside and bully its inhabitants. Others stole land and property from the Church, driving monks from their monasteries and nuns from their convents. And those who felt they had claims to rule the duchy themselves also flexed their muscles, not necessarily with the intention of seizing power – or not immediately, at any rate – but to size up the degree of resistance they might expect if ever they marched against Robert in earnest.

The young duke had been obliged to learn fast. First he appointed Osbern Herfastsson as his steward and adviser, choosing him for his experience, his honesty and his standing within the family. Osbern was closely enough related to feel a sense of kinship, yet not so close as to have any thought of seizing the throne for himself. Next Robert took personal command of the Norman Militia, a brotherhood of professional soldiers, noble knights and civilian volunteers sworn to defend the duchy and its duke. These he wielded as an ever more effective weapon against his enemies, so that little by little he imposed order upon his lands.

But war could not be waged without the money raised in peace. So Robert made it his business to learn about the administration of the duchy. Normandy's position astride the mouth of the Seine meant that any seaborne merchant who wanted to take his goods to Paris and the French hinterland first had to pay duties at Robert's ports. There were tolls and duties levied on traders who travelled the duchy's roads. And the huge, fertile estates first won by Rollo the Strider and expanded by his successors produced revenues that poured into the ducal coffers in Rouen.

Robert was a very rich man and he could afford to be generous. It was the custom at the time for gifts to be given on a person's name day: the feast of the saint with whom they shared a name. People had long travelled from across the duchy to Rouen on the duke's name day, knowing that anyone, no matter how lowly, would be allowed into the great hall of the ducal palace to offer their gift in person to their lord. Merchants who sought business from the palace and nobles currying favour competed to see who could produce the most lavish, extravagant presents: bolts of silk from Damascus; furs from the frozen lands of the north; jewelled swords, or fine stallions.

St Robert's Day was 30 April, when the final frosts of winter were giving way to the warmth of spring and the orchards of Normandy were white with apple blossom. On Robert's first name day, a blacksmith was among the earliest arrivals. He knelt and held out two knives that he had forged. Robert was touched. It was obvious from his shabby clothes that the smith was not a wealthy man, and the dried mud on his boots and hose showed that he had made his way on foot. Yet here he was, offering up the products of his own labour, time and materials he could ill afford to waste, expecting nothing in return.

'What is your name?' Robert asked.

'Jean of Beauvais, Your Grace,' the smith replied.

'Beauvais? That's a fair walk from here.'

'Two days and nights, Your Grace.'

'Then I thank you, Jean of Beauvais. These are fine knives and I'm honoured that you've given them to me. But a man should not be expected to work without a fair reward.' Robert summoned one of the palace chamberlains and ordered him to give the blacksmith one hundred silver pennies, a sum far in excess of what the knives were worth – more, indeed, than the smith could expect to earn from years of toil.

Jean was overjoyed as he stepped away from the duke and joined the other spectators who had gathered to watch the ceremony. The next man to come before Robert was a nobleman leading two magnificent horses, mighty enough to pull any plough or carry the heaviest knight in battle. Robert took care to be gracious in his thanks to the nobleman, but then added, 'Sadly my stables are already full. I think these fine creatures would do better service if they went to one who has more need of them than I. Jean of Beauvais! Come here!'

The smith emerged from the crowd and walked nervously towards the ducal throne, wondering why he had been singled out. He feared that the duke might have had a change of heart and be about to ask for his money back. Instead, Robert said, 'You are not a rich man, yet you came here to give me knives that you might have sold to someone else. So now let me give something to you. Please accept these two horses, as a sign of my gratitude.'

The smith could not believe what he had just heard. At first he thought the duke was making fun of him, so he laughed, as if going along with the joke. When no one else joined in the laughter, he feared that he had made a grievous mistake and fell to his knees, his hands clasped together, imploring the duke to forgive him. But Robert said, 'There's nothing to forgive. I meant what I said. The horses are yours.'

The smith took hold of the horses' bridles and, still not quite trusting in his good fortune and fearful that the duke might yet change his mind, led them as fast as he could out of the hall.

Herleva had been watching from a gallery that ran along one side of the hall. That night, lying in bed with Robert's arms around her, she said, 'I love you so much for what you did today. You've never been poor. You can't imagine what the money and the horses will mean to that smith and his family. They won't go hungry. They'll have a roof over their heads. Their whole lives will be better because of you.'

Robert kissed her head. 'It wasn't any great kindness on my part. Jean of Beauvais went to much more trouble making those knives and bringing them here than I did giving him money I can easily afford, and handing over some horses that weren't even mine to begin with. And I was doing it as much for my good as his.'

'How do you mean?'

'Well, at least a hundred people were there this morning and saw what happened. So what do you think people were talking about in all the taverns this evening? What will Jean be telling everyone when he gets back to Beauvais? If I ever call on him to fight for me, I know he'll answer my call, and bring his brothers, his sons and his friends along with him. If I want people to give their loyalty and even their lives to me, I have to give them something in return. It's simple common sense.'

Robert was right. The story of his generosity to the blacksmith

240

from Beauvais was talked about, sung about and then written about by chroniclers. And so while those who hated him still called him Robert the Devil, his followers dubbed him Robert the Magnificent.

Herleva's family, too, found their lives transformed by association with the duke. Fulbert was appointed steward of Falaise Castle. Meanwhile Doda, who could still not quite believe that a grandson of hers would one day be Duke of Normandy, ensured that her two sons, Osbern and Walter, were trained in the arts of riding, hunting and swordsmanship. Soon their status had been elevated to the point that noblemen's wives began to see two young men who had spent most of their lives in a humble cottage beside a filthy tannery as potential husbands for their unmarried daughters. For Fulbert and Doda of Falaise, there were no words glowing enough to express their gratitude for what Duke Robert had given them.

But their rise had come at the House of Bellême's expense. And Robert had long since learned that the most risky thing a man in his position could do was to do nothing at all. There was nothing to be gained by waiting until Bellême was on the march. The problem had to be dealt with. And the time to do that was now.

2

Alençon, the County of Bellême

When the Count of Bellême was shaken out of his drunken stupor, three powerful sensations struck him in quick succession. The first was that he felt as though someone were smashing a battering ram against the inside of his skull. The second was that his steward was standing over him shouting something incomprehensible about the duke. And the third was that the pounding that was sending such vicious bolts of pain through his head was coming from outside, too.

He pulled himself up into a sitting position, adding nausea to his troubles as he did so, and looked at his steward through bleary, half-opened eyes. 'Wha . . . whassappening?' he mumbled.

'The Duke is here! Duke Robert! His men are smashing down the door to the keep!'

'What d'you mean, he's here? How? The walls . . . how'd he . . . ?'

'His men came over the walls in the darkness. They took the gatehouse. Now they're here!'

Now the message got through. Bellême staggered from his bed, giving the serving girl who'd been sharing it with him a hefty kick as he did so. He grabbed his sword and ran from the chamber, still barefoot and dressed only in the long undershirt that doubled as a nightgown, shouting, 'Warin! Fulk! Bertrand! Talvas! To arms, boys! To arms!'

When all four sons had gathered round him, Bellême had to

yell his orders over the sound of the ram against the splintering wood and the shouts and screams from the castle's terrified inhabitants. 'Warin, you're in charge. Get every man you can. Arm as many as possible with bows and arrows. Send half of them up to the battlements. Keep the rest to set up a defensive position here. Any man who comes through the door, I want him prickled like a hedgehog. I'm going up top to see what the hell's happening out there.'

He raced away up the narrow, twisting stone staircase to the castle roof, his hangover forgotten. But when he got there and peered through the open embrasure between two battlements, he was met with a sight that twisted his innards and tightened his throat anew. The open space between the castle walls and the foot of the motte on which the castle keep stood was filled with men, their shields and banners all bearing the golden leopards. More of them were massed on the path that led up the motte to the thick, iron-studded door against which the ram, protected beneath a canopy of ox hides stretched over a wooden frame, was being deployed. Boulders, flaming arrows and burning pitch would all wreak fatal damage on the frame and the men beneath it, just as they had done at Falaise. But the attack had caught Bellême entirely unawares and unprepared, so none of those weapons was available. A handful of Bellême men were sheltering behind the battlements, but if one of them ever dared leave their cover for long enough to aim and shoot an arrow down at the attackers, he was met by a volley from Robert's bowmen that sent him scurrying back for cover.

The battering suddenly stopped and the unexpected silence that followed was broken by the shouted words 'I see you, Bellême! Come out, and we will talk.'

The count was all too familiar with Duke Robert's voice, and the sound of it only added to his bile.

243

He stepped out into the open, where everyone could see him, and raised his own voice. 'The hell with you, Normandy! Show yourself, like a man, and then maybe we'll talk.'

The mass of men in the yard below seemed to split in two and Robert walked along the path between them like Moses through the parted seas. He stopped at the foot of the motte and looked up at Bellême. 'I'm offering you a choice,' he said, 'and a fairer one than you ever offered me. Defy me and I will finish the job I've just started. I will lead my men into your castle. I will overpower whatever defences you may set up against me and I will kill every last member of your family if I have to. Look around. See my army. You cannot win. But I am not a bloodthirsty man. I take no pleasure in death. So here is my offer: surrender. Come out of your castle with your saddle on your back. Crawl to my feet and swear your fealty to me, and I will spare you, your family and all your people. I will even let you keep the castle of Alençon, though it is a ducal property and you only hold it by my permission, as you did by my brother and father's permission before me. So there you have it. You surrender, or you and your family die. What is it to be?'

'Go fuck yourself, Normandy!' Bellême roared back. 'I'd rather die than surrender.'

He received no reply to his cry of defiance. But as he looked down at Duke Robert, he saw him give an order to one of his men, a short, solidly built lad he recognised from the Falaise campaign. The young man immediately ran up the motte and disappeared for a moment beneath the leather canopy. An instant later, the battering ram smashed against the castle door and Bellême had to duck behind a battlement as a storm of arrows arced up from the castle yard and split the air precisely where he had been standing a moment before.

'Shoot back, you gutless cowards!' Bellême screamed at his cowering men. He scuttled across the roof and back down the stairs to the great hall, where his sons and the men they had rounded up were waiting.

'I'm sorry, Father, but there wasn't time to send anyone up to you,' Warin said.

'No matter. They're better off down here. We need every man we can get to keep that arrogant pup at bay.' Bellême looked around at the motley band of castle guards, family retainers and servants, some in armour and bearing proper weapons, others just brandishing carving knives and pitchforks. 'We are the men of Bellême!' he cried. 'And we fight to the bitter end!'

The weak, ragged semblance of a cheer that greeted him was lost amidst the cacophonous pounding of the ram against the door. Then Bellême noticed the presence of his youngest son at his elbow. 'Talvas!' he exclaimed. 'Have you come to fight at your father's side?'

'No, I've come to tell you not to fight at all,' Talvas replied. Bellême's immediate reaction was to damn him for his cowardice. But Talvas had said the words so calmly, without any trace of fear or panic, that the charge of spinelessness suddenly seemed absurd.

'Of course I'm going to fight!' Bellême told him. 'Would you rather have me crawl out of here on my knees?'

'Yes,' said Talvas, looking him right in the eye. The first serious cracks were appearing in the door. The wood was bowing before the battering ram's assault. It would not be long before it gave way. But Talvas went on, apparently unperturbed, 'I would rather that you, and I, and even my idiot brothers all lived than throw away our lives on a battle we cannot possibly win. Fight on and the House of Bellême perishes today. Surrender and we will survive. And whatever insults you suffer now, you'll have the chance to make Robert of Normandy repay you twice over in the future.'

With a deafening crack, a great splintered hole appeared in the door, and for a second Bellême could actually see the ram's iron head lunging into the hall before it disappeared again.

Warin threw himself against the yielding wood, screaming at the men around him to do the same. Now the only thing keeping the Normans at bay was the straining limbs and shoulders of the desperate defenders.

'Surrender,' Talvas repeated.

Bellême knew that his son was right, and though it went against every fibre of his being, he found himself forming the words. 'I yield! Throw down your weapons, men. Step away from the door. I yield!'

Warin looked at his father with uncomprehending disgust, but he had always obeyed his commands and he took two paces back, just as he had been told. His men did the same. The door burst open. Robert's troops surged in. The siege of Alençon was over before it had even begun.

The Countess of Bellême was standing on the grassy bank of the motte with the servants when her husband emerged from the castle keep on all fours and made his slow, painful way like a cumbersome beast of burden down the path to the flat ground on which Robert of Normandy stood. Bellême's saddle, a bulky, heavy construction of wood and padded leather, had been fastened around his chest by the two girth straps, and the stirrups hung down and dragged in the dirt to either side of him. His four sons walked behind him, three heads downcast, with only Talvas looking around him with cool, unflustered deliberation. Bellême's humiliation was so absolute that it seemed to shock the assembled forces on both sides into something close to silence, with only the occasional catcall or foul-mouthed insult from the victors and a feeble cheer or two from the castle's vanquished defenders.

246

As for the countess, she could barely breathe for all the emotions surging within her. Despite everything that had happened and all the mistreatment he had heaped upon her, she felt profoundly distressed to see her husband so degraded. She had grovelled on her knees before him often enough – so often, in fact, that she had come to take herself at his estimation and even believed that she deserved whatever punishment he meted out to her – yet still it pained her to see a man she had once loved and looked up to brought so low. At the same time, however, another part of her was exultant, thrilled by Bellême's slow, ungainly progress before so many eyes. He finally halted at Robert's feet and the countess heard the young duke ask, 'Do you swear to give me your absolute fealty as my loyal vassal?'

The count's reply was inaudible.

'Speak up, so that all can hear, and please refer to me as "Your Grace",' the duke insisted. 'So, do you swear to be my loyal vassal?'

The countess could see the effort it took for Bellême to raise his head and call out for all to hear: 'Yes, Your Grace, I swear it.'

'Do you swear to obey me?'

'Yes, Your Grace, I swear.'

'Do you swear never to rise in rebellion against me?'

'Yes, Your Grace, I swear.'

The countess heard no trace of the usual arrogance, assurance or scathing contempt in her husband's voice. He sounded beaten and pathetic. And yet even as Robert said, 'Very well, then I accept your vows,' there was still worse to come.

The duke pointed at the four sons of Bellême. 'Step forward and undo this saddle,' he commanded. They gathered round their father, who had to remain motionless on his hands and knees while the boys fiddled with the buckles of the straps around his chest, got in one another's way and finally lifted the saddle off his back. Only then could he get to his feet and stand before the duke, back bent, shoulders hunched and wincing from a mass of aching joints and muscles.

'You have kept your word; I will keep mine,' Robert said. 'Take your sons, your men and your household back into your castle. You may keep your title and all your lands. Let the whole world see that I will act at once to stamp out any hint of rebellion or disloyalty, but I will act with mercy to those who repent their misdeeds.'

The countess knew full well that Bellême had not repented. He would spend the rest of his life trying to wreak his revenge on the man who had bested him so publicly. And in the meantime, he would appease the fury stoked within him by his own degradation by subjecting her to ever more terrible debasement. But she could stand that, a thousand times over, now that she had seen what a real man could do to the craven bully to whom she had to be a wife.

Duke Robert went back to Rouen, his palace and his family. In many people's eyes Herleva was nothing more than his concubine, barely more respectable than a common whore, and William a mere bastard. But Robert treated them as his true wife and son. The Viking peoples from whom he was descended had been pagans and as such had no equivalent to the Christian concept of marriage. A man simply took a woman, often by seizing her as booty in a raid. These unmarried partnerships were known as *more danico*, or 'the Danish way', and as Robert well knew, virtually all his predecessors from Rollo onwards had had relationships of this kind that produced children, including sons who would themselves become dukes.

So far as Robert was concerned, he was simply following his forefathers' traditions. But these were different times and there were some in Normandy who believed the old ways could no longer be tolerated. Soon Robert discovered that while he could defeat his enemies on earth easily enough, it was quite another matter to take on his master in heaven.

3

Fécamp, Normandy

A chilly wind had set in from the sea, carrying with it a fine yet persistent drizzle that swirled around the graveyard at Fécamp Abbey as they laid Lady Gunnor to rest beside her husband and oldest son. The prayers of the abbot and the chants of the choir were blown away on the breeze and the cold black earth piled beside the grave, though newly dug, was already hardened by frost.

Herleva shivered and pulled her cloak even more tightly about her as the last amens were said. Robert put an arm around her shoulder and held her close. 'Let's go inside,' he said. 'There's a roaring fire and plenty of hot spiced wine to warm us all up.'

'Wine! Wine!' chirruped William excitedly, tugging at his mother's spare hand.

Robert smiled affectionately at his son. The boy was only three, but already no one could doubt that he was a true product of the House of Normandy: tall for his age, and thickset, with a fiercely determined, competitive nature and a temper as hot as his flame-red hair. When he was happy, William could light up the darkest palace chamber with his smile. But if ever he should be denied what he wanted, his scowl could put any gargoyle to shame.

'No wine for you,' said Robert sternly, causing William to fix him with a furious pouting stare, which disappeared in an instant as William noticed his father winking at him and knew that he was going to get what he wanted.

'I think I'll stay here for a few minutes,' Herleva said. 'Lady Gunnor was always so kind to me. I don't think I'd have been able to manage without her. I just want to pray for her soul and give thanks to God for bringing her to me.'

'Of course,' Robert said, giving her shoulder an affectionate squeeze. Herleva smiled at him. She knew that he was a fierce warrior, well capable of killing another human being, but all she could see in his eyes now was the affection and kindness of a man looking at the woman he loved. More than four years had passed since they had first set eyes on one another, but still their passion was as intense as ever and the bond between them grew deeper with every day that passed.

'Thank you,' she whispered and reached up on tiptoe to kiss him on the cheek.

'Don't worry, my lady, I'll take care of Master William,' said Judith, who was now employed more as a nanny than a hand-maiden. She took the boy's hand, then looked back at Herleva, rolling her eyes, as her young charge solemnly informed her, 'I have wine now.'

'Oh will you now?' replied Judith, leading him away.

Herleva stood alone by the graveside, remembering her conversations with the dowager duchess. Though she had been far senior in rank as well as age, Gunnor had never been condescending towards Herleva. Instead she had paid her the great compliment of unfailing honesty, never stinting in compliments when she deserved them, nor sparing her criticism or tough advice when that might be called for. As a result, Herleva had always trusted her and counted on her calm, clear-sighted wisdom to help her cope with her dizzying ascent from being the daughter of a humble tanner to the mistress of one duke and, quite possibly, the mother of another.

She was still lost in her thoughts when she heard a voice say,

'Excuse us, milady, but we got to fill it all in before it gets dark.'

She looked up to see two gravediggers, carrying shovels, regarding her with the deference of mere peasants towards a high-born lady. She looked at them in their filthy tunics and rough wool cloaks. Her own cloak was lined with fur, and the dress beneath was made from the finest cloth that Flanders had to offer. Yet it was not so long since she had been almost as poor as these two men.

'By all means, get on with your work,' she said, and they bobbed their heads and thanked her for her kindness.

Herleva walked towards the abbot's house, where the funeral guests were being given their refreshments in the main hall. She stepped into an atmosphere heavy with the damp, doggy smells of drying clothes and the smoke from a blazing fire and a myriad candles and torches. But it was gloriously warm and bright and the first sips of spiced wine soon removed any chill from her body. She looked around for Robert, but before she could find him amidst the press of bodies, she heard his furious voice cutting through the hubbub.

'That's enough, Uncle! Let me remind you that I am the Duke of Normandy. I am master in this land, and my personal affairs are no business of yours!'

A sudden quiet descended, as every other voice in the hall fell silent. Every voice bar one, for now the archbishop, his voice tight with barely suppressed rage, replied, 'And let me remind you that I serve no master but the Lord God Almighty, and if you will not answer to me, rest assured a day will come when you will most assuredly answer to Him.'

There was a gasp, a collective intake of breath as the mourners took in this unmistakable threat of divine retribution, soon followed by an even greater hum of chatter as everyone tried to make sense of what had just transpired. Herleva had followed the sound of the voices, and now she saw Robert making his way through the crowd towards her. She quailed as he stared at her with eyes like burning coals beneath his lowering brows. She'd never seen him this angry, not even on that terrible afternoon outside the walls of Falaise Castle. He finally reached her, and she waited for a moment, letting him cool down a fraction before she very gently placed a hand on his arm and screwed up the courage to look him in the eye. 'What is it, my darling?' she asked.

Robert took a deep breath and relaxed just a fraction. 'My dear uncle Robert wants me to get married. He says I have to, now that I'm duke.'

Herleva frowned. Was that really such a terrible idea? Just a short while earlier Robert had been so loving towards her. Why was he rejecting her now?

She tried to make light of his words. 'Well I don't mind if he wants me to be a duchess,' she said, with a brittle smile.

Robert's expression softened. He reached out to stroke her cheek. 'Oh, my love, to me you already are my duchess and I want no other. But Uncle Robert refuses to bless any union between us. He says I have to think of my position and the future of our family. You . . . you aren't a good match for a duke of Normandy. I must take another great noble's daughter, or even a princess for my wife.'

Herleva felt sick. She could hardly breathe. 'But he can't say that!' she pleaded, gasping for air. 'And you . . . please tell me you wouldn't do that. I couldn't bear it.'

Robert grabbed both her arms to support her. 'Listen to me,' he commanded. Herleva raised her head. Robert looked her in the eye, willing her to believe him as he said, 'You won't lose me. I told him I loved you, and I'm going to stay with you.'

'Oh, thank God . . .' gasped Herleva, collapsing against his chest. 'I love you so much.'

'And I love you too . . . more than anything,' Robert replied.

'That's what I told my uncle. For pity's sake, he actually married Richard and Adela. He must have known, just looking at them, that they were going to be miserably unhappy. What possible good would it do making me be miserable too?'

He suddenly realised that every person in the room had their eyes fixed upon him and Herleva. He looked around and in an icy voice said, 'Leave at once, all of you. I would have some privacy.'

The mourners milled about, unwilling to step back out into the cold, but uncertain where else to go. Then the voice of the abbot rang out, 'If everyone would just follow me . . .' and they all filed out, trailing him into some other part of the building.

'As you can see,' said Robert as the last of them left the hall, 'I am the duke and what I say goes.'

Herleva managed a little laugh.

'That's better,' Robert said, wiping a tear from her face with a linen kerchief.

'I don't understand how your uncle can talk about dynastic marriages,' she said. 'Not today of all days. Lady Gunnor was his father's concubine. They were together because they loved one another, and because his father was Duke of Normandy and . . .' she smiled at Robert with a glimmer of flirtation in his eyes, 'whatever he said went too.'

'Precisely!' grinned Robert, pleased to see Herleva back to her usual self. 'That's exactly what I told him.'

'So what did he say?'

'That times were changing. We weren't just a bunch of Vikings any more. We had to act like respectable nobles.'

Herleva tilted her head and gave him a coy, not so innocent look. 'And are you respectable, Your Grace?'

'Not with you, my lady,' said Robert, fixing her with a look of undiluted lust that made Herleva melt like butter in a red-hot skillet. She longed for him to take her in his arms and kiss her hard. Instead he carried on as though nothing had happened. 'Anyway, my uncle said he was drawing up a list of suitable brides.'

'I'll kill them if they ever set foot in Normandy!' snapped Herleva, with all the intensity of her frustrated passion.

Richard laughed. 'I can't imagine any delicate little princess being a match for you.'

'So . . . what are you going to do about it?' Herleva asked.

Robert was about to reply when a door at the far end of the hall slammed open and William raced into the room, hotly pursued by Judith.

'Mama! Papa!' he cried. Then he caught sight of all the goblets and flagons left behind by the departing mourners, and a huge smile split his rosy cheeks as he added a final word: 'Wine!'

4

For a fortnight or more, the arguments raged back and forth, with Robert refusing to set Herleva aside and the archbishop insisting, 'You're a duke now, and your duchy matters more than your cock. Forget that woman and concentrate on your duty – to God, to Normandy and to our family.'

In the end, after yet another furious row that achieved no more than any of the others that had gone before it, the older man threw up his hands in frustration. 'The hell with this, I'm going to Evreux. I'll spend a while hunting, playing with my children and bringing pleasure to my wife. And when I return, we'll finish this debate once and for all, or you will suffer the consequences.'

'Are you threatening me, Uncle?'

The archbishop paused, working his jaw as if physically biting back the first, furious words that came to mind. Eventually, still struggling to control his temper, he said, 'No . . . Your Grace. I am trying to explain the realities of the situation to one who seems disinclined to accept them. In the end, you will do as I say, not because you want to, but because you will see that there is no alternative course of action. Now, if you will excuse me, it will soon be time for the midday service, over which I must preside before I leave for Evreux. I take my duties seriously, even if you do not.'

Robert watched his uncle stalk away. The archbishop must have been more than fifty years old, and his hair had all but changed from gold to silver, yet he still stood tall and strong, his massive shoulders had not yet begun to stoop and there was the energy of a much younger man in his walk. He was not a man that anyone would choose to fight, unless . . .

Robert's eyes widened. His face broke into a grin. That was it! A fight was precisely what he would pick with his uncle. But not on the old man's terms, for no one could match him as a politician, diplomat or strategist. He thought like a chess player, knowing all his moves in advance, without giving any hint of them to his opponent. Yet for all the archbishop's gifts, the one thing he had never been was a soldier. His father, Duke Richard, had spotted very early that his second son was exceptionally intelligent, and so had raised and trained him for the Church, keeping him at his books while his brothers were off with their swords and staffs. There was no need to teach a man of God to defend himself with weapons and armour, for no man who valued his immortal soul would dare harm, let alone kill a priest.

That assumption, Robert realised, was the archbishop's greatest weakness.

After lunch, he asked his steward Osbern Herfastsson and Herluin to join him for a walk in the palace gardens. 'There's a matter I wish to discuss.'

'Couldn't we talk indoors, in front of a blazing fire?' Osbern asked. 'Your Grace might be more comfortable. It's perishing cold outside.'

Robert laughed. 'Are you going soft in your old age, cousin? Find a cloak and some good stout boots and you'll be warm enough.' He lowered his voice. 'What I have to say cannot be overheard by anyone.'

Osbern nodded. 'Outdoors it is, then.'

Robert had to admit that this really was not a day for a slow, contemplative stroll round a garden. A light dusting of snow had fallen, making the stone paths cold and slippery beneath their feet, and the feeble afternoon sun could only occasionally be seen behind a thick grey veil of cloud. So he got straight to the point. 'I intend to march on Evreux, capture the town and the castle and force my uncle to give way – at the point of my sword, if I have to. He's always telling me about the consequences of defying him. Well, it's time for him to discover what happens when *he* defies a duke.'

'But you can't!' Herluin gasped. 'You can't make war on an archbishop. It's blasphemy, sacrilege . . . It's just wrong.'

'He's right, Your Grace,' said Osbern, more calmly. 'Your enemies already spread enough lies about you. It wouldn't be wise to give substance to their slanders.'

'You mean the people who say I killed Richard, the ones who call me Robert the Devil? Well let me assure you, Osbern, that I had no part whatever in my brother's death, unless you hold me responsible for the fever that struck him while he was besieging my castle. And I'm no devil, either. I wouldn't dream of attacking an archbishop.'

'But you said . . .' Herluin began.

'I said I want to march on Evreux. And there's a very particular reason why I want to confront my uncle there: because Evreux is the one place in the world where he doesn't consider himself an archbishop. In Evreux he's a count, with a wife and family, which an archbishop who had sworn vows of chastity couldn't possibly have. So if he is to enjoy the pleasures of being the Count of Evreux, he'll have to put up with the same threat that any baron has to live with – the very real possibility that someone will come along and try to take it all away from him.'

'If you mean to harm the . . . the count, then I will have to leave your service,' Osbern said. 'He is my cousin. His late mother was my aunt. I'm not going to attack my own kith and kin.'

'I understand, Osbern,' Robert said, 'but I'm hoping that he won't be foolish enough to fight us. I don't want to hurt him, any more than I wanted to hurt Richard. I have no interest in killing other people; I just want what I want. There would never have been a siege if Richard had let me have Falaise in the first place. And there won't be any bloodshed in Evreux if my uncle accepts that I want Herleva and no one else.'

'What if he doesn't?'

'Then he will learn that no mere count can defy a duke's will and expect to get away with it.'

When the archbishop rode out of Rouen, he was not dressed in his gaudy clerical robes, but in normal clothes, and over them a thick woollen cloak whose wolf-skin collar covered the entire breadth of his shoulders and upper back. Only the golden ring with a centre of blood-red cornelian hidden beneath his leather gauntlets revealed his true status. A sword hung from the belt around his waist, for even if he lacked the skill to defeat a trained warrior, he was well able to swing a long, heavy blade with enough force to overcome lesser opposition.

Two trusted retainers rode alongside him. The man to his left, protecting his more vulnerable flank, was called Ranulf of Damville. His face was as craggy and tough as pine bark and the stubble on his chin as white as the snow beneath his horse's hooves. But he was fully clad in a coat of chain mail, with a steel helmet hanging from his saddle, and his eyes were always moving, checking his surroundings for any sign of trouble. For more years than he could remember, Ranulf had kept the archbishop safe on his travels around the duchy. Until recently he had shared this duty with an equally gnarled old campaigner, Thierry of Breuteuil. But Thierry had recently succumbed to a sudden illness, as even the toughest soldiers could do, and his place had been taken by a much younger man called Orbec, whom Ranulf watched almost as closely as he did the strangers

259

they met along the way, or the land through which they travelled. Orbec seemed a sound enough lad, but in Ranulf's opinion he still had a great deal to learn.

The road to Evreux ran due south from Rouen, but as they left the city, the three men took their bearings from the sun and bore right, towards the south-west. When dusk fell, they rode on for a while until they came to an inn, where they stopped for the night. Ranulf led the horses away to the stables with the easy certainty of a man who knew his surroundings well, while Orbec trailed in his wake. And when the archbishop walked into the hall where passing travellers ate, drank and, if needs be, slept, the innkeeper recognised him at once as a loyal customer, though he knew him as Robert of Fécamp.

The following evening, after a long, hard day's ride through worsening weather, they stopped at another inn, where they were greeted with equal familiarity. Late on the third afternoon they came to the village of Gacé. A few peasant houses were scattered on either side of the track, which had by now been reduced to a treacherous strip of mud and slush. One of the hovels had a sign outside that proclaimed it to be a tavern, but the archbishop and his two companions ignored it and rode on as flurries of snow whipped around them.

In the winter light there seemed to be no colours anywhere but white, grey, black and various murky tones of brown. Ahead of them, beyond the half-built beginnings of a defensive wall, a few more buildings were ranged around the base of a great circular mound on top of which stood a wooden castle keep.

The three riders stopped just short of the mound, dismounted and led their animals to a stable where two grooms were waiting to take care of them. The grooms greeted them with cheerful hellos and banter for the two soldiers and a more respectful 'Good afternoon, my lord' for the archbishop. Then another servant appeared to take the riders' baggage, though he seemed far too ancient and scrawny to be given such a task, and lead them up the mound to the keep. Its timbers were dark and sodden with all the rainwater and melted snow that had seeped into them over the winter. But the front door at least was hard enough to make a noise when the servant beat upon it with his fist, shouting, 'Oi! Let us in, we're freezing out here!'

The wizened, virtually toothless old man looked round at the archbishop, whose face was almost hidden behind the upturned collar of his cloak. 'Sorry, your lordship, don't mean to be rude. But round here you've got to shout just to get anyone's attention.'

The door was opened by an unkempt, slack-jawed minion, who looked at the new arrivals with dull eyes and gave a jerk of his head to indicate that they could all come in. He paid no attention to the archbishop or his two companions, preferring to hold the door open with one hand while the index finger of the other rummaged around in his right nostril in search of something to eat.

A smouldering fire was filling the dark, dank space that passed for a great hall with smoke, while failing to add either heat or light. Like figures emerging from a fog, a man and a woman came forward to greet the archbishop. He removed his riding gloves and they knelt to kiss the ring that he presented to each of them in turn. The couple were as unprepossessing as everything else in this dismal, godforsaken place. Both were well past their youthful prime, assuming that either had ever had one. He was unshaven and greasy-haired, with a large boil on his chin from which grew two long, wiry black hairs. She had the pinched features of a woman whose individual discontents had merged to create a single, unbroken air of disapproval and resentment.

'Good day, Godfrey, Lady Judith,' the archbishop said, without any great enthusiasm, as the two of them got back to their feet. 'Is the boy here to see me?'

261

Lady Judith darted her head from side to side, peering through the murk like a bad-tempered crow. 'Ralph!' she squawked. 'Come here! Now!'

A boy appeared, making his way round the side of the hall, running his left hand along the wall as he went as if afraid to let go completely and plunge into the centre of the room. He was small, skinny and quite startlingly ugly. Two watery, bulging eyes peered out beneath a shapeless mop of dull brown hair. His ears were big, his nose was long and his lips were stretched over protruding upper and lower teeth. He had very little chin at all.

The archbishop looked upon the boy as if examining an inexplicable mystery, a miracle in reverse. Ralph's mother had been a serving girl at the ducal palace in Rouen, back in the reign of the archbishop's brother Richard. She was a lovely young woman, with a body so beautifully formed and so full of life and energy that it had hardly seemed possible that she could have expired giving birth to a creature such as this.

'He doesn't get any less ugly,' said Lady Judith, spotting the look on the archbishop's face. 'The village children call him Donkey-Head.'

Ralph was close enough to hear every word. He flinched at the sound of his nickname and stopped dead in his tracks.

'Come closer,' the archbishop said. 'I won't bite.'

Ralph shuffled forward to within touching distance of the archbishop, then stopped and stood there, head bowed, his eyes fixed firmly upon the floor.

'Look at me, boy.'

The archbishop's voice was uncharacteristically gentle, his words sounding like an encouragement rather than an order. They produced the desired effect.

'Hello, Ralph,' the archbishop said.

'Hello, Father,' said the boy.

5

Evreux, Normandy

The archbishop spent but a single night at Gacé before he and his men set off for Evreux. Two days after their arrival there, Robert, Herluin, Osbern and around a hundred armed knights appeared outside the city walls. These were little more than a wooden palisade, and only a handful of guards were stationed at the main gatehouse. They greeted their duke's arrival without any sign of alarm, assuming that his visit was a friendly one. Before Robert had even demanded admission, the gates were opening and his expeditionary force was riding through them, en route to the castle where the archbishop and his family lived.

By now the archbishop had been told of his nephew's arrival. He was taken completely by surprise and for once in his life found himself unable to work out precisely what was going on. For Robert to arrive with such a strong force was a very clear sign of aggressive intent. But having already waged war against his own brother, he surely couldn't be mad enough to fight his uncle too. Yet that certainly seemed to be the case.

The archbishop ordered the gates of the castle to be barred, and when the first of Robert's knights ventured too close to the stone fortress, he found his horse rearing up as an arrow buried itself in the ground right between the steed's forelegs.

Robert sent Osbern forward under a flag of truce to negotiate on his behalf. The archbishop received him affectionately and offered wine and pastries. 'I dare say they'll be welcome,' he said, doing his best to muster up his usual imperturbable attitude. 'You must have been on the march for days.'

Osbern accepted the refreshments gratefully. 'His Grace the duke wishes you to know that he does not desire or intend any harm to come to you,' he began.

'Then why are he and a large number of armed men camped outside my walls?'

'He's simply making it plain that he's serious. He insists that his wishes must be respected, and he refuses to back down on that score. But he has no desire for anything beyond his right to choose his own wife.' Osbern leaned forward and spoke more informally. 'Listen, cousin, Robert may be young, but he knows his own mind. The way he sees it, there are certain things that matter to him more than any others. As long as he gets his own way in those things, he won't raise a finger against you or anyone else in anger. But if he doesn't get his way, then he'll fight and, as we both know, he'll win.'

'But he can't fight me. I'm his uncle. And what's more important, I'm an archbishop!'

'Everywhere else, perhaps, but not here,' said Osbern, reverting to his emissary role. 'His Grace the duke reminds you that you choose to set aside the rank of archbishop here, preferring to live as the Count of Evreux, a layman who has a wife and two strapping sons. As a count, you are the duke's vassal. And when a vassal refuses to obey his lord, it is the lord's duty, as well as his right, to discipline him.'

The archbishop smiled, then chuckled quietly to himself and finally burst out laughing. 'Well I'll be damned. That young sprig isn't quite as green as I'd imagined. Tell him from me that I'm impressed by his reasoning. But it doesn't alter my view. Look, Osbern, you must see this. It's taken us a hundred years, but we're finally being accepted by the court and king in Paris as a proper ruling dynasty rather than a bunch of jumped-up Norse vagabonds. If Robert makes this tanner's daughter his wife, I don't care how pretty or charming she is, we'll be a laughing stock. And before you say anything, yes, I know I'm a fine one to talk about common blood, or choosing one's own wife, come to that. But I'm not the duke. It's different for him.'

'You realise Robert doesn't give a damn what anyone in Paris or anywhere else thinks of him?'

'Of course he doesn't. He's a headstrong, arrogant, prideful boy. He has it in him to be a great duke, and he knows it. But it won't happen unless he accepts that there are certain rules that even we sons of Rollo have to obey if we want to prosper.' The archbishop sighed in frustration. 'For God's sake, Osbern, I'm not saying he can't fuck the girl. She just can't be his wife.'

If the archbishop expected that his man-to-man approach would elicit some sympathy, he was about to be disappointed. Osbern looked back at him, stony-faced. 'When I agreed to become Duke Robert's steward, I not only swore loyalty to him, but also to Lady Herleva . . .'

'Lady Herleva is it now?'

'. . . and she has given me no cause to regret my decision. So I'll thank you not to talk of her in that way.'

'I see. Well then, perhaps you will at least tell His Grace the duke that I would be very grateful if he'd consent to meet me here, in private, so that he can say his piece and I can say mine. I dare say neither of us will be swayed by the other's arguments. But I want to make one last attempt to settle this matter before one or other of us does something we both may later regret.'

Robert accepted his uncle's invitation. Once inside the castle, he made a point of visiting his aunt and her son Richard, the heir to Evreux. Then he made his way to the chamber where his uncle awaited him. Once again the archbishop provided food and drink, laid out on a table between his chair and the one reserved for his guest, though naturally it was of finer quality than Osbern had received.

Robert ate a perfectly roasted chicken leg, threw the bone on to the floor for the dogs to eat, washed the meat down with some freshly brewed ale and began. 'Osbern said you wanted to discuss our differences.'

'Indeed I do,' the archbishop replied. He sipped some wine as he gathered his thoughts. 'I think I should disabuse you of two misconceptions that appear to have taken root in your mind. The first is that you can persuade me to let you do something I consider fundamentally wrong. Let me assure you that you cannot.'

'I may not be able to persuade you. But you seem to forget, Uncle, that I am the Duke of Normandy and you are not. So I can damn well order you to approve my marriage to Herleva and conduct my wedding service, just like you conducted my brother's.'

'And that is your second mistake. Let me use your own logic to defeat you. As the Count of Evreux, yes, I am your vassal. But if I'm in church, conducting or even discussing a wedding, then I must be Archbishop of Rouen and thus bow to no man but His Holiness the Pope. You are young, Robert, and inexperienced. You have yet to discover the limits of your power. So let me warn you, as your uncle who loves you, do not set yourself against the Church. The Roman Empire could not defeat the power of Our Saviour Jesus Christ. Neither the Huns and Vandals, who destroyed Rome, nor our own Viking forefathers, who terrified Christendom for centuries, could overcome the power of the cross. We would not be Christians ourselves if that were not true. Kingdoms and empires rise and fall, but the Church survives them all.'

Robert hammered his hand on the table, punctuating every word as he said, 'I . . . will . . . not . . . back . . . down.'

The archbishop's face bore the look of a disappointed parent. 'Ah, Robert, I hoped you'd be a better duke than your brother. Have I really misread you so badly?'

'What you've misread is the depth of my love and the strength of my determination. I won't marry any woman but Herleva, and nothing can ever change that.'

'I fear you're wrong, Robert. And if I'm forced to show you just what the Church can do to you, the people you love and the land over which you rule, then that charming girl of yours and your fine young son may very well suffer more grievously than anyone else. For their sake, I beseech you: do what I say.'

Robert leapt to his feet, knocking over his chair and sending his tankard of ale crashing to the floor. 'How dare you threaten my woman and my son?' he raged. 'Get out! Leave Normandy and go into exile. From this moment on, you are no longer Count of Evreux. Your castle and your lands and their revenues are forfeit. I'll take them all!'

The archbishop remained motionless and impassive in his chair. His voice was calm as he said, 'Don't do this, Robert, or I swear you'll regret it.'

'Enough!' Unable to contain the energy burning inside him, Robert stalked away across the room, then turned and jabbed a finger at his uncle. 'I won't listen to any more of your empty threats. You must leave immediately, with a single horse for yourself and a mule for your baggage. I will send a dozen men to escort you as far as the border with France. Your family may remain here as my guests.'

'May I ask how long you expect me to remain in this exile?'

'Until you accept Herleva as my duchess.'

Now the archbishop stood up. 'I don't think that will be the reason I return to Normandy, Robert,' he said, walking across to his nephew. 'In fact, I am entirely confident of returning on my terms, and at a time of my choosing. In the meantime, if you wish to communicate with me, send envoys to Chartres. I shall stay there with Bishop Fulbert. He has a magnificent kitchen, so I shall comfort myself with the thought that even if I am forced to be away from the land and the people I love, at least I shall be very well fed.'

'Go . . . just go,' said Robert, with an angry flick of his hand, as if the archbishop were a particularly large, annoying wasp.

The archbishop did not move. 'You're making a terrible mistake, Robert. I have tried to stop you, but . . . ah well, it's always good to learn from one's experiences. And you are about to learn a very painful lesson from this one.'

Robert pointed towards the door. 'For God's sake, get out . . . now!'

6

Warin of Bellême emptied his tankard of ale and looked around the great hall at Alençon Castle. Beside him his father was picking at a joint of lamb. There had been a time when the count would have cut himself a great slab of meat, still pink and oozing blood, skewered it on his knife and held it up in front of his face so that he could tear it apart with his teeth, stuffing his mouth till it was almost too full to chew, while the juices ran down his chin. Now the old man had lost his appetite. Robert of Normandy had unmanned him twice over, first by forcing him to surrender on his knees, and a second time by letting him keep the castle. It would have been better for the family to wander the roads like a band of vagabond mercenaries, better even to die than to stay here knowing that their continued tenancy was only a result of the duke's generosity.

Did Robert expect them to feel grateful for his mercy? Warin wondered. Did he imagine that they would be singing his praises and telling all and sundry that he was really a very good man, once you got to know him? Well fuck that. The House of Bellême hated Robert more than ever, and the only thing on which they all agreed was the burning need to avenge their humiliation.

Warin ordered a serving girl to refill his tankard and then slapped her hard across the backside as she bent to pour the ale. He took no pleasure in the feel of her body beneath her dress, the squeal she emitted or the look of genuine pain – for he had struck her hard enough to sting – in her eyes. He did not even relish the fact that it was she who then apologised, for spilling some ale over his half-eaten trencher of bread, and enquired whether she had offended him, though they both knew that she had not. He just wanted someone else to feel as bad as he did, and she was the nearest candidate.

Warin emptied the tankard, and then another. The drink did nothing to cheer him. In fact it served only to add to his bitterness. He found himself spoiling for a fight. He needed the release that only violence could bring. And then he heard something that had long been absent from mealtimes at Alençon Castle: the sound of laughter. It infuriated him. How dare anyone mock the family's suffering? What right had they to be happy when the House of Bellême, which employed them, housed them and fed them, had been brought so low? Warin searched for the source of the offence and found it at a table directly opposite the one at which he sat. One of the castle soldiers, Gonthier, was doubled up, banging the wood in front of him with the flat of his hand, desperately trying to control his hilarity enough to be able to speak to the man next to him.

Gonthier was an honest, brave, utterly reliable man who'd served the House of Bellême with distinction for almost twenty years. But the sight of his good humour drove Warin over the edge from bilious irritation to blind rage. He climbed up on to the table in front of him, then clumsily made his way across it, stepping in plates of food and knocking over glasses and tankards as he went. The two retainers who had been sitting opposite him scrambled out of his way as Warin clambered down from the tabletop on to the bench on which they had been sitting and from there to the floor. He staggered past another table towards the one at which Gonthier was seated. The soldier saw Warin coming and grinned. 'Good day, my lord,' he called out. 'Have you come to hear our joke? It's a good one!'

A few of the men around him made a cursory attempt at a nervous chuckle. Warin ignored them. He kept on barging past the diners sitting on their benches and the servants attending to them until he reached Gonthier. His steps were lurching and unsteady, his breathing was laboured, his eyeballs were bulging and his face was flushed deep red, almost purple.

Gonthier was now looking at him with a puzzled expression, as if unable to believe that he could possibly be as enraged as he seemed with so little provocation.

'Joke?' Warin finally replied. 'I'll give you a fucking joke.'

He pulled out his sword, lifted it high into the air and then without a second's hesitation brought it down again, backhanded, slashing at Gonthier with every ounce of his strength.

The soldier, trapped between the bench and the tabletop, could not get out of the way of the heavy steel blade. He gave a desperate cry of 'No!' as he held up an arm in a futile bid to protect himself, but Warin's sword brushed it aside, swept down to the very bottom of the stroke and sliced deep into the side of Gonthier's neck. Blood spurted from the wound, spraying across the table and the men on either side, who were desperately trying to get away from Warin, his sword and the flood of gore from Gonthier's neck.

Seconds later, Gonthier was dead, his body slumped across the tabletop, and the blood flow had slowed to an oozing trickle. But Warin was not finished. Seized by a crazed, berserker fury, he kept hacking at the soldier's neck, screaming, 'Laugh at this! Go on, laugh . . . laugh, you fucking traitor!' Within half a dozen blows, Gonthier's head had been separated from his body and was rolling across the table, his eyes wide open in the blind stare of death. But Warin did not stop swinging his blade until finally he slashed it so hard into the oak tabletop that it became stuck.

He pulled at the sword. He wrapped both hands around its hilt, placed a foot against the table and jerked his whole body backwards. But the steel remained embedded and unmoving. He swore and shouted in a paroxysm of incoherent anger. He jerked again, then a third time, without any success, and was just about to make one more effort when his whole body began to shake.

With his hands still holding his sword, Warin convulsed like a fish on a hook. Then his grip loosened and he fell to the floor, thrashing and twitching in an uncontrollable fit. His eyes rolled up in his skull. A foam of white spittle appeared at the corner of his mouth. A woman screamed. Someone shouted, 'Demons!' and other voices joined in: 'He's possessed! God help us! Get the priest!'

All through the assault on Gonthier, Warin's father and brothers had looked on with chilly indifference. If he felt like killing one of their men, who were they to stop him? But now they rushed down from the high table and joined the onlookers, who had formed a rough circle around Warin, unable to help him and unwilling to risk any contact with the demon that had him in its grip.

Finally a priest in a dirty black cassock burst through the crowd. Standing nervously a pace away from Warin, he offered up a prayer for his salvation and sprinkled holy water in the general direction of his shuddering, spasm-racked body.

Suddenly Warin was still. 'God be praised,' murmured the priest and knelt down beside the motionless form of the heir to the House of Bellême. He put his fingertips on the skin between Warin's neck and his jaw, hoping to feel the steady beating of life. There was nothing. He placed his ear over Warin's open mouth, but neither heard nor felt any breath. With growing desperation, he laid his head on Warin's chest, but the heart within it was still. Finally he looked up, caught the Count of

Bellême's eye and said, 'God has taken your son, my lord. He rests in heaven now.'

'I sincerely doubt that,' muttered Talvas, though his words were drowned by a howl of pain and grief from the count that echoed around the hall. Bellême rushed to where Warin lay, kicked the kneeling priest out of his way and sat down on the floor, cradling his son's corpse in his arms and rocking back and forth, moaning like a wounded dog.

At last he let go of the body and got to his feet again. He stumbled over to his sons, Fulk and Bertrand, who were standing side by side. 'Robert of Normandy did this to us,' he rasped. 'I am too old to fight. You will have to make him pay.'

7

As an exile, the archbishop could not return to Rouen to negotiate with his nephew, so Fulbert, Bishop of Chartres, went in his place. Before he left, the bishop assured his old friend that he would do everything he could to persuade Duke Robert to rethink his stubborn refusal to follow the archbishop's very reasonable suggestions. 'You have my complete sympathy, Holy Father,' he said. 'You've suffered most grievously, especially since the duke owes so much to your faith in him.'

'More than he knows,' the archbishop agreed.

'You can comfort yourself with the thought that though he may have taken away your material possessions, he can't take what's in your soul. What's more, by God's grace you have the means to bring back anyone who goes astray and the sanctions, provided by the Church, with which to punish them too.'

'You must make it very clear to him that I intend to use those sanctions. Leave him in absolutely no doubt.'

Fulbert gave his friend a cold, tight, satisfied smile: the look of a man about to provide an enemy with a very nasty surprise. 'Have no fear, Holy Father. We will have Duke Robert crying out for absolution. And I will not rest until he is on his knees, confessing his sins and crying out, "Thy rod and thy staff, they have comforted me."'

'Oh yes,' said the archbishop. 'After what that ungrateful whelp has done to me, I want him to feel that rod and staff. And I hope that when he does, he will be suitably chastised.'

A week later, having paused for a night in Evreux to give his greetings to the archbishop's wife and children and hand them a letter from him, Fulbert arrived in Rouen. He found quarters in the priory of Saint-Gervais and the following morning went to the ducal palace for his audience with Robert of Normandy.

Fulbert was, like the archbishop, a sophisticated, not to say cynical observer and manipulator of events. The two institutions he knew best, the Church and the French royal court, were both snakepits of ambition, intrigue and deceit. But Fulbert had survived them both very comfortably. He was a man who took pleasure in the bounty that God provided. With his thick head of silver hair, his shrewd eyes, his surprisingly plump, unlined cheeks and his lavishly embroidered episcopal robes, he looked distinguished, well fed and immaculately dressed. Standing before Robert, who was seated on a high-backed chair, raised on a dais, he saw the sort of young princeling with whom he was all too familiar: handsome enough and not lacking in physical courage, but cocky, overconfident, impetuous and fundamentally unsuited to the kind of contest in which he now found himself.

Fulbert felt entirely confident of victory, but that was, of course, in no way evident from the way in which he began the conversation. 'Your Grace,' he said, in a pulpit-trained voice that never strained for volume yet somehow reached every corner of the audience room, 'I have come as an emissary of His Grace the Archbishop of Rouen. He sends you his greetings and wishes you to know that he is praying nightly that the Lord will send you wisdom and guidance to help you through this unfortunate time.'

Robert acknowledged the greeting with a little nod of the head and replied in kind. 'Thank you, Bishop Fulbert. Please assure the archbishop that whatever quarrel we may be having now, he is still my beloved uncle, and that I too ask the Lord to keep him in good health, and to open his heart to the justice of my case.'

He smiled politely at Fulbert. The bishop smiled back, then got down to business.

'Your Grace, I fear it is my sad duty to inform you that His Grace the archbishop remains adamant that neither he nor the Church, nor the Lord God Almighty Himself, can condone the state of concubinage that exists between yourself and Herleva of Falaise, the mother of your son, William. Furthermore, His Grace reiterates his strong advice to you that you must, at the earliest opportunity, seek out a true and proper marriage with a bride whose nobility matches your own. Should you do this, you may be assured of his blessing and the blessing of all who love the Lord.'

'Does he now?' Robert replied. 'Well then I fear he will remain your guest for some considerable time. For I have no intention of betraying the woman I love, nor the son she bore me. Nor would I dishonour the rite of marriage by entering into so sacred a union with a bride chosen for reasons of political advantage rather than the true and lasting love that is its proper foundation.'

Fulbert nodded thoughtfully. 'I see . . .' he murmured, as if digesting what Robert had just said. Then he went on, 'May I ask Your Grace: do you understand what is meant by the term "interdict"?'

Robert shrugged. 'I have heard the word. I confess I do not know its precise meaning.'

'Then allow me to enlighten Your Grace.' Suddenly there was a colder, steelier tone to Fulbert's voice. 'An interdict is a formal instrument of censure, used by the Church to punish individuals or groups who have in some way done wrong, by forbidding them from taking part in the sacred rites of the Church. No person who is the subject of an interdict may celebrate Mass, make confession, be baptised, or marry. The only exceptions to this rule are that, for the good of their immortal souls, the dying may receive the last rites, and interdiction may, at the discretion of local bishops, be suspended for a few of the most significant feast days: Christmas, Easter and the like.'

Osbern, Herluin and a couple of Robert's other close advisers were also in the room. As Fulbert outlined the devastating impact of an interdict, they could not hide the shock from their faces, for there was absolutely nothing more terrifying to any of them than the thought of being cast aside by God. Robert, however, managed to maintain his composure. Fulbert knew that the young duke must have been as horrified as the others; that he had the self-control not to show his fear was a mark in his favour. The bishop made a mental note not to underestimate his opponent.

Robert, meanwhile, betrayed not a trace of concern in his voice as he said, 'Thank you for that explanation, Bishop. I think I understand. But why are you telling me this?'

Now Fulbert struck his blow. 'Because His Grace wishes me to inform you that, with the full knowledge, approval and authority of the Holy See itself, he is placing the entire Arch-diocese of Normandy under an interdiction, to commence from this moment on.'

There was an audible gasp from the onlookers. Even Robert could not hide the shock that flickered very briefly yet noticeably across his face. Fulbert went on without a break. 'I have with me letters addressed to all the bishops under the holy father's authority instructing them that until further notice, and with the exceptions of which I have already informed you, only they, their clergy and their brothers and sisters in monasteries, convents and so forth may continue to celebrate the sacraments.'

'The whole of Normandy?' Robert asked, his anger rising.

'Are you telling me that just because my uncle disapproves of the way in which I choose to live with the woman I love – a form of union, incidentally, to which he owes his very existence, since his own parents also conceived their children out of wedlock – he intends to deprive the entire duchy of the comfort of the Church?'

Ah, the young pup is losing his temper, Fulbert thought. And when he does, he'll lose his judgement too. He looked Robert right in the eye and said, 'Yes, that is exactly what I am telling Your Grace. I should point out, in the interests of clarity, that an interdict does not prevent a member of the Church from praying. They may still speak to their Father, their Lord Jesus Christ, the Blessed Virgin Mary and all the saints. Whether they will get a hearing, of course, I am not in a position to say.'

'But what will my people do if they cannot eat the Lord's flesh, or drink His blood, or confess their sins, or bring their children into the Church through baptism?'

'They and their souls will suffer grievously, Your Grace,' Fulbert said. 'That is the purpose of an interdict.'

Robert's jaw was clenched and his face was tight with tension. 'And what will it take to persuade my uncle archbishop to lift this interdict?' he asked.

'That you submit to his will in the matter of your concubine, whose presence in your life is, you must agree, a proper concern for a man of God such as His Grace; that you return all his properties, titles, honours and so on; and that you agree to make a sincere and honest endeavour to find a suitable wife at the earliest opportunity.'

Robert shifted forward to the edge of his seat and glared down at Fulbert. 'So I must sacrifice the woman I love just to please an old hypocrite, or the people of my duchy will suffer a grievous spiritual punishment?'

The bishop stood his ground. 'I strongly object, on His Grace's behalf, to the use of the word "hypocrite", and I cannot comment on whether you do or do not love the woman in question, but in essence, yes, that is the situation.'

Robert rolled his eyes and then looked up towards the heavens. 'Is this what you want, Lord?' he cried. 'Well . . . is it?'

Before God or Bishop Fulbert could reply, the tension was broken by the unexpected arrival of a palace official, accompanied by a man whose cloak and boots were covered in mud. As he pulled a rain-sodden hat from his head, to reveal a receding head of dark ginger hair that hung almost to his shoulders, he looked exhausted, yet jittery with nervous energy. Evidently he'd come a long way, and now, having arrived at his destination, was desperate to justify the journey.

'What's the meaning of this interruption?' Robert snapped.

The official cringed as he stood before the ducal dais. 'Your Grace, there is a merchant here to see you,' he said. 'He has come from Alençon. He says he has news that he must impart to you in person. It concerns the Count of Bellême.'

Robert gave a sigh of irritation. 'Please excuse me for one moment, Bishop Fulbert.' The bishop gave a little bow, then retreated away from the dais. Robert looked the merchant up and down. 'So, who are you?'

The merchant smiled nervously and twisted his fingers to and fro in the fabric of the hat. 'My name is Thurstan, Your Grace – Thurstan of Coutances. I am a fishmonger.' He straightened up a fraction and added proudly, 'I specialise in all forms of preserved fish: dried, salted and smoked. That was why I was in Alençon, you see, to sell my fish. And that's how I saw the murder.'

Robert hadn't been expecting that. 'What do you mean, murder?'

'It was Warin of Bellême, the count's eldest son, that did it,

279

Your Grace. He just went mad. He heard someone laughing and took offence. So he got up from his place, came over to the man, and killed him, bosh, with his sword. The poor fellow didn't get no warning, couldn't defend himself or nothing. One minute he's happy as a clam, the next he's stone dead.'

'That's unforgivable,' said Robert. 'Did the Count of Bellême do anything to punish his son?'

'Well no, Your Grace, he couldn't,' Thurstan said. 'Warin's dead too. The same demon that drove him mad killed him. He had a terrible fit, fell to the floor and that was it.'

'Well this is very serious, disturbing news. Thank you for bringing it to my attention.'

It seemed that Robert was bringing the meeting to a close.

'But Your Grace, that's not why I'm here,' Thurstan pleaded. 'See, the Count of Bellême, he blames you for his son's death, says you've brought nothing but misery and shame to his family.'

'He brought that on himself.'

'Yes, Your Grace, but the thing is, the count told his other three sons, the ones that are still alive, to attack Normandy. He told them to make you pay for Warin's death. So they're going to do as much damage as they can. Any property you own, or that belongs to someone loyal to you, they're going to try and destroy it, or burn it down, or just mess it up however they can.'

'When did all this happen?' Robert asked.

'Eight days ago, Your Grace. I packed up and got going for Rouen quick as I could. But I still had most of my fish on my cart, Your Grace, and my ox isn't as young as he used to be.'

'You did well, Thurstan of Coutances,' said Robert, clearly meaning it. 'You've come a long, long way to tell me your news. Let me make your journey worthwhile.' He cast an eye across the room to his men. 'Osbern!'

'Yes, Your Grace?'

'Tell the cellarer that we'll take all this excellent fishmonger's produce. And Osbern . . .' He gestured at his steward to step right up to the chair, and then whispered, 'Whatever the stuff is worth, pay him twice as much. For what he's told us, it's cheap at the price.'

Robert stood up. The audience was over. 'I must apologise, Bishop Fulbert, but my people's lives and their property are threatened. I must deal with this at once.'

'And what about the threat to their souls, Your Grace?' the bishop asked.

'I would hope that, with your indulgence and my uncle's, that threat might be delayed a short while. My intention is to put an end to this incursion on my territory by striking a single, decisive blow. With God's grace I will be back here within a fortnight, possibly sooner. When I return, I will have an answer for you and my uncle.'

Fulbert was unmoved. 'You could give me an answer now, Your Grace. Your simple consent to His Grace the archbishop's terms is all I require.'

Robert frowned. He had not expected the bishop to be so unbending or unreasonable. 'You must surely understand that I have not had time to consider his proposals,' he insisted.

'On the contrary, Your Grace, you are very familiar with His Grace's desires. The only thing you learned today was how he intends to enforce them.'

'Yes, by threatening the immortal souls of innocent men and women who have nothing whatever to do with our quarrel. That is a low, ungodly blow, Bishop Fulbert, and I will not let it beat me just yet. For now, my answer is no. Perhaps I will change my mind while I am on campaign. You are very welcome to stay here, or at the archbishop's palace, while I am away. I will give orders that you are to receive every possible comfort.

Now, if you'll excuse me, I have a war to fight and a traitor to defeat. Herluin!'

'Yes, Your Grace?'

'Assemble the militia. We need provisions for them and food for their mounts. Our friend the fishmonger made it here from Alençon in eight days. We'll cover the same ground in four. Go!'

Herluin raced from the audience chamber, but Fulbert was not yet finished. 'Your Grace . . .'

Robert dragged his attention back to the sleek, unflappable priest. 'Yes, Bishop Fulbert?'

The bishop looked at him coldly. 'I am no general, but I can give you one piece of advice about battle. No matter how many men you assemble, how many horses and how many swords, no army on earth can defy the will of God. Think on that, Your Grace, as you ride away to war.'

8

Four days had passed since Robert had left. By his own estimate, he should have found the Bellêmes' raiding party by now. Herleva knew her man. Once he had the enemy in his sights, he wouldn't waste time shadow-boxing. He'd go straight in for the kill, and though she had never, from the moment she met him, doubted his courage or his fighting skill, the very thought of him riding into battle filled her mind with terrifying images of him lying dead or terribly wounded. She had to do something to distract herself, and since it was market day in Rouen, she summoned Judith, told her to wrap William up nice and warm and informed Osbern, who had been left behind to mind the palace in Robert's absence, that she was going out.

A look of concern spread across the steward's face. 'Are you sure that's wise, my lady?' he replied, sounding as though he felt very strongly that it was not.

'Whyever not?' Herleva asked. 'I often take a walk around the market. Don't worry, I won't spend all the duke's gold while he's away.'

Osbern managed a hint of a smile. 'Of course not, my lady. It's just that, well, circumstances are unusual at the moment.'

'You mean, the duke being away?'

'Among other things, my lady.' Osbern looked at her pensively. 'I suppose it should be all right. I can't imagine there'll be any danger . . .'

'What, just walking round the marketplace? Don't be silly, Osbern!'

Herleva giggled at the absurdity of it all, but Osbern paid her no attention. 'Still, I'd be happier, and I'm sure Duke Robert would be happier, if you had someone to look after you,' he said. 'I'll fetch one of the guard. If there's the slightest sign of trouble, he'll bring you back at once.'

Now Herleva's laughter stopped. 'What's happening, Osbern?' she asked. 'You're worrying me.'

'I'm sure it's nothing. I'm probably just being overcautious. But the duke is away and I'd hate to have to tell him that anything had happened to you while he was away.'

'Oh, we'll be careful, won't we, Judith?'

'Yes, my lady,' Judith replied, though Herleva could have sworn her old friend had exchanged glances with Osbern as if they both knew something she didn't. No, she decided, she must be imagining it. And then William started charging towards a set of steep stone steps, shouting, 'Look at me!' and Herleva had no other thought in her mind but getting to her boy and stopping him – no easy task with his precocious size and strength – before he hurtled headlong to his doom. Together she and Judith managed to subdue him, weather his instant temper tantrum and take one of his hands each as they set off down the stairs, with William raising his feet off the ground and trying to swing as they went.

'The guard will be waiting for you by the main gate!' Osbern called after them.

Sure enough someone was there to meet them, but Robert had taken the best of his fighting men with him, so this was a far from impressive specimen: paunchy, unkempt and with a surly, uncooperative expression. He glared at Herleva so resentfully that she had a mind to reprimand him, but she didn't want to get a reputation for high-handed behaviour, so she bit her tongue. He was large, wore a coat of chain mail and carried a large sword: that was the main thing.

They set off into the heart of the city, towards the market square.

Edward of England took pride in two things above all others. The first was his royal blood. He had recently taken to calling himself King Edward, and Robert, having no desire to argue with his cousin, was happy to command that the ducal household should give Edward all the honour due to a true monarch, and treat his younger brother as a prince. The second of Edward's virtues, in his own eyes, was his piety. He spent many hours deep in Bible study, seeking to find an even closer connection to God and also, while he was at it, to discover new reasons for disapproving of other people's failings.

Edward took Communion every morning, confessed his sins on a daily basis and attended Vespers in the evening, too. For the past two weeks he had been in retreat at the abbey of Fécamp, cut off from the world outside and leading the simple, silent life of a penitent sinner. Now he was looking forward to getting back into the swing of palace life. He went to the chapel, expecting to eat the flesh and drink the blood of his Saviour, Jesus Christ, but to his surprise, the door was locked. Strangely, however, he could hear the sound of voices within, declaiming the words of the confession. Edward was almost certain that he was not late. He was never late. But even if he were, the doors should not be barred against him, or anyone else.

He tried the door again, leaning against it with all his weight. Still it would not budge.

This was absurd.

He knocked on the door, gently at first, so as not to disturb the priests at their prayers. But then it occurred to him that unless he disturbed them they would not know that someone was outside, needing to get in. So he slapped the flat of his hand against the thick oaken door, and then again, more loudly, and then three more times in quick succession, until his palm was stinging.

Finally he heard the sound of a sliding bolt, the door opened a fraction and a young priest peered out. 'Oh, Your Majesty,' he said. 'Please excuse me. I'll fetch the chaplain for you.'

Then he closed the door again and before Edward could do anything the bolt was pushed back into place and the entrance was barred against him once again. He felt a fury born of frustration, humiliation, incensed dignity and sheer regal outrage boiling up inside him.

The door was unbolted a second time and pulled very slightly ajar. This time Edward was not caught napping. He stuck out a foot and planted it between the door and the frame so that it could not be closed again.

'I demand to be let in,' he said, loudly enough to be heard over the voice of a priest saying a prayer of penitence. He shoved against the door.

'I do apologise, Your Majesty,' came the voice of the palace chaplain, who was on the other side of the door, trying equally hard to close it, 'but that won't be possible.'

'What do you mean, it won't be possible?' asked Edward, his voice rising in disbelief. 'I am the rightful King of England. I hold my title by the grace of God and I demand to be let in.'

'I'm afraid you can't come in, Your Majesty, by order of the archbishop.' The chaplain's voice was by now becoming breathless and showing signs of strain. 'Quick! Someone help me!' he cried.

Edward could hear the sound of pattering footsteps on stone and suddenly there was a much greater weight pushing against him and he cried out in pain as his foot was trapped. Even so, he was not ready to give up just yet.

'Don't be ridiculous, man. The archbishop is my uncle. He would never deny me the Sacrament.'

'But he has placed an interdict on the whole of Normandy. Has no one informed you of this?'

'No, they certainly have not. And on what grounds, may I ask, has this interdict been declared?'

'It has to do with His Grace the duke's personal affairs, sire. More than that I cannot say.'

'You mean his sinful coupling outside the bonds of marriage with that vile Jezebel, the tanner's daughter of Falaise?' Edward was forcing out his words between desperate gulps of air. His foot hurt most damnably.

'It is not for me to interpret my holy father's intentions. My duty is simply to continue to pray to God's glory with my brother priests and monks, while denying the sacrament to the laity . . . Your Majesty, might I suggest that we refrain from further exertions? Perhaps if we were both to take one step back from the door . . .'

For a second Edward toyed with the thought of deceiving the chaplain by agreeing to step back only to force his way into the chapel. But no matter how great his shock or disapproval at this entirely unexpected turn of events, he could not, as a king, be seen to behave so boorishly.

'Very well,' he agreed.

The chaplain and his fellow priests retreated, the pressure on Edward's foot eased and he withdrew it with a little wince, took a single pace back, then sat down on the floor and began rubbing his battered toes.

'How long is this appalling state of affairs to last?' he asked, as the strains of the Kyrie Eleison wafted from the chapel.

'Until His Grace the duke repents of his ways.'

'Huh!' grunted Edward. He had a lot of time for his cousin – it was not Robert's fault that he had been led astray by an evil temptress – but he knew his own kin, and not one of them ever willingly gave way in an argument or a fight. Edward, however, was more open to reason. 'Very well then,' he said. 'My argument is not with you, chaplain. I look forward to taking Communion with you again very soon. In the meantime, my quarrels lie elsewhere.'

The door closed. The bolt was put back in place. And Edward, the landless King of England, hobbled away down the palace corridors in search of the slut of Falaise.

9

Despite the winter chill and the lowering grey skies, there was always a bright, warm, cheerful feel to market day. Throngs of farmers, merchants and local people had travelled from leagues around to buy and sell, meet old friends, exchange gossip, and drink late into the night in the taverns that ringed the square. Confectioners tempted sweet-toothed passers-by and the grubby fingers of thieving little boys with colourful arrays of pastries, sweetmeats and fruits preserved in rich honey syrup. And through the hubbub wandered pie-sellers carrying trays of piping hot pastries, sweet and savoury alike; minstrels, jugglers and clowns; old peasant women offering to read fortunes or sell sprigs of lucky heather; tricksters and purse-snatchers; scampering children and barking dogs, both groups equally overexcited.

Viking traders were there in numbers too, drawn to Normandy by blood ties with its people as well as the hope of profit. Some sold goods from the north: ivory and ornaments carved from walrus tusk, amber beads, strong ropes and timber, delicate feathers and casks of salted fish. But others concentrated on exotic items brought back from the faraway lands, in the known world and beyond, over which the Vikings had roamed. They stood behind tables on which were arrayed shallow pots filled with Oriental spices whose dazzling colours and pungent aromas overwhelmed the senses. Or they shouted out enticing descriptions of precious metals and jewels from Spain, Germany and Constantinople, or rugs from the souks of Arabia. The furriers' stalls displayed pelts of every size, made into all manner of cloaks, coats, capes, hats and rugs. There were huge white bearskins from the far north; grey wolf skin and red fox; pale brown beaver and deep black mink brought by Varangian travellers from the lands of the Rus. Elsewhere there were silks whose vivid dyes and patterns made even the jewels and spices look dull, and precious objects as mysterious as they were beautiful.

Herleva adored the market. It reminded her of home. She had worked at the family's leather stall in Falaise since she was a little girl of six or seven, so small that she could barely see over the countertop. She'd learned to haggle, to talk customers into paying the best price and to know when they had reached their upper limit and it was time to strike a deal. Over the years the market folk had become a second family to her. So as she walked through the stalls, she spotted merchants and artisans who also plied their trade in Falaise and called out greetings to them as they passed.

Normally she could be assured of a cheerful reply, often laced with the kind of affectionate teasing she seldom received now that she was the Duke of Normandy's woman. She loved the way the market folk still treated her as one of their own, and the evident pride they took in her success. But this morning something was different. A few of the stallholders responded to her in the usual way, but most managed no more than a surly grunt or even turned their backs on her, blanking her as she walked by.

The townspeople, too, seemed different. Herleva was the beautiful mistress of a handsome young duke. She had produced a son, albeit an illegitimate one, to ensure that the House of Normandy had a successor. And she was one of them, a commoner who had won the heart of a mighty lord. All these things combined to ensure her popularity. Or at least they had in the past. But not today. There was a sullen resentment as people made way to let her pass. Men and women alike glared at her. Some even spat on the ground beside her.

'Man angry,' William said as they passed one well-dressed burgher.

The man coughed, but Herleva could swear that he said, 'Slut!' as he did it.

'Why man angry, Mama?' William asked.

'I don't know, darling.' Herleva looked at Judith. 'Do you know what's going on? Why's everyone acting like this?'

'I'm sure I don't know, my lady,' said Judith so shiftily that Herleva stopped dead in her tracks.

'Yes you do,' she said. 'I can tell. Answer my question, or I swear I'll make you regret it.'

Judith looked at her almost as sullenly as the guard had done, with no more kindness in her eyes than the townspeople had shown. Herleva felt as though she had been plunged into a nightmare. Why would nobody talk to her?

'For God's sake, Judith, please. I'm your oldest friend, tell me what's happening!'

'Go on, tell 'er,' someone called from the crowd. 'Tell the duke's bitch what she's done to us.'

'You! Shut your face!' the guard shouted. Snarling malevolently he took a step towards the crowd that had gathered around them, his hand on the hilt of his sword, sending people fleeing in all directions like frightened starlings.

Herleva had burst into tears, overwhelmed by the inexplicable hostility all around her. She felt a hand grabbing her arm and heard Judith say, 'Back to the castle,' and suddenly they were hurrying back the way they had come. William, alarmed by his mother's distress as much as the chaos around them, had started to cry as well. Herleva wiped her face and picked him up in her arms as they ran between the stalls, trying to ignore the mounting jeers of the crowd. As they left the market square and

291

set off down the street that led to the palace, she felt something hit her dress and heard laughter behind her. She turned to look and saw a pair of boys picking up horse manure and clods of mud from the road and throwing it in their direction, much to the approval of the crowd.

The guard had given up trying to protect them. He was running as hard as he could for the palace guard, yelling for help as he went. There were shouts from the battlements above the main gate, and a few moments later, three or four more guards emerged. Herleva ran desperately towards them as more townspeople started hurling rotten vegetables, bread rolls and even the contents of a chamber pot, emptied from a first-floor room, that mercifully only landed close enough to splash the hem of her dress.

William had recovered his good humour. He was wriggling in Herleva's arms, trying to look all around and crying out in glee at every new development in what clearly seemed to him like an excellent game. Herleva caught a sudden look in his eye, a combination of excitement, determination and sheer aggression, and she suddenly knew with absolute clarity that this would be her son's life, that he would never be as completely at ease anywhere else as he was on the battlefield. A shock of fear sliced through her at the thought of her boy fighting for his life and killing other women's sons. But there was no time to think about that, for now there were strong arms grabbing her and others taking William as she was picked up and carried through the rapidly closing gate and back into the palace.

Finally they were safe. Herleva retrieved William, who was wide-eyed with excitement. 'Soldier carry me!' he told her proudly. 'I fight!' He swung an imaginary sword in front of his face. 'I kill bad man!'

Herleva couldn't bear it. She had only gone out in the first place to escape thoughts of death. With tears pricking her eyes again, she handed William over to Judith. She was just about to go off in search of Osbern, intending to force an explanation out of him, when she heard a roar of 'Jezebel!' and there, coming towards her, was King Edward of England, his face scarlet with rage. 'I have been denied God's holy flesh and blood, and it's your fault,' he shouted as Herleva dropped into a curtsey, head bowed as she fought back the sobs. Having escaped the fury of the commoners outside, now she was suffering the hatred of a king.

Still keeping her head lowered, she raised her eyes to look at him. 'Your Majesty, I . . . I don't understand . . . Have I offended you?'

'Your very existence offends me. Your sinfulness offends me, the sins of all your wicked, impure sex!'

'But what have I done wrong?' she cried, desperate for someone to tell her what terrible crime she had committed to provoke so much dislike.

'What have you done wrong?' Edward reached down and grabbed Herleva's arm hard enough to hurt. He dragged her to her feet and shoved her round so that she was face to face with William, who was himself struggling to get out of Judith's grasp.

'Look at your bastard,' Edward sneered. 'Consider the act of filth and degradation by which he was conceived. What more do you need to know?'

For a moment Herleva was dumbfounded. Then she was seized by an emotion she had never felt before, a furious determination to protect her child, no matter what the cost. 'Let me go!' she shouted, and with her free hand lashed out at Edward, raking her fingernails down the side of his face.

He howled in pain and let her go, then dabbed at his cheek with his fingertips. 'You've drawn blood, my royal blood,' he said in disbelief. 'By God, I'll kill you for that.'

He stepped forward, his right fist clenched. But before he

could deliver a blow, Prince Alfred's voice rang out. 'No, Edward, don't!'

The next thing Herleva knew, the king's younger brother was holding him from behind and physically dragging him away from her.

'Are you mad . . . Your Majesty?' Alfred hissed in Edward's ear. 'If you even touch her, Robert will never forgive you. He'll have us both kicked out of the duchy, assuming he doesn't just hand us over to Canute. For God's sake, leave her be.'

Alfred released Edward and left him standing simmering with pent-up aggression while he walked over to Herleva. 'Are you hurt, my lady?' he asked.

She shook her head.

'Good, I'm glad,' Alfred said.

Herleva was pitifully grateful that someone was finally being kind to her.

'Come here,' Alfred said, and hugged her comfortingly while she gathered herself together again. He looked back at Edward. 'I think it would be best if Duke Robert never heard about this,' he said. 'My lady, I hope you will accept His Majesty's apology for any hurt his words may have caused you. And sire, I suggest that you and I pay a visit to the falconry. The sight of such magnificent birds is sure to raise your spirits. Though I have heard that their claws can cause quite a scratch if one is not careful. Who knows, that might happen to you.'

'Thank you, Your Highness,' said Herleva, stepping out of the hug.

'It was my pleasure.'

As the two rightful heirs to the throne of England walked away, Herleva wiped her face and tidied her dress and her hair. Then she set off to find Osbern, feeling more determined than ever to force an explanation out of him.

He was in the audience chamber, talking to a young soldier

from the palace guard. Herleva caught the words '. . . return as fast as possible,' and then Osbern saw her and fell silent.

She walked towards him, feeling angrier with every step. 'You knew what would happen at the market, didn't you?' she shouted.

'I feared it, yes,' Osbern replied.

'So why did you let me go? Tell me . . . what have I done . . . why do they hate me?'

Osbern sighed, and with a terrible sadness in his voice said, 'Because, my lady, they think you've condemned them to an eternity in hell.'

10

*Alençon, the County of Bellême, and the Valley
of Blavou, Normandy*

It took several days for Fulk and Bertrand of Bellême to mount
their raid on Normandy. Their brother Warin had to be buried
first, and even by the standards of funerals held on cold, wet
winter days it was an exceptionally grim occasion. Their mother
was hidden behind a heavy black veil and not just because she
was mourning her son, for their father had given her a
particularly brutal beating that had left her virtually sightless in
one eye, so severe was the vivid red and purple swelling all
around it. Very few of the people of Alençon turned out to
watch the funeral procession from the castle to the church. It
was not a day for standing still by the side of a road, and Warin
had hardly been a popular young man. That he had died in the
immediate aftermath of committing an unprovoked murder
only made public affection for him all the more meagre.

So the family and their closest retainers stood in the
unrelenting rain while Warin's brother Ivo, Bishop of Sées,
committed his soul to God's keeping. The count himself had
been swaying unsteadily on his feet, making a soft, moaning
sound through much of the ceremony, but as the coffin was
lowered into the grave he cried out, clutched his face and fell to
his knees on the soggy turf before keeling motionless on to the
ground.

Talvas, watching, could not believe his luck: first his brother
dead, now his father as well. With every corpse there was one

fewer family member between him and the title and lands of Bellême. But then the old man groaned piteously and made a desperate attempt to get back to his feet. As he raised his head there was a collective gasp of horror from the mourners gathered around him, for his face was twisted into a grotesque rictus, so that one side of his mouth pointed up while the other drooped towards his jaw. His eyes, too, were caught in a frozen wink, with one wide open and the other half closed, the eyelid unable to move either up or down.

'It's the demon,' whimpered Fulk. 'It's left Warin and taken Father instead.' He looked around with wild, panicked eyes. 'We're cursed! Take him away! For pity's sake! Before the demon attacks us all!'

The count staggered about helplessly, his arms hanging limply by his sides, making incoherent pleas for help. No one dared approach him until the countess took his hand and led him away like an oversized gibbering infant.

'We've got to get out of here,' said Bertrand. 'Just round up the men and go.'

'Someone's got to mind Father and the castle,' Fulk pointed out.

They both looked at Talvas.

The youngest of the Bellêmes had no desire whatever to go on what was evidently a reckless unplanned expedition calculated to provoke Robert of Normandy into furious retaliation. But there was no point letting his brothers know that. 'No! Don't make me stay,' he pleaded. 'There's nothing I can do here. Mama can look after Father until he gets better. I want to be with you, fighting for the colours of Bellême.'

For a terrible moment, Talvas worried that he might have overdone it and actually persuaded them to let him come. But then Fulk sneered, 'You just don't want to stay here. You're scared of that demon.'

'And you're not?' Talvas replied, wanting to annoy his brothers.

'Watch your tongue, little brother,' said Fulk menacingly. 'We give the orders and if we say you're staying here, that's what you have to do.'

'You can't make me,' Talvas whined.

Fulk stepped up and grabbed Talvas by the neck. 'Yes we can!'

'That's enough, Fulk, let go of him!'

Bishop Ivo, who was only three years older than Talvas but had the authority of a bishop's rank, stepped between his warring brothers. 'You!' he said, pointing at Fulk. 'Do what Father has commanded you and fight back against Robert of Normandy. And you, Talvas, obey your brothers and remain here in Alençon where you are needed.'

Fulk darted a sharp, angry look at Ivo and Talvas in turn, then stalked off, shouting orders at his men as he went. Talvas stood still, doing his best to look sullen and uncooperative, until Ivo chided him, 'For the love of God, Talvas, don't just stand there looking miserable. Go and see if Mama needs any help.'

'Me? Help her?' Talvas asked, genuinely astounded by the very suggestion.

'Yes,' Ivo insisted. 'You are her son. It's your duty.'

Talvas found it hard to understand why he should offer assistance to a woman who had long since been reduced to the level of a mere menial. But Ivo clearly had a sentimental attachment to the old bitch and there was no need to shatter his illusions, so he just said, 'Of course, I'll go to her right away.'

'God bless you. And please let her know that I will send a priest to exorcise the demon from Father's soul. It is a special skill, but I know just the man.'

Sure enough, a couple of days later an elderly priest, stick thin with chalky white skin stretched across the bones of his cadaverous face, arrived at Alençon Castle and made his way to the chamber where the count lay drooling and muttering garbled words whose meaning no one could understand. The priest burned incense, said prayers, doused the count in holy water and commanded the demon to depart. But none of it seemed to do any good, and when the priest left, after two further attempts at exorcism, Talvas was delighted to see that his father's condition was if anything getting worse.

His brothers, meanwhile, were making their way across the southern reaches of Normandy, looting, sacking and raping as they went. There was no clear direction to their line of march, nor any real purpose, other than the desire to cause as much harm and damage as they possibly could. Wherever they and their fifty or so men found food they took it. Where they found wine or ale they drank it. And where they found women they fucked them.

They ended up describing a ragged circular path that took them up to the north-west of Alençon before they turned right and headed eastwards, then right again on a southerly bearing and right again south-west back to Alençon. By now their progress was slowed by carts heaped with booty, as well as the mules, horses and human captives that followed in their wake. They were not helped either by the replacement of military discipline by drunken debauchery. Half the men were reeling in their saddles. There were no scouts ahead, or to the flanks of the column, and fights had started to break out as the men squabbled over the human and material loot they had acquired along the way.

On the eighth day out from Alençon, sundown found Fulk, Bertrand and the men of Bellême in a narrow valley between two ridges, atop one of which was the hamlet of Saint-Quentin-de-Blavou. There was some debate among the men about whether it was worth going up to the village to see what might be on offer there. But the ridge was steep and high and there seemed no easy path up it, so the exhausted, bleary-eyed raiders got down from horses that were all in desperate need of proper feeding and grooming and half-heartedly set about finding wood for fires to warm them on this bitterly cold night.

Robert and Herluin had left their men camped just outside the village and were looking down from the ridge. Two days ago they had come across the first signs of the devastation the Bellême raiders had wrought – a burned-out manor house strewn with corpses, some horribly mutilated – and had been following their trail ever since. Robert was disgusted by the pointless destruction, and the slovenly carelessness of the men who'd carried it out only deepened his contempt.

'I'm tempted just to hit them tonight, kill them all while they're lying there in a drunken stupor,' he said.

'Do you want me to tell the men to get ready?'

Robert gave a long sigh as he thought it over and then shook his head. 'No,' he said, reluctantly overruling his own impetuous instincts. 'The horses are tired and hungry and so are the men. And if we went in on a pitch-black night like this, we could easily kill as many of our own men as theirs. No, we'll get them at dawn. And this is how we'll do it . . .'

11

A grey half-light had already broken over the top of the ridge, while the valley floor below was still plunged in darkness. Robert had his men awake and fed while those of Bellême still slept, and now they were silently making their way in two columns, curving round like horns to sweep down into the valley on either side of the enemy's encampment.

The ridge did not run straight along the side of the valley, but undulated in and out like the short, pudgy fingers of a giant hand. So Herluin, riding at the head of one of the columns, could take advantage of the folds in the landscape to bring his men down from the heights unobserved, even supposing that there was a sentry awake and on lookout.

'Your task is to be a hammer, smashing down on those bastards of Bellême,' Robert had told him. Now, as he reached the valley floor, Herluin prepared to strike. He had some forty men and he spread them out in a line about a hundred paces wide, right in the middle of the valley. When they were all assembled, he led them forward in a walk, that changed to a trot, then a canter, until finally they were riding at full gallop directly towards the camp, thundering out of the gloom towards their unsuspecting prey.

Fulk of Bellême had fallen asleep roaring drunk and was only woken by the combined discomfort of a swollen bladder and an aching head. As he pissed, he looked at the snoring, farting men ringed around the barely warm grey embers of what had been

301

their fire. Then he stopped. He could hear something, a thundering somewhere in the distance. And he could feel a tremor in the ground beneath him. It took a second or two for the meaning of those signs to penetrate his befuddled brain, but then he was pulling up his hose, grabbing his sword and shouting, 'To arms! To arms! We're under attack!'

His boot lashed out at the sleeping bodies around him, ignoring their muttered complaints as he screamed, 'Get up!' and wondered why the bloody hell he was having to rouse the men. What had happened to the sentries? The pounding of hooves was clearly audible now, and shouts of 'For God, Robert and Normandy!'

A toxic mixture of rage and fear rose in Fulk's gorge as he realised that his family had once again been outwitted by the House of Normandy. He dashed for his horse, passing several of his men, some stumbling around in the semi-darkness trying to find weapons or bits of armour, others looking frightened, uncertain and on the verge of breaking completely.

He leaped into his saddle and tried to rally his men around him. His squire had found the lance to which the standard of Bellême was tied and was running with it towards his master. But another veteran campaigner, already up and mounted, intercepted the boy and took the lance from his hands before riding up to Fulk. 'Well?' he asked. 'Fight or run?'

Fulk peered up the valley into the slowly lightening gloom. He could see the Normans now, looming out of the morning mist and streaming between the overladen carts and wagons, cutting down anyone in their way. There was no hope of stemming their charge. The best he could do was to get his men away in reasonably good order before the valley became a deathtrap. Some of them were already in full retreat, not even bothering to mount their horse but running away pell-mell, as if a man on foot could possibly hope to escape a charging horseman.

'Around me!' Fulk shouted, trying to make himself heard over the chaos as the Normans bore down on him. They were close now, almost within range of a well-thrown lance. It was time to go. With a cry of 'Retreat!' he turned his horse and led the small band of mounted knights who had rallied to his side away through the camp, leaping over fires and tents and barging runners out of the way, trampling any that fell in their path.

As he burst out from the far side of the camp, Fulk screwed up his eyes. The sun had just risen over the horizon and its dazzling rays were shining directly in his face, blinding him. He turned to look back at his pursuers. Now the sun was his friend, for it perfectly illuminated the Normans. They were being held up by the sheer chaos of the camp, and though the panicked, befuddled Bellême soldiers running to and fro before the onslaught were putting up little if any resistance, still they took time to dispose of. Fulk smiled to himself. He might yet get away.

And that was when he ran into Robert of Normandy.

'Your task is to be the hammer,' Robert had said to Herluin, and then added, 'I'll be the anvil'.

His men had formed the second Norman column and had come round behind the Bellême camp. They remained hidden behind an outcrop until Herluin's detachment had smashed into the camp and, as Robert had expected, forced Fulk and his men into full-scale retreat. Only then did he swing his own column out into the centre of the valley and launch a charge straight at the fleeing rabble.

Robert at once spotted the standard of Bellême and recognised Fulk riding beside the man who was carrying it. He pointed his charger and galloped directly at the enemy, coming out of the sun with his sword out and swinging . . . and slicing through Fulk of Bellême's neck, taking his head clean off with a single blow.

* * *

Barely half a dozen of the men who had left Alençon on the raid into Normandy survived the slaughter in the Valley of Blavou and made their way back home. One was Bertrand of Bellême, who somehow managed to ride through the deadly melee with barely a scratch on him. By midday he was back at Alençon Castle. The first person he met when he raced into the great hall was his youngest brother, Talvas. When Bertrand told him what had happened, Talvas reacted with words of horror at the description of Fulk's death and was suitably enraged when told that his killer was the family's mortal enemy, the Duke of Normandy. A more perceptive man than Bertrand of Bellême, or one less overwhelmed by loss, defeat and exhaustion, might have noticed that whatever Talvas said, there was no emotion whatsoever in his eyes. But Bertrand wasn't concentrating on his brother. He was too busy racing through the castle to the chamber where his father lay in bed, his face still frozen in that contorted grimace and his arms flopping limp and useless.

'Father, Father, terrible news!' he exclaimed as he burst into the room. 'Fulk is dead. That bastard Robert of Normandy cut his head right off. We lost everything – all our men, our treasure, everything!'

Talvas, following his brother at a calm, steady pace, arrived at the scene just in time to witness his father's wild-eyed stare, the look of a man facing the slavering jaws of the hounds of hell, and to hear his strangled attempt to speak, though no sound emerged beyond a wordless, crow-like cawing. Then the Count of Bellême gave a final, convulsive shudder that shook him from head to toe before his eyes rolled in his head, his mouth emitted one last gruesome rattle and he dropped back on to his pillow, stone dead.

Bertrand stood there for a few seconds – his jaw had actually dropped open, almost as feebly as his father's, Talvas noticed –

completely unable to cope with yet another death. Then he threw himself on to the bed, his arms around his father's cooling corpse, sobbing helplessly.

Talvas, meanwhile, made sure that there was no one around to see him and then allowed himself the luxury of a smile. When he'd sat down to lunch on that fateful day barely two weeks earlier, there had been four men between him and the title of Count of Bellême. Now there was just one. And as he watched Bertrand's incontinent response to their father's passing, Talvas felt pleasurably certain that he wouldn't be too hard to remove.

12

Robert had hardly wiped the blood from his sword when the messenger Osbern had sent from Rouen caught up with him. The young man was exhausted and his horse lathered in sweat. Still buoyant in the afterglow of a battle survived and won, Robert ordered one of the squires to take the animal away and make sure it was properly fed and watered. He thrust a wine flask into the messenger's hand and, frowning, now said, 'You've ridden hard.'

'Day and night, Your Grace, as my lord Osbern commanded.'

'So what do I need to hear that can't wait until I return?'

'That you must hurry back at once, Your Grace, with all your men.'

'Why, what's happened?' Robert asked, his mind whirling with visions of a French army marching on his capital in support of the archbishop.

'It's the townspeople, Your Grace. They've heard rumours that they're being punished by the Church, and that it's all the fault of your . . . your . . .' The messenger looked around in desperation, as if he might somewhere find the right word to describe the duke's woman.

'My what?'

'Lady Herleva, Your Grace. She was walking through the market when people started shouting insults at her. Then some boys threw things at her. She ran for the castle and—'

Robert gripped both the messenger's arms, hard enough to make the lad wince. 'Was she hurt?'

'No, Your Grace. Some soldiers from the palace rescued her and your son.'

'William?' Robert gasped. 'You mean he was there to see his mother insulted?'

'Yes, Your Grace. But he wasn't hurt. He wasn't even frightened. I heard he wanted to go and fight the townspeople himself.'

For a moment, Robert's mood lightened. 'That's my boy!' he laughed. 'He's a born soldier, that one.' Then he got back down to business. 'What was happening in Rouen when you left? Were the people up in arms?'

'No, Your Grace, but they weren't happy either,' the messenger said. 'They're frightened, Your Grace. There are all sorts of rumours going round. Some people say the Pope has condemned everyone in Normandy to hell. Others think that bodies will be left to rot in the open air or thrown into pits because they can't be buried in proper graveyards. And they don't know why exactly this is all happening, just that the Church has done it because of Lady Herleva. I stopped into an inn to get something to eat and I heard someone say that Lady Herleva was . . . was a witch. I mean, I don't think that, Your Grace, of course I don't. But that's what they were saying.'

'If anyone says that in my hearing, I'll tear their tongue out myself.' Robert grimaced. 'Damn! I wanted to deal with Bellême once and for all, but it'll just have to wait. Herluin!'

Robert gave orders to get the men readied for a hard march back to Rouen.

'Yes, Your Grace,' Herluin replied. 'But what do you want done with all the booty that the Bellêmes looted? We can't just leave it here?'

'Well we can't give it back,' Robert pointed out. 'We have no idea who it belongs to.' He thought for a moment. 'Leave twenty men to load it all up and bring it back to Rouen. We'd better give some of it to the men. They won't fight if there's no profit in it for them. The rest I'll keep, but I'll send alms for anyone who was robbed by the Bellêmes. Anyone still alive, that is.'

Herluin went off to organise the march. But Robert's conversation with the messenger had been overheard. Only a couple of soldiers had been in earshot and they had not caught all of what was said. But they heard enough to start passing on a garbled, misunderstood story that Duke Robert's concubine was a witch, the Church had forbidden the dead to be buried and they were all going to go to hell because of her.

The whispered rumours then took another twist when someone asked, 'What about the men that died here today?' For though the defeat of the Bellêmes had been swift and over-whelming, two militiamen had been killed in the fighting and another three lay injured, one of them on the verge of death. If they couldn't have a proper Christian burial, what would become of their souls?

A mood of unrest descended on the Valley of Blavou, just as it had done on the marketplace at Rouen. A deputation was sent to talk to Duke Robert. They stood before him looking nervous and shamefaced – for every man there knew him to be an astute, courageous and fair-minded commander – before plucking up the courage to ask if the stories were true.

Robert said nothing, but walked across to one of the Bellêmes' carts and climbed up on to it. 'Gather round!' he shouted, then stood with his back straight, his head held high, giving no hint of any doubt or uncertainty as his soldiers ran to hear what he had to say. When they were all gathered in front of him, he said, 'How many of you were with me at Falaise?'

A few hands were stuck in the air and there were shouts from other veterans who had fought through the siege.

'And how many fought with my brother Duke Richard?'

There was another show of hands and more shouting.

'Then you will remember a young woman, heavy with child, who was kidnapped in the forest and threatened with death in the hope that I would rather admit defeat than see her suffer. That woman was Herleva, the tanner's daughter, and the child she bore was my son William. So . . . did she look like a witch to you? Did she scream curses, or cast spells over her enemies? Did demons fly down from the sky to her aid? No. None of that happened. Because she's not a witch. And I will strike down any man who dares suggest that she is with the very same sword I used to cut off Fulk of Bellême's head.'

A voice shouted out from the crowd. 'What about the burials?'

'What about them?' Robert asked. He turned to the friar who had travelled with the war party to act as chaplain. 'Friar Martin, have you been given any orders from your prior to deny the last rites to the dying, or a proper burial to the dead?'

'Not that I know of, Your Grace,' the friar replied.

'Very well then, you will stay here to make sure that no man, on either side, goes unburied or unblessed. I will leave you a purse so that you can pay the men of the village to help you. As to the rest of you, I will say this: it is no secret that my uncle the Archbishop of Rouen and I are in dispute. But our disagreement concerns a matter of state. It has nothing to do with witchcraft, or black magic, or any other kind of devilry. And the sooner we are on the march, the sooner this dispute can be settled. So move, all of you, now!'

Robert seemed to have won his men over. As the long journey back to Rouen began, the mood was good-humoured and the talk turned back to the battle and stories of individual enemies slain or put to flight. Robert had extra rations of wine distributed to the men that night: enough to keep their spirits up without leaving them too drunk to wake early and get on their way at dawn.

It was Sunday, the fourth before Lent, a fresh, bright morning with the sun rising into a deep blue cloudless sky and the air cold and crisp enough to clear the foggiest head. This was a day that reminded men who had recently faced death of the sheer joy of being alive. So it took an hour or more before a question occurred to one of the soldiers. 'What's happened to all the bells?'

Every Sunday morning, without fail, the people were summoned to Mass by the ringing of countless bells across Normandy's towns, villages and countryside, as they were across the whole expanse of Christendom. A Sunday without church was as inconceivable as a morning without sunrise. And yet this morning there was silence.

They came to a village where peasants had gathered round the locked door of a small wooden church. The place looked familiar and Robert realised that they had passed this way a few days earlier, on the way to fight the Bellêmes. That day, he and the militia had been greeted as heroes, come to save the people from the threat of violence and robbery. Now the faces that looked up at the long line of armed, mounted men were sullen and resentful. None of them dared do or even say anything, for fear of a retribution they could not hope to resist, but their silence told Robert all he needed to know.

His men were no happier than the peasants. The Church had closed its doors to the people of Normandy. God had turned His back on them. The Norman Militia had no fear of any man or army on earth, but this rejection terrified them.

For three more days they rode north. Robert drove them harder with every league that passed, wanting to get the journey over, desperate to escape from the angry eyes and muttered insults of his people. The militia kept their discipline. They still obeyed his orders, but their spirits had been crushed and their affection for him as a leader dashed.

On the third night of the march, Robert sat by a campfire, a goblet of wine in one hand, staring at the dancing flames as if the answers to all the problems that beset him were somehow hidden there. He turned his head at the sound of footsteps and saw Herluin standing a few paces away.

'May I?' he asked, pointing at the ground next to Robert.

'Be my guest.'

The two men sat in a tense, uneasy silence, drinking their wine. Robert was the first to speak. 'What is it?'

Herluin sighed, grimaced and rubbed the back of his neck with his hand, trying to find the right words. Then he asked, 'May I speak with you as a friend?'

'Of course,' Robert replied.

Herluin's face screwed up once again. 'Look, Robert . . . Your Grace . . . I've known you all my life, and as long as we both live, you can count on my loyalty. Any battle, I'll be there beside you. Any argument, I'm on your side. You know that.'

Robert nodded, his eyes fixed firmly back on the fire.

'And Herleva's a beautiful girl. She's always stood by you, no matter how bad things have been. And she's given you a son that any man would be proud of.'

'I know,' said Robert, picking up a piece of wood and jabbing it hard at the fire.

'But . . .' Herluin took a deep breath as he summoned up the courage to say the words they both knew were coming next, 'you can't keep her. You know your uncle won't ever back down. And if he keeps the interdict in place, the whole of Normandy will rise up against you . . . and God knows what they'll do to Herleva. I'm sorry, Robert, I really am.'

Robert said nothing, just kept poking the fire. 'You remember when Fulbert of Chartres came to deliver my uncle's demands, and his threats? That fishmonger arrived with the news from Alençon and I sent you off to summon the militia . . .'

'Yes.'

'Well, after you'd gone, Fulbert said that it didn't matter how big an army I had, I could never beat God.'

'Well he's right.'

'But if God's against me, why did He let me defeat the Bellêmes? That doesn't make sense.'

'I don't know. It's not for us to understand or explain His will. But you'll never win back the love of the people as long as the church doors stay locked, that's for certain.'

'But I can't give her up . . . I just can't . . .'

Herluin put an arm round Robert's slumped, disconsolate shoulders. 'I know. If I were you, I couldn't give her up either . . . But what else can you possibly do?'

The question was asked without any expectation of an answer. But Robert spent several more hours sitting by the fire, prodding away at the dying embers with his stick, until, shortly before dawn, the first inklings of a plan came to his mind. By the time he mounted his steed to lead the final march to Rouen, he knew exactly what he had to do. Others might not agree with him, but if there were any objections, he had a reply already in mind: can you think of anything better?

13

Rouen, Normandy

Robert arrived back at the ducal palace late that afternoon. He found Herleva in the solar, the private room decorated with beautiful tapestries and intricately patterned rugs where she spent her days with the other women of the household. She was standing by a window with the shutters wide open, heedless of the cold draught as she looked out, lost in thought. Robert slipped into the chamber as quietly as he could, trying not to disturb her, and stood for a moment by the doorway, just to watch her. He wanted to paint a picture of her in his mind, an image he could keep with him for the rest of his life, whether she was with him or not. He wished his uncle could see her now. Surely he would see that she looked fit to be a duchess.

A soft, private smile crossed her face and his heart ached at her perfect beauty. She was wearing a veil that covered her head and fell across her shoulders. But a few locks of her wonderful golden-red hair had somehow escaped and they shone against the deep emerald green of her dress, which was cut by some magic of the seamstress's art so that it clung to the upper half of her body, emphasising the glorious contrast between the fullness of her breasts and a waist that was still as slender as the day Robert had first set eyes on her.

William was sitting on the floor in front of a huge open fireplace filled with blazing logs, playing a game with his grandmother, Doda, who had journeyed from Falaise to be with her daughter at her time of crisis. He spotted Robert and

313

pointed at him, crying out, 'Papa!' before jumping to his feet and racing towards his father. Robert reached out and grabbed William in both hands, then swung him up into the air, provoking shrieks of excitement. 'Again, again!' William squealed, and this time Robert let go when his arms were at their furthest stretch, tossing the little boy into the air before he caught him again and put him back down on the floor.

'Again!' demanded William, more crossly this time.

'No, that's enough,' said Robert.

'Please, Papa, please!'

'I said no,' Robert repeated, in a tone that made it clear he wasn't open to argument. He reached down and ruffled his son's mop of red hair. 'I need to speak to Mama,' he said.

'Come along, William,' said Doda, taking his hand. She bobbed her head, murmured, 'Your Grace,' and led her reluctant grandson out of the room.

Herleva had spotted Robert doing his best to enter the room unnoticed, but chose not to go to him right away. She wanted time to stretch out as slowly as possible, so that every instant she had with him could be savoured and treasured. She knew he was looking at her and imagined his hands caressing her body as his eyes were now doing. The discovery that love could be such an overwhelming, all-consuming pleasure had transformed her whole existence. To have him inside her; to feel his hands and his mouth on her; to know the countless ways that he could bring her to a point of ecstasy and abandonment – how could she possibly live without that? The dress she had chosen for his return was so perfectly fitted that Judith had been obliged to sew her into it, and a smile crossed her face as she wondered how Robert was going to solve the problem of taking it off.

Then William had noticed his father and responded with typical energy and exuberance, so that Herleva could no longer

314

pretend to be unaware of Robert's presence. She saw his face light up as he played with his son. This was surely what God had intended: a man, a woman and a child, all united by love. How could it possibly be sinful? She put the thought aside. There would be time for questions later. For now she wanted nothing but Robert in her mind and her heart. And so, as he put William down and watched Judith take him away, Herleva turned and walked towards her man.

Neither of them said anything. As their lips met in a burning, desperate kiss, there was no subtlety or even tenderness, just a raw hunger born of the knowledge that they had to take one another now and somehow try to satisfy their insatiable longing completely, for who knew how many more chances they might have? Herleva ran her hands over his face, frantic for one last touch of his skin beneath her fingertips and the abrasive scrape of his stubble. Robert clawed at her dress, trying to find a way to undo it until finally he growled, 'The hell with this,' and simply lifted her off her feet, carried her across the room and laid her down close to the warmth of the fire on a soft Persian rug.

He kneeled down next to her, never taking his eyes off hers. Then he reached down, put one hand on each of her legs, just below the knee, holding them through the fabric of her dress, and parted them a little.

He took out the dagger that hung from his belt. 'Don't move,' he said. 'Stay completely still.'

Herleva nodded, her eyes fixed on the dagger, whose blade glinted gold, orange and scarlet in the firelight.

Robert plunged the dagger into the dress in the gap between her thighs and she gave a little moan. He grabbed the skirt with his left hand and pulled in one direction while his right hand dragged the dagger in the other, ripping the fabric of the dress and the linen chemise beneath it. He put the dagger down, then reached into the hole he had just made, grabbing either side of the tear and pulling them apart until the whole dress had been split from top to bottom. One final cut of the knife slashed through the hem. He threw the skirt open, leaving Herleva completely naked and exposed from the waist down.

She moaned again and her hips squirmed.

'I said don't move,' Robert repeated. Then he pulled off his boots, his long woollen gown, his undershirt, his breeches and his hose.

Herleva looked him up and down, saw the evidence of his desire for her and said just a single word: 'Now.'

Robert had been a boy when Herleva had first shared his bed, and she an innocent, utterly inexperienced girl. Now he was a man. His body had filled out and hardened, so that he was broader in the shoulders, more solidly muscled in his torso and limbs. His callow, nervous uncertainty had been replaced by the confidence that came from years spent learning how to please a lover. And she for her part had lost any shame about her desire for him. She gloried in it. As their bodies joined together, fusing so perfectly and naturally that they seemed to share a single existence Herleva felt at one and the same time completely exposed to Robert, utterly at his mercy, and yet entirely safe. She had absolute trust in his love for her, and an equal certainty in her own power to inflame him with desire and satisfy his needs as well as her own.

There had been nights when they had drawn out their loving as long as possible, withholding the final release for so long that the need for it became an exquisite agony. But now there was no time for that. Now they made love with a fierce, unrelenting intensity, Herleva's moans rising to screams before her back arched and the muscles deep in her belly fluttered. As her body and mind were struck by a lightning bolt of pure joy, she heard

316

Robert groan and then felt him subside, and they were left silent, breathless and overwhelmed by what they had, and what they would lose.

Robert rolled over on to his back and Herleva moved with him, wrapping herself around his body, with one of his thighs between her legs and her head on his chest. She listened as his heartbeat slowed and his breathing became calmer.

'My darling,' Robert began, 'I don't know how to say this, but—'

'Sshhh . . .' Herleva put a finger on his lips to silence him. 'You don't have to say anything. I understand. I know what has to happen. You have to abandon me. All I ask is, please, make sure that William is safe and properly cared for.'

'No!' Robert lifted his head and, cradling her in his arms, looked down at her face. 'I will never abandon you. Even if we cannot be together, I'll always make sure that you are looked after, and I'll always recognise William as my firstborn son, no matter what happens.'

'But how?'

Robert gently laid her back on the rug and got to his feet. 'I'm going to talk to Bishop Fulbert. You'd better find another dress. I'll meet you before supper and then I'll tell you everything.'

14

The moment Robert walked into the audience chamber and announced that he was giving up Herleva and restoring all his uncle's titles and properties, Bishop Fulbert's entire demeanour was transformed and the smooth, ruthless negotiator was replaced by an affable man of the world. 'My dear boy,' he said, putting an avuncular arm around Robert's shoulder, 'you are making a wise and truly noble decision. Besides, there's no reason why you can't still enjoy the young lady's charms, which I gather are all too apparent. Mother Church is very understanding. She knows that great demands are placed upon those whom God has called to be temporal leaders of His people, so special dispensations are required. If you uphold the sanctity of marriage in public, show due courtesy to your wife and provide her with children, so that her maternal instincts are properly fulfilled, then your private affairs are of no concern. Provided you confess to them in full, of course. That's tremendously important.'

Robert pulled away in disgust. 'First you ask me to betray my woman. Now you want me to dishonour her too. Be grateful that you wear a bishop's ring, Fulbert of Chartres. If you did not, I'd make you pay for those words.'

'Forgive me, Your Grace, I meant no offence. I was merely suggesting that your sacrifice need not be quite as great as you imagine.'

Robert had more important things to do than argue with this smug, slippery cleric. It was time to bring the conversation to a close. 'Please convey to my uncle my sincere desire to resolve any outstanding problems that may exist between us, and my humble and heartfelt request for the lifting of the interdict that has been placed upon the people of Normandy. They have suffered enough for my stubbornness.'

'I will be glad to do so,' Fulbert replied. 'And please be assured that my holy father the archbishop and I will both pray for you, giving thanks to God for your change of heart and beseeching Him to grant you such wisdom that you will never again stray from the path of righteousness, but will strive at all times to further the glory of His name.'

'Thank you, Bishop Fulbert. That will be all.'

Once the bishop had left, Robert sent servants to Herluin and Herleva, telling them to meet him in the audience chamber. 'Please ask my lady Herleva to bring her silver wine strainer,' he added.

Another member of the household staff was dispatched to fetch the finest bottle of wine that the cellarer could provide. Robert supervised the arrangement of three chairs in a rough circle, with a table near them on which the wine and three golden goblets, one even more lavishly bejewelled than the others, were placed.

'So, what's all this about?' asked Herluin as he walked briskly into the room and looked around at the unexpected arrangement.

'Take a seat,' Robert said, waving at one of the chairs.

A moment later, Herleva arrived. She had changed into a simple, unadorned dress of plain brown wool with an equally austere white wimple on her head. Yet for all the nun-like purity of her appearance, Robert had to make a conscious effort to quell the lust that stirred in him as soon as he clapped eyes on her.

'Perhaps you will do me the honour of serving the wine,' he said, trying and failing to sound casual.

Herleva unclasped the chain from which the strainer hung

and poured the rich, red vintage through it into Robert's personal goblet.

'Thank you,' he said, politely but with no endearment at the end of the sentence. Normally he would have called her 'my love', or smiled at her with eyes that made no secret of his desire, and Herleva bit her lip to try and distract herself from the sharp dart of pain that had cut into her at this evidence that everything between them had changed for ever. She tapped the strainer on the table to remove the grounds that had settled there and filled another goblet for Herluin. Finally she saw to herself, pouring a smaller, more ladylike portion than she had allowed for the men. Over the past four years she had acquired the habits and mannerisms of a gentlewoman. She wondered what new role would be in store for her now.

Robert took a long sip of his wine, using it to buy time while he composed his thoughts. Then he looked at Herleva and Herluin in turn. 'In all the world there are three people whom I truly love,' he began. 'One of them is William. You are the other two. So now I want to recognise and reward you, Herluin, for your friendship, your loyalty and your bravery in my service. I am raising you to lordly status, giving you the title of Viscount of Conteville. It's a lovely place, near to Honfleur, by the mouth of the River Seine, and I'm granting you and your heirs an estate there worthy of your new rank, along with permission to raise a castle.'

Herluin blushed scarlet, and Herleva smiled as she saw the pleasure in Robert's face and the overwhelming emotion in Herluin's. 'Thank you . . . thank you so much, Robert, Your Grace . . . I'm lost for words. Thank you.'

'Now I must ask you one more favour.' Robert paused for a second. 'I want you to take Herleva as your viscountess.'

'What?' Herleva gasped, though she barely had breath enough to make a sound.

'Your Grace . . .' Herluin began, but then had no idea what to say next.

Robert continued, regardless, with a desperate enthusiasm. 'I really believe this is the best thing for all of us. I want you both to leave Rouen and live in peace, away from all the politics and plotting of court life. Your soldiering days are over, Herluin. I won't ever again call on you to fight by my side. Just gather your crops and breed your cattle. Raise a family. If you are a good husband to Herleva and as loyal to her as you have always been to me, you'll be doing me the greatest service I could ever ask.'

Now Robert turned to Herleva, who was as wide-eyed and startled as a doe suddenly cornered by hounds.

'My darling, Herluin doesn't need me to tell him that you're the most beautiful woman in all of Normandy. I know how . . .' Robert searched for the right phrase and could only manage, 'how highly he thinks of you. But I want you to know that he is the most honest, trustworthy, decent and brave man that any woman could wish for.'

Robert looked at his lover, then his friend, then back again, knowing that he was asking the impossible, but determined to carry the idea through, for want of any better solution. 'I can't order you to love one another,' he said. 'But I hope you'll care for each other as a husband and wife should, respect one another and support one another. Perhaps, with God's grace, love will grow between you.'

Robert could see he wasn't getting anywhere. 'Look, I didn't want any of this to happen, but it has and now we have to make the best of things. I want you to know, Herleva, that your family will keep all their privileges. It doesn't matter what my uncle says, I'm still the duke, Falaise Castle is still my possession and your father's still going to be the steward.'

Herleva said nothing. She was still trying to come to terms

with the way Robert was disposing of her and mapping out her life with someone else, as though her feelings and her will had nothing to do with any of it. He's worked the whole thing out, she was thinking. He must have known he was going to say this, even when we were together in the solar. Why didn't he say anything, or warn me, or . . . ?

And then Herleva was hit by something Robert hadn't mentioned, that he must deliberately have been avoiding. 'What about William?' she asked, with quiet despair. 'Do you still want to be his father?'

'Of course!' Robert exclaimed. 'He's my only child, my son . . . I want him to be my heir.'

A faint tremor of hope returned to Herleva's expression and voice. 'So you'll see him from time to time, and maybe you'll see me, too . . .'

'My dear, I'll see him all the time. If William is to be the next Duke of Normandy, he has to be brought up here, at court. The people have to be able to see him. My barons need to know that my mind is made up. William will succeed me, whatever claims anyone else may make on the duchy. And he has to be trained so that he's ready to—'

'No!' Herleva cried. 'No, you can't! You can't take my boy! I can't lose you, and him too . . . I just can't!'

She leaped to her feet and ran weeping from the chamber.

Robert drained his goblet and threw it across the room. 'Damn!' he shouted. 'Damn, damn, damn!'

Herluin got up and walked across to where the goblet was lying. He picked it up, then walked back via the table where the wine jug stood. He filled the goblet and gave it back to Robert, and poured some more for himself. Then he sat down, looked at his despondent friend and said, 'Shall I order more wine, Your Grace? We're going to need it.'

15

Life as the mistress of a palace filled with courtiers and servants had taught Herleva the importance of controlling her emotions in public. The slightest sign of distress was enough to set tongues wagging. So she remained outwardly calm for as long as it took to find her mother in the solar, warming herself by the fire. Only then did she break down. Doda took her daughter in her arms and began a gentle interrogation, trying to assemble a coherent story out of the fragments of information, like the individual pieces of a scrambled mosaic that Herleva provided through her tears.

The gist of it was soon clear enough. It had been obvious to Doda from the moment she'd arrived in Rouen and felt the tension and hostility inside the palace, let alone on the streets of the town, that Duke Robert would have to back down. The only question in her mind was how he was going to do it. In the event, he'd tried to do the right thing, even if he hadn't found the right way to tell Herleva, assuming there actually was a right way, which Doda very much doubted. So now it was up to her to talk her daughter into accepting an offer far more generous than a common-born mistress of a great lord had any right to expect. She took Herleva's hand, looked her in the eye and kindly but very firmly said, 'My darling, you must obey the duke and marry Herluin, or you'll spend the rest of your life wishing you had.'

'But Mama—'

'But nothing. Listen to me, girl. Robert could never have

323

wed you, and he knows it. The archbishop is right. A duke can't take his bride from the tanneries of Falaise.'

Herleva shook her head, trying to deny the truth before she asked, 'But how can he just give me away to Herluin?'

'He's not just giving you away, though, is he?' said Doda, leading her daughter over to an ornately carved settle strewn with embroidered cushions on which they both sat down. 'He's doing everything he can to provide for you. He's giving you a husband and a title and land enough that you'll never want for anything as long as you live. And he's making your son his heir . . . My God, girl, think what kind of life you'd have had if you'd never met Robert of Normandy. You'd have ended up like me with a smelly old tanner for a husband, living by a dungheap. Ugh!'

There were tears in Herleva's eyes, but her mother's exaggerated expression of disgust forced a snuffly giggle out of her. 'Your life wasn't that bad!'

'Well, no, I suppose not, but I'm a lot happier in the steward's house at Falaise, I'll tell you that.'

'Don't worry, Mama. Robert's going to let you and Papa stay at the castle.'

Doda patted Herleva's hand. 'He's a good man, that one. But it's not me I'm worried about. Sweetheart, what do you think will happen to you if you turn Robert down? Do you really want to be out in the wide world all on your own, with people whispering behind your back, calling you a witch, blaming you for leading their young duke astray?'

'But I didn't!' Herleva protested.

'Of course you didn't, but that won't stop folk saying you did. But if you go off to Conteville with Herluin, as a proper lady, people will have to treat you with respect. And if they see you with their own eyes being a good wife to Herluin, raising children and looking after all the people on your estate, they'll

324

soon forget anyone ever had a bad word to say about you. You're a lovely girl. Anyone who knows you loves you.'

'But what about William? I can't leave my little boy, Mama . . . I just can't.'

'I know, sweetheart, I know. But William's not just your little boy, is he? He's going to be the Duke of Normandy. That kind of rank comes with its own burdens and sacrifices, and we just have to accept them. I mean, just think of Our Lady, the Blessed Virgin Mary. She had to see her son, our Saviour, sacrificed for our sins. Take comfort and inspiration from her . . . Ah, there there, my darling, don't cry . . .' Doda reached out as her daughter nestled against her.

'I can't bear it, Mama. We were so happy,' said Herleva, lifting her eyes to look at her mother. 'And now . . . now I'm losing everything!'

'I know, I know.' Doda stroked Herleva's back. 'It hurts now, that's only natural. But you'll still be able to see William from time to time. And you'll have a new life to think about. You can't imagine ever loving Herluin now, of course you can't. But who knows what will happen in time? The men we fall desperately in love with when we're young girls aren't always the best ones to look after us and our children when we get a little older.'

'I'll always love Robert, so how can I ever love anyone else?'

'Because we do. Maybe not in exactly the same way, perhaps, but it's still love. And sometimes that peaceful, gentle kind of love is the deepest love of all.'

'But I don't ever want to love anyone more than Robert. I'd hate that. It would feel like betraying him.'

Doda sighed. 'Oh, my poor, sweet Herleva, seeing you like this makes me glad I'm not young any more. Now . . . go to Herluin and tell him that you consent to be his wife. And don't sound too miserable when you're doing it. He knows he's second best in your eyes, but there's no need to make it obvious. The only way this will ever work is if you sincerely try to make the very best of it, so you might as well start as you mean to go on.'

Doda got to her feet. 'Now then, stand up,' she said briskly. She handed Herleva a linen kerchief. 'Here, wipe your eyes and your nose. Now let's get a splash of cold water on your face. We can't have you going to your husband-to-be looking all red and blotchy, can we? Come on, stand up straight, young lady. Head up! Deep breath! Ready?'

Herleva steadied herself. 'Yes, Mama.'

'Then go and meet your new husband.'

Herleva returned to the audience chamber and announced, without looking at her intended groom, that she was willing to take Herluin's hand in marriage. Robert thanked her with the exaggerated stiffness of a drunk man trying to maintain the appearance of sobriety, then swiftly left the chamber, telling the other two that he was leaving them to talk in private. The truth was that he could not bear to see Herleva with anyone else, not even a man he had chosen for her. His heart was breaking too. But he was the Duke of Normandy. He could not afford to let a single weakness show.

Herluin had not kept pace with the duke's consumption of wine. He'd decided that Herleva was bound to come back to them with an answer. The chances were that she'd turn him down, but he wanted to have his wits about him, just in case she agreed to Robert's scheme. As for himself, he needed a clear head to think his own position through. He was being offered a title, an estate and the hand of the loveliest woman in Normandy. Only a madman would turn that down. Yet it would surely be just as foolish to condemn himself to a lifetime with a wife whose heart and body had already been given to another man. When he and Herleva were finally alone, they stood for a while in uncomfortable silence, neither knowing quite how to start the conversation until Herluin said, 'The trouble with dukes is that they always expect to get their own way.'

Herleva laughed gratefully, relieved that he'd not tried to win her over by claiming a sudden new-found passion.

'Robert's always been clever,' Herluin went on. 'He knows how to turn things to his advantage.'

'He kept Falaise Castle.'

'Exactly. Bellême thought he'd won. He'd captured you. He'd threatened your life. But Robert still found a way to win.'

'Is that what he's doing now, do you think: winning?'

Herluin shook his head sadly. 'No. He's losing you. He doesn't want to show it, but I've known him half my life, I was with him when his father died, and I've never seen him hurt this badly. He loves you with all his heart. He loves you so much he's prepared to make me a viscount and send me away from his side just so you can have everything he can possibly give you.'

'But what about you?' Herleva asked. 'What do you want?'

'Does it matter? Robert is my liege lord. I'm sworn to his service. If he commands me to dedicate myself to you, that's what I'll do.'

'Is that what this is then, an order you've got to obey? It's all Robert this and Robert that. Don't you care about me at all?'

'Of course I care,' Herluin said, with an intensity that caught Herleva completely off guard. 'I was there the day he met you. I saw the same girl he did. Believe me, if he'd been any other man in the world, I wouldn't have let him take you without a fight.'

Herleva frowned. There was no mistaking the sincerity in Herluin's voice. 'I never knew that,' she said. 'You never showed any interest in me at all.'

'How could I? You belonged to Robert.'

327

'And now I suppose I belong to you.'

'Don't say it like that, as if you don't have any choice in the matter.'

'But I don't.'

'You do. If you really can't face the idea of being my wife, turn me down. Look, I don't expect you to love me right away. I just want you to give me a chance . . . give *us* a chance. If we're going to be married, then we should act as if we mean it.'

'You sound like my mother,' said Herleva. 'That's what she said.'

'Then you should listen to her, she's a very sensible woman. So . . . ?'

Herleva could still feel the after-effects of her lovemaking with Robert. Just to think of him ripping her dress in his desperation to take her was enough to reawaken all the ecstasy of being with him and the raw wound of losing him. But she had no choice. She said, 'I'll try. I promise you, Herluin, that I'll try,' and she let him enfold her in a brief, passionless hug. And so, in the space of a few hours, her whole life changed for ever.

Robert's heart was broken twice over: once by watching Herleva leave, and a second time by the sight of William's helpless incomprehension. The poor little boy couldn't understand why his mama was crying. Her sadness frightened him and her tears made him cry too. She was dressed in her outdoors cloak, the one she wore for travelling. And she was crouching down in front of him, kissing him and telling him to be a good, brave boy. And William couldn't understand what was going on.

Robert and Herleva had told him that she was going away, but neither of them had been able to give him a decent answer when he'd asked, 'Why?' William had watched Judith packing up all Herleva's clothes into great big wooden trunks and had stood by as the servants had piled them on to a big wagon, with two oxen to pull it. But he couldn't understand why none of his own clothes or his toys had been packed too. He kept pulling at Judith's hand and shouting, 'We go! We go with Mama!' while Judith tried to explain through her own tears that they were staying here. Judith wasn't going with Mama because she was here with William, and she was crying too.

In truth, Robert's own feelings were little different from William's. Why did he have to stand here like a silent, motionless statue and watch the woman he loved hold Herluin's hand for balance as she stepped up into the carriage that was taking her away? He watched William trying to pull himself away from Judith's grasp so that he could run to the carriage. Judith was holding him so hard that William cried out in pain, then he started to cry and shout, 'Mama! Mama! I want my mama!'

Herleva leaned out of the carriage and gazed back at William. Then she looked up at Robert, silently pleading with him to do something. But he couldn't. The only way he could stop himself from breaking down and crying like his son was to detach himself completely from everything that was going on around him, to remain the stern, impassive duke. The mask was crumbling, though. If that damn carriage didn't get out of the palace yard and through the gate soon, he was going to collapse completely.

Now Herluin had mounted his horse and ordered the wagon driver and Herleva's carriage to get going. Six soldiers rode alongside, to act as escort on the road to Conteville. At last the carriage was going towards the palace gate. There was no turning back. She was leaving them.

William gave one last, extra-hard tug and suddenly he was free and running as fast as he could after his mama's carriage, shouting and shouting, begging her to stop and come back.

But she didn't. And when he got right up to the gate, a

guard caught him and carried him back to where Judith was waiting. William kicked and punched as hard as he could, but the guard just laughed. Then Judith took him and this time she didn't let him get away.

'Come on, William,' she said. 'Let's go and see if we can get you some nice bread and milk.'

She took the boy to the kitchens and they found bread and milk, and a handful of currants too. William ate them and felt a little bit better. But when he went to bed that night, he asked Robert why Mama hadn't come to kiss him good night. 'I prayed and prayed,' he said, 'so why won't she come?'

Robert had no good answer to that question either. All he could say was, 'Don't worry, Will, you'll feel better soon. We all will.' But he knew he was lying. William would see his mother again one day. Maybe that would help. But for Robert, the joy had been taken from his life, and he feared that it had gone for good.

Book Four:

Sacrifice and Redemption

Summer 1034–February 1037

1

Winchester, England, and Rouen, Normandy

Canute the Great, monarch of a northern empire encompassing England, Denmark, Norway and a substantial portion of Sweden, leaned across to his wife, seated on the throne next to his in the great hall of Winchester Palace, indicating that he wanted her to move towards him too. When their heads were almost touching, Canute held up a hand to prevent sharp-eyed attendants from observing what was said and whispered, 'Is this any of your doing?'

'I promise you, Your Majesty, I had nothing whatever to do with it,' Queen Emma replied.

'You've not been corresponding with that brother of yours in Rouen, or your sons?'

'I've never had any contact with Edward and Alfred, not once in all these years,' she said, trying very hard not to let the pain she felt creep into her voice: the last thing Canute wanted was an emotional, nagging wife. 'I made that promise to you, and I've kept it. And yes, Archbishop Robert of Rouen and I do write to one another. But never about this.'

'Huh, I see. So this is all the duke's doing, then?'

'I couldn't say for certain, Your Majesty. But this is a formal embassy from Normandy, so that's a reasonable assumption.'

Canute nodded and sat straight again. 'Very well, approach the throne,' he said.

A bishop in full regalia, complete with mitre and staff, stepped forward, accompanied by a monk in a simple brown habit, and two finely dressed noblemen. They all bowed before the king and queen, and then the bishop spoke.

'Your Majesty, I greet you most humbly on behalf of His Grace Duke Robert of Normandy, who in turn beseeches you in the name of Edward and Alfred, the sons of King Ethelred of England.'

At the mention of Ethelred and his sons, Canute became visibly more tense. 'Proceed,' he said, in a voice that dripped menace.

The bishop was taken aback by the evident hostility the names had aroused in the king. Clearing his throat nervously, he unrolled a parchment, held it out before him and began to read, in a quavering voice.

'Whereas Edward and Alfred of England, who were born princes – or as their own people do call them, "athelings" – were driven from their home some sixteen summers ago; and whereas they have lived ever since in exile in Normandy; and whereas I look on them now not just as cousins, but as brothers and bearers of a common blood; and whereas it grieves me to see them bereft and deprived of their land and birthright, I plead with Your Majesty, look upon these sons of England with kindness and mercy and allow them to return to England, to swear their fealty to you and to live among their people once again. Praying God for his grace and mercy on you and your people, I remain your most humble servant Robert, Duke of Normandy.'

The bishop seemed relieved to have come to the end of the words on the parchment without any serious mishap. But they did not appear to have had much effect on Canute. He sat in stone-faced contemplation for a few seconds, then asked, 'Tell me, Bishop, are these the duke's own words?'

'Oh yes, Your Majesty. His Grace took great care in their composition and personally supervised the writing of them too.'

'And he is sincere in calling these athelings his brothers, and pleading on their behalf?'

'Oh, absolutely, Your Majesty. His Grace has known King Edward and Pr—'

'King Edward?' Canute exclaimed. 'King of what, exactly?'

'Well, that is simply how he is known in Normandy, Your Majesty.'

'Is he King of Normandy, then?'

'No, Your Majesty.'

'Has he been crowned? Has he been blessed with sacred ointment in the sight of his people, like a true monarch?'

'Well, no, Your Majesty, nothing like that.'

'And yet he calls himself a king, does he? Well not in this land, not as long as I have breath in my body!'

Canute stood up and drew himself to his full height before glaring down from the dais at the bishop, who had to crane his head to look the king in the eye. 'Go back to Normandy, all of you!' he roared. 'Tell your duke that I reject his plea. Tell him that it is only out of my mercy, and my respect for their mother . . .'

Emma sat rigid and unblinking, looking straight ahead of her, doing everything she could to keep her face as still and expressionless as a mask as Canute's words ripped her heart from her body.

'. . . that the sons of Ethelred are alive at all. They should be grateful for that alone. Now be gone! Get out of my sight and return home to Normandy, and be sure not to tarry, or I'll have you all killed and send nothing back to your duke but your heads.'

Canute glowered at the Normans' departing backs as they all but ran from the hall. Then he looked around at the other plaintiffs, courtiers, nobles and servants, muttered, 'I've had enough for one day,' and stalked away to his private chambers, leaving his queen alone and ignored behind him.

335

Emma breathed deeply, straightened her back and raised her head. With every ounce of queenly dignity she still possessed, she took her time about rising from her throne and leaving the hall. She made sure not to catch Godwin's eye. The last thing she needed if she wanted to keep her tears in check was even the faintest suggestion of sympathy. She had just descended from the dais and been met by three of her ladies-in-waiting when Harold Harefoot, the younger son of Canute's association – Emma refused to label it a marriage – with Elgiva of Northampton, barged his way past the other women and stood directly in her way.

Harold hadn't become any more handsome or civilised over the years. He was sweaty, spattered with mud and reeking of alcohol, the evidence of another day devoted to his two favourite activities: hunting and drinking.

'Well that went well,' he sneered. 'So sorry that I won't have the chance to get to know your boys. Oh, by the way, did you hear about my dear mother?'

Emma said nothing. This was, very obviously, not a conversation she wished to pursue.

Harold went on regardless. 'It seems that the good people of Norway don't appreciate her charms. They've threatened to kick her and my brother Svein right out of their godforsaken country. Svein's thinking of going to Denmark. I don't know why. Maybe he wants to get rid of your boy Harthacnut and have it for himself. But if Mother has to leave, she's coming back home.'

'I'm sure I'll look forward to seeing her again,' Emma said.

'Ha! Bet you can't wait,' Harold sneered with clodhopping sarcasm. 'Just think, she'll be here at court. And I'll be the only son of Canute or Ethelred present in England. So if anything should happen to my father – though God forbid, of course – well, there'd only be one possible person to succeed him: me.

I'm going to be your next king, Your Majesty, and no, before you have any mad ideas, I certainly won't marry you the way the last two did.'

'Thank you for that assurance,' said Emma.

'But not for much else, eh?' said Harold. 'Not for very much else at all.'

Emma forced her way past him and walked stony-faced to the solar. Only there, in the company of her ladies, did she finally give in to her grief.

Robert's deputation returned home to Rouen and told him of their humiliation, and by extension, his. He stalked off to his chamber, slamming the door in the faces of all the courtiers who followed him and raged in private. For years he'd put up with Edward moaning at him to do something to help him get back to England. It had taken months to persuade the self-proclaimed king that his only chance of going home was to return as Canute's humble subject. Now that hard-won concession had been thrown right back in Robert's face. Well to hell with that. He was Duke of Normandy, a proud scion of Rollo the Strider's line. He wasn't going to let anyone insult him like that.

'That arrogant Dane calls himself Canute the Great,' Robert told his barons at dinner that night. 'Let's see just how great he is when he matches his sword against some proper Norman steel.'

2

Fécamp, Normandy

More than three years had passed since his mother had left the ducal palace and gone off to marry Viscount Herluin. Now William was a sturdy young pup of six – or as he insisted, almost seven years of age – standing on the cliffs above the bay at Fécamp, on the north-east coast of Normandy. As far as he could see, the water was covered with ships, hundreds of them, some with prows carved into the shapes of angels, dragons or sea monsters; others whose sails were emblazoned with crests, or dazzling patterns of stripes or sunrays; others again – the ones belonging to the very richest nobles – adorned with gilded prows and stern posts so that they shone with dazzling brilliance in the bright spring sunshine. Alongside the warships, with their lean whippet lines and hulls topped with rows of shields to protect their warrior oarsmen, lay the fatter, more ungainly merchantmen that would carry the supplies and horses on which a waterborne army would depend. Smaller craft scuttled between the longboats, ferrying men, food and weapons. William watched, entranced, as a line of men passed one bundle of arrows after another from one of the little ferryboats up to the most magnificent of all the vessels, his father's flagship, which Robert had named the *Lady Judith*, after his mother. A golden leopard roared from the prow, and its sails were coloured a deep, imperial purple.

William thought the *Lady Judith* was the most wonderful thing he had ever seen in his life. A day earlier, he had actually been allowed to go aboard and had looked on wide-eyed as Airad, her captain, and commander of the whole fleet, whose thick black beard was long enough to rest on his barrel chest, had told him, 'This beauty is so big, Master William, that your father, God bless His Grace, and six of his knights can come aboard with their horses, without the need for one of those slow old transports to stick the beasts in.'

Airad patted the mast, as thick as a tree trunk, that reached way up into the sky. 'Look at this here – the tallest mast, with the biggest sail on the ocean. Our *Judith*'s the fastest ship for a thousand leagues around. And if the wind doesn't blow, no matter. We can row her. Can you count all the oars, Master William?'

William frowned with concentration as he went along the line of oars, lost count at nine and had to start again.

Airad laughed at the lad's frustration. 'I'll save you the trouble, young 'un. There's eighteen pairs of blades and thirty-six strong men to pull 'em. Only the best for His Grace the duke.'

At that moment, there was nothing in the whole world that William wanted more than the chance to set sail with his father on the *Lady Judith*, and a day later, absolutely nothing had changed.

'Please can I go with you to England, Papa?' he pleaded.

Robert, who was examining the same scene with a much more calculating eye, looked down at his only child, on whom the hopes of his family dynasty rested, and ruffled his hand through that thick mop of blazing red hair. His mother's hair, thought Robert, the wound of losing her still unhealed.

'Pleasepleasepleaseplease!' William insisted.

Robert dragged his mind away from the thought of Herleva. 'No, William, for the five hundredth time, you can't,' he said. 'And don't look at me like that, young man, or I'll put you over my knee and give you a sound thrashing, right in front of the soldiers.'

William ignored the threat, knowing that the argument still had a long way to go before there was any danger that his father might actually carry it out.

'But Papa, why can't I come? Cousin Alfred's going with you. Why am I always, always left behind? It's not fair!'

'Because Cousin Alfred is a grown man and you're a small boy, that's why.'

William fixed his father with outraged eyes. 'I am NOT small!' he piped, his voice rising in pitch as well as volume.

'Maybe not for a boy your age. But next to a proper grown-up man, yes, you're still very small. And this is not an expedition for boys.'

Robert bent down and lifted William up on to his back, so that their heads were side by side, then pointed out towards the sea. 'All those ships are here for a very, very serious reason. We've got to sail to England, which is dangerous enough. When we get there, we may have to fight the English, and you are much, much too young to be getting into real battles just yet. There'll be plenty of time for that when you're older.'

'But I'm not going to be older for ages and ages, Papa,' said William impatiently. Then another question struck him and he forgot all about how horribly long it was taking him to grow up. 'Who are you going to fight, Papa? Will you fight King Canute and kill him so that Cousin Edward can be king?'

'If Canute wants to have a battle, I won't run away, and if we fight, then he may get killed, because that's what happens in battles.'

'But you won't get killed, will you, Papa?'

Robert laughed. 'I hope not! I've been in lots of battles and no one's killed me yet.'

'Good,' said William, with a finality that suggested the matter had been settled to his satisfaction. As Robert lowered him back down to the ground, William asked, 'Papa, does each kingdom only have one king?'

'That's right, why do you ask?'

'Well, if each kingdom only has one king and King Canute is King of England, how can Cousin Edward be King of England as well?'

'Good question, William. And the answer is, because even though your great-uncle Canute is actually King of England now, Edward ought to be king.'

'Why?'

'Because Edward's papa Ethelred was king years ago, but Canute stole the throne away from him.'

William had an image in his mind of a man stealing a chair so that he could sit on it and say that he was king. 'Is that why you're going to England, to get the throne back again?'

'Not exactly,' said Robert, loving his boy and the way his mind worked.

'But will Edward become the proper King of England, with a crown and everything?'

'I suppose so, yes.'

William's face lit up. 'Maybe you could be king, Papa, instead of Edward! And you could wear the crown and tell all the English what to do and they would have to obey you!'

'Maybe I don't want to become a king. Maybe I've got enough to worry about just being Duke of Normandy.'

William looked at his father as if that was the most ridiculous idea he'd ever heard. 'I want to be a king,' he said. 'Being a king wouldn't worry me at all!'

'No, I can see that!' laughed Robert.

'But I don't understand, Papa . . . If you're going to make Cousin Edward the King of England—'

'I didn't say I was. I said that might happen.'

'All right then, if you might make Cousin Edward King of England, why isn't he coming to England with you? Why is Alfred going instead?'

'Because Alfred is a soldier and Edward isn't. He's a man of God. He likes to change the world by prayer, not by war, and maybe that's better.'

'No it isn't,' said William, shaking his head. 'Fighting is fun!'

Robert sighed. 'No, William, fighting isn't fun. Sometimes it's necessary and sometimes it's unavoidable. But it isn't fun.'

'I think it is.'

'Well if all you ever want to do is fight, then you won't be a very good duke. Come with me, young man. It's time you got a taste of the other duties that you'll have to attend to when it's your turn to rule Normandy. Do you remember when you came with me to the abbey of Préaux?'

'Was that the really new one that hadn't even been finished yet?'

'That's right. I signed a charter – a big piece of paper – so that everyone could see that it was a proper abbey because I said so.'

'Yes, and you let me carry it up the steps, in front of everyone, and put it on the top of the altar.'

'Well, today I'm going to sign another charter, but this time you're not going to put it on the altar . . .'

'Oh,' said William, sadly.

'You're going to sign it too.'

William's face lit up. 'What, just like a real duke?'

Robert smiled down at his son. 'Yes, exactly like a real duke.'

3

Fécamp, Normandy, and Rennes, Brittany

As Robert led William away, he thought about his son's notion of his expedition to England. In truth, the six-year-old's image of two men fighting over a stolen throne wasn't that much more childish than Robert's actual justification for going to war. The circumstances were, on the surface, perfectly straightforward. Canute's recent actions could only be seen as a deliberate insult. England was holding Normandy in contempt. Since peaceful negotiation was evidently impossible, it had not been hard for Robert to persuade his assembled nobles and knights that the only acceptable response to such provocation was by inflicting a military defeat that would teach Canute some manners and force him to take Normandy as seriously as she deserved.

And so this great fleet had been assembled and men recruited from all over the duchy and beyond. It was never hard to find volunteers for an attack on England. It was one of the richest countries in Europe, and though the sea acted as a partial protection, its endless leagues of coastline had long provided landing spots for imperial armies bent on conquest; pirates seeking slaves and plunder; and Norsemen who had, in England as in Normandy, spent centuries despoiling the kingdom but ended up ruling it.

Robert's plan was simple. He intended to do to England what the sons of Bellême had attempted to do to Normandy, but with a much larger, well-disciplined, properly led force. He would beach his fleet on the south coast and then advance inland, stripping the towns and countryside of anything portable, valuable or edible. For all William's enthusiasm for kingship, Robert was not planning a conquest. If Canute marched against him with an overwhelmingly larger army, he would avoid battle and circle back towards his ships. On the other hand, if Canute looked beatable, Robert would lead his Normans into battle, and if they should defeat the English and slay their king, well, then anything might be possible. At the very least, the English would have to give him a very great deal of gold to go away.

When Robert had told his troops and sailors that they could look forward to a short, hard-fought campaign that would weigh down their longboats with booty, he had been cheered to the echo. His senior commanders and naval captains were equally satisfied that their duke knew what he was doing. Most of them had fought with him, or in a few cases against him, and had learned through experience that Robert of Normandy brought victory to his own side and destruction to the enemy. There seemed no reason why he would not defeat the English as crushingly as everyone else he had encountered.

What Robert had not told anyone, for he could scarcely even admit it to himself, was that the whole great campaign, which had brought hundreds of ships and many thousands of men to this normally tranquil bay and emptied his treasury of gold and silver on the promise of profits to come, was really little more than an exercise in distraction. In truth, he was heartsick, listless and still numbed by the crushing sense of pointlessness and failure brought on by the futile struggle against the archbishop and the God he represented here on earth.

With Herleva gone, Robert walked through the world like a ghost, visible to the whole world yet empty and lifeless inside. The one person who could make him forget his melancholy and bring him warmth, laughter and any feeling of joy was William.

Fathering him was Robert's greatest and only pleasure. The moment his son was out of his sight, the cold, numb darkness descended again. In the absence of anything or anyone else that could bring him to life again, he found himself requiring ever more dramatic, excessive means of diverting his mind from its troubles.

And that, in the end, was why he was invading England.

William was bored. He'd been perfectly happy watching the ships and the sailors and soldiers going about their business, getting ready for the war against England, even if it had been a huge disappointment when his father had told him that he couldn't go too. But spending hours on a hard wooden seat listening to bishops and abbots talking about things he didn't understand was no fun at all. So far as he could see, there was a big argument going on about some land that used to belong to the monks at Fécamp Abbey and someone had taken it from them and now they wanted it back. Just like Cousin Edward wants his throne back, William thought to himself.

The self-styled King Edward of England was actually sitting alongside William, listening to all the arguments go back and forth, as was the archbishop, who always took a great interest in matters involving Fécamp, since he had been born there and, like his father, brother and mother, would one day be buried there too.

Finally, to William's huge relief, the talking came to an end. His father consulted briefly with the adults alongside him and declared that the abbey could have its land back. A monk transcribed the judgment in Latin, and Robert, Edward and the archbishop all signed the parchment, thereby conferring on it the status of a legally binding charter. Then the duke turned to his son and said, 'Now, William, you can be a witness too. Just think, this is your very first charter!'

William had only just begun to learn his letters, so he couldn't write his own signature, but Robert showed him where the monk had written his name and William carefully put an X there.

Robert clapped proudly, and the rest of the court, including both parties in the dispute, promptly burst into applause, all loudly telling one another what a fine young lad William was. Only a few also muttered under their breath, 'Even if he is a little bastard.'

William was still basking in the grown-ups' approval when Captain Airad burst into the hall and told Robert that the wind had changed and was blowing in the right direction. In an instant the charter was forgotten, and all other business for the day cancelled. Suddenly there were men running to and fro, barking out orders, and the next thing William knew, Robert was giving him a big hug, and a kiss goodbye, and telling him to be good while he was away.

William was sad to see his father go, but soon cheered up when Osbern the steward said that he could watch all the ships sail away. He watched until the entire fleet had left the bay and the *Lady Judith* was already so far away that he could only just see a little black dot, far out to sea. As they walked back towards the abbey from the cliff edge, Osbern said that he had a nice surprise for William. Fécamp, he revealed, was not very far from Conteville, where Herleva – or, as she was now formally titled, the Viscountess of Conteville – now lived. William was to stay with his mother and her husband Herluin until his father returned from England.

And that made William feel much, much better.

William was not the only onlooker as Robert of Normandy's fleet set sail for England. A crowd of monks, peasants and townspeople had gathered on the cliffs to watch the magnificent spectacle. Among their number was a Breton called Guerech of Dol. He passed himself off as a travelling knife-grinder, and he could indeed hone an axe, sword, carving knife or scythe to a razor's edge. But his real purpose as he made his way through Normandy was to be the eyes and ears of his master, Count Alan of Brittany.

Word that Robert was raising a great army and fleet had reached Alan's court at Rennes. Alan wanted to know whether he should regard Robert's military preparations as a threat – since they might, conceivably, be directed at him – or an opportunity. For if the duke were to leave his duchy, taking many of its finest men with him, this would surely present Alan with a perfect opening for an attack of his own, on Normandy itself.

It was not that Alan had any personal grudge against his twice-times cousin Robert of Normandy. They could scarcely have been more closely related if they were brothers, and Robert had always seemed to like Alan better than his actual brother Richard. But the two men were also, like all great lords or monarchs, in constant need of land and treasure with which to reward their followers and ensure their continued loyalty. That meant they had to increase their territory. Since they ruled lands that shared a common border, it was thus inevitable that each would try to shift that border to his own advantage, and at the other's expense.

There was one particular prize that Alan coveted above all others: the monastery of Mont Saint-Michel. It stood on a mighty throne of rock just off the coast at the mouth of the Couesnon river. Charles the Bald, King of the Franks, had granted the monastery and its land to Count Salomon of Brittany more than one hundred and fifty years ago. But the rulers of Brittany, who had once called themselves kings, so great were their dominions, were weakened by disputes amongst themselves and constant wars against the Franks and the Vikings. William Longsword of Normandy had taken advantage of their decline and seized great swathes of Breton territory, including Mont Saint-Michel. The loss had festered in the guts of the lords of Brittany ever since, and Alan had always harboured a secret ambition, bordering on obsession, to be the man who finally avenged his forefathers' loss. This might be his chance to do just that. He gathered his lords together and told them to expect an order to march on Normandy. But first he had to know exactly what Duke Robert was up to. So spies were sent out to get the answers their lord needed, and one of their number was Guerech.

Two days after the fleet's departure from Fécamp, having ridden his own horse until it dropped, stolen another and galloped that, and another again, into the ground as well, Guerech presented himself at the gates of Count Alan's palace at Rennes. He persuaded the guards that he had a message of vital importance and was escorted to a chamber where the count and a number of his most senior aristocrats were deep in a heated debate about the possible dangers of a march into Norman territory.

'My lord, I saw the Norman host with my own eyes. I saw the fleet lying at anchor at Fécamp. I saw the duke and all his men go aboard. And I saw them sail away to the north-west, to England.'

'By God, this is the news I have been praying for,' said Alan, hardly daring to believe it. 'Are you sure . . . are you absolutely sure that your eyes did not deceive you?'

'Quite sure, my lord. The people there all said the same thing. Duke Robert feels slighted by King Canute. He wants to teach His Majesty a lesson. And he's sailing to England to do it.'

'Then it's settled. We march on Avranches at once. Have

faith, my lords, we'll teach my haughty cousin the exact same lesson he wants to give to Canute. And, by God, we'll walk right into his duchy to do it!'

The Breton army marched from Rennes that same day. But even as the rearguard was passing through the city gates, towering thunderclouds had started to mass in the sky above them. Soon afterwards the first rain began to fall, and by the time the army had reached open countryside, the heavens had opened and the great mass of armed men, filled with confidence and purpose and advancing to the sound of pipes and drums, had become a miserable mass of bedraggled humanity, up to their ankles in mud, soaked by a torrential downpour and frozen by biting wind.

4

The storm that drenched Count Alan of Brittany's army had hit Duke Robert's fleet first. Their voyage had been frustratingly slow, for the fresh breezes that had sent them briskly on their way from Fécamp had dropped so much that the only way to make any progress at all was to get out the oars and order sailors and soldiers alike to take their turn at manning them. It was hard labour that exhausted the men without gaining much distance in return for their aching muscles and blistered palms.

One of the knights who sailed on the *Lady Judith* with Robert went by the single name of Rabel. He held no title, was far too dangerous for any man to dare give him a nickname and, having gone on his first campaign when he was little more than a boy, could not remember where he had been born and weaned. So Rabel plain and simple he remained. He was not a large man, in height or build, but he more than made up for any lack of size with his courage, determination and hard-bitten, leathery toughness. A scar ran down the left side of his face, from his hairline, past his eye and almost down to his jaw. It was not a pleasant sight, but as Rabel would growl at anyone foolish enough to point it out, the rotting corpse of the man who gave it to him looked a great deal worse.

Rabel had fought for three Dukes of Normandy. At the siege of Falaise he had distinguished himself in Richard's service. When Robert became duke, Rabel was equally loyal to him. No one could possibly doubt his devotion to the golden leopards emblazoned on his shield. And so it fell to him to point out the obvious to his leader: 'Your Grace, if the men have to keep rowing all the way to England, they'll be no damn use to you when they get there.'

Robert tried to argue. 'But we can't be far from the coast now. If they can just summon up one last effort . . .'

But his argument lacked conviction. He knew he could not deny the sense of Rabel's words. So the oars were shipped and the sails left to capture what faint wafts of wind they could. For half a day, the fleet sat becalmed. And then the wind began to freshen and shift its direction. At first, as the sails finally filled and the ships picked up speed, the changing conditions seemed like a blessing. But as the wind direction swung from west, to north and then north-east, the temperature dropped and the breeze became a gale and then a tempest. Now that blessing was a curse.

The storm went on for two days and nights, though the skies were so black that there were no dawns or sunsets and little distinction between midnight and midday. The waves that had been mere ripples on the surface of the water became furious, surging monsters that picked ships up, lifted them high into the sky and then hurled them down again into the maelstrom, smashing the hulls so hard and so often that even the strongest timbers were bound eventually to sunder. Some hulls simply disintegrated, reduced to little more than fragments of driftwood, bobbing about in the foam. Everywhere masts were torn down and rigging was swept away. Rare were the ships that didn't lose men overboard, and those who remained were reduced to exhausted, shivering, starving husks as they tried to keep themselves and their craft intact in a hellish world where seasickness was a constant companion and sleep a distant memory.

Finally the rain stopped, the clouds parted, the wind fell and a dawn broke that saw a blissfully bright and warming sun rise over a swelling but no longer raging sea scattered with the remnants of the fleet.

'Where in God's name are we?' Robert asked Airad.

The *Lady Judith*'s captain seemed as unbowed by the storm as his vessel's mighty mast, which still towered overhead. He scratched his great black beard and admitted, 'Can't rightly say, Your Grace. We've been blown a fair old way, but where we've been blown to, well, I'm afraid your guess is as good as mine. But I do know this,' he went on, before Robert could express the disappointment that was written on his face, 'the wind's coming from the west. If we just run before it, we're bound to sight land sooner or later. Then it's just a matter of recognising it.'

'Could it be England?' Robert asked, his spirits rising with the hope that his plan might not have come to nothing after all.

'Yes, could be. But if you don't mind me saying, Your Grace, we'd better hope that it's not. If Canute's ships should ever find us in this state, they'd finish us off before we even put a toe on shore.'

By noon, land had been spotted on the eastern horizon, and as it drew closer, Airad gasped in wonder. 'By all the saints, I think that's Jersey. We've been blown in a great circle, along the Channel and right around the Cotentin. Your Grace, this is as good a landfall as we ever could have hoped for.'

Jersey had been part of the duchy of Normandy since William Longsword's day. Its people were delighted to provide shelter and provisions for their duke and his men, and the island's shipyards had everything required to patch up the battered vessels that limped one by one into port. Miraculously, the bulk of the fleet had survived. Robert dispatched men to the mainland to find out how many of the missing ships had managed to sail back to the coast of Normandy. Even now, he still hoped that his army could be reassembled and the attack on England made after all. But then news reached Robert's headquarters on Jersey that dashed those plans in an instant.

Alan of Brittany was on the march. His army stood at the gates of Avranches. If that stronghold fell, the entire duchy would be at his mercy.

Robert had been seated at a table with Alfred, Rabel and his other senior commanders when the news arrived. After the storm and the near-destruction of his fleet, this was more than he could bear. He slumped back in his chair, all energy gone, his face drawn and ashen with fatigue. 'God has deserted me,' he said, in a blank, emotionless voice. 'I am still not forgiven.'

'No, Robert, don't say that!' Alfred implored him. 'Can't you see, God has saved you. If He had not brought the storm, you would be in England by now and Normandy would be without its duke and most of its army. But God sent the storm that blew you away from England here to Jersey. And what better place could there possibly be for you? You have the men and the ships to strike at Alan when he least expects it, from a direction he could never foresee. Just when he thinks his victory is certain, you are going to defeat him.'

Robert raised his downcast eyes. 'Maybe . . .' he said, without any sign of enthusiasm.

'No, Your Grace, not maybe – certainly,' Rabel said. 'Prince Alfred is right. If you divide the army in two, you can send one half to relieve Avranches while the other lands on the coast to Count Alan's rear. He'll have no choice but to retreat all the way back to Rennes or be butchered where he stands. Either way, he loses.'

Now Robert sat up. 'You're right, both of you. Thank you for keeping your faith when I had lost mine. There's no time to waste. I will deal with Avranches. Rabel, you will command the assault on the Breton coast.' He rose from the chair and leant forward with his hands on the table. 'Lay waste to all the land between Dinan and Mont Saint-Michel. Let your men take from Brittany what they would have had from England. Burn what you cannot take with you. Set the whole land ablaze. I want the people of Brittany to feel abandoned by their lord and master. I want them to feel the sting of Normandy's sword. Alan thinks he can betray me, his own cousin. Well . . .' he slammed a fist down on the table, 'I will crush him for his treachery.'

Robert paused. The emotion of the past few minutes seemed to have drained his meagre reserves of energy. 'I just pray that Avranches does not fall,' he said, much more quietly. 'Everything depends on that. Whatever else happens, Avranches must not fall.'

5

Avranches, Normandy, and Brittany

The fortress of Avranches was under the command of Nigel, Viscount of the Cotentin, and his lieutenant Alfred of Gavray. Nigel was a greybeard, no longer possessed of the strength he had once taken for granted. More than twenty years earlier, the English had landed in the Cotentin, hoping to march from there into the heart of Normandy, capture old Duke Richard and bring him alive back to England. Nigel had met the invaders with a small force of his knights, augmented by a great mass of the common people, men and women alike, armed with a motley collection of farm implements, blacksmiths' hammers, knives, cudgel and a few bows and arrows. The raw savagery of their attack overwhelmed the English, and only a handful of survivors returned to England to tell the tale of a land where the men were ferocious warriors, and the women took the stout poles from which they usually hung their family's water jugs and used them to smash their enemies' heads.

Nigel had no such Amazons to help him now. But his military mind was still sharp enough, and his lack of physical prowess was more than made up for by the man standing beside him on the ramparts of Avranches. Alfred of Gavray was more commonly known as Alfred the Giant. Normandy was a land of tall, well-built men, but Alfred dwarfed them all. He was a veritable Goliath. His neck was as thick as most men's thighs, and there were prize bulls sold for stud in the cattle markets of Rouen that would envy his barrel chest and the massive slabs of muscle bunched around his shoulders, back and tree-trunk limbs.

Like the great Rollo himself, the Giant ran rather than rode towards his foe, striding into the fray swinging a fearsome two-headed axe whose shaft was as long as many men were tall, and whose blades were bigger than ploughshares. His presence on a battlefield was enough to plant courage in his comrades' hearts and terror in his enemies'.

The Giant looked out at the approaching host, who were now about a league away. He could see the spears and pennants of the mounted knights and the mass of men walking behind them – the crossbowmen for whom the Bretons were both famed and feared. You could tell a great deal about an army by the way it marched to war, and this one was clearly well disciplined, strong and purposeful.

'So what do you think?' Nigel asked.

'I think that if we ever let them establish their siege, they won't leave till we're beaten,' Alfred the Giant replied in a thin, high-pitched voice that was totally at odds with his appearance. 'They must have half as many men again as us, and if those bowmen get set, they'll be picking us off the moment we poke our heads above the parapet.'

'Then what do you suggest we do?'

'Attack, obviously. Look at them, strutting and prancing down the road. They think they've got us beat, that we're all shitting ourselves with fear just looking at them. Last thing they'll expect is for us to come charging out the gates when they're still strung out on the march, all tired after a day in the saddle, or, even worse, walking. They won't know what's hit them.'

Nigel slapped Alfred halfway up his back, not being tall enough to reach his shoulder. 'That's the spirit! Makes me feel years younger just talking to you. Round up the men. Get them armed and mounted. My orders are simple – ride hard and fast straight towards the enemy. Kill as many of them as we can. Then just hope to God they don't kill more of us. Any idiot should be able to understand that.'

It did not take long to assemble the defenders of Avranches, for there were not very many of them. They were a motley bunch to be sure: a company of Nigel's own men from the Cotentin; local knights from Avranches and the surrounding manors; others who had been driven to the city by news of the Bretons' approach. Just as he had done all those years earlier, Nigel had spent the final days before the inevitable conflict recruiting townsfolk and peasants to supplement the regular soldiers. Now he stood up in his saddle at the head of his troops and shouted, 'Open the town gates!'

His command was obeyed and the gates swung back on their hinges to reveal the Breton vanguard, still advancing, but now barely fifty paces from the walls.

'There are your enemy!' Nigel shouted. 'They have come here to take this city, burn your homes and rape your women. But we won't let that happen. We're going to kill them first . . . all of them! Now, men of Avranches, men of the Cotentin, men of Normandy . . . charge!'

The aged viscount spurred his steed and raced away, straight towards the enemy. Alfred ran beside him, his great axe in his hands. And the rest of the men, outnumbered but undaunted, followed behind them, thundering through the gates, plunging into the Breton army, knowing that they were going to save their city or die in the attempt.

Robert's column, marching to the relief of Avranches, was still three leagues from the city when his scouts, riding ahead of the main force, came across the first corpses. From the way they were scattered across the road, many with arrows sticking out of their backs, it was evident that they had been cut down as they fled pell-mell from a crushing defeat. They had all thrown away their shields in their hurry to get away, and there were no banners to be seen. As a result, the scouts could not be certain whether the dead men were Bretons, slaughtered after their attack on Avranches had been repelled, or Normans, desperately escaping a fallen city.

Uncertain of what they should report back to Robert, the scouts rode on a little further, their horses picking their way through the corpses as they went. They passed through a dark, sunless copse where mangled, eviscerated bodies hung from branches, like dripping fruits of a satanic vine, and out into the light beyond.

A dozen soldiers were methodically stripping bodies of weapons, armour and valuables, under the supervision of two men. One was silver-haired, the other a great bear in human form.

'I know him,' said one of the scouts. 'That's Alfred the Giant. He's one of ours!'

The riders called out greetings and rode up to the two men.

'Do you come from Duke Robert?' asked Nigel of the Cotentin.

'Yes, my lord,' the leader of the scouting party replied. 'His Grace is marching on Avranches to raise the Breton siege.'

A huge, gap-toothed grin spread across Alfred the Giant's face. 'Then tell His Grace there's no need to hurry. We raised it all by ourselves.'

Robert spent a night in Avranches. He rewarded Nigel, Alfred and their men with titles, grants of land and gifts of gold, and then marched on into Brittany. Just as Rabel was doing to the west, Robert embarked on a campaign of devastation and savagery. He took the town of Dol and laid it waste. There was a grim, implacable set to his jaw and a callous lack of any human feeling about the merciless efficiency with which he led his men as they slaughtered, robbed, burned and raped their way towards Rennes.

One horrific story after another reached Count Alan and the remnants of the Breton army. Everyone had known Robert to be a warrior, fierce in the pursuit of victory, but this deliberate, unrelenting cruelty was something new. He was acting like a man possessed, and Alan grew fearful that nothing would stop him until he had visited total destruction upon the land and people of Brittany. In desperation, he summoned his spy Guerech.

'This is a letter to Archbishop Robert, pleading for his assistance,' Alan said, handing Guerech a folded, sealed parchment. 'You must get to Rouen as fast as possible. Ride day and night. At all costs avoid capture. Just get this message to the archbishop. Implore him to come and make peace between me and my cousin before it is too late. And tell him from me to make haste, for the sake of God Almighty. For what is happening here is surely the work of the Devil.'

Almost three weeks passed. Many more lives were lost, and more farms, villages and towns were laid to waste. Finally the archbishop arrived in Brittany and summoned his two nephews to meet him, informing them as he did so that he would not let them leave his presence until a just and lasting peace treaty had been signed and a reconciliation effected, not just between Normandy and Brittany as warring lands, but between Alan and Robert as men.

A pavilion was erected in the middle of a meadow that lay in neutral land between the two armies. The archbishop was not surprised when Alan entered it looking exhausted and downcast; that was only to be expected. What shocked him, however, was Robert's demeanour. He had feared that the duke might be overbearing and triumphal in the wake of his crushing victory.

359

But the man who stepped under the awning and walked towards the round table at which the archbishop and Alan of Brittany were already seated had bloodshot eyes sunk deep into a pale, bloodless face. Robert normally took pride in his appearance, but his clothes were unwashed, torn in places and besmirched with the stains of blood, smoke and every kind of malodorous filth. He collapsed into his chair and sat, round-shouldered, scratching away at an itch on his left shoulder. He looked like a man being eaten from within, with both his mind and body on the verge of total collapse.

'My God, Robert, what's happened to you?' Alan asked. He had expected to feel anger when he saw Robert, even humiliation. Never had he imagined that his principal emotion would be pity.

'I don't know whether to call for a physician to heal you or a priest to exorcise you,' the archbishop observed.

The table had been set with wine. Robert poured some for himself, ignoring the others, drained the goblet in one, wiped the back of his hand across his mouth and sneered, 'Look to yourself, Uncle. You were the one who made me like this. I'm a heartless, soulless wreck, thanks to you.'

The archbishop leaned across and slapped Robert hard across the face. 'Grow up. Stop feeling sorry for yourself and act like a man. And don't you dare tell me you've embarked on this barbaric campaign just because you lost a woman years ago and are still wallowing in self-pity. You're trying my patience, Robert, and God's too. Now pull yourself together. The people of Brittany deserve to live in peace. They're counting on us to give it to them.'

The treaty was a simple one. Robert agreed to withdraw all his forces from Brittany. Alan, in his turn, pledged his allegiance and that of his house to Normandy, accepting Robert as his lord. The archbishop implored them to remember that they were kin and had once been friends. 'We all have enough real enemies in the world, without making enemies of one another.'

Just before the archbishop began his journey back to Rouen, Robert came to him. 'For God's sake, help me,' he begged.

The archbishop withdrew his left foot from the stirrup in which it had just been placed. He looked his nephew in the eye and placed a hand on his shoulder. 'No, Robert,' he said. 'For God's sake, and yours, help yourself.'

6

'Please, Mama, can I hold the baby?'

Herleva smiled at William, who was standing over the cradle where his new half-brother lay sleeping. 'Not just now,' she said. 'Robert's sleeping. But when he wakes up, maybe you can hold him then.'

'Robert's got the same name as Papa.'

'Lots of people have that name.'

'Is that why you called him that?' William persisted. 'Because of Papa?'

'That's one reason, yes,' Herleva agreed. 'But my lord Herluin has relations called Robert in his family, too, so the baby is named after them just as much.'

'Do you still love Papa?'

'He's your father so I love him because of that, just as I love you. But Herluin is my husband, and I have vowed to be his wife, so I must be loyal to him above all men, and honour him, and obey him, just as he loves me . . . And just as you will love your wife one day.'

'Ugh!' spluttered William, with a look of absolute disgust on his face. 'I'm never going to get married. I'm going to be a soldier, and a duke. And one day I'm going to be a king!'

'Are you now?' said Herleva, laughing as she gathered her oldest son into her arms. Moments like these were so precious. She and William spent far too little time together, and when they did, there was often a distance between them, as if he were

362

keeping part of himself hidden away where she couldn't see it. A sliver of ice had entered his nature since they'd been separated, and along with it a new kind of anger. He had always had a hot temper, but those rages vanished as quickly as they began. But now there was something else, a sense that he might be capable of storing away his fury, unforgotten, until the time came to take his revenge. She worried how that anger might manifest itself if he should become Duke of Normandy, and who might suffer as a result. And then a memory came to her of her dream on the night that she and Robert had first made love: the night, she was certain, that William had been conceived. She thought of the tree growing from her belly and spreading its branches over Normandy, France and even across the sea to England, and suddenly she understood the dream's meaning.

William was to be a king. His children would form a great dynasty of kings and queens, all of them growing from a seed planted in her belly when she was just a common village girl of sixteen. The thought filled her with awe, but also dread, for she had a fearful premonition that kingship would bring more troubles than delights, and that the crown would weigh heavy on her son's brow, and those of his sons to come.

'Run along!' she said, releasing William from her hug. 'Go and find Odo. I'm sure he wants to play with his big brother.'

Herleva had given Herluin two fine sons, and the experience of being parents was steadily turning what had started as an artificial arrangement, established by ducal command, into a genuine, heartfelt marriage. Nothing could ever match the overwhelming passion of first love that she and Robert had shared. But as the years had gone by, Herleva had come to appreciate that what she had originally seen as an act of abandonment had actually been the proof of Robert's love for her. For his was a true sacrifice that had left him alone, while bringing Herleva and Herluin together for life. And if she could not have her first love, Herleva had no reason to complain about the second.

Herluin was not as handsome as Robert, nor as dashing, nor was he possessed by the wild, impulsive passion with which Robert had swept her away time and again. His virtues were quieter. They did not shout to make themselves known, nor would they ever take her breath away with excitement or lust. They simply persisted, day after day, month after month, year after year, until one day Herleva realised that her entire life was now built on the foundations Herluin had given her. Without even thinking about it, she had come to take his strength, his loyalty, his honesty and his kindness for granted. She felt completely safe at the centre of the world he had created for her: the castle he had built; the land he had cultivated; the people who respected him as a benevolent, merciful master and loved her as their mistress; and the sons who bore the name of Conteville – his name, and now hers too. Whatever she might have lost in starry-eyed passion, she had gained in peace and contentment.

Robert of Normandy was alone and in torment. But Herleva of Conteville was, to her surprise, very happily married.

Other women, however, were not quite so fortunate.

7

Alençon Castle, the County of Bellême

'My lord, your bride awaits you,' said the chamberlain of Alençon Castle.

'And she shall have me,' said William Talvas, Count of Bellême, adjusting his fur-trimmed wedding cloak, 'just as soon as I have spoken to her father.'

'But my lord, Baron Arnulf is with Lady Hildeburg. He will escort her to the castle chapel just as soon as you arrive there.'

Talvas glared at his argumentative underling. 'I'm sure he will, but not before he has spoken to me. Now, enough of your insolence, just go and fetch him.'

Talvas' life was taking a definite turn for the better. His brother Bertrand, having learned precisely nothing from the House of Bellême's catastrophic defeat in the valley below Saint-Quentin-de-Blavou, had gone off on another plundering mission, this time into the county of Maine. He'd been taken prisoner and thrown into a dungeon beneath Ballon Castle, half a day's ride north of the town of Le Mans. While Bertrand was trapped in his cellar – and Talvas was finding endless reasons why he was, sadly, unable to pay a ransom for his older brother – a group of Bellême men, acting in his name, hanged an old soldier called Walter Sor and two of his sons. Sor, however, had three other sons, who happened to be near Ballon when they heard the news of their father's death. They rode to the castle, demanded entrance, went down to the dungeons and smashed Bertrand of Bellême's head in with axes.

Talvas thus inherited the title of Count of Bellême and all the lands and castles that went with it. With his wealth and status assured, he then went in search of a wife, and Hildeburg, a delicious fifteen-year-old virgin, seemed to him to be an ideal choice. Once he'd dealt with her father, of course.

Talvas' self-satisfied musings were disturbed when a furious Baron Arnulf came bursting through the door. Arnulf was not as senior a noble as Talvas, but he had served successive Dukes of Normandy with distinction, had been rewarded with considerable estates and was deservedly respected throughout the duchy. Arnulf was a man's man. His handshake was strong, his word was never broken and the two things that made him happiest were the love of his family, and the company of his friends while hunting, feasting or slaughtering their enemies. He had no time at all for Talvas of Bellême, who struck him as a duplicitous, conniving backstabber. But for some reason his daughter seemed to find the man charming, and there was no denying the prestige the marriage would bring. So, against his better judgement, Arnulf had gone along with the idea. Now he feared that all his suspicions were about to be justified.

'What in God's name do you think you're doing, Bellême? Half of Normandy's waiting in the chapel, and my poor girl's weeping her heart out because you won't come and marry her. What's going on?'

'Why don't you join me in a goblet of wine, Arnulf? It may soothe your temper a little.'

A scarlet flush spread across Arnulf's face and his balding, close-cropped scalp. 'There's no time to be sitting sipping wine like a couple of old women. Clearly you're up to something. Just be good enough to tell me what it is.'

Talvas gave a regretful sigh. 'Very well then, since you refuse my offer of hospitality, I will answer your question. I want to talk to you about your daughter's dowry.'

Arnulf frowned. 'But that was all agreed months ago, before the betrothal was announced. I've brought the gold, the deeds to the properties and a wagon filled with dresses, rugs, tapestries and candlesticks. After the service, at the wedding feast, I'll happily give them to you before the eyes of all your guests.'

'I'd like them now, if you don't mind,' Talvas said.

'Are you suggesting that I would break my word? By God, I've killed men for lesser insults than that.'

Talvas looked unimpressed. 'I'm sure you've killed men for all sorts of reasons, but that's no concern of mine. Besides, you're unarmed and, oh look, there happens to be a dagger just lying on the table next to me. So, back to the point. I want everything we agreed to in my possession before I marry your daughter. And I'd also like something else: that woodland of yours just outside Argentan. It looks like excellent hunting country to me.'

'But I'm leaving that to my oldest son.'

'No you're not. Well, not unless you'd like your daughter to be sent back to your castle as a rejected bride. Or I could marry her, fuck her senseless, divorce her on the grounds of adultery – trust me, it wouldn't be hard to find someone willing to claim that he'd seduced her – and return her to you with her reputation ruined. So, do you agree to my terms?'

'I'm not going to give my daughter to a treacherous, heartless bastard like you.'

'Yes, actually, I think you are. If you insult me now by breaking off the betrothal, I'll have no alternative but to come and seize my lovely bride-to-be, like Menelaus chasing after Helen of Troy. And even though things haven't gone quite as well for the House of Bellême as we might have liked in the past few years, my forces would still be more than enough to crush you and your family and raze your castle to the ground. Now, give me your famous word that the woods are mine, have the

367

dowry placed in my treasury and we can all get on with the wedding.'

The whole day went splendidly so far as Talvas was concerned, though many of the guests did comment that Baron Arnulf looked surprisingly sour-faced for a man whose daughter had just won a great nobleman's hand in marriage. Talvas and his new wife ascended to their bedchamber accompanied by their most valued guests, their marriage bed was blessed and finally they were alone.

Hildeburg really was a very pretty little thing, Talvas thought: such innocent big brown eyes, such rosy cheeks, such sweet soft lips. And her father had been right: she really did love him. It was obvious from the way she looked at him and the guileless adoration in her voice as she spoke her marriage vows. She really wanted to be the best wife she possibly could be. He imagined that his own mother must have been much the same on her wedding day. So a precedent had been set.

'Tell me, my dear, are you a pious soul?' he asked.

Hildeburg gave a shy, modest smile. 'I hope so, William, I—'

The slap hit her right on the side of her face, catching her completely by surprise.

'Don't ever call me William, or even worse, Talvas,' he said. 'In future you will address me only as "my lord". You will never speak unless spoken to, save to ask my permission to do something, or to enquire how you may best please me. Now, stop snivelling and answer this simple question: do you understand?'

The hurt in Hildeburg's eyes went far deeper than her stinging cheek. 'Yes . . . my lord,' she answered.

'Good. Now take off all your clothes, and when you have done that, kneel before me, sitting on your heels, with your eyes cast down and your hands resting on your legs in front of you.'

When his new wife had done as she was told, Talvas looked at her appraisingly, greatly pleased by the slenderness of her waist and the plump, inviting curve of her hips. He pulled her thick chestnut hair back so that it did not fall in front of her face, then, having presented her to his satisfaction, said, 'There was a servant handing out food to the guests. You would not have seen her, for she is far too lowly to be allowed near the high table, and besides, she is old and ugly and would have put guests off their food. That servant is my mother. She was my father's wife and thus was the Countess of Bellême, just as you are now. My father took pleasure in humiliating her. It pleased him to rob her of everything she had: her beauty, her social position, her every possession. He took it all. And he beat her cruelly for the very slightest infraction.

'As you can imagine, I was horrified by his behaviour. I swore I would never treat my wife like that. I refused to be so unforgivably . . . unsubtle, so crude or so obvious. That is why you will always be treated, in public, with all the honour and dignity befitting a Countess of Bellême. You will never lack for any luxury. When we have children, they will be raised to respect and obey you. But in private, just between you and me, things will be very different. I am going to degrade you in ways that you cannot begin to imagine. You will spend your days in secret, unspoken terror of what awaits you at night, and the thing you will fear most is the possibility that you will somehow fail to please me, for your only hope of mercy is to satisfy my every whim, no matter how bestial it might be.'

Talvas saw that Hildeburg was quivering. 'Now, I am going to ask you a question and you are going to answer it without raising your eyes. You will never raise your eyes to me when we are alone together, any more than you will speak, unless I command it. So, wife . . . are you afraid?'

Hildeburg's arms were shaking and her fingers dug into the

369

soft bare flesh of her thigh as she replied, 'Yes, my lord.'

'And what do you fear most?'

He knew that she feared the pain. She feared the terrible, shapeless threat of the unimaginable cruelties that lay in store for her. And she feared the lifetime of torment to which she had somehow been condemned. But if she had any sense, if she valued her life at all, she feared saying any of that to him now.

Hildeburg had to force her answer out between the sobs racking her body. 'That . . . that . . . that I fail to please you, my lord.'

'Good girl. That was the right answer. Now place your forearms and elbows on the ground in front of you, crawl over to the bed – keep your knees wide apart, I want you properly displayed – and let's find out quite how pleasing you can be.'

8

Fécamp, Normandy

Once again Robert had summoned the great men of Normandy to attend him at Fécamp. In the days leading up to the appointed date, the fields around the abbey saw a flowering of brilliantly coloured tents and pavilions. Stable lines were set up for the horses brought by the barons and their attendant knights and squires, and blacksmiths and feed sellers from leagues around gathered to attend to the animals' needs. The humans, too, were well looked after. Food sellers lit cooking fires and set up stalls to sell chickens, roasted six to a long steel spit; or choice cuts from the carcasses of sheep, goats, cows and even great oxen slowly cooked over pits of burning charcoal and wood. Wine and ale merchants sold their wares by the barrel. Minstrels and poets supplied entertainment, while all manner of women, from haughty, expensive beauties to cheap, disease-ridden slatterns, provided other comforts.

Yet as the sun set on the eve of the great assembly, not one man there knew why it was that they had all been summoned. Many assumed that Robert, having seen one attempted invasion of England frustrated by the weather, was about to announce a second attack. Why else would he have brought them to exactly the same place? Others maintained that his peace treaty with Alan of Brittany was just a ruse and that they would soon be returning to that ravaged land to complete the job they'd started a year earlier and place it all under Norman control. This theory took a beating when Alan himself arrived in Fécamp with a small group of his most trusted barons, clearly coming in peace. But to some cynics it was just proof that Robert was bent on mischief, for Brittany would be helpless and vulnerable if its count and leading aristocrats were either lying dead on a field in Normandy, or languishing as prisoners in one of Robert's dungeons.

The abbey itself was filled to bursting with abbots and bishops from all over Normandy, headed by the archbishop himself. Priests and monks being incorrigible gossips, the speculation was just as rife and often even more outlandish at the refectory's high table as it was around the ale barrels outside. Only a very few of the most perceptive souls on either side of the abbey walls pointed out that Robert had not in recent months borne much resemblance to a man bent on conquest. On the contrary, all his old ebullience and dash had disappeared and he had become an ever more brooding, solitary presence. His energies were all directed inwards, and they seemed to be eating him alive.

Robert himself arrived at the abbey late at night, accompanied by William, proudly riding a pony beside his father's stallion. Also with him were Osbern Herfastsson, Brother Thorold – the monk appointed as William's tutor – and such a small party of guards that they were able to ride right through the barons' camp and into the abbey courtyard before the slightest attention had been paid to their arrival. Robert, his son and his steward ate a light supper and then retired to bed in the abbot's house, which they had sequestered for the night, leaving no one, not even the archbishop, any wiser as to the reason for their presence.

The only place big enough to hold the hundreds of people who had gathered at Robert's command was the abbey church. The barons packed the front rows of pews, with lesser knights behind them and the most junior personnel forced to stand wherever they could find the slightest bit of space. The archbishop and his senior clergy occupied the choir stalls, and as with their secular equivalents, the lesser priests and monks were obliged to perch on steps or cram into side chapels.

When the church was filled to capacity and beyond, there was a blare of trumpets, the main doors were flung open and the ducal party, led by Robert himself, came marching down the aisle. At once, a spontaneous burst of applause burst out. For all the rumours and suspicions that still surrounded the manner in which Robert had inherited the dukedom after his brother's sudden death, and the chaos into which Normandy had descended in the first years of his rule, the great majority of the people in the church had reason to thank him. Normandy was prosperous and at peace. The duchy was regarded with respect by its neighbours, and any who tried to fight it were invariably taught a swift and very expensive lesson. As a leader, Robert was just and merciful whenever he could be, and ruthless when he needed to be. Meanwhile William had become something of a mascot to the warriors of Normandy, who had no doubt at all that he would grow up to be a man after their own hearts.

William, Osbern and the men with them took their places in the seats that had been reserved for them right at the front of the congregation. Robert himself mounted the steps that led to the pulpit and stood before his subjects like a priest about to deliver a Sunday sermon.

'In a short while,' he began, 'I will be leaving Normandy on a journey that will take me at least a year, possibly two. I'm going on a pilgrimage to Jerusalem. For some time now my heart has been troubled and my soul has not been at peace. I have sinned, as we all have sinned . . .'

At the back of the church, one rustic knight from an obscure hamlet hidden away in the depths of the Cotentin turned to his neighbour and whispered, rather more loudly than he was, perhaps, aware, 'Bloody hell, he did murder his brother after all.'

'I don't know about that,' the man next to him said.

'Well, what other sin could it be, eh? What's he done apart from that to warrant a fucking pilgrimage?'

'Hey, you two, keep your voices down!' someone else hissed at them. 'And you can stop swearing in church, too, while you're at it.'

If Robert was aware of the commotion, he ignored it, and continued with his announcement. 'The only way to wash this sin from my conscience is to visit the very place where Our Lord Jesus caused himself to suffer and die for all our sins. There I will pray for forgiveness and hope that God Almighty hears my prayers and sees fit to answer them. When I feel that I have redeemed my immortal soul through prayer and acts of charity, I will return to Normandy a better, wiser and, I hope, happier man.'

He stopped and looked around the church. And now the silence was filled with a hubbub of voices. Most of them were asking, 'Why, Your Grace?' or, 'What sins have you committed?' Robert ignored them, but then another voice called out, 'Who will rule us while you are away?'

Robert lifted his arm to signal silence and gradually the noise died down. When the church was quiet once again he said, 'It is my intention, with his agreement, of course, that my uncle the Archbishop of Rouen will oversee the government of Normandy. Both his wisdom and his experience are unmatched, as is his determination to do what is best for this duchy and to overcome anything or anyone he believes to be a threat to Normandy or its people.'

Robert gave a wry smile and added, more quietly, 'And I speak from personal experience.' Then, more loudly, he added, 'But of course my uncle is not and cannot be the Duke of

Normandy. I am intending to return here and continue my rule. Only a fool, however, would pretend that there are not great dangers lying in wait for any pilgrim. Many who set off for the Holy Land never return. If I should be among them, someone else will have to take my place. That is why I now intend to nominate my successor . . .'

Suddenly an absolute silence, laden with suspense and expectation, fell over the congregation.

'In the event of my death on pilgrimage, or for any other reason, the next Duke of Normandy will be my son, William.'

The tension broke with a crashing wave of noise. Some men applauded and called out, 'God save William!' Others booed, others again yelled objections: that he was too young; that he knew nothing about warfare or government, and, above all, that he was a bastard.

Robert heard the slurs and leaned forward in the pulpit. 'How dare you?' he shouted. 'William is my son. I am his father. There is no doubt at all about his parentage. That's legitimate enough for me.'

He took a few seconds to cool his temper and let the excitement in the church subside. 'I am aware that my son is but a boy. He cannot possibly rule unaided. So I am now calling upon my uncle archbishop, my cousin Alan of Brittany, my cousin and steward Osbern Herfastsson and my son's tutor, Brother Thorold, to guide him in my absence and to do everything in their power to maintain the governance of this duchy, its peace and its prosperity, on William's behalf and mine.'

Robert looked round at the choir stalls. The archbishop was glaring at him in furious disapproval. Robert knew that he would have outraged his uncle twice over: first by weakening the duchy by leaving it without a duke, and second by making and announcing his plans without even telling the old man, let alone asking his advice. But there had been no other possible way of doing this. Had the archbishop known, he would have found a way to stop him leaving for Jerusalem. And since that was something Robert was not prepared to countenance, he had been obliged to keep his intentions secret.

Stepping down from the pulpit, Robert stood at the head of the aisle. He looked towards his son and said, 'Come here, William.'

The boy got up without the slightest hesitation and strode towards his father, who turned him round to face the hundreds of aristocrats and soldiers crammed into the church.

'Hold up your right hand, Will, so that everyone can see your palm,' Robert said. 'Like this, look.'

Keeping his elbow tucked into his side, Robert raised his hand so that the palm was level with his shoulder, and William copied him.

'Well done,' Robert said. 'Now repeat after me . . . I, William of Normandy . . .'

'I, William of Normandy,' William muttered, looking shyly down at the ground.

'Say it again, Will, but this time keep your head up and speak as loudly and clearly as you can.'

'I, WILLIAM OF NORMANDY!'

'That's much better . . . do solemnly swear . . .'

'Do solemnly swear . . .'

Line by line, William was taken through his oath, promising to serve Normandy and its people for all his life; to be fair and just in his judgments; to seek peace whenever possible but never shirk from war when there was no other option; to protect and defend all who were his vassals; and to be faithful to God, Jesus, the Holy Ghost and the Virgin Mary.

When the oath had been completed, Robert told everyone in the church, clergy and laity alike, to get down on their knees.

Then, reminding them that they were speaking in the sight and hearing of God and all His angels, he made them take a vow of their own. In this case, they promised to be faithful vassals to William; at all times to serve and obey him as the rightful heir to the dukedom, and likewise those who acted in his name; to answer his call to arms, whenever it might come; to set aside thoughts of treachery, rebellion or insurrection; and always to act for the good of Normandy, rather than seeking personal advantage for themselves.

Many of the assembly were reluctant to say the words. Objections were raised, to murmurs of approval or heated dispute. Robert required all his powers of persuasion, and every ounce of his authority as a leader, to drive the men, like a herd of disputatious sheep, from one end of the vow to the other. But at last it was concluded.

'Know this,' he said. 'You have all sworn a solemn oath. To break that oath is to commit treason. And treason is punishable by death. So let no man be in doubt what the consequences of his actions will be should he take up arms against William's person, or the duchy itself. Remember, too, that you have sworn in God's name. If you defy William, you also defy your maker.'

With that, he took William by the hand and strode back down the aisle and out of the abbey church, leaving a silent, bemused and far from happy assembly behind him. No one had imagined that they had been brought here to be told they were, as many of them saw it, being deserted by their duke, still less that Normandy would now be in the hands of a boy who had yet to see his eighth birthday. One man, Drogo of the Vexin, stopped Robert on his way out to say, 'If you will allow me, Your Grace, I would be honoured to accompany you on your pilgrimage.' The rest, however, were in such a foul mood that if there had been a challenger strong and determined enough to have seized the moment, he might well have persuaded the barons and bishops alike that Normandy needed a new duke, and that he should be it. But there were no challengers, simply a crushing sense of anticlimax and a sullen resentment that they had all been dragged across the duchy for no good reason at all.

The archbishop was no less angry than the rest. 'Are you out of your mind?' he raged at Robert when he came upon him at the abbot's house. 'Throwing away your dukedom on a wild goose chase!'

'You of all people should not use those words to describe a pilgrimage to the site of our Lord's crucifixion,' Robert replied.

'But why do it? And why now, after everything that we've been through – everything *you've* been through?'

'Because of everything I've been through, that's why.' Robert set his hands on the archbishop's shoulders and looked him in the eye. His uncle's flesh seemed weak and flabby beneath his fingers and his bones somehow flimsier. Old age was finally taking hold of him. But this was not the time to worry about that. Robert had to explain something that he could barely understand himself.

'I've been half dead for months,' he said, 'as if I were already consigned to purgatory.'

'What ails you, my boy?' the archbishop asked, his anger giving way to concern. 'This can't just be about that woman.'

'Nothing . . . and everything. I feel responsible for Richard's death, though I swear to you, Uncle, that I did not have him killed. He would not have been sick if we had not fought. And we would not have fought if I had not seized Falaise Castle against my father's wishes.

'I feel heartsick that I did not have the strength to defy you, marry Herleva and make William my legitimate son in the world's eyes as well as my own. And yet I am even more guilt-ridden by the harm I did to my own people by putting my desires before their well-being and causing you to place that

378

interdict on Normandy. How many souls will not be saved because they could not take Mass or confess their sins before God? I cannot live with that burden on my conscience. I must go to Jerusalem, throw myself before God and pray that He will forgive me.'

'But you may die before you even get there,' said the archbishop gently.

Robert shrugged. 'If that is God's will, then I will know I am not forgiven and I will accept whatever punishment He has in store for me.'

The archbishop looked at Robert and saw not a proud, impulsive, headstrong duke, but a confused young man who had been orphaned before he was twenty and now, still four years short of his thirtieth birthday, found himself overwhelmed by the trials that Fate had set for him. For once in his life, the patriarch of the House of Normandy set aside ambition, calculation and the iron will with which he had sought to shape his family's destiny, and let an uncle's love and compassion rule his heart.

'If that is what you must do, then go with my blessing,' he said. 'And I will pray to God every day for your safe return.'

9

Paris, France

'Papa, what's a bastard?'

They were three days out from Rouen, on the road to Paris. Robert had decided to take William along with him on that first, short leg of a very long journey. They were riding side by side, proceeding at little more than a walk. The pace of the journey was determined by the ox carts carrying baggage, tents and provisions that rumbled along at the back of the column. So there was plenty of time to talk.

Robert looked down at his son. 'What makes you ask a thing like that?'

'You know how I do my lessons with Brother Thorold and three other boys, Fitzosbern, Roger and Guy?'

'Yes . . .'

'Well sometimes, if we're having a fight, they call me William the Bastard. Why do they do that?'

Robert felt a surge of protective anger. 'Because they're very naughty, rude little boys. I've got half a mind to turn round, ride back to Rouen and beat some manners into them right now.'

William looked baffled. 'But why, what's so bad about it?'

Robert tried to think of a way of changing the subject, or perhaps he would simply not give William an answer, but he could see he wouldn't get a moment's peace until he told the boy what he wanted to know. 'A bastard is an illegitimate son,' he said. 'That means a son whose mother and father weren't

380

married when he was born. And I wasn't married to your mother, so that's why they say it.'

'So is it bad to be a bastard, then?'

'Sometimes, yes.'

'Why?'

'Well, sometimes an illegitimate son can't inherit his father's property or title. But you will inherit my title. When I die, you will become Duke of Normandy. That's why I made everyone swear their loyalty to you at Fécamp, so that they would know that as far as I am concerned, you are my true son and heir, even though Mama and I were never married.'

'But why didn't you marry Mama? Didn't you love her?'

'I loved her with all my heart, William. I always will.'

'So why didn't you marry her?'

'Because I was a fool and I didn't think I needed to. I thought I could do anything I liked, but I was wrong.' Robert rode on for a few more paces in silence, then said, 'I want you to make me a promise, William.'

'What sort of promise?'

'That you won't make the same mistake I did. This is very, very important. You must promise me, on your honour, that you won't get married until you've found someone you truly love. But when you do find her, marry her no matter what, even if other people don't want you to. Do you promise?'

William couldn't really understand what his father was going on about, but this was clearly very important to him, so he said, 'I promise.'

'Good lad, that's the spirit!'

As they travelled on, Robert did his best to fit all the lessons he might have taught William over the years he was growing up into the few days they had together. He wanted very badly to return from his pilgrimage, but there was every chance that he would not, so he had to prepare his son for life as Duke of Normandy.

'Your people must know two things: that they will be rewarded generously if they do right, and that they will be punished severely if they do wrong. If all you do is reward them, they will become lazy and spoilt and lose their respect for you. If you only ever treat them harshly, they will hate you and support anyone who rises up against you.

'As for friendship, if you are very, very lucky, you will have a friend as good and loyal and trustworthy as Herluin of Conteville was to me. But you can't count on friends. In the end, most of them will put their own interests ahead of yours. So you have to be able to rely on your family – *our* family, the House of Normandy. I'm sure that your mama and Herluin will bring up your little brothers to love you and support you, just as Cousin Osbern is teaching his son Fitz to be true to you too.'

'Sometimes me and Fitz fight,' William said.

'I'm sure you do. I fought with my brother Richard and Cousin Alan of Brittany. I fought with your great-uncle Robert, too. In the end, though, we all made peace, because we knew that we were part of the same family so we had to stick together. That's why, if one of your family ever does something wrong to you, you should always give them a chance to say sorry and then be nice to each other again. Do you understand, Will?'

'Yes, Papa.'

'Good, but remember this too: if you give them a chance and they betray you a second time, show them no mercy. If you do, you will only be storing up danger for yourself in the future. And one other thing, William . . .'

'Yes, Papa?'

'Your mama is a viscountess now, but she came from a very humble home.'

'I know. Grandpa Fulbert was a tanner. His house smelled of poo!' William giggled.

'Shh, you mustn't say that!' Robert scolded him, though he

was laughing too. 'Anyway, it doesn't matter what the house smelled like,' he went on. 'From the day I first met Mama, she always behaved like a true lady, and treated others as a lady should. So if anyone ever, ever mocks her, or seeks to use her background as a way to mock you, punish them for it. Punish them so harshly that no one will dare to mock you or Mama ever again.'

'Is that another promise?' William asked.

'Yes,' his father replied.

'Then I promise that if anyone's nasty about Mama, I will make them very sorry.'

There was an expression on William's face as he said those words, something about the set of his jaw and the unflinching look in his eye, that suddenly showed Robert what his son would look like as a man. And seeing it, he knew for certain that anyone fool enough to cross William of Normandy would live to regret it, though not, perhaps, for very long.

William had never met a king before. But when they reached Paris, his father took him straight to the royal palace to meet King Henry I. Papa had said that he and the king were about the same age, but Papa was much bigger than the king, who was quite small, with short hair, a wispy beard and sad-looking eyes. But he seemed like quite a kind man, and after William had bowed and said, 'Good day, Your Majesty,' like Papa had taught him, the king asked, 'Did your father tell you why he's brought you here?'

'He said I was coming to pay homage to you.'

'And did he explain what that means?'

'That you would become my master and I should be good and do what you say.'

'That's right. You will become my vassal, and must do me service if I call on you. But I have to look after you too. So if you ever have serious trouble and no one can help you in Normandy, come here to Paris, and I will do what I can to solve your problems, or defeat your enemies.'

William didn't think that Henry looked like he'd be very good at defeating enemies, but he knew that it would be rude to point that out, so he said, 'Thank you, Your Majesty.'

Now William had to kneel down in front of King Henry's throne and say a vow, quite like the ones that everyone had said to his father when they all gathered at Fécamp. In return, the king said that he recognised William as the rightful heir to Normandy and that any man who tried to harm him, or take the title of duke for himself would have the King of France to answer to.

'Thank you, Your Majesty, for showing my son such favour,' Robert said, sounding as though he really meant it.

'You're very welcome, Normandy. You gave me shelter and help when I needed it. One day, perhaps, I'll return that favour to your son. In the meantime, I wish you a safe journey to Jerusalem. Be sure to pay me a visit on your way back home. I would very much like to hear about the holiest of all cities. To think you will tread the same ground as Our Saviour – I envy you, Normandy, truly I do.'

That night Robert and William dined at the king's table and the women of the court made a great fuss of William, but he did his best not to show how embarrassing it was listening to them all say what a sweet, handsome little boy he was. Some of them even pinched his cheek and gave him little kisses and mussed up his hair. William hated that.

The following morning, he said goodbye to Papa and made him promise that he would come back safely. 'Don't worry, Will, I'll come back. And when I do, I'll tell you stories about all the places I've gone to, and the extraordinary people and magical creatures and monsters I've met along the way.'

That sounded good, but even so, William couldn't help but say, 'Please don't go, Papa.' But finally it was time for Papa and Cousin Drogo of the Vexin and all the people who were going with them to set off on the road to Jerusalem.

William had told himself he absolutely wouldn't cry when Papa went, but he couldn't help it. And then it was time to make the journey back to Normandy. All the way, William hoped that they would turn a corner and Papa would be sitting there on his horse, smiling and saying he'd changed his mind and ridden back to be with him again after all. But they went all the way to Rouen and still his father hadn't come home.

10

One year had ended and winter had given way to spring when Brother Thorold came into the classroom at the ducal palace in Rouen with an excited look on his face, clutching a rolled-up parchment. 'I have wonderful news for you, boys, and especially for you, William. A brother monk has written to me from his monastery in Constantinople, sending word of His Grace Duke Robert's progress. It seems that he made a splendid entrance into the city. Now, the walls of Constantinople were built by the Emperor Theodosius, more than five hundred years ago. They stretch for leagues all the way around the great city. They rise up to the sky and they're so mighty that no army has ever breached them. And inside the walls, Constantinople is the biggest, richest, most magnificent city in all the world, filled with wondrous churches and palaces and ruled by a mighty emperor. This whole town of Rouen would only be one very small, poor district of Constantinople.'

The four boys gasped, just trying to imagine a city that size.

'I tell you all this so you will understand that the inhabitants of Constantinople are not easily impressed. But His Grace certainly managed to make his mark. In fact, a story is going round the city that when Duke Robert approached the gates of Constantinople, he ordered that his horse should be re-shod with horseshoes made of gold. And he told his men that if one of the shoes came off as they rode through the streets, they should not try to pick it up, but just leave it there for the people to take away.'

'Does your father really put gold shoes on his horse?' Fitz whispered.

'I don't think so,' William hissed back. 'Maybe he got some on the way.'

'According to the story, our duke was concerned that the French had a reputation for being greedy for gold,' Thorold went on. 'So he wanted to be seen to be letting other people take his gold, and then they would know that it did not matter to him.'

'Please, Brother Thorold, is that story really true?' William asked.

'Well, your father is known for being generous, William. But in my experience he is also prudent and he knows that it's a sin to waste the bounty God has provided, so I'm not sure he would actually use gold to shoe his horse. But I do have more stories about what His Grace did in Constantinople. Would you like to hear about how he met the emperor himself?'

'Yes please!' the boys chorused.

'Very well then, I shall tell you. But only after we've worked on some Latin declensions together. And the harder you work, the sooner I'll tell you the story.'

For the next hour, William and his classmates worked harder than they had ever done, until finally Brother Thorold was satisfied.

'Now,' he said, picking up his scroll again, 'it seems that Duke Robert paid a visit to the palace of the Emperor Michael, whose huge empire stretches from the south of Italy, across Greece and the lands of the Serbs and the Bulgars and the Thracians, through Asia Minor and Armenia, right up to the Persian Empire in the east, and almost down to the Holy Land in the south.'

None of the boys had the faintest idea where any of these places might be, any more than Thorold did, but they certainly understood the gist of what their teacher was saying. The Emperor Michael was a very great and powerful ruler indeed.

'So, our duke went right up to the emperor and sat himself down in the chair next to his,' the tutor continued. 'The emperor took one look at what my brother monk calls Duke Robert's "honest face and handsome appearance" and thought he must be the King of France himself!'

The boys fell about laughing and William said, 'I think my papa looks much more like a king than King Henry does.'

'Hush, boy!' exclaimed Brother Thorold. 'You mustn't say such things about His Majesty, though I agree with you that your father does have such a regal manner that he might persuade anyone that he was a true monarch. But in this case, an interpreter was found and Duke Robert was able to tell the emperor that he was just one of the great magnates of France, on his way to see the relics of Christ and worship at the Holy Sepulchre. He said that he did not want to march through the emperor's lands without seeking his permission first, for fear that people might think he was arrogant. The emperor was very pleased by this show of respect and ordered his servants to supply Duke Robert and his men with as much food and drink as they needed for as long as they wished to stay in Constantinople. The emperor's officials, acting on their master's orders, also offered the duke gifts of gold, beautiful clothes and sumptuous goblets, serving jugs and chalices. But Duke Robert did not want to impose upon the emperor's generosity, or appear to be begging from him, so he politely declined the gifts.

'When the emperor heard, he was furious. He felt slighted that anyone had refused gifts that he had freely offered. So he decided to force Robert to accept them by sending out an imperial decree to all the merchants of Constantinople, forbidding them to sell anything to Robert or his men, or to buy anything from them. When the duke's servants went out to buy wood to make cooking fires, they found that no one would sell it to them. But the duke had noticed that it was the habit of the people of Constantinople to nibble on almonds and walnuts and then throw away the shells. So he sent his men out into the streets to gather up all the shells they could find and make fires out of them instead. When the emperor heard how clever Duke Robert had been, he was greatly amused and gave him full permission to journey onwards to Jerusalem under his imperial protection.

'And that,' concluded Brother Thorold, 'is the end of my friend's letter and of my story.'

'Where do you think my father is now? Has he got to Jerusalem yet, do you think?' William asked.

'I don't know for sure,' said Brother Thorold, 'but this letter took more than two months to get here, and I should have thought that Constantinople is perhaps about halfway to Jerusalem. So he might well have done.'

William said nothing. But that night he thought about his father praying by the cave where Jesus' body was buried, and then he gave a little prayer of his own: that his father should decide that he had prayed enough and it was time to go home.

11

Jerusalem, the Holy Land

It was unseasonably hot for the first week in April and the sweltering temperature was only made worse by the effort required to manhandle the heavily laden wooden pallet through the teeming streets. Everywhere the market stalls were surrounded by hordes of haggling, gossiping, arguing customers. Arabs, Palestinian Jews, Byzantine Christians, tradesmen from every corner of the eastern Mediterranean and the Levant: all manner of men and women were here, along with their camels, donkeys and horses. In the midst of them came four tired, sweaty, parched Normans, dressed in woollen hose and heavy robes that were utterly unsuited to the conditions, carrying a fifth man between them. They spoke none of the myriad tongues being babbled all around them and so had no means of cutting through the crowd, other than barging their way and gritting their teeth at the insults, indignant shrieks, waved fists and even the occasional blows that they received in return for their rudeness.

Their companion, lying on the pallet, was painfully thin, and though his skin was, like the others', slick with perspiration, his bloodless complexion suggested a chill as cold as the grave that would soon be claiming him. With every bump, every jostle of the pallet, he clenched his teeth in pain. He was desperately trying, even now, not to cry out. He didn't want the others to feel that they were failing him. Not now – not when they were finally so close.

For months they had journeyed over mountains, across rivers, seas and arid deserts, and now their destination awaited them at the end of this street.

One of the carriers looked down at him. 'Almost there,' he said, doing his best to muster an encouraging smile. 'We'll take you right up to the sepulchre if they'll let us – maybe we can go inside.'

'What better place to die than Our Saviour's tomb, eh? And on Good Friday too,' said the sick man, so quietly that his friend had to bend right down to hear him over the hubbub of the street.

'In your own bed, many years from now, after you've got better and gone home,' came the answer, though both men knew it was nothing but fantasy.

Finally the crowds thinned and the men reached the most sacred spot in all Christendom: the Church of the Holy Sepulchre, built over the twin sites of Golgotha, where Christ was crucified, and the tomb where he was buried. They laid the pallet down on the ground in front of the church and then gently raised the sick man's shoulders and head so that he could gaze upon . . .

. . . a ruin.

Where once a great church had stood, now there were just a few short stretches of ragged wall, rising to a fraction of their former height. Scaffolding had been erected alongside some of the brickwork and a few more new courses laid, but there was no sign of any further activity. Here and there an occasional column marked where the aisle must have been, and part of the portico still stood, but the roof had vanished completely.

The men looked on, at once too overwhelmed by disappointment and too outraged by the desecration to speak.

Duke Robert of Normandy wiped the back of his hand across his forehead and contemplated the sight for which he had risked his fortune, his duchy and his life. Then he looked down at the pallet. 'Oh Drogo,' he sighed, 'I am so, so sorry.'

But Count Drogo of the Vexin had finally succumbed to the fever he had been battling since they left Damascus, more than two weeks ago.

'Are you lot Franks?'

The language was Frankish, though the accent was unlike any Robert had ever heard. The speaker was almost as emaciated as Drogo had been, but through lack of food rather than illness. His clothes were as ragged as any beggar's and his hair, which hung to his shoulders, was as matted and unkempt as his beard. But both were a very dirty yellow in colour. Whatever else he might be, this was no native of Jerusalem.

'We are Normans,' said Robert. 'You?'

'They call me Otto of Cologne.'

'And I am Robert of Normandy. My companions and I have come here on pilgrimage. Are you a pilgrim too?'

'Not really,' Otto said, with an apologetic grimace. 'Tell you the truth, I didn't come here to pray. I came to make my fortune. I'm a mason by trade, and there's always someone who needs stonework. Well, that's what I thought, anyway, but it's not worked out like that, though God knows they could use a mason.'

'What happened here?'

'About twenty-odd years ago, the caliph – that's, like, the ruler of all the lands from here to Egypt and beyond – well, he ordered all the Christian churches in Jerusalem to be torn down. This one included. Then a new caliph took over and he said the church could be rebuilt, but they ran out of money. The Byzantines are supposed to be paying for it, but they're still haggling with the caliph over what he'll give them in return.'

'But what about Golgotha, and the sepulchre?'

'Oh they're still here, underneath it all. Tell you what, I can show you round, if you could spare me a few pennies for my trouble. You'll never find your way through the rubble without me.'

Robert reached into the leather purse that hung from his belt, pulled out a coin of gold and held it in front of Otto's staring, hungry eyes. 'Take me to the sepulchre and this is yours. But if you try to deceive me, then I will give you steel instead of gold. Do I make myself clear?'

Otto's eyes darted to the broadsword in its scabbard on Robert's left hip.

'Completely clear.'

'Good, then lead the way.'

The Normans took up their positions at each corner of the pallet and lifted it. Otto looked at them in bemusement. 'What are you doing with him? You're not going to bury him in the tomb, are you?'

'No,' said Robert. 'But we are going to fulfil our promise to take him there. Even if his body is dead, his soul still lives.'

Otto led them to the far end of the ruined church where a second, much smaller ruin stood. 'This is what they call the aedicule,' he said, pointing at the pile of rubble. 'See, when the church was first built, the Romans cut away all the rock around the cave where Jesus was buried. All they left was the floor of the cave and the actual tomb where Our Lord was laid. Then they covered that with the aedicule. There was an outer section, where they had part of the stone that blocked the tomb – the Angel's Stone, it's called – and then the inner section was the tomb. Now if you just put your friend down and follow me over these bits of masonry here . . .'

They laid Drogo's pallet on the dusty, debris-strewn surface of what had once been a beautiful marble floor and climbed over the remains of a wall.

Otto stopped and pointed down at a large carved marble box

that had been toppled on to its side. 'You can't see it, but inside there is the Angel's Stone. And if you just climb down here . . .'

They followed him into the heart of the ruined aedicule, crawling on hands and knees to make their way beneath a partly collapsed arch. There before them was the unmistakable shape of a stone tomb, topped by a slab of marble.

'That's where the body of Christ was laid,' Otto said. 'Right there, on this very Friday all those years ago.'

Robert fell to his knees and prayed with an intensity he had never before experienced. He begged forgiveness for his sins. He pleaded for his son's health, happiness and long life, and for Herleva, too. He prayed for the souls of his parents and brother. Then he stood and gave Otto his coin, and another besides.

'Go and get the others,' he commanded his men. 'They must see this. And make arrangements for Drogo to be buried as soon as possible. I will be there when he is laid to rest. But for now I want to stay here, alone.'

12

Eight days Robert of Normandy spent at the sepulchre, deep in prayer. By day he barely ate: just a few morsels of bread at sundown and sunset and the occasional scrap of dried fish or goat's cheese. He refused all offers of wine and ale and drank only water from a nearby well. At night he laid his cloak down on the stony ground and slept within a few paces of the tomb, out in the open where God and His angels could see him.

There were times when his meditations became so intense that he could no longer distinguish between the dreams that came to him while sleeping and the visions that filled his waking mind. One evening his men came to be with him, and as they sat around the fire he told them, 'I was visited by the souls of my dear dead mother; my father, whose will I defied, and my brother Richard who was once my enemy.' His eyes shone in the light of the flames as he went on, 'I felt their presence, their love and their forgiveness, and the living spirits of my beloved Herleva and my son William came to me too and gave me their blessing.'

The men, sons of a world in which spirits and devils were as real to them as any living thing, murmured in awe at their duke's revelations, and some even fell to their knees and began to pray themselves as Robert went on, 'With every one of these visitations I felt the presence of God, and Mary and Jesus, so that the redemption bestowed on me by my own family was bestowed by the Holy Family too. I tell you, a great weight has been lifted from my heart and its place has been taken by the power and joy of the Holy Spirit.

'Pray with me now. Give all that you can spare to provide for the building of a new church here, and for every penny you give, I will give ten more. Soon we will be going home again, back to our families and our worldly lives. And when we return, we will each be able to say, "I have been to Jerusalem. I have prayed at the Saviour's tomb. And I have been redeemed!"'

So it was that when Robert left the Holy Land, and took the road north, towards Asia Minor and Constantinople, he travelled in far better spirits than those that had assailed him when he first departed Normandy. He was a man in the prime of life, still to reach his thirtieth year. He had spent eight years learning to command armies, defeat enemies and rule a duchy. His mind was clear. His body felt strong and filled with an energy he had not experienced in years. It seemed to him that his pilgrimage had given him an entirely new kind of wisdom, a deeper, more mature understanding of what really mattered in life. Now, he felt sure, he was equipped to give Normandy the leadership it deserved, to leave his son a legacy that would do them both proud and to find a woman he could love as much as Herleva. Now, at last, he knew how to live.

13

Rouen, Normandy, and Trondheim, Norway

One of the many things that his brother Alfred did not appreciate, in Edward's opinion, was the heavy burden that he had to bear as head of the English royal family in exile. It was all very well endlessly gallivanting off on ill-considered military expeditions, but someone had to stay behind to accomplish all the tedious but necessary tasks that the likes of Alfred, or even Duke Robert, considered beneath them.

His sister Goda, for example, required a new husband. Drogo had died on the way to Jerusalem, leaving three sons, of whom the eldest, Walter, had now inherited the title of Count of the Vexin. As a vassal of the House of Normandy, Walter could be assured of protection against his enemies, so his position, and Drogo's legacy were secure. Goda's situation, however, was a lot less certain. She was still a relatively young woman, so she could hardly be expected to spend the rest of her life in widow's weeds. There were therefore only two options open to her: find another husband, or retire to a nunnery.

Goda resembled a slightly inferior version of her mother: tall, blonde and attractive enough, without being truly beautiful. She had no interest whatever in forsaking worldly pleasures for a monastic existence, but unlike Emma she had neither the courage nor the bargaining power to negotiate her own marriage treaty. She had come to Rouen so that Edward could find a suitable groom and conclude an agreement on her behalf.

'Are you sure you wouldn't rather be a nun?' Edward had

pleaded, when first told what Goda expected of him. 'It seems to me that poverty, chastity, modesty and seclusion are precisely what women require. If there were more of you in monasteries, fewer men would have to suffer the peril of being led astray by the temptations placed in their paths by the wanton daughters of Eve.'

Goda gave an exasperated sigh. 'You know, most men don't actually require much tempting. They want us more than we want them. How else do you think Drogo sired his sons?'

Edward blanched. 'Don't say another word. The very thought of such carnal degradation disgusts me.'

'Oh come on, Edward. Are you really saying that you have no desire for women at all?'

'Absolutely none.'

'Do you prefer boys, then?'

'Enough! I won't have such talk in my presence. Let us just conclude this unpleasant business and you can be on your way.'

Letters were written and sent to royal and ducal houses known to have sons who were of marriageable age but not yet betrothed. Weeks passed before any replies were received and more weeks still before one arrived bearing a positive response.

Edward summoned Goda. 'Are you familiar with Eustace of Boulogne?'

'Of course,' she said. 'His father is Count Baldwin. But Eustace is married to Matilda of Leuven. I've met her. She's not died, has she?'

Edward frowned. 'The Eustace of Boulogne I'm talking about is certainly not married. His parents think it's about time he was, and they have no objection to you being his wife.'

Goda looked appalled at the very idea. 'You mean Baldwin's grandson? But he's just a boy! Has he even started shaving?'

'Oh yes, I know that for certain because I'm told he has a

very impressive moustache. And he's now in his twentieth year, so he's hardly a mere boy.'

'That makes him eight years younger than me. For God's sake, Edward, I'm a grown woman. I've had three children by a strong, virile man. If I'm to have another husband, I want to be his wife, not his nursemaid.'

'What you want has nothing to do with it. If age is the issue, Baldwin is the one who has a right to be concerned. He needs his grandson to marry a woman who'll give him sons. The fact that you've had three is some reassurance. But can you produce any more at this time in your life? That's the question.'

'You can tell him from me that I can.'

'How do you know?'

Goda rolled her eyes at her brother's absolute refusal to confront the business of making babies. 'The same way every woman knows. I bleed. And if you and he really must know, I do it as regularly as before I first became pregnant with Walter. Does that satisfy you?'

'Frankly, no, it horrifies me. But if you are still fit to breed, then the House of Boulogne will take you. You may consider yourself betrothed to Eustace, subject of course to Baldwin and myself reaching agreement over your dowry.'

'What will you have to pay him to take me?'

'More than I can afford, but not so much that Normandy can't pay it.'

'Do I have any choice in the matter?'

'No,' said Edward bluntly. 'So far as I am concerned, the entire matter has been satisfactorily concluded.'

It was freezing cold on the quayside at Trondheim, where Elgiva of Northampton and her son Svein were boarding the ships that would carry them away from Norway. After years of dissatisfaction and threats of rebellion, the Norwegian people had

399

finally risen up against them, led by Magnus, son of Olaf, the king whose downfall had allowed Canute to seize power.

'I won't be sorry to leave this godforsaken place,' Elgiva said, wrapping a thick cloak even more tightly around her to ward off the bitter wind blowing up the Nidelva river from Trondheim fjord. 'I just can't bear the thought of the smug look on that hag Emma's face when she hears that they kicked us out.'

'You did what you had to, Mother,' Svein said. His body was seized by a harsh, rattling cough that made Elgiva look at him with worry in her eyes. Svein gave a brusque jerk of his hand as if to brush her concerns away, then pulled himself together and went on: 'No ruler can afford to be lenient or indecisive, and you were neither of those things. Your laws were harsh, but they were reasonable. The people complained, but they had no right to do so.'

'That's Norsemen for you,' said Elgiva. 'The truth is they can't abide to be ruled by anyone.'

'As for Queen Emma,' Svein went on, 'she's getting very old now. She must be fifty . . .'

'At least.'

'Well then, she'll be dead soon and you won't have to worry about her.'

'Now there's a happy thought,' Elgiva said, almost managing a smile. She was a woman whose beauty had been marred by the sourness of her disposition, which was evident by the suspicious look in her eye and the disapproving expression on her tight-pinched lips. But though she could nurse a grievance for decades, she never did so at the expense of planning for the future.

'Listen to me, Svein,' she said. 'I want you to be King of England one day. Now, Emma's desperate to put Harthacnut on the throne, but I'm not sure he wants it as much as she does. My guess is he'd rather win back his father's possessions up here in the north. I think there's a deal to be done, so go to him and make it. If you cede him full power over Scandinavia, he'll leave England to you, just mark my words.'

'And what will you do?'

'Me? I'll go back to England and try to knock some sense into your idiot brother Harold. If anything happens to you, he'll be next in line, but you'll be ten times the king he ever would. So make sure you stay safe and sound, do you hear me? Take care of your health, and don't look at me like that, it matters. Now give your old mother a kiss.'

They embraced and boarded separate vessels. Svein ordered his skipper to set a course for the Jutland peninsula. When he arrived in Denmark, he went straight to Harthacnut's palace and was warmly received. The two half-brothers agreed that when the time came, they would divide their father's empire exactly as Elgiva had predicted. But it was not long before Svein's sickness worsened. Monks trained in the healing arts did their best and apothecaries supplied their finest herbs and potions, but within a few months of leaving Norway he was dead.

Elgiva received the news of her son's passing with as much fury as grief. Losing Norway had turned out to be a blessing in disguise. Now that she was back in England, she was much closer to the centre of Canute's power. Svein had secured the deal she'd wanted. Everything was going even better than she'd planned. But now her brightest hope had gone and the future rested with Harold. Thank God Canute was still a relatively young man. There should at least be time to train her son to be something approaching a half-decent king.

There was one more task Elgiva had to undertake before she could put Harold on the throne. A man who would be King of England had two ways of claiming the crown. The first was to win it by conquest, as Canute had done. The second was to win the support of the Witenagemot, or the Witan as it was informally known: the formal gathering of the English nobility and most senior clergy. Without their approval it was impossible for any one man to control the far-flung kingdom. To win the Saxon aristocracy over, a claimant had to persuade them that his rule would be in their best interests. He had to offer the prospect of rewards, advancement, low taxes and the assurance that he would be strong enough and man enough to maintain a firm, fair grip on the kingdom and his subjects.

Harold was hardly ideal material to provide any of those things, and he was outnumbered three to one by Emma's sons, Edward, Alfred and Harthacnut. Even Elgiva would admit that they were all better men than Harold. But her boy had one great, precious advantage. He was in England. And if the Witan should ever meet to choose a new king, he alone could stand before it.

His case, of course, would be made with Elgiva's help. The lords and bishops would cast their lots for Harold. But as they and she all knew, Elgiva of Northampton would be England's actual ruler.

14

Winchester, England

Canute was dead, taken ill on a royal tour of the West Country and his life snatched away with a shocking suddenness. On hearing the news, Harold Harefoot decided that he was not prepared to wait for the Witan to decide that he could be king. As if to prove just how speedy he could be, he wasted no time in making his first move.

The only man entitled formally to consecrate a monarch was the Archbishop of Canterbury. That consecration required the use of the crown and sceptre that were the symbols of royalty. Harold intercepted the caravan bringing Canute's body and possessions back to Winchester and seized the crown jewels. Then he rode to Canterbury, where he leaped off his horse at the doors of the cathedral, marched up the aisle and confronted Archbishop Aethelnoth.

'Take these,' he said, holding out a leather bag in which the priceless treasures had been carried from London. 'Now crown me king.'

Aethelnoth had begun his career as a humble monk at Glastonbury, but he was anything but low-born. He was descended from the kings of Wessex. His father, Aethelmar Cild, had held the ancient title of Earldorman of the Western Provinces during the time of King Ethelred. His late brother Wulfnoth was thegn, or lord, of Sussex. And his nephew was Godwin, Earl of Wessex, ally of Queen Emma and supporter of Harthacnut's claim. He had also been Canute's personal chaplain, and had even been present when the once-pagan king was confirmed as a Christian. He had thus spent many years in close proximity to the royal family and developed his own ideas about who did or did not deserve to be Canute's successor.

Aethelnoth took the crown and sceptre from the bag and carried them towards the cathedral's high altar. There he knelt and said a solemn prayer, beseeching God to guard these symbols of earthly majesty, before rising to his feet and placing them on the altar itself.

Harold watched all this with great satisfaction. So far as he was concerned, Aethelnoth was just a soft old fool, like all priests. But if it made him happy to indulge in this ludicrous mumbo-jumbo before he got on with the coronation, then Harold wasn't going to interrupt him.

Now Aethelnoth turned away from the altar and came back down the steps to Harold. 'I would, of course, be willing to consecrate you, my lord,' he said.

'Don't you mean Your Majesty?' Harold asked.

'Not yet, my lord – not until the ceremony has been completed.'

'Then get on with it, man!'

Aethelnoth shrugged and gave a regretful smile, like a tailor explaining why his customer's robes weren't ready. 'As I was saying, I would be happy to consecrate you. But I cannot consecrate you without the crown and sceptre. And as you can see, my lord, they are on the altar, where no man may touch them without my permission: not a layman, not a priest, not a bishop, not even the man who wishes to wear the crown and hold the sceptre.'

'Don't be ridiculous!' Harold exclaimed. 'Let me get them.'

He tried to barge past Aethelnoth. But though the archbishop was a much older man, he was well built and still perfectly capable of standing his ground. After a brief tussle, he pushed Harold away and fixed him with a basilisk stare. 'The altar is sacred. To defame it is to condemn yourself to an eternity in hell. To get to it, you must first go past me, and to do that you will have to kill me. That will assure you of execution in this life and even fouler damnation in the next one. So I suggest you leave now, son of Canute. If the Witenagemot declares you the rightful ruler of this kingdom, then I will consecrate you as my king, and do it gladly. Until then, however, the crown stays on the altar.'

Harold twisted his face into a contemptuous sneer and spat at the archbishop, spattering saliva over the stone between his feet. 'That's what I think of damnation,' he said. 'You won't find me in any congregation, not on Sunday or any other day. The hell with your religion. I'd rather be on a horse, with my dogs, chasing deer, than on my knees prattling to God.'

'Then I shall pray to Him for you, Harold. For if someone does not plea for your soul, there will only be one fate awaiting it when the Day of Judgement comes.'

'So what's the final decision?'

Emma's voice seemed to have lost its majesty, just as her circumstances had done. One day she had been Queen of England, dressed in royal robes and bedecked with dazzling jewels and rich golden ornaments, her husband's consort, a voice in his government and a force in the land. The next she was a widow, her power gone with her husband's life. She was struck down by grief, robbed too soon of the one man she had ever truly loved. She wanted to be able to mourn him, as any other bereaved wife might do. But that luxury was not afforded to her, for now, at her weakest, she was plunged into a battle with Elgiva as both women fought for control of the throne of England. Their weapons were their sons. And as the Witan

405

finally met at Oxford to consider the succession, Elgiva had the upper hand.

'There hasn't been a decision yet, or not a final one at any rate,' Godwin told her, having ridden hard all day on the journey from Oxford to Winchester. 'I stood for Harthacnut, of course, and all the southern nobility were with me. Leofric of Mercia supported Harold's claim, with the men of the Midlands and the north behind him.'

'Of course Leofric supported Harold,' said Emma bitterly. 'Elgiva was his lover for years. I wouldn't be surprised if he was the boy's real father.'

'Well, Elgiva was certainly a far greater threat to us at Oxford than Leofric. Every day, when it was just the men debating the issue, we were able to swing opinion towards Harthacnut. But every night, Elgiva organised feasts. She stuffed people's faces with food and practically drowned them in wine. She knew exactly who stood where, and who was wavering. And if there was anyone she thought she could win over to Harold's side, she'd sidle up to him, acting all sweet and charming, telling him how wise and strong he was and how much he impressed a helpless female like her.'

'That woman's as helpless as a pack of rabid wolves.'

'I'd rather face the wolves any day,' said Godwin. 'Elgiva's a sorceress. She was promising everyone she met that Harold would give them land and gold and senior positions at court, and the damn fools were falling for it, one after the other.'

'How was it left, then?'

'I managed to buy us some time. The Witan's agreed to split the kingdom in two. For now there'll be no single king. Harold will control the northern earldoms. Harthacnut will have power over Wessex and the south. All mints south of the Thames have been told to stamp coins with Harthacnut's image. But Emma, you've got to persuade him to come back to England. You and

I can be his regents in the short term, but if he's not back here soon – a few months at the very most – then Elgiva will make sure that the Witan gives Harold the whole country, and the crown along with it.'

'I've tried. He won't come,' Emma admitted. 'He's been in Denmark so long he thinks of it as his true home. And says he's fully occupied there, fighting Magnus of Norway. He's worried that if he leaves to come to England, Magnus will invade Denmark. Then if Harold somehow wins the fight for England, Harthacnut will be left with nothing at all.'

'If he's here, with Wessex behind him, Harthacnut can't lose. He's a better man than Harold, with a better claim to the throne. He is Canute's legitimate son. Harold isn't. As you say, we don't even know if Canute was really his father at all. Elgiva could have had a baby by another man and then just pretended it was Canute's. I wouldn't put it past her.'

'I'll do my best,' Emma sighed.

'You'll have to do better than that. Whatever happens, I'm not going to let anyone take Wessex from me. But I can't keep it without the support of the king, whoever he is. So if you want me on your side, find me a king. And find him fast.'

15

Herluin had taken William out for his first day's hunting, along with another nobleman from a nearby estate and a cheerful group of lesser knights from the neighbourhood, all attended by falconers, kennellers, and local peasants happy to come and act as beaters in exchange for a good loaf and plenty of ale. They had ridden out into the marshlands that lay alongside the river as it drew close to the sea, looking for cranes, the most prized of all trophy birds.

'Why is a crane so special?' William had asked Herluin as they set out that morning.

'Because it's the biggest bird you'll ever see,' his stepfather replied. 'A big one stands as tall as you, and however tall it is, its wings are twice as wide.'

'Maybe if we find one, I can ride on it and fly away.'

Herluin laughed. 'I don't think anyone's ever done that. But I'll tell you what you *can* do if we catch a crane . . . eat it! We'll take it home and hang it in the larder till the meat is ready to cook, and then we'll have a feast, so that everyone in the whole castle can have a helping.'

They made their way along the maze of paths that picked out the land firm enough to support a man or a horse, wending their way between the reeds and grasses. Often the horses went up to their knees in the water, which was chest high for William's much smaller pony. His boots and hose were soon soaked through, an unpleasant prospect on a cold autumn day.

But Herluin was impressed to discover that the boy did not once complain about his discomfort. In fact, he paid no attention to it at all. He was too entranced by the sight and sound of the beaters as they floated out into the marshes in small round coracles, smacking their hands against the surface of the water, blowing horns and banging tambours.

The racket sent great flocks of ducks, geese and waders into the air, and then the falcons were loosed to dart up into the sky. The hunting birds hovered for a moment as they chose their prey, looking for the smallest and weakest. Then, folding their wings behind them, they plummeted down on to their unsuspecting targets, which struggled for survival in mid-air fights to the death that ended with the prey either somehow managing to escape the falcon's grasp, or, much more likely, tumbling down to the marsh, to be retrieved by the waiting dogs.

William had only recently begun to learn the art of falconry, but he was given a leather gauntlet. Then the falconer placed a goshawk on his wrist, and when the next flight of ducks sped into the pearl-grey skies, William let it loose. The goshawk was unlike all the other birds being used that day since it attacked from behind and below its prey, striking upwards into its target's vulnerable underbelly. But the thrill of seeing it take down one of the ducks was no less for that, and Herluin was just as warmed by the excitement on the boy's face as if he had been his own son. William was the creation of two people Herluin loved: how could he not love him too?

Hours went by. They broke for a hearty lunch and then went back out into the marsh. But though the falcons remained fully employed, there was still no sign of the birds they had come here to find. Herluin was about to call an end to the day's activities when, far off to the west, flying out of the low rays of the setting sun, there came a flight of three grey cranes. Their long, black-tipped wings seemed almost to wave, rather than beat, so graceful was their progress through the air. Their heads and long necks were black too, though streaked with white.

'Aren't they magnificent?' Herluin said, pointing the cranes out to William. 'See how still their heads are. Their necks and bodies move in time with their wings, but their heads remain absolutely steady.'

'They're huge,' gasped William.

'Wait till they get closer and they'll look even bigger. That's why you need a very special breed of falcon to go after them.'

'The eagle!' William cried, clapping his hands in excitement.

'Sshh!' Herluin put a single gloved finger to his mouth. 'Redclaw is very fierce – that's why I named him after a great hunting dog I used to know – but he doesn't like to be startled by unexpected loud noises.'

Now the falconer produced a bird that put all the others to shame. Redclaw the golden eagle was Robert's wedding gift to Herluin. He was a creature fit for an emperor. His wings and body were a deep, rich brown, but there was a dash of gold in the plumage around his fiercely proud, glaring eyes.

'Look at his talons,' Herluin said. 'They can bring down a young deer – I've seen him do it.'

William examined the eight claws digging deep into Herluin's thick gauntlet. Each was longer than his own fingers, curved like a Saracen's scimitar and just as deadly sharp.

'I've even heard hunters' tales of golden eagles being used to hunt wolves and foxes,' Herluin went on. 'I can believe it. Redclaw's wings spread wider than my outstretched arms. I doubt there's a finer hunting bird in all of Normandy. But he's still smaller than those cranes over there. So, can you guess how he makes his kill?'

'The crane's neck,' said William with grim relish. 'It's very long and the crane can't fight if its neck is being cut, and strangled, and killed by Redclaw's talons . . . like this!' He clenched his fingers into eagle's claws and then squeezed them tight as if round a crane's long neck.

When Herluin let him loose, there was a grim inevitability to Redclaw's pursuit. The cranes scattered across the sky when they saw him coming, but there was no escaping the eagle's inexorable determination, as implacable as Death itself as he fell upon his chosen victim.

'We're going to have a feast,' said William matter-of-factly when the crane's fatally wounded body splashed into the water.

Herluin was surprised by how calm the boy was. He had expected him to be shouting and clapping with glee, as he had done earlier in the day. But now, when the most important quarry had been taken, the excitement had given way to a quiet yet intense satisfaction at a job well done. This eight-year-old boy was reacting less like a soldier, wildly celebrating after a hard-fought battle, than a general soberly assessing the true worth of his victory and already thinking ahead to the next step in the campaign.

As they made their way back to Conteville Castle, William's mood changed once more and he became a small boy again, chatting and laughing about all the funny things that had happened during the hunt, but pausing every once in a while for a surreptitious yawn when he thought Herluin wasn't looking. It had, after all, been a very long day and the poor lad was exhausted. By the time they made their way through the castle's outer gates, he was almost asleep in the saddle.

Herluin felt drowsy enough himself. He'd drunk a fair amount of fortified wine to warm his spirits since they'd first set out that morning and it was starting to take its effect. So he didn't really notice the half-dozen unfamiliar horses being attended to by his grooms, and when Herleva came racing out of the keep to meet him, he assumed she was simply excited to see her menfolk's return. Only when she came closer did he realise that the expression on her face was actually one of distress.

He dismounted and took a few steps towards her as she dashed into his arms.

'What's the matter, my love?'

'Something awful's happened. The archbishop is here, with Gilbert of Brionne, Osbern Herfastsson and William's tutor, Thorold. They've been here since mid afternoon, but they won't tell me why they've come. It's obvious, though, just looking at them, that it must be bad news.' She looked up at Herluin. 'They won't say anything until William is there to hear it.'

'The poor lad's half asleep,' he said, not wanting to think about the implications of what Herleva had just said.

'Don't worry, I'll take him.'

Herleva walked across to William's pony and he fell from the saddle into her arms. She tried to stand him up. 'Wake up, darling. Some people are here to see you.'

'Don' wan' see anyone,' William mumbled.

'You must. It's Great-Uncle Robert, Gilbert and Osbern Herfastsson. They've come all the way from Rouen just for you.'

William huffed crossly and screwed up his face in protest. Gently Herleva coaxed him into a walk and led him by the hand to the castle keep. The archbishop and the men who had come with him were in the great hall, warming themselves by the fire. When he saw William walk through the door, the archbishop turned and led them towards the boy. When he was a few paces away from his great-nephew, he fell to one knee, those behind him following suit.

'Your Grace,' he said, 'I have very solemn news. On his way back from Jerusalem, your father Duke Robert was taken ill in the town of Nicaea, in Asia Minor. God in his infinite wisdom chose to take him from us and welcome him into heaven.

William, your father is dead. You are the new Duke of Normandy.'

A shout of 'Long live the duke!' echoed around the hall.

William himself stood stock still. He said nothing, nor did any emotion register on his face. Many who were there, recounting the story later that evening or in the days to come, would say that the poor child was simply too tired to understand what was happening.

But Herleva saw something else. She saw William hiding his loss away, deep in his soul, where only he could ever know it existed. And when she wept, it was not just for the loss of the man who had been her first and greatest love, but for her son, who was one more step removed from her, and one step further down the lonely road to his destiny.

16

Winchester, England

The twice-crowned Queen of England sat among the debris of her lost existence and counted all the reasons why she hated Elgiva of Northampton. For the past three days Winchester Palace had been ransacked by men sent by Harold Harefoot, who now styled himself King Harold, there being no other putative monarch who wanted the crown badly enough to come to England and get it. The treasury that contained all the coins, jewels, ornaments and relics that Emma and Canute had accumulated over the years had been emptied. Tapestries, carpets and silks had been torn from the walls, lifted from floors and piled onto carts to be taken back to Tamworth, the ancient capital of Mercia, where Harold and his mother now held court.

Emma had not let Harold's men into the palace without a protracted stand-off between them and the housecarls, all men still loyal to Canute's memory, who formed her bodyguard. She had no intention of allowing a fight to break out. The housecarls were outnumbered, and for her sake as much as their own she did not want to see them all killed. But the delay had afforded her enough time to take some of the treasure – pieces chosen for their small size and great value – and hide it, wrapped in a cloth, in the short pipe down which the faeces produced by the palace's inhabitants were conveyed through the wall, to drop down to a midden below. Whatever happened, she would never be reduced to penury. Nor, though, was there any current prospect of her regaining her old influence or prestige. Harthacnut still refused

414

to leave Denmark. That left her with but one alternative. She had long avoided contacting her sons in Normandy, partly because she knew how much it would infuriate Canute, and also because she suspected that messages from her would not be welcomed. Sending her children away had been both a political necessity and the only way of ensuring their survival. But they might not see it quite the same way. Still, there was nothing else for it now: she had to find a way to bring them into the fight against Harold.

One Sunday, after Mass at the cathedral, she had a quiet word with Aelfwine, the recently installed Bishop of Winchester. Aelfwine had, like his old friend Aethelnoth of Canterbury, been one of the priests who ministered to the royal family. He had always liked and admired Emma, and even feared her a little, too: never a bad thing, in her opinion. She knew she could count on his discretion.

'I wonder if you could do something for me, Bishop,' she began.

'Of course, Your Majesty,' said Aelfwine enthusiastically. 'I am always delighted to be of service.'

'Thank you so much. I simply need someone to write a letter for me. One of the monks of the cathedral priory would be perfectly capable of doing it, I'm sure. But it has to be someone completely reliable – a man who can be trusted absolutely.'

'Hmm . . .' Aelfwine rubbed his chin thoughtfully. 'May I be frank, madam?'

'Of course. Speak freely. I need good advice more than flattery or unthinking obedience.'

'Well, the priory monks are a law unto themselves. They've always run the cathedral, both the actual services and the administration of the place, and I believe that they resent the fact that I, who have never been a monk, am now in charge. So I'm not sure I can trust them to act in my best interests, or in yours.'

'I see. Can you think of anyone you *can* trust?'

'Yes, my lady, I will write your letter, and you may be absolutely certain that its contents will always be safe with me.'

A few days later, Aelfwine met Emma in one of the few chambers at the palace that she still used and wrote down the letter that she dictated to him.

'Emma, queen in name only, sends motherly greetings to her sons Edward and Alfred,' she began. She looked at Aelfwine. 'Does that sound too formal, do you think? I'm not sure what else I can be. I hardly know them, after all.'

'It sounds perfect, Your Majesty. And if I may say so, "queen in name only" is both a most elegant phrase and a most distressing state of affairs. The country is going to rack and ruin since His Majesty's tragic death.'

'I was just about to make the very same point. So, to continue . . . Since we all lament the death of our lord the king, and since you, dear sons, are deprived with every passing day of more and more of the kingdom that is your rightful inheritance, I wonder what you are planning to do about it . . .'

'Might I suggest that you just end with "do", Your Majesty? The following words are superfluous and I think they sound – quite unintentionally, I'm sure – as though you are hectoring your sons.'

'Well I am, Aelfwine, but I agree it's probably not a good idea to make that too obvious. No, actually, I *will* make it obvious. Next line . . . The delay arising from your procrastination is simply helping the usurper of your rule, who is constantly going round villages and towns and making the chief men his friends by gifts, threats and even prayers. I'm sure that they would rather be ruled by one of you than have to suffer Harold's power.'

'I wouldn't mention his name, Your Majesty. That alone would condemn you if the letter ever fell into the wrong hands.

If you permit, I will write "than have to suffer the power of him who now commands them".'

'Good idea, Aelfwine. There's no need to make life any easier for that vile man and his mother. So, after that say: I'm therefore asking one of you to come to me speedily and privately, so that I can give you my best advice. Please let me know how you plan to make this happen. Send word back to me with the messenger who has brought you this letter, whoever he may be. Farewell for now. I love you both with all my heart.'

The letter was written and the wax that closed it stamped with Emma's personal seal. A housecarl disguised as a pilgrim on the road to Rome sailed from Dover on a boat bound for Calais, and walked from there to Rouen. Four weeks later he returned bearing two letters: one from each of Emma's sons.

Edward's was terse. It concluded:

I shall therefore return to claim the kingdom over which I am already the rightful ruler. We shall meet and jointly decide how best to regain the throne, since this is in both our personal interests. I will, of course, treat you with the respect due to one who has been Queen of England. But forgive me, madam, for any filial feeling that I may once have felt for you died, at your hands, long ago.

Alfred's, though, was very different.

Edward refuses to allow me to join him on his voyage to England. He says that one of us has to stay behind, in the safe shelter of Normandy, to ensure the survival of Ethelred's line. I, however, believe that he does not want me to stand alongside him, for fear that others might decide that they would rather be ruled by me. I have decided to come to England anyway. I long to see you, my beloved mother, and if I can help to rally the people to the cause that you and I both cherish, then I will know that I have done my duty by you and my late father. I have contacted our sister Goda in Boulogne. She thinks that Count Eustace, her new father-in-law, might be willing to help me with men and ships. So I am going to recruit as many men as I can here in Normandy, then ride north to Boulogne. I hope to be in England soon and to have the reunion with you that I have dreamed of for so many years.

Your loving son, Alfred

That night, Emma went to the cathedral for evensong and lit candles for her sons. She prayed to God that Edward might become king, and then begged, 'Gracious Father, watch over my youngest child, my beloved Alfred, and bring him safely to me. I have been without him for so long. Grant me the blessing of his presence before I die.'

When the service was over, she left the cathedral and walked alone back to her empty, echoing palace.

17

The South Coast of England

Edward spent much of the journey to England leaning over the side of the longboat and puking into the Channel. The rest of the time he was on his knees praying to God for deliverance from the tribulations of wind and sea. Rabel had to admit that the prayers seemed to work, for the journey from Harfleur to the Isle of Wight passed without the slightest mishap, with breezes fresh enough to fill their sails yet not so fierce as to create rough waters. Their destination was Southampton, which stood by the mouth of the River Itchen at the head of a long inlet that cut several leagues into the coastline. From there it was barely an hour's hard ride to Winchester, where Queen Emma awaited them. But as they rounded the easternmost point of the Isle of Wight, one of the lookouts spotted horsemen riding along the clifftop, keeping pace with the fleet.

Edward seemed alarmed when their presence was pointed out to them. 'Oh dear, do you think they've seen us?' he asked.

'I would imagine so, Your Majesty,' Rabel replied. 'They'd be pretty feeble watchmen if they hadn't.'

'But will they be able to warn anyone that we're coming?'

'That'll be their aim, sire. If they send a rider to the north of the island, find a skiff to get them across the water to the mainland, then ride hard from there, they can sound the alarm up and down the coast. But they won't be far ahead of us. Not if we put our backs into it.'

Rabel gave the order to man the oars, and word was passed

419

from boat to boat. Soon they were all gaining pace. 'There you are, sire,' said Rabel. 'What did I say?'

Edward did his best to sound enthusiastic. 'Well that's very impressive, Rabel, it really is. Good work. But I can't help wondering whether we may find ourselves at a disadvantage when we come ashore.'

'I don't follow Your Majesty.'

'I mean, there may be a considerable number of English defenders massed against us, and ours is a relatively modest force: barely five hundred fighting men, and only mounts for a small number of those. Perhaps it might be best to change course and scout out a more propitious landing spot, where we won't be observed.'

'Hmm . . .' Rabel brought his hand to his chin and adopted a pose intended to suggest that he was giving the king's suggestion the most earnest consideration. In fact he was biting his tongue for fear that if he spoke, he might just tell the king what a gutless, feeble, lily-livered old woman he was. Having waited for his temper to subside a little, he replied, 'Well that's a very interesting and, if I may say so, well-considered suggestion, sire.'

King Edward smiled benevolently. 'Well, it was just what came to mind.'

'Quite so, sire. But if I may say so, it's just possible that there may be unforeseen difficulties.'

'Really? What sort of difficulties?'

'Well, sire, suppose we bear west and land further down the Wessex coast. We'll certainly evade those Englishmen we might encounter if we stick to our present plan. You're absolutely right about that. But we will end up a lot further from Winchester. That will mean it will take us longer to get there, so . . .'

Rabel left the sentence hanging, hoping that the king would pick it up. And Edward duly obliged. 'So our enemies would

420

have more time to organise and oppose us, making the danger even greater.'

'Your Majesty, you are a born general. You spot strategic strengths and weaknesses in an instant.'

The king looked suitably flattered. 'Thank you, Rabel. I confess I am not by nature a warrior, but I have read widely on the subject of war and I believe I understand its most important elements, better, perhaps, than one who has been so busy fighting that he has not had the time to study.'

'Undoubtedly, sire, your strength lies in your wisdom, not your sword arm.' Rabel smiled as engagingly as his scarred and pitted face would allow, wishing all the while that he could be talking man to man to a proper soldier, not mincing his words like a limp-wristed courtier with this kingdomless king.

'Yes, nicely put,' said Edward agreeably.

'As for our present plans, sire, I don't think we have any cause for alarm. They won't have time to muster a large force against us. Fewer than a thousand men, certainly.'

'A thousand . . . ?'

'Exactly. And any one of my men is worth at least three English, isn't that right, lads?'

A ragged, slightly breathless cheer rang out from the oarsmen.

Sure enough, the last few leagues of their progress up Southampton Water were accompanied by English soldiers, on horseback and on foot, tracking them along both banks. 'Bear right!' Rabel commanded, and the fleet headed for the eastern shore. There were beaches up ahead, broad enough to take all forty boats, and now a race began between the oarsmen and the English to see who could gain control of the shoreline first.

Edward watched the contest with a sickness born of tension and fear, worse than anything the sea had inflicted on him. One moment it seemed as though the English must surely get to the beach ahead of them and force them to turn away without even attempting a landing. The next the oarsmen had upped their stroke rate even further, put on more speed and might yet be able to establish a foothold on English soil.

The shore was now so close that he could hear the sound of the docile inland water lapping against the pebbles. The English vanguard was racing across the last clumps of marram grass that grew atop the low bluff at the far end of the beach.

Edward realised to his horror that Rabel had placed their ship at the very head of the fleet. They were still a few paces from the shore, but now there came a rasping sound as the keel ran up against the sand and stones beneath them.

Tens of English soldiers were now charging down the beach towards the onrushing boats, wielding swords, spears and mighty double-handed axes. Some of the Normans rushed to the bows of their boats, clutching bows, and loosed off arrows at point-blank range. Others leaped over the side into the knee-deep water and raced to engage the enemy.

Edward stayed aboard the ship. He found the sights and sounds of battle – the clash of steel against steel, the bellowed battle cries of the warriors, and the terrible shrieks of the wounded – unbearable, and yet he could not turn his eyes away as bellies were pierced, throats cut and limbs severed. He was appalled and yet enthralled by the way the English axemen swung their weapons in a figure-of-eight motion that created a ceaseless whirling storm of steel around them. At first, as the axes sliced into one Norman after another, reducing shields to kindling and cleaving right through chain mail, Edward feared that these men were unstoppable. But then he realised that the axes required the soldiers to grip them with both hands. That made it impossible for them to carry shields. If one could only get past the blades and inside the circles they described through the air, then the axemen were suddenly defenceless. The more experienced Normans clearly understood this, for they were able to time their counterattacks to evade the axehead, or simply drop to the ground and roll beneath it.

For a while the battle hung in the balance, as the weight of the English piling in from the beach matched the impetus of the Normans leaping from the incoming ships. But then, like a branch that bent under pressure until it finally snapped, the English gave way. Once the solid line of their advance was broken, the disciplined force became a mass of frightened, panicking, vulnerable individuals. One by one they were picked off by the Norman bowmen, pierced by the lances of the first mounted troops to emerge from the ships, or cut to pieces by the infantry. The sand was stained with their blood, which ran down in little rivulets to the sea and foamed around the longships' bows.

The battle was won. Rabel returned to the boat with a broad grin on his blood-spattered face. 'Great news, Your Majesty: the English have been routed, and we've only lost around twenty men. If we press on to Winchester, we can reach it well before nightfall and meet up with Queen Emma's bodyguard. Together we'll be strong enough to see off anything the English are likely to throw at us. And Earl Godwin has always been an ally of Her Majesty's, so like as not he'll come over to your side. By the time the sun rises tomorrow morning, you'll be King of England and the people will be rallying to your cause.'

'I already am the rightful King of England,' Edward replied coldly.

He did not seem particularly pleased by the success of their landing. Rabel had expected to find a man champing at the bit to get to Winchester, meet the mother he'd not seen in twenty years and establish his position as ruler of England. Instead, there was a peevish, pursed-lipped expression on Edward's face.

'Shall I give the men the order to march, sire?' Rabel asked.

'I think not,' Edward replied. 'We may have won this

skirmish, against a hastily mustered force. But what will happen when we face the greater battles to come? I do not trust Godwin. He may rally to me, but he might equally cast his lot with the pretender, Harold Harefoot, if it profits him to do so. And my mother's bodyguard is comprised of Canute's former housecarls. Their loyalty will still lie with their old master, and after him his son Harthacnut. To them I will seem like an interloper.'

'But Your Majesty—' Rabel began, only to be silenced by Edward's upraised arm.

'That's enough! I have made our decision. We have fought here and won. Honour has been satisfied. Your men may take whatever booty they can find from the bodies of the dead. When that has been done, we will sail back to Harfleur. So far as I am concerned, this has been a most successful expedition. You have served me well, Rabel. Please thank the men for their efforts on my behalf.'

The king had given his orders and Rabel had no choice but to obey. The men gathered up whatever weapons, trinkets and coins they could. Then they boarded their forty ships and rowed back down Southampton Water, past the Isle of Wight and out into the open sea.

And as they rowed, the soldiers asked themselves, and their companions, the same question: What the hell was the point of that?

18

*Boulogne, France, and the countryside of
Southern England*

Alfred recruited a company of Norman knights and men-at-
arms with the promise that they would get rich at the expense of
the English. Most of the men had been on Duke Robert's
abortive invasion of England, and though they had done well
enough from the plundering of Brittany, they still hungered for
the wealth that England could provide. Then he led his men to
Boulogne. Goda's new husband Eustace seemed to Alfred to be
interested in nothing beyond his falcons, his horses and his
extravagantly long and bushy moustache. But when Alfred
asked him whether there was anything the House of Boulogne
could do to help his claim on the English throne, it soon became
plain that there was more to Eustace than met the eye.

'It would be to my family's benefit to be associated with the
King of England, that's obvious,' Eustace said, thoughtfully
stroking the thick black pelt of hair that stretched from his top
lip right across to his ears. 'But what guarantee do we have that
you will succeed in your quest for the throne? There are other
claimants, after all. And at least two of them, including your
own brother, actually style themselves king. It seems to me that
your chances are not good.'

'I disagree,' retorted Alfred. 'My brother may be the eldest of
us four, but he lacks the courage to seize an opportunity.'

'Really? I hear he's getting ready to sail from Harfleur, bound
for Southampton.'

This was news to Alfred, but he did his best to hide his alarm. 'Yes, but what will happen when he gets there?' he asked. 'Edward is no soldier, so he can't fight his way to power. He's not a charmer, or an orator either, so he's hardly likely to talk anyone over to his side. So far as I'm aware, my half-brother Harthacnut is in Denmark – or has he set sail for Southampton too?'

Eustace laughed. 'No, you're right. He's in Denmark, and my father for one is convinced he'll stay there. Why wouldn't he? He's spent most of his life there. I doubt he even speaks English.'

'Then that only leaves me with Harold Harefoot, the courtesan's son, to worry about,' Alfred said.

Eustace did not seem to think that Harold would be much of a problem. 'I've heard that Canute wasn't actually his father. They say his mother Elgiva took her pleasures wherever she could find them. Apparently the father could be any one of a dozen men.'

'Well, whoever's son he is, Harold Harefoot's not fit to be a king. If he were, Godwin would have taken his side. But Godwin's still my mother's ally. Whichever of her three sons gets to Winchester first will win her support, and with it Godwin's. I'm going to make sure that I win the race. And when I do, I'll control the whole southern half of England. Harefoot will be stuck up in the north and I can finish him off at my leisure.'

Eustace nodded. 'Very well, I accept that you have a good chance of success. So what do you want from Boulogne?'

'Simple: men, horses and ships – as many of all of them as possible.'

'And in return we get?'

'The friendship of the King of England. I will be in your debt, and one day, when you are in need, you'll be able to call on me, ask for a favour, and that debt will be repaid.'

'I see, so we give you men, horses and ships in exchange for a promise of something, we don't know what, at a later date, but we don't know when. Huh . . . I doubt my father will find that a very good offer. But don't worry, Alfred of England, I will ask him anyway. You're my brother now, after all. It's my duty to help you.'

Two days later, Eustace gave Alfred an answer. 'My father says that he will give you what you need. But he's not interested in any promises. He wants something now. And what he wants is Dover. We'll sail straight there, and when we arrive, you'll declare that the town is now the property of Boulogne.'

'So before I've even been crowned King of England I'll be giving part of my kingdom away?'

'A very small part, Alfred. Just one coastal town. Think how many more towns like it will still belong to you.'

'Yes, but Dover is the closest English port to the mainland.'

'Quite so,' Eustace agreed. 'And if we control it and Boulogne, we'll be able to dominate trade back and forth across the Channel. That's quite a prize, which is why we're prepared to give you thirty ships, and their crews, and soldiers to fight in your name. But then the crown of England is also quite a prize. Which is why you will say yes to our offer.'

'Sixty ships,' said Alfred.

'Fifty.'

'Very well, we have a deal.'

The port of Dover was guarded by a strong force of Englishmen, so Alfred's men were not able to come ashore there. Instead they sailed north, landing unopposed further up the coast. They marched inland, spreading the word that Alfred the Atheling, son of Ethelred, had returned, and with him the true line of English kings.

Early one morning, when they were still a good few days'

march away from Winchester, a small group of riders came racing towards them. A red pennant with a golden dragon flew from one of their lances. Alfred recognised it as the symbol of Wessex, and his heart soared. These must be Godwin's men, come to greet him.

The first of the riders pulled up in front of the column and called out, 'I have a message for Prince Alfred!'

Alfred rode out to meet him, and the rider leaped from the saddle, went down on one knee and bowed his head. Then he stood and said, 'I bring you greetings, and a warning from Godwin, Earl of Wessex. He bids you stay your journey a while until he can join forces with you. He wishes to discuss a possible change to your plans that will, he believes, bring you great benefits.'

'What change is this?'

'It is not for me to say, but the earl was most adamant that he was thinking only of your best interest and of England's.'

Alfred was uncertain. What mattered to him above all else was to reach Winchester, and his mother, before Edward could get there. 'Tell me,' he asked Godwin's messenger, 'has my brother Edward arrived in Winchester yet?'

'No, Your Highness. King Edward landed briefly near Southampton, but then he . . .' The messenger seemed unable to find the right words. 'He determined, in his royal wisdom, that this was not the right time to bless England with his presence and departed once again.'

'You mean he got to England, thought about it for a while, and then decided to go straight back to Normandy?'

'Well yes, that might be one way of describing it.'

Alfred was convulsed with laughter. He could just imagine Edward losing his nerve and hear the words he would use to excuse his weakness. He felt the tension of the past weeks drain from his body. He had told Eustace that he would be the one to get to Winchester and take advantage of the power that his mother and Earl Godwin could bring to bear. But only now could he afford to believe his own words. Only now did he dare believe that his dream of kingship might come true. He pulled himself together, wiped a tear from his eye and said, 'My apologies. It's quite wrong of me to find my brother's conduct amusing. So, take me to see Earl Godwin. I'm sure we have much to discuss.'

Godwin greeted Alfred as if he were his own long-lost brother. 'I can't believe my eyes. To think that you were just a babe in arms when they smuggled you out of London. Your mother the queen will be so proud when she sees what you've become.'

'How is my mother?' Alfred asked.

Godwin grimaced. 'I must be honest, Your Highness, these last months have been very hard for her. She's lost so much and suffered so greatly. But she'll be overjoyed to see you.'

'Then let's go to her at once.'

'That may not be the wisest course,' said Godwin, clapping his hands together and wringing them, as if wrestling with a powerful dilemma. 'Of course, I quite understand your eagerness to see Her Majesty again, after so long apart. But would you rather see her as a pretender to the throne, as you are now, or as a king, which you could be if you allow me to advise you?'

'As a king, of course,' Edward said.

Godwin smiled. 'Your answer proves your fitness for the throne! If only your elder brother were so bold, he might be king today.'

'So what's this advice of yours, Godwin?'

'Simply this, Your Highness: divert your march towards London. The city is the richest and biggest in England. It has the men and money you'll need if you're going to face Harefoot in battle. Even more importantly, London doesn't support his claim. If you, the son of Ethelred and Emma, should call upon it for backing, you can be sure your call will be answered. You already have the power of Wessex at your back. With London too, you will be far too powerful for Harefoot.'

'Well, you have given me a lot to think about, Godwin. It certainly sounds like a fine plan.'

'Thank you, Your Highness. Now, if I may make so bold, we'll reach the town of Guildford by tomorrow night. I'll send men ahead and have a feast prepared for our arrival. We'll talk some more and drink toasts to our alliance and to your mother, for whom I have the very greatest regard. Then in the morning you can give me your decision and we'll either march north to London, or carry on westwards to Winchester, as we see fit.'

Alfred gave a nod of assent, and there was a broad smile across his face as he said, 'Very well then, lead the way!'

19

Alfred spent most of the next two days deep in conversation with Godwin, exchanging his descriptions of life at the court of Normandy for Godwin's insights into the political situation in England. All the while, more messengers were being sent off in every direction to spread the word of Alfred's arrival and summon men to join him. On the afternoon of the second day, that summons received its first answer. As they were riding along the banks of the River Wey, with Guildford almost in sight, a large party of around a hundred men came riding over the grassy downland to join them. They were tough, surly and very obviously battle-hardened, and when they came to pay their respects to Alfred, they spoke in a heavily accented dialect.

'I can't understand a word they're saying,' Alfred muttered to Godwin, who was riding beside him.

'Don't worry.' He grinned. 'No one else can either! They're Mercians, from the Black Mountains of Herefordshire. It's border country, practically Wales. They're savages, but by God they can fight.'

'Mercians? But isn't that Harold Harefoot's stronghold?'

'It is, but there are plenty of folk up there who can't stand Harefoot any more than the rest of us can. Rest assured, these lads'll do their duty when the time comes. They'll get their blades nice and red all right.'

They feasted that night in the town's great hall. Whole sheep and pigs were roasted on spits. Great barrels of ale and wine were rolled into the hall, swiftly emptied and replaced. Toasts to King Alfred, Queen Emma and the House of Godwin were followed by speeches ringing with love of Wessex and England. At the end of the evening Alfred was escorted to the largest house in the town, the property of a local wool merchant. He had drunk so much that he could barely stand and had to be helped up the stairs to his bedchamber. He undid his sword belt and collapsed on to his bed still fully clothed, just managing to kick off his boots before falling into a deep sleep filled with drunken dreams that transformed into a nightmare. His mind was possessed by visions of violence and slaughter. He felt overcome by fear. He heard shouts and the terrible screams of men who had been wounded in combat. And then he realised that he was not dreaming. He was awake. The town was filled with a hellish commotion of running feet, smashed-down doors, burning buildings and fighting men.

Alfred got out of bed, feeling the poisonous effects of all the wine he'd consumed swilling around his guts and pounding against his skull. He scrabbled around on the floor for his boots, but stopped short as he heard the sound of footsteps rushing up the stairs. Before he could dive for his sword, the door to his chamber was smashed open and four of the Mercians piled into the room. One of them was holding a burning torch, the only source of light in the room. He thrust it at Alfred's face, and the prince had to close his eyes against the dazzling glare and put his hands to his face to protect him from the torch's flames.

He was helpless, defenceless. He did not even see the club that one of the Mercians held in his hand. He just felt a crashing blow against his temple, and then he was unconscious again and there were no dreams or nightmares, just an empty nothingness.

When Alfred came to, it was light outside, but he was still lying on the bed. The first face he saw was Godwin's, peering

432

down at him like a parent examining a baby in its cradle. 'Ah, he wakes,' Godwin said.

Alfred groaned as the pain of his bruised skull combined with the sore head he'd acquired at the feast. He tried to bring his hand to his face, but he couldn't. He was still so dazed that it took him a moment to work out that his hands were tied behind his back. His feet were bound too. Now he felt the ache in his shoulders and arms, and the chafing from the rope at his ankles and wrists. The light from the open window was shining right in his eyes, so that they hurt too and he could hardly see, but so far as he could tell, he and Godwin were alone in the room.

'Wha' . . . what's happening?' he asked feebly. He felt so dizzy. He couldn't think properly, or make any sense of anything around him.

Godwin moved closer so that he blocked out the sun and all Alfred could see was his shadowy, looming presence. 'You have been arrested for conspiring with the Count of Boulogne and others against King Harold, rightful ruler of England.'

'That's not true! I came here to see my mother, Queen Emma,' Alfred protested, knowing how pathetic he sounded. 'It was you who talked about marching on London and seizing the throne.'

'On the contrary, I simply feigned support for your treachery in order to make you reveal its full extent. You traded away the king's port of Dover. You invaded his realm with your Norman knights and Frankish mercenaries, hoping to incite rebellion among his subjects. Your brother Edward had the same intent, but he was sensible enough to realise that he had no hope of success, so he turned tail and fled.'

'But . . . but . . .' Alfred screwed up his eyes and tried to think clearly, 'you were supposed to be on our side.'

Godwin's face took on an exaggerated look of astonishment.

'Me, the king's loyal servant, find common cause with an invasion of England mounted by our foreign enemies? How dare you suggest such a thing?'

'I'm not foreign. I'm as English as you are!'

'I hardly think so. You were born to a Norman mother and you've lived in Normandy since you was just a snot-nosed brat.'

'I was born to a King of England and his queen. Unlike Harold, whose parents were a Dane and his mistress.'

'I shall tell him what you think of his parentage. Or maybe you should tell him yourself. You'll see him soon enough.'

Alfred grimaced as another wave of pain and nausea swept through him. 'But why have you gone over to him, Godwin? Why desert my mother now?'

'It's very simple. I serve the King of England. I fought alongside King Edmund, the one the people called Ironside. Then I fought for his conqueror, Canute the Great, gave him my counsel and helped govern the country in his absence. I made no secret of supporting Harthacnut, but he seems reluctant to press his claim, so now I have pledged my loyalty to Harold.'

'You're the damn traitor, not me!'

'No, Alfred, I am not a traitor. I am a realist. I take note of events and act accordingly. That's why I continue to prosper as Earl of Wessex, while you have not the faintest chance of ever becoming king. So now it's time to take you to meet a real king.' Godwin stepped back from the bed, opened the door to the chamber and shouted, 'Men!'

'Wait!' Alfred called as heavy footsteps thundered up the stairs. The first man came into the room. Godwin held out a hand to stop him, then looked back down at Alfred. 'Yes?'

'What's happened to all my men? Where have you taken them?'

'To a place called Guildown,' Godwin said, and the man by the door gave a little laugh.

Alfred frowned. 'What's so funny?'

'Typical soldier,' said Godwin. 'Such a crude sense of humour. No remotely civilised man would find anything amusing about an execution site, let alone hundreds of men being put to death, some hanged, some beheaded, many of them horribly mutilated before they died. Noses and ears sliced off. Hands chopped from arms. Some of them even castrated, balls and pricks gone for ever . . . For pity's sake, man, stop laughing!'

But the soldier couldn't help himself. He was doubled up, hardly able to breathe at the hilarious thought of all the atrocities Godwin had described. Godwin himself was smirking, barely able to suppress his own amusement. 'I'm sorry,' he said, 'very rude of me, but I just couldn't help myself.'

'No!' cried Alfred. 'You can't have killed them all! It's not possible. Even you couldn't be that barbaric.'

'You're quite right. We aren't killing them all. One man in ten will be spared, then given to the executioners to sell into slavery. It's a nasty business, executing that many. They deserve a reward for all their hard work.'

Godwin sat down on the edge of the bed and gave Alfred an avuncular pat on his shoulder. 'So now you know everything. Time you went on your way.' He got back up and spoke to the soldier. 'I want you and your men to march this traitor down to the river. There's a boat waiting to take him to London. Make sure he gets there safe and sound. His Majesty can't have the pleasure of ordering an execution unless the accused man is alive. But don't feed him – just the occasional sip of ale is quite enough. Don't wash his face or hands, don't loosen his bonds and don't change his clothes. Let this pretender to the throne be soiled by his own piss and shit, as filthy and hungry as the lowliest beggar, when he stands before a true king.'

* * *

Harold Harefoot and his courtiers were feasting on great piles of shellfish and platters of eels when Alfred was dragged into the chamber. He was still bound at the wrists and ankles and his condition was just as squalid as Godwin had intended. 'Dear God, it stinks!' said Harold, wrinkling his nose in disgust and provoking peals of sycophantic laughter.

He got up from his place at table, still holding an oyster in one hand and a short-bladed knife in the other, and walked over to Alfred, who was being held in place by two of the Mercians.

'Do you suppose it's even human?' asked Harold, turning his head to address the table. 'I'm told that in her younger days, when she wasn't quite such an ugly old bitch, its mother, the Queen of Sluts, was so desperate for cock that she'd fuck anything, man or beast.'

'Don't insult my mother!' croaked Alfred through parched, cracked lips.

'Oh! It does talk!' Harold cried, setting off another burst of sniggering. 'It can't hold its bladder or wipe its own arse, but it can talk . . . in a strong Norman accent!'

Harold looked at Alfred as the crowing of his sycophants subsided. 'So, traitor, about this mother of yours . . . I hear from Earl Godwin that you claim the only reason you came to England was to see her.'

Alfred said nothing.

'It's been twenty whole years since you and the wizened old crone were last together, isn't that so?'

Again Alfred did not respond.

'Oh dear, the beast appears to have lost its voice,' Harold mocked. He stuck his knife between the two halves of the oyster shell, opened it and let the slippery flesh slide into his mouth and straight down his throat in one. 'Mmm . . . delicious!' he said, with a mocking smack of the lips, as he threw the shell to the floor.

He kept looking at Alfred. 'So tell me – speak up and be honest – do you long more than anything to clap eyes on your dear old mother . . . just once? Well . . . do you?'

Still Alfred was silent.

'Speak to me, traitor!' Harold shouted, losing his temper. 'I am your king. I command you to speak!'

'You're no king,' Alfred finally replied. 'You're the bastard son of a whore.'

Harold's face tightened till his lips were white with rage. He stepped right up to Alfred, holding the oyster knife to his face. 'What did you say?' he hissed.

Alfred didn't flinch. 'You heard me. Or is your hearing as feeble as your claim to the throne?'

Harold reached out and grabbed the hair at the back of Alfred's head. 'Do you see this knife?' he said, placing the tip of the blade on Alfred's cheekbone, just below the corner of his left eye. 'It's made to prise open a shell. But it can prise your eye open just as easily. Let me show you . . .'

Harold pressed the knife into Alfred's skin and drew a drop of blood that ran down his face like a crimson tear.

'No!' Alfred gasped.

'Oh yes,' said Harold. He glanced at the Mercians to either side of Alfred and said, 'Hold him tight.' Then he dug the knife deeper into the socket of Alfred's eye.

Alfred screamed in pain. He writhed desperately, frenziedly, like a rabbit in a snare. Harold clenched his left fist still tighter round his prisoner's hair, to hold his head in place.

The knife went deeper.

Alfred's voice echoed off the stone floor and walls of the chamber, rising ever higher in pitch as Harold twisted the knife, forcing the tip into Alfred's left eyeball. He pulled, forcing the eyeball between Alfred's eyelids and out of his skull, stuck to the end of his knife yet still connected by a string of nerves;

437

then he gave a sharp tug that snapped the nerves. He flicked the eyeball off his knife and let it fall to the flagstones, where it bounced and rolled until it came to rest close to the discarded oyster shell.

'Excellent,' said Harold. 'Now for the other one . . .'

20

Winchester, England, and Rouen, Normandy

The seventy monks of the cathedral priory regarded Aelfwine, Bishop of Winchester, as an unwelcome intruder foisted on them for political rather than religious reasons. He found it hard to be taken into their confidence, or to play much of a role in the priory's communal life and conversation. Still, there was some gossip that even he could not avoid overhearing, which was why he was making his way to the royal palace on a chilly February night, dressed in a hooded cloak over a plain priest's cassock, hoping very much that he would not be recognised along the way.

Only when he reached the main gate did he reveal his name and title, proven by the bishop's ring on the fourth finger of his right hand, to one of the handful of Canute's former housecarls who still stood guard over his widow. On his last visit to the palace, when he had written Queen Emma's letter to her sons in Normandy, Aelfwine had been surprised by the modesty of her circumstances. In the months since then, however, her situation had become even more desperate.

Emma was living in just a few small chambers with only a single servant and a cook to look after her. A profusion of candles and torches had once lit the palace at night, and there had been great fires and braziers to keep it warm, but now it was a dark, cold place. Aelfwine had to make his way by the glow from a solitary candle, which he held out in front of him as he made his way through the deserted corridors and halls. All around him, high on the walls, ran the great sculpted friezes of scenes from Scandinavian mythology commissioned by Canute. The flickers of light from the guttering flame cast shifting shadows across the stonework, so that the monsters and warriors seemed to move and loom over him and he found himself muttering frantic prayers to ward off their pagan evil.

When Aelfwine finally found Queen Emma, sitting in a heavy cloak and woollen mittens beside a meagre fire, he was shocked by the change in her appearance. It was understandable that she should have been marked by her husband's passing, but over the past few months she seemed to have aged a decade. Her haughty, majestic beauty had vanished. Now she was thin, drawn and all but overwhelmed by suffering. And yet as he examined her more closely, it seemed to Aelfwine that bereavement and the humiliating loss of power and wealth that had followed it had given Emma a deeper nobility, that of a martyr rather than a monarch, so that now she looked almost saintly.

She smiled at him, and even that expression was suffused by sadness. 'I must apologise, Bishop, but I cannot offer you the level of hospitality that a man of your eminence deserves. Still, the cook has made me some barley broth for my supper. You're very welcome to share it if you like.'

'That is most kind of Your Majesty, but I have already eaten. I come bearing news.'

Her face brightened. 'Oh! Do you have word of Alfred? Godwin told me that he had met my son on the road to London, but that was months ago and I have not spoken to Godwin since . . . or anyone, really. All the people who used to be desperate for my friendship or assistance seem to have disappeared like swallows in winter. Oh dear, I'm afraid I'm rambling – an old woman's failing! – so, please, what is it you wished to tell me?'

Aelfwine had been dreading this moment. With every step

he'd taken on the way to the palace, he'd had to fight the urge to turn back. But he felt a certain responsibility for what had happened, given his role in drafting the letter that had brought the queen's sons to England in the first place, so he owed it to her to make sure that she heard the news from his lips.

'Your Majesty, I do have word of Prince Alfred, but I fear it is not good.'

Emma's face fell and she whispered, 'No, please God, not my baby . . .'

Aelfwine swallowed hard. 'As you know, the cathedral priory is a Benedictine house and the prior makes a point of maintaining regular correspondence with his opposite numbers in some of the other prominent Benedictine houses. These include Ely. I don't know if you're familiar with Ely, Your Majesty . . .'

'I've heard of it, of course, but I've never been there.'

'Well, the monastery sits on an island, surrounded by flooded fens and marshes. The waters are rich in eels, hence the name of the place, and the monks regularly go out to check on their eel traps, which provide food for the monastery. On one of these expeditions they came to one of the smaller islands that rise above the water, and there, on the shore, they found a man lying by the water's edge.'

Emma stifled a sob. Aelfwine noticed and stopped his story. 'Your Majesty . . .' he murmured.

'No, please, carry on,' Emma said, recovering her composure with a difficulty that was painfully obvious to Aelfwine. Nevertheless, he did as he was commanded. 'At first they thought the man was dead, for he did not appear to be breathing and . . . and . . . Your Majesty, I know no easy way to say this, but his eyes had been gouged from his face. The holes where they had been were suppurating and the man's forehead was burning with fever.'

441

Emma could restrain her emotions no longer. She was weeping, but though she could not bring herself to speak, she motioned at Aelfwine to keep going.

'The monks at once forgot their traps and placed the man in their boat, then returned to the monastery as fast as they could. The man was taken to the infirmary, his wounds were cleaned and he was given a little broth to drink. After three days he had recovered enough to be able to speak. He told them he was Alfred the Atheling, son of Ethelred. But before he could say how he came to be so mutilated and abandoned, he tired. The following day, however, he told the monks a little more of his story. It seems he had sailed from Boulogne, landed on the Kent coast and made his way towards London. On the way, however, he and his men were intercepted by Earl Godwin . . .'

Even though the palace was all but empty, Aelfwine looked around, as if fearful of being overheard, and lowered his voice before he went on. 'Godwin pretended to be Alfred's ally and said he would escort him to meet you here in Winchester. But he betrayed Alfred, killed all his men, and handed him over to Harold Harefoot. Alfred could not remember the circumstances of his blinding, nor how he came to be in the vicinity of Ely. One can only assume that the king wished to dispose of his enemy as discreetly as possible, so he was left on a tiny, remote patch of dry land, where he would either die of exposure and starvation, or drown if he attempted an escape.'

'Is he alive then?' Emma asked, praying for some small glimmer of hope.

'I fear not, Your Majesty. It seems that the exertion of telling his story proved too much, and he succumbed to his wounds and his fever. But his end was peaceful, he received the last rites and the monks said a Mass in his honour, so his soul is at rest and his place in heaven is surely secure. That is some comfort, I hope.'

'Yes,' said Emma, 'and more comfort than Harold intended to provide. Thank you, Aelfwine. I realise how hard it must have been for you to come to me, knowing what pain you would cause. But I am grateful to you. At least I know what happened to my boy. And now I see that I am in mortal danger. Harold has already come for my treasure. It won't be long before he comes for me too. My only hope is to leave England. There is nowhere safe for me here now.'

'Will you go back to your family in Normandy?'

'No. I've been too long away. Most of the people I grew up with are dead, and those few that live are strangers to me now. And if Edward already knows that Alfred is dead, he will surely hold me responsible.'

'Why should he do that?'

'Alfred said he was coming to see me, didn't he? If he had stayed in Normandy, he would be alive today. I blame myself for that – I'm sure others do too.'

'So where will you go?'

Emma sighed. 'I have other relatives in other lands. I'll just have to hope that one of them is prepared to take me in.'

A short while later Aelfwine left Emma's chamber. He did not see her servant hiding in the pitch-black shadows outside her door. But she saw him, and recognised him as the gentleman who had visited Her Majesty a few months earlier. That made two secret meetings, both after dark. And even a humble servant girl without a shred of education could work out what that meant. And tell her family about it, too.

When news of Alfred's death and the slaughter of his followers reached Normandy, it was greeted with outrage and fury. Plenty of voices were raised in the ducal council chamber insisting that the only possible way of avenging this appalling crime was to mount an invasion like the one Duke Robert had once planned, taking as big an army as Normandy could muster to England and making Godwin and Harefoot pay for their acts of treachery and murder with their own blood. But who could lead such an army? Duke William had yet to celebrate his tenth birthday. Nor was anyone prepared to trust any of his guardians enough to place an army at their command: who knew what they might do with it when they returned to Normandy?

Suggestions that the exiled King Edward of England might wish to avenge his brother's death were met with short shrift by those who knew what had happened on his last, brief excursion to the English coast. Edward himself declared that he was too deep in mourning and too fully occupied in ceaseless prayers beseeching the Lord to grant Alfred's soul a place alongside his angels in heaven even to consider a military expedition. And it was true that he was indeed spending a great deal of time on his knees in the palace chapel and before the great altar at Rouen Cathedral, where all the world could witness his piety, and that some of his prayers really were offered up on Alfred's behalf. It was also the case that Edward had made a private resolution that if he ever took his rightful place on the throne, he would make Godwin pay for his shift of allegiance. But the emotion that gripped him most firmly as he mourned Alfred's passing was one of profound satisfaction.

He was not so unsubtle as to say 'I told you so' – not quite – but he was often to be heard expressing his great sorrow that Alfred's courage, his passion and his admirable longing to fight for his family's birthright had led him into such a foolhardy course of action. 'If only he had let me advise him!' Edward wailed. 'I had been to England myself. I had discovered how malicious and ungrateful its people were when confronted with their true-born king. I saw at once that the time was not right. Poor Alfred! How can I forgive myself for letting him take such a fatal risk?'

But really, when one thought about it, how fortunate that he had. For Edward was still alive. His claim to the crown still stood. Now there was one fewer rival to prevent him grabbing hold of it. All he had to do was wait, be patient, and everything might yet work out to his advantage.

21

Bruges, Flanders

'Welcome, Your Majesty.' Adela, Princess of France and Countess of Flanders, dropped into an immaculately graceful curtsey as she greeted Emma at the door of her palace in Bruges.

'Your Highness,' Emma replied with a little nod of the head, deeply gratified by the honour that Adela had paid her and the combination of perfect manners and human sympathy it embodied.

She looked at the elegant, confident young woman standing before her in a dress of the finest Flemish weave and tried to imagine her as the plain, shy, mistreated maiden whom her brother the archbishop had described in his letters telling the story of Adela's disastrous marriage to Richard of Normandy. Emma's mother Gunnor had written about Adela too, though her accounts had always been far more sympathetic to a girl she had always thought would grow into a fine adornment to Normandy if she'd ever been given the chance. Well, Normandy's loss had been Flanders' gain, for Adela was rapidly developing an international reputation for both her learning and her political acumen, just as Emma had once done. She too was one of her husband's closest advisers and a regular signatory to his charters.

'It's very good of you to make me welcome here,' Emma said. 'My departure from England was a little hasty, I'm afraid. And though I would love to return to Normandy, I'm afraid it's been a very long time since I could call it home. I fear my

446

presence might, well, complicate matters . . .'

'Oh, I quite understand. And it's absolutely our pleasure to have you here,' Adela said, leading the way towards the women's quarters of the palace. 'Your niece Countess Eleanor came with me to Bruges to marry my father-in-law, after I had gone to Normandy to marry her brother. So our two families could hardly be more closely connected.'

'You know, Eleanor wasn't even born when I left Normandy. Goodness, that seems a lifetime ago now.'

'We get on very well, she and I, and almost think of ourselves as sisters. It's so nice to have an ally of one's own age, don't you think?'

'I only wish I knew,' sighed Emma. 'Both my husbands had previous wives, so the other women at court in England were more likely to be my enemies than friends.'

'You sound just like my mother! When I was growing up in Paris it was fighting, fighting, all the time.'

Most of it started by your mother, Emma thought, though she said nothing. She had never met Queen Constance of France, though she knew of her by reputation, as half Christendom did, and had a sneaking admiration for her shameless lust for power and intrigue. Perhaps it would be best to change the subject. 'It's particularly kind of you to be so hospitable to me here when you were welcomed so poorly to Normandy.'

'Oh, that also seems like another lifetime. My marriage was unhappy, I admit. But I could not be happier now. God has treated me very kindly and I give thanks for His mercy.'

They entered a chamber draped in tapestries of such fine silk, such vivid colours and decorated with such beautiful designs of animals and flowers that they far exceeded anything that had hung in the palace at Winchester. The air was warmed by a roaring fire and heady with the scent of candles, mulled wine and spiced pastries. Here, thought Emma, was a place of sanctuary, somewhere cosy, inviting and utterly feminine. She smiled as two little girls ran towards Adela, shrieking with delight. Behind them walked a young woman, and for a moment Emma felt the eerie sensation of watching her own younger self brought to life before her eyes.

'Your Majesty, may I introduce the Dowager Countess Eleanor?' Adela said.

Emma accepted her niece's curtsey and then, quite spontaneously, held out her arms and embraced her. It had been so long since she had held someone in a simple hug, and it felt so good, so reassuring that she found herself blinking away a tear. But then there were small hands tugging at her dress, and more high-pitched shrieks and giggles assaulting her ears, suddenly broken by a sharp command of 'Silence!' as Adela brought the children to heel.

'Behave yourselves, girls,' she went on as Emma and Eleanor disentangled themselves. 'This is Queen Emma of England . . .'

The two girls gasped and looked open-mouthed.

'Is she a real queen?' one of them asked.

'Yes, Matilda,' Adela replied. 'And how do you greet a queen?'

The two girls grabbed hold of their skirts and gave such elaborate curtseys that they knocked into one another and almost fell over, providing Emma with another sensation she'd almost forgotten: laughter.

Adela was laughing too as she said, 'Your Majesty, meet my daughter Matilda, who so rudely questioned your royal status.'

'And this is Judith,' said Eleanor, 'who is my daughter, Matilda's aunt, Adela's cousin and your great-niece!'

'Goodness,' said Emma, 'that's an awful lot of things for one little girl to be.'

'Come and see our dolls!' said Matilda, more as a command

than a request, and Emma let herself be led away across the room.

She could, she realised, pass the rest of her days in this palace, acting as motherly friend to Adela and long-lost aunt to Eleanor. She could, perhaps, allow herself to be happy and enjoy all the simple pleasures of a woman's life, the pleasures that she had long been denied.

But that would mean accepting Harold Harefoot, the man who had killed her son, as King of England and, even worse, Elgiva of Northampton as Queen Mother. Emma could not even countenance that. When she went to bed that night, the very thought of Harold and his mother crowing over their triumph was enough to wake her in the early hours and keep her wide-eyed and restless till dawn.

One of her sons was dead. Another had turned and fled at the first sign of danger. But she still had a third son to call upon. And so, once again, she pleaded with Harthacnut to leave Denmark and take up his crown in England. When he wrote back giving her reasons why he would not do as she asked, she wrote again, and again, and kept writing, knowing that in the end her will would prevail because it was stronger than any man's. Emma had been a single step away from the throne of England for almost thirty-five years. She was not about to walk away from it now.

She would see her son consecrated as King of England, whether he wanted the crown or not.

22

Archbishop Robert of Rouen had outlived four Dukes of Normandy and was now controlling the reign of a fifth. But even he, with all his wiles, could not forever defy the passing years. Slowly his strength ebbed away and his body became ever more vulnerable to pestilence and evil vapours. He was weakened by a series of fevers. The flesh melted away from his body, so every one of his ribs could easily be counted, and his cheeks were sunken into his toothless maw. Finally he took to his bed at the ducal palace in Rouen – where, it was felt, his wife and children might more easily visit him than if he were in a religious establishment – with the exhausted resignation of a man who knew that he would never now rise again.

William was summoned to the old man's bedside. 'I am not long for this world . . .' the archbishop began.

The boy's eyes widened. The transformation of his great-uncle's face into a living death's head had been frightening enough. His words scared William even more. 'Please don't die,' he pleaded.

The archbishop managed the glimmer of a smile and reached out a bony hand to pat William's arm. 'I'm afraid I don't have any choice in the matter,' he said. 'God is calling me, and I go knowing that my place in heaven is secure. So don't you worry about me. You're the one person who matters now. The fate of our family, and of Normandy itself, is riding on your young shoulders, my boy. One day you will be old enough and strong enough to rule the duchy and defeat its enemies in your own name. But for the next few years you must depend on other men to do it for you. It's very important for you to know exactly which men you can trust to help you, and which will only be interested in helping themselves. It won't be easy. Your enemies will often pretend to be your best friends. They'll try to trick you and deceive you. You have to be very, very careful. Do you understand, William?'

He nodded, solemnly. 'Yes, Great-Uncle.'

'Good. Now, I am going to tell you the names of all the good people I know you can trust, and all the not so good people that you must be wary of. And we're going to repeat those names every day until you remember them all.'

'Like Brother Thorold makes me repeat the catechism until I remember it?'

'Exactly like that.'

'Can I trust Brother Thorold?'

'Yes, you certainly can.'

'Good. So who else can I trust?'

'Well, you should always trust and love your mother and, of course, your stepfather Herluin of Conteville. He would never betray you. Your mother's brothers Walter and Osbern, though they may just be commoners, can also be relied upon. And when you grow older, I'm sure your own half-brothers Odo and Robert will always be at your side.'

'They're my friends.'

'Exactly. You can always count on your steward, Osbern Herfastsson, too.'

'And William Fitzosbern!' William piped up. 'He's my friend as well!'

'Quite so . . . And I can also name two cousins who are on your side: Alan of Brittany, and my brother Godfrey's son, Gilbert of Brionne.'

'What about King Henry? When we went to see him and I promised to be his vassal, he said he would always look after me.'

'And he will do . . . for now. As long as you are weak, it is in his interests to protect you. You see, you are his vassal, so you must obey him, and in return, he has a duty to protect you.'

'What if I become strong and I don't need him to protect me?'

'Oh, well done, William, that's a very good question indeed. The moment you become strong, you'll be a threat to Henry, because you might decide not to obey him any more. So then he'll be frightened about what you might do, and that will make him angry and it might lead to war.'

'A war between me and the King of France?'

'One day, maybe . . . but not yet, not for a very long while! Now, we must stop for the day. I'm exhausted. But come back tomorrow and I will test you on all the people you learned about today, and tell you all about the bad men that you can't trust at all.'

'If they're bad, will they go to hell?'

'Almost certainly.'

'Excellent!'

The next day, William returned to his great-uncle's bedchamber and recited again and again the names of all the good people he could trust. The archbishop corrected him if he left any out or gave an incorrect name, until it was clear that they were fixed in his mind. Then they moved on to the list of William's potential enemies.

'My brother Richard, your grandfather, had two wives. One was Judith, your grandmother, who died before you were born. The other was called Papia of Envermeu, and she gave him two sons, your uncles Mauger and William. They're a few years older than you and they'll soon reach the age when young, ambitious men start looking around for ways to get ahead. Beware them both, my boy!

'I fear, too, that my own sons may seek to gain control of our family and all that comes with it. Remember the name Ralph of Gacé. He is of my blood, though not of my raising. Had I been there to train his mind, I would have no concerns, but he has become bitter and resentful in my absence. Watch him. And watch the House of Bellême. They fought your father and he defeated them. But he did not destroy them, and as long as that line remains intact, its sons will seek their revenge.'

William's head was spinning with all the enemies he was supposed to remember. But the archbishop wasn't finished.

'You will face threats from inside the duchy and from the other lands that surround us. Brittany is safe for now. As long as Alan lives, he will be loyal. But he and his ancestors fought us, so I have no doubt his successors will too. And beware Anjou and Maine. Flanders should not be a danger, but . . .'

The old man fell back on the bed and groaned. 'So much to tell you, but I'm so, so tired . . .'

A woman came in carrying a tray with a small earthenware jug and a crystal goblet upon it. She bowed to William. 'Excuse me, Your Grace, but I have a soothing draught for His Grace the archbishop – herbs prescribed by the apothecary to soothe his fever and ease his pain. After that he will sleep a while.'

William did not recognise the woman. She was quite old – as old as Mama, at least, maybe even older – but very beautiful, with golden hair, and the way she walked and talked wasn't at all like a normal servant. When he'd still been a very little boy, Judith had told him stories at bedtime, all about kings and queens, and knights and beautiful damsels, and this woman looked the way he'd imagined the women in those stories would look.

'Do you want me to go?' he asked her, quite forgetting that he was a duke and she just a humble serving woman.

'I think that's a very good idea,' she said, in a voice that was soft and gentle, yet somehow so certain that William could not even imagine disobeying her.

'Very well,' he said, looking into her deep blue eyes and doing exactly what he was told. As he left the room, it seemed as though he were in a sort of dream, from which he might wake up at any moment. But then his friend Guy of Burgundy came racing up, shouting, 'William, William, come and look at my new slingshot!' and suddenly William snapped out of his dream world and ran away after Guy, the beautiful woman quite forgotten.

The woman sat on the edge of the archbishop's bed and placed the crystal goblet to his lips. 'Drink, Your Grace,' she said, as a sweet, warm aroma of honey, berries and spice enveloped them both.

'Thank you, my dear,' he replied, doing his best to manage a feeble smile. He raised his hands to the goblet, but the woman retained her hold on it, knowing that her patient was too weak to bear its weight. The archbishop bent his head and took a feeble sip.

'That's very good,' the woman said. 'Now try to take a bit more. It will make you feel so much better.'

With patience and great tenderness, she helped the dying man drink more than half the goblet's contents. Only then did she ask, 'May I ask Your Grace, have you made your last confession?'

The archbishop raised his head. 'What an extraordinary question,' he said, a spark of animation returning to his voice. 'The answer, as it happens, is no. But why on earth would you ask me such a thing?'

She smiled. 'Because it seemed to me that now that you are at the very edge of the abyss, with one last chance to make peace with your God, you might feel the need to tell him, and the priest by your side, the secret that only you and your guardsman Thierry of Breteuil ever shared.'

A quiver of alarm crossed the archbishop's shrivelled face. 'Thierry's dead,' he said.

'I know,' said the woman. 'I killed him.'

The archbishop's eyes widened in alarm. He opened his mouth to cry for help, but the woman covered it with her hand.

'Sshhh . . . it's too late,' she murmured. 'I've killed you too. But don't be afraid. I've been merciful. Yours will be a peaceful, painless death, just as Duke Richard's was. Tell me . . .' She withdrew her hand. 'Why did you decide that he had to die?'

'I decided no such thing!' the archbishop gasped.

She smiled indulgently, letting him have his little pretence. Then, with quiet insistence, she repeated, 'Tell me.'

The archbishop gave a sigh of defeat. 'He was a disaster,' he admitted. 'If he had been duke for any longer, the duchy would have been torn apart by civil war and then consumed piecemeal by its neighbours. Robert was our only hope.'

'But now he is gone. Now all your hopes rest on the shoulders of a nine-year-old boy.'

The archbishop's eyes closed. 'I know,' he sighed. 'And he can't possibly survive. My whole life's work has come to nothing. But . . .' With a final effort of will, he fought back against the soft, velvety blackness that was now enveloping him and opened his eyes to stare at the woman. 'I don't understand. I sent Thierry to commission Jarl the Viper to murder Richard. Does the Viper always send women to carry out his killings?'

'No,' she said. And then she lowered her head, placed her lips to the archbishop's ear and whispered, 'I am Jarl the Viper.'

The archbishop did not respond. His eyes had closed again

and the Viper knew that it would not be long before he had passed from this world into the next. But she wanted to send him to his eternal sleep with a little story. 'Poison is such a feminine weapon, don't you think?' she said. 'It requires no strength, merely the skill to grow beautiful flowers, then gather together their seeds and berries and the sap from their stems. One must scour marketplaces, too, and seek out the very particular merchants who deal in the powders and liquids that combine to form fatal draughts. Then one must select and blend one's chosen ingredients, and heat them or liquefy them, as the recipe for each particular poison requires. Finally one must possess the guile and imagination to devise a means of inducing one's victim to consume, or touch, or breathe that which will kill them.

'All these are women's talents and I learned them as a little girl, albeit a girl who had to live as a boy, for how else could her master take her as his apprentice? He gave me his knowledge and I gave him my body, though he took me as he would take a boy. And in the end, when I had learned all I needed, I took his life . . .'

The Viper stopped and looked at the motionless, unbreathing form of Robert, Archbishop of Rouen and Count of Evreux. 'As I have taken yours,' she said softly to herself. Then she gathered up the goblet, the jug and the tray and slipped quietly from the room.

Jarl left the palace through the same side entrance through which she had come on her way to kill the archbishop and, a decade earlier, Duke Richard before him. On the way to the gate, she passed through a small garden where William and three of his friends were playing, all waving wooden swords at one another.

The poisoner had heard some of what the archbishop had

been saying to his great-nephew about the enemies he would face. The old man was right, she thought sadly, looking at the boy duke, whose shock of bright red hair marked him out so clearly from his playmates. All your life there will be someone trying to destroy you. There will always be enemies.

She looked at the other three boys. They were all engaged in a mock fight, playing at knights and pretending to kill and be killed. One of the boys stuck his sword into William, who grabbed his belly with a great groan and rolled around on the ground, while his friends fell about laughing.

One day those swords will be steel, thought Jarl. One day some of those friends will be enemies. One day one of those boys may come to me asking me to kill you.

She sighed, feeling the strange weight of responsibility that came with her occupation, then very quietly she said, 'And then what am I going to do?'

Author's Note

This book is the result of a personal passion – virtually an obsession – dating back almost fifteen years. It began with an episode of Simon Schama's TV series *A History of Britain* in which he vividly described the bloated, half-naked body of William the Conqueror lying at the priory of Saint-Gervais in Rouen, deserted by his family and allies, stripped of anything valuable, including his clothes.

This image of the mighty Conqueror brought so low struck me very powerfully. I realised that while I had known his name since I was a child, I knew virtually nothing about his life, beyond the Battle of Hastings and the Domesday Book. Next morning, I went online and started looking for information about him.

I soon discovered that the actual history of William's life is frustratingly incomplete. For example, no one knows for certain when he was born; not even the year. The relationship between his parents, Robert of Normandy and Herleva (whose father is variously described as a tanner, an embalmer, a steward and Robert's chamberlain), is variously assumed to be anything from a one-night stand to something close to a marriage. And was William's father really a murderer? Robert inherited the dukedom when his older brother Duke Richard III died suddenly. In the malevolent, often paranoid world of Norman politics, rumours immediately spread that Robert was responsible for Richard's death. But there is no conclusive evidence, one way or the other. Richard might have died naturally. Or someone else might have ordered his assassination.

Throughout William's life one comes across similar moments of incredible drama or emotional intensity that are only partially described by the very limited number of more-or-less contemporary accounts of the period. Even so, there's still some extraordinary material for a novelist to work with. For example, the story of how a Viking raider called Rollo the Strider acquired the duchy of Normandy by humiliating a king of France; the various sudden deaths of members of the House of Bellême; and even the pathetic attempt by 'King' Edward the Atheling to invade England are taken directly from medieval sources.

Likewise, while I have reset the scatological Moriuht poem declaimed by Warner of Rouen as a series of dirty limericks, the basic content is exactly what the real-life Warner wrote. He really did dedicate the work to Archbishop Robert and his mother Gunnor, along with the King of France, and it really was written after the death of Richard II of Normandy, but while both his successor Richard III and his younger son Robert were alive. So the fact that I have Warner reciting it at a wedding feast is an invention, but one based on fact.

Speaking of that wedding, Richard III of Normandy is said to have married a bride called Adela of France. Baldwin V of Flanders certainly married Adela, daughter of King Robert and Queen Constance of France. But whether these two Adelas were one and the same woman is not known. I have taken the liberty of assuming that they were. Others may disagree, and possibly with good reason, but there's no definitive proof, one way or the other.

Even when events are described in the chronicles, the accounts are often fleeting. For example, the entire story of the dispute between Robert and the archbishop that led to the imposition of an interdict on Normandy occupies less than a paragraph in the *Gesta Normannorum Ducum* (*The Deeds of the Dukes of Normandy*), the most important chronicle of the time. No reason for their fight is given. The rebellions of the House of Bellême and the deaths of Warin, Fulk and the Count of Bellême himself are described immediately after the conflict between Robert and his uncle, and both sets of stories are done and dusted in a single page's worth of text.

To expand these fragmentary sketches into an entire book I relied on imagination, guided by a few basic rules. The first was that although I tried to make the story as dramatic as possible, and though the timing of some events had to be adjusted to fit the story, I tried very hard not to write anything I flat-out knew to be wrong. There is, for example, no evidence whatsoever that the archbishop had his nephew Richard murdered. But since no one knows how or why Richard died, there isn't any evidence that he didn't, either. Still, I have to admit that Jarl the Viper is entirely my own creation, so I gave myself a fair amount of latitude. That's why this book is listed under 'fiction'!

My second rule was to follow what I thought of as the emotional logic of people's relationships. In the case of Herleva and Robert, for example, we know that they must have had sex, because they produced a son. But they certainly didn't get married, since there is no record of such a union and William was known as 'the Bastard' all his life. We also know that Herleva married Herluin, described in the *Gesta* as 'a certain honourable soldier' and that they had two sons, Odo and Robert, who went on to become the Bishop of Bayeux (and Earl of Kent) and Count of Mortain respectively. This marriage, according to the *Gesta*, took place after Robert's fatal pilgrimage to Jerusalem, though the English chronicler William of Malmesbury says that, on the contrary, Robert was still alive when Herleva and Herluin wed.

What conclusions can be deduced from all that information?

Well, Herleva and Robert's relationship must have been a significant one, or else he would not have named William as his heir. But whatever the *Gesta* may say, it must have been over before Robert's pilgrimage, because Odo became Bishop of Bayeux in 1049, and even in eleventh-century Normandy he would have had to be at least eighteen at the time, and thus born in 1031 and possibly conceived in 1030, when Robert was still very much alive.

So Herleva and Robert split, but she was allowed to marry a man who either was, or soon became, a viscount. She must, therefore, have had her former lover's favour and been considered a good enough match for a man of high social standing. Here was a commoner who became a duke's lover and a viscount's wife, and gave birth to a king, a bishop-earl and a count. As David C. Douglas, author of the finest biography of William the Conqueror, drily remarks: 'She was a remarkable girl.'

But what of William himself? Well, he was no more than six or seven years old when he witnessed one of his father's ducal charters for the first time. So he must by then, if not earlier, have been living at the ducal court in Rouen and been part of his father's household. On the other hand, he always treated Odo and Robert de Conteville as his brothers – hence the titles of Bishop of Bayeux and Count of Mortain they later respectively acquired – and there are also references to the help he received from his uncles on his mother's side. All that suggests he remained close to his mother, her family and her children by Herluin.

Those were the thoughts in my mind as I created my picture of Robert and Herleva's love affair, and similar thought processes went into, for example, the dysfunctional mother–son relationship of Queen Emma and Edward. My next decision was: how should they talk?

Our most powerful sense of how medieval figures spoke comes from the characters in Shakespeare's plays. But their speeches were written more than half a millennium after the period described in this book: William Shakespeare is closer to us in time than he was to his namesake the Conqueror. So there was no point in trying to put some kind of cod-medieval language in my characters' mouths. I took the view that while the way people speak changes over time, the fundamental nature of the emotions and desires they talk about remains eternally constant. So I gave them modern speech, with the one important caveat that characters should never use images or metaphors that could not possibly have applied nine-hundred-plus years ago. Thus, for example, people shoot arrows, because 'shoot' comes from an old Anglo-Saxon word. But they do not 'fire' arrows, because the notion of a shot being fired depends on the existence of gunpowder, which was around in eleventh-century China, but certainly had not made its way to north-western Europe.

Finally, a brief note about names, which, to be honest, drove me crazy. The essential problem is that so many people had the same ones. So we have Duke Robert of Normandy, and his uncle Robert, Archbishop of Rouen, and King Robert of France, one of whose sons was called Robert, as was Robert of Bellême, whom I have renamed Bertrand simply to avoid confusion when he and Robert – by which I mean Robert of Normandy – appear in the same scene.

Every Count of Flanders seems to have been called Baldwin. The Counts of Boulogne were mostly Eustaces. Count William of Bellême had a son called William Talvas. William the Bastard had a half-uncle, William of Arques, and one of his closest friends was William Fitzosbern. As if that were not enough, when Emma of Normandy married King Ethelred, she was given the honorary Saxon name Aelfgifu, which was also the same name as Ethelred's first wife Aelfgifu of York and Canute's first wife Aelfgifu of Northampton, or, as I have called her, Elgiva.

I have done my very best to find ways of naming the characters that are reasonably simple to follow. Please forgive me if in this, as anywhere else, I have failed.

Finally, of all the historians whose work shaped my research, there were three in particular without whom this book could not have been written. I have already mentioned David C. Douglas and to his name I would add Professor Elisabeth Van Houts, translator, editor and annotator of the *Gesta Normannorum Ducum* and *The Normans in Europe*, and Harriet O'Brien, whose book *Queen Emma and the Vikings* was essential to my understanding of the life and character of Emma of Normandy.

David Churchill

Timeline

The dates below reflect the timeline of the book and in a very few cases – notably the appointment of Elgiva of Northampton as regent of Norway – do not precisely conform to the actual date of the event in question. However, it is very hard indeed to be sure of the dates of many of the key moments in Norman history. For example, I have placed William's birth in September 1027, but it may have occurred up to a year later. Similarly, historians differ as to the exact date on which Duke Robert announced his intention to go on pilgrimage, and the date on which he departed. Some place the start of the pilgrimage in late 1034, others in early 1035. Nor are any of the dates in the life of William's mother Herleva, the tanner's daughter who became the Viscountess of Conteville recorded. All that said, this timeline does provide a basic chronology to the key events in the book.

911
- Rollo the Strider becomes the first Duke of Normandy following a treaty with Charles the Simple, King of the Franks

1002
- Marriage of Ethelred of England and Emma of Normandy

1016
- Death of Ethelred in England

1017
- Canute marries Emma of Normandy, Edward and Alfred of England exiled to Normandy

1026
- (August) Death of Duke Richard II of Normandy. He is succeeded by his son who becomes Duke Richard III. His second son, Robert, becomes Count of Hiémois
- Robert takes up residence at Falaise Castle

1027

- (January) Marriage of Duke Richard III and Adela of France
- (Spring/Summer) Siege of Falaise Castle
- (August) Richard dies and Robert becomes Duke of Normandy
- Birth of William of Normandy
- Canute makes Elgiva regent of Norway

1028

- Siege of the Bellême's castle at Alençon
- Marriage of Adela and Baldwin V, Count of Flanders

1030

- Death of Lady Gunnor in Normandy
- Robert II, Archbishop of Rouen, places Normandy under an interdict

1031

- Herleva marries Herluin de Conteville

1034

- William signs his first charter
- Robert sails to invade England but lands in Jersey
- Alan of Brittany marches on Normandy, Robert's army returns and launches counterattack
- Archbishop Robert negotiates a truce at Mont Saint-Michel where Alan swears allegiance to his cousin Robert
- Robert names William as his heir and departs on a pilgrimage to Jerusalem

1035

- Death of Svein, Canute and Elgiva's eldest son, in Denmark
- (July) Death of Robert in Nicaea, William becomes Duke of Normandy
- (November) Death of Canute in England, Emma is exiled, Harold Harefoot assumes the English throne
- Prince Edward travels to England, defeats the English defenders on the coast, but returns immediately to Normandy
- Prince Alfred journeys to England, independently of his brother

1036

- Death of Alfred in England

1037

- Death of Archbishop Robert in Normandy